FAILURE DRILL

JAMES TARR

BOOKS

Vinci Books

vinci-books.com

Published by Vinci Books Ltd in 2025

1

Copyright © James Tarr 2017

The author has asserted their moral right to be identified as the author of this work in accordance with the Copyright, Designs and Patents Act 1988.
This work is a work of fiction. Names, characters, places and incidents are the product of the author's imagination or are used fictitiously. Any resemblance to actual persons, living or dead, places and incidents is entirely coincidental.
All rights reserved. No part of this publication may be copied, reproduced, distributed, stored in any retrieval system, or transmitted in any form or by any means, including photocopying, recording, or other electronic or mechanical methods, nor used as a source for any form of machine learning including AI datasets, without the prior written permission of the publisher.
The publisher and the author have made every effort to obtain permissions for any third party material used in this book and to comply with copyright law. Any queries in this respect should be brought to the attention of the publisher and any omissions will be corrected in future editions.
A CIP catalogue record for this book is available from the British Library.
Paperback ISBN: 9781036701086

Printed and bound in Great Britain by Clays Ltd, Elcograf S.p.A.

By James Tarr

James Tarr Conspiracy Thrillers

Failure Drill
Splashback
Splits and Transitions
Whorl
Waiting for the Kick
Ghosts and Madmen
The Subsection

AUGUST 2000

Chapter One

THE RAM'S HORN

My stomach ached. The nagging, worrying feeling that had been bothering me all day, the twisting in my gut, hadn't gone anywhere. Why not?

I sat in my car and reflected on the day. There wasn't much to reflect on. I'd gotten out of bed at the usual time and headed for the office with an acceptable amount of enthusiasm. There was the normal amount of paperwork to get done, then the call from Scott to meet for lunch.

What, then, was this burrowing worm of unease? I was receiving all the internal signals that something was wrong, that I was in for a bad day. Was there some bill I'd forgotten to pay? Some call I'd neglected to make?

Perhaps it's possible to have a bad day without anything bad actually having to happen. That theory certainly held true when it came to people. I'd met a number of people in my life that I'd just known were bad, with a capital B, but not all of them had done something in front of me to prove it. I just *knew*.

Take, for example, the two clowns I was watching from

my car parked in the lot of the restaurant where I was supposed to be having lunch with a friend. Instead of eating, I was watching two guys telegraph all the signals I associated with "bad guys". I was sitting in my car watching them sit in their car and watch the people moving behind the glass of a Ram's Horn Restaurant.

Their car was a blue Chevy, still on the good side of ten years old and in reasonably good shape. Nothing untoward there. The man in the driver's seat was in his forties. Black hair, slightly hooked nose. A bit grizzled, and a few acne scars, but most women would probably think he was handsome. It looked like he was wearing a broken-in leather jacket. His companion barely looked twenty. He was skinny with curly red hair and patches of freckles on his pale skin. He wore an olive drab army jacket with a frayed collar. It was cool for August, but even so they seemed overdressed for the sixty degree weather.

The redhead was talking animatedly, gesturing abruptly with his hands to emphasize his words. The driver seemed to be ignoring him as he moved his eyes back and forth over the people in the restaurant. He seemed quite cool and relaxed compared to his passenger, who was a hyper little squirrel. I don't know what it was, but there was something about them . . . .

I sat and watched them for about five minutes, then got sick of waiting for something to happen. I'd been late when I arrived, and sitting in my car listening to the engine click wasn't going to make me any earlier.

I left Heckle and Jeckle in their Chevy and walked into the restaurant. There wasn't any line and no hostess came to seat me as I looked around the room for my friend. I spotted him in a booth near the back corner of the dining room. Ignoring the hostess who appeared in front of me just when I didn't need her, I made my way toward my old friend. He was dressed in a grey, low profile, low budget suit and white shirt, with a navy blue tie that was pulled away from his neck. The top button of his shirt was undone but the tie still seemed to chafe him. He'd have to rebutton it before he went back to work, but I knew him and he'd put it off until the last minute. I used to do the same thing when I had to wear a tie.

I stopped in front of the table and watched him scowling at the menu. He looked up at me and back down at the menu.

"John," he said.

"Scott," I replied. Bantering fools, us two.

He was sitting with his back to the wall in a spot where he could watch the door. Among cops it was known as the Wild Bill Hickok Syndrome, and it had saved many a cops life.

"Nice choice of booths."

He looked up at me again, not scowling anymore but with the lines from the frown still etched in his face. They matched the deep lines in the corners of his eyes behind the thick lenses of his glasses and the grey-white hair at his temples. He looked forty-five. He was thirty-three.

"I've never been shot in the back," he replied. "I'd like to keep it that way. I may be paranoid but that doesn't mean they're not out to get me." He went back to scowling at the menu. I smiled -- I had a tendency to keep my back to the wall in restaurants too. I slid in across from him, feeling my jeans stick briefly to the vinyl cushion.

I played with a fork while I waited for a waitress to notice me and bring over a menu. And waited. They could still be too deep in shock from my good looks to approach, but I wasn't betting on it. Scott attracted bad waitresses like flowers attract bees, and I gritted my teeth in anticipation. Seeing a grand total of nine other people in the restaurant, I figured our waitress had her work timed out to the exact second so she could smoke as many cigarettes in the kitchen, over the food, as possible. My entrance probably ruined her whole plan, and she was still fuming and plotting revenge.

A few minutes later, a plump adolescent wearing an ugly polyester uniform came over to our table and plopped a menu down in front of me. There were zits on her chin that she'd tried to cover with too much makeup, and her jaw muscles stood out like golf balls as she loudly chewed her gum.

"Ready to order yet?" she said in a loud, nasally voice.

I looked down at the unopened menu in front of me and then at Scott. For a brief second his scowl hinted at becoming a smirk, then returned to its normal formation. He ignored her. I smiled at the waitress and said, "No, we're not quite ready to order yet, thank you."

She turned on her heel without a word and walked into what looked to be the kitchen, loudly chewing her gum. I looked back at Scott and shook my head.

"I don't know how you do it," I said. "Every single goddamn time."

"It saves me tip money." Both of us laughed for a while and then he went back to scowling at the menu.

"The prices are going to stay the same no matter how long you try to intimidate them," I remarked profoundly. He sighed and closed the menu.

"It's not the prices," he said, inspecting a fingernail, "it's finding something I like."

"Since when have you not cared about price?" I jabbed. "And anyway, you do the same damn thing every time we go out. Here, Denny's, anywhere. You scowl at the menu for a while, ask the waitress what she recommends, then order a hamburger with the works. Every time."

"Well, I like order in my life," he said. I snorted.

The waitress arrived and took our orders. I got a steak sandwich and Scott got a hamburger with the works, after asking the clueless waitress what she recommended. He ignored my snickering.

As I ate I looked around the room. The nine people occupied a total of four tables. Not bad, considering ten a.m. was early for lunch. I'd been keeping weird hours lately and Scott had to take his when he could get them. As it was, he got paged twice and had to trod off to the pay phone near the restrooms as the battery on his cell phone was dead. The calls turned out to be about improperly filed paperwork. I could hear him across the room as he informed the second caller that if his lunch was interrupted again for a non-emergency the person responsible would have a hard time sitting down due to *seriously* misfiled paperwork.

"Can't you just flush that beeper?"

He gave me half a smile. "I wish. They'd grab another one out of a drawer and bill me for the one I lost before I could get out the door. There's no escape. *Many have tried, all have failed*," he finished in a ridiculous, deep, melodramatic voice.

Halfway through the meal I had to excuse myself to the bathroom, stepping around three men dressed in mechanics' coveralls as they got up to leave. In the john, the toilet paper roll was full and the graffiti was amusing, which was all I could realistically hope for from a public restroom. Someone once wrote that you could judge how a society was faring by the condition of its public restrooms. If so, our country is in trouble.

As I washed my hands in the sink I heard someone yelling just outside the door, using profanity that would have been out of line at a bachelor party. Between the sheer volume of noise and the apparent anger with which the tirade was being delivered I began to suspect bad things were going to happen. And soon. I shut off the light, leaving myself in darkness, and cracked the door.

Out past the imitation wood paneling partition that was designed to conceal the restroom doors my pudgy waitress was standing stone still behind the cash register, looking up, frozen in fear. Someone I recognized was standing on the counter holding a sawed-off shotgun that wasn't quite aimed at her and yet wasn't quite pointed away. He had pale skinny arms disappearing into the sleeves of an army fatigue jacket and red hair under the pantyhose he'd pulled down over his head. I didn't think anybody did that with pantyhose anymore.

"Gimme the money. Gimme the fucking money! Get it or I'll fucking SHOOT!" Red waved the sawed-off pump vaguely in her direction.

The adrenaline rush hit me then. My hands began to sweat and it felt like my eyeballs were throbbing in time to my rapidly accelerating pulse. My face flushed with heat. Pucker factor eight. I opened the bathroom door a few inches wider so that I could almost get my head through and craned my neck to try and see past the partition.

Mr. Acne was there too, in the middle of the dining area with a large automatic in his right hand. He held the pistol down at his side, finger out of the trigger guard. It looked as if he'd been born with it in his hand. Not good.

"Everybody up. I want you to move over to the far wall

and start emptying your pockets on that table there." Mr. Acne's voice was even and steady, and he was a lot calmer than Red.

Most of the people were terrified and did exactly as he said. An older man in an expensive suit sitting with his back to the door didn't respond and Acne reacted by pointing the automatic at his nose. There was a noted lack of expression on Acne's face, another bad sign. The man was holding a glass halfway to his mouth, probably not realizing it was still in his hand.

I noticed Acne was wearing gloves. Red wasn't, and it almost looked like the two of them weren't aware of each other. Red was engrossed in yelling at the terrified waitress, while all of Acne's calm and quiet attention was centered on the motionless man in the suit. For all of Acne's lack of expression, the guy in the suit seemed just as unfazed, maybe even a little resigned -- like this happened to him every day and he was expecting it.

"I said stand up!" Acne said to the well-dressed man, his voice rising. Mr. Suit was looking at him and didn't move, but the glass in his hand began to tremble.

I pulled my pistol out of its holster on my right hip and cocked the hammer. It was a SIG P230 automatic, small and light and easy to carry. Small and light and easy to carry, however, meant not much bang. I'd sacrificed stopping power for comfort, and boy was I regretting that decision as I looked at Red's shotgun. I'd have gladly traded the little Sig for a shotgun of my own, or better yet a Thompson submachinegun.

I looked out the door again, but still couldn't see Scott. Acne was the closest person to him, and even though he was now shouting animatedly at the man in the suit (Look at me. I SAID LOOK AT ME!) he looked too alert to jump. If

Scott made any sudden moves he'd probably get a bullet in him if Acne was even halfway talented with a gun. And Scott hadn't bothered to wear a Kevlar vest since he'd worked the road. Speaking of Kevlar vests, Acne's jacket looked mighty thick, and was zipped up all the way to his neck.

The panicked waitress finally managed to get the drawer to the cash register open and started handing wads of bills to Red. In the dining room, Acne had apparently reached some turning point in his one-way dialogue with the man in the suit. The two were staring at each other now, Mr. Suit still sitting, looking both terrified and somehow resigned to his fate. "You…you don't…" he said halfheartedly. The muzzle of the gun was only inches from the man's forehead. If Acne pulled the trigger the room would get a new paint job.

I swung open the bathroom door and stepped out into a crouch, pointing my SIG at Red, who had one hand full of cash and the other full of shotgun as he turned toward me. I shot him three times in the chest as he raised the shotgun. He looked confused, then fell off the counter onto the floor.

Before Red hit the carpet Acne was already moving. He pivoted and fired a shot at me that ended up in the men's bathroom somewhere, then turned his gun back on the man at the table. I fired twice at Acne, center mass, just as he was squeezing off a round that would've blown the man's head apart. Instead, my bullets threw off his aim enough so that the round from his gun blew the drink out of the man's hand. Razor sharp glass shards flew through the air.

Acne looked stupidly at the dark holes in his jacket and lurched drunkenly toward the door, all thought of killing the man in the suit forgotten. As the muzzle of my gun came down from the recoil of the second shot I raised my sights, took an extra quarter second to aim, and cranked off a third round at Acne's head. My bullet hit him in the throat at the same instant I heard a double tap from Scott's automatic. One of the two rounds from Scott's gun hit Acne just under his raised right eyebrow. His body slowly collapsed forward, his finger following a too-late command from his brain and firing the pistol once into the floor.

The body hit with a sickening wet thud. I covered Scott while he approached the corpse and kicked the gun out of its hand. It was then that I noticed the blood and brain matter sliding slowly down the fractured window that looked out onto the parking lot.

I backpedaled into the bathroom and puked noisily into the sink.

Chapter Two

AFTERMATH

I stood next to Scott on the sidewalk outside the Ram's Horn, watching the police scurry around like ants. Only the bored expressions on their faces gave away their true feelings about all the activity that seems so intriguing to citizens. The lab guys had already done their once-over: photographing and fingerprinting everything, vacuuming the carpet, tables, and probably my puke in the sink. Two paramedics began loading the black body bags, one at a time, into an ambulance. Apparently the Medical Examiner's meatwagon was busy elsewhere and had to miss the fun.

The county detectives had already taken statements from us. Scott knew most of the responding officers personally so there was very little hassle and they only gave my concealed pistol license a cursory glance. After I gave my statement they left me pretty much alone and talked to Scott.

The county lab techs and forensics guys were packing up their things. There hadn't been much for them to do other than to verify our story. They went through all the motions anyway, taking hundreds of photographs, drawing diagrams of the scene, plotting bullet trajectories, and conferring noisily with the detective in charge of the case. Scott and I had already turned over our guns to the Firearms and Toolmarks expert. It was his job to verify that our guns were the ones that fired the killing rounds. He had to see which bullets from what gun went where, and whether their placement jibed with our story. Standard operating procedure for cops is to assume *everybody* is lying to them, so I couldn't take the treatment personally, but I still disliked being on the wrong end of the investigator's pen.

The lab techs had done as much as they could with the blue Chevy that Red and his friend had been sitting in, then towed it away to their controlled access garage for more in-depth examination.

The usual rubberneckers and gawkers had congealed in clumps on the sidewalk, but there wasn't much for them to see. Even the two uniforms pulling line duty mostly just stood around. Once the sirens had died down a lot of the street spectators had left, probably disappointed. All the good stuff, like pools of blood and crumpled bodies, had been inside and hard to see. A few news crews were milling around with cameras, but the cops kept them so far away from the scene they'd just about given up hope of ever getting any gruesome video for the six o'clock news.

I shook my head and spat on the sidewalk, the acid taste of vomit still in my mouth. The vomiting had taken me by surprise. I'd seen people shot before -- hell, I'd shot people before. Maybe it had been the brains sliding down the window. I hadn't been expecting that. Seeing a corpse was a lot different from seeing someone killed, and that's light years from actually pulling the trigger, but I'd seen a lot of bodies in worse conditions and never lost my lunch.

I'd made myself look at the bodies and remember why I had to kill them. It had been their decision, not mine. I had fewer nightmares that way.

I'd shot people before, in two different situations; it hadn't been glamorous or turned me into a stressed out wreck. It had been terrifying, exhilarating, and necessary. I just wished I hadn't glanced at that window.

As I stood there, I remembered looking at Red and what was left of Acne and thinking that all freshly dead look alike. Skin that didn't look real once it was immobile, loose joints, and glassy eyes over startled expressions. Except for Acne, whose eyes had been about eight inches apart when we finished with him. Christ.

I sucked in a lungful of air and let it out, slowly. The faint smell of automobile pollutants tickled my nostrils. Scott finished talking to two plainclothes county cops and walked over. He reassumed his position beside me and pulled in a lungful of his own of pure city air, then coughed slightly.

"Well," he said, "one of the county dicks knew the redhead on sight, so at least we've got that mystery solved already. They'll double-check his prints against the records in AFIS, but it's a pretty sure bet that he's one Leroy Hawkins, better known as Red, or RedMan. Big chewing tobacco fan, apparently. That stuff'll kill ya."

I pinched the bridge of my nose and looked at Scott.

"The other guy we don't know yet," he went on. "No one recognized him, but then being shot in the head'll do that to you. We'll run his prints and see what shakes."

"What was he saying to that old guy in the suit, the one he was going to kill?"

"I couldn't hear too well from where I was sitting but what I did hear didn't seem to make much sense. At first it seemed like he was mad at the guy for not moving fast enough, but then it seemed like he was going to kill him anyway, no matter what."

"So what did Mr. Suit have to say about why people are so eager to donate lead to his bloodstream?"

I watched the ambulance pull away with half the lab boys in it, followed by a marked county cruiser with its flashers spinning silently. I looked at my watch. It had only taken the cops three hours to process the scene, a record time. The owner of the restaurant probably didn't mind the lost business; when the story hit the news he'd have hordes of people beating down his doors in hopes of seeing a bloodstain. When Scott didn't answer I looked over at him. He had a wry smile on his face.

"Let me guess," I said. "He got away."

Scott nodded. "Probably slipped out when I called the cavalry, while you were still redecorating the bathroom."

I sighed and pinched the bridge of my nose again, then sipped at the cup of coffee the restaurant manager had provided to responding law enforcement. "So what's the story on Red?"

"Career loser," Scott explained. "Tough guy that doesn't mind carrying a gun. He's done a little time for assault with intent, that kind of stuff. Been in and out of jail since his teens."

"This whole thing is screwy," I said. "None of it makes any sense. Acne looked and acted like a professional, except for the company he was keeping and the little jig with the old guy in the suit. He was wearing gloves and I bet the spent cases from his gun the lab guys bagged are clean of prints, but Red got his prints all over everything and didn't seem to care."

Scott nodded. "Either 'Acne', as you call him, was just

renting the kid 'cause he needed a body, or he wanted the job to look amateurish and the kid fit the bill. This was either a slightly fucked up robbery with way too much firepower, or a botched, *really* fucked up hit on the guy in the suit." He shrugged. "Either way, we'll send his description and prints out over the wire and see what pops up. Acne, that is. I'll see what I can find on the guy in the suit, too. I had the techs dust his chair and table in case he left any good prints, but I doubt it. It's not my case, but they'll damn well keep me informed."

"Man, I thought for sure Acne was wearing a vest," I confided to Scott. "That's why I failure drilled him."

"You what?"

"What?"

"What the fuck's a Failure Drill?" he asked me.

"A double-tap to the body, two shots, followed immediately -- without a pause -- by a shot to the head. You know, because you think the guy's wearing a vest or something, and have to assume any shots to the body will fail to stop him."

"The *'Anything That Can Go Wrong Will Go Wrong'* school of gunfighting. I'm familiar with the technique," he said. "I'd just never heard it called that before."

"I think it's also called a Mozambique Drill," I told him.

"Why?"

"Fuck if I know. I look African to you?" I snapped. Acne's ruined face kept popping into my head. The coffee wasn't going down very well, and I could still taste the vomit in my mouth.

Scott shrugged and smiled at my outburst and said "Easy......Go back far enough, we're all Africans." While I blinked at him he called out to the two remaining county cops. He told them he'd be heading back to the station in a few minutes and they nodded, then drove off in their cruiser.

Scott and I said goodbye and I watched him walk to his car and drive off. I'd known him since high school and I hoped the lines in his face weren't mirrored in my own. He'd just made lieutenant, one of the youngest ever in his department, and he'd been so busy lately our lunch was the only time he'd had free to see me. As Wonder Boy of the department he was having a lot of shit piled on him. An officer involved shooting was just one more hassle he didn't need.

I sighed again. It was getting to be addictive, but I promised myself that as soon as my bad day was over I'd quit cold turkey.

I climbed into my car after one last look around and headed out toward my office on Big Beaver Road in Troy. I was leasing an office out of a shiny, modernistic building that looked like it was covered in tin foil. On Big Beaver they all did, victims of the bug that had afflicted architects about fifteen years before and hadn't quite faded away yet.

My office was halfway up the twelve-story monument to food wraps, stuck in the middle of tax offices, moderately successful attorneys, stock brokers, and investment counselors. There was also a cut-rate travel agency that fit in about as well as I did.

The lettering on the pebbled glass door said THE J. PHAULT AGENCY, and below that in slightly smaller letters, Security Consultation and Investigation. I'd worked hard on coming up with just the right wording that was aggressive yet classy, exciting yet discreet. I don't know if I'd been successful, but it brought in the clients, most of whom could pay. I rode up in the elevator alone. Most of the upwardly mobile types I shared the building with were working hard at four in the afternoon, closing deals, selling shares, or practicing their golf strokes.

The elevator and the hall on the sixth floor, like my office, were done with the same style and grace exhibited on the exterior of the building. Chrome, glass, and blocky aluminum fixtures dominated, with the walls done in white, off-white, beige, light cream, café au lait, or ivory -- whichever one of three dozen names for the white family the interior decorators had been using that week.

I unlocked the door to my office and went in. The building's mail delivery service hadn't been by yet, or maybe they had and I was still unloved by the Postmaster General. I was prepared, though. I sat behind my desk that was too ugly to be the stylish its designers had hoped for and caught up on some paperwork I'd been putting off. I had a few letters to type up, and it took me a lot longer than it should have. I kept seeing Red, the confused expression on his face when I shot him, the clumsy way he fell off the counter. Over and over it played in my head, until my temples began to throb.

At about four thirty there was a rattling on the window behind me, and I turned in my chair to see pea size hail coming down in thick sheets. The cars down on Big Beaver were switching on their lights in the gathering gloom. I shook my head. It was typical Michigan weather. For the previous two weeks everyone had been sweltering in humid, 90- to 100-degree heat that was the average for August in Michigan, then just two days previous the temperature had plummeted to sixty and was expected to stay there for at least a week. Now there was hail. It just proved what people always said about Michigan weather: If you don't like it, just wait a minute.

Thinking of home, I grabbed the phone, remembered finally to look at the answering machine for messages, found none, and dialed. After two rings a female voice answered. I breathed obscenely into the receiver for about ten seconds, slurped once, then hung up. I drummed my fingers on the desk for about a minute, then snagged the phone on the first ring.

"Phault Chauffeur Agency," I said. "Bend over, we'll drive."

"I knew it was you. I'd recognize that desperate panting anywhere."

"Desperate? Madam, I'll have you know they line up at the door just for the chance to gaze upon my shapely backside. What's for dinner?"

"I don't know, what're you going to make?"

"Wait a minute. *You're* the wife. You're supposed to greet me naked at the door with dinner already on the table. Besides, you're the one that's home already, babycakes, not me."

"Sounds like a good way for the dinner to get cold. All right, all right, you whiner. When you get home I'll have something ready for you. When're you leaving?"

"Now, I think. It's dead here." Bad choice of words. Red's face popped into my head again, but I shoved it back down through sheer force of will.

"Okay. See if you can hurry it up, though. I love you."

"I love you too."

We hung up at the same time, me with a big smile on my face and my bad day forgotten, at least for a while.

I rode down in the elevator with a group of young urban professionals that looked at me sideways since I was the only one not wearing a suit. I thought about showing them my gun, but then remembered the police had confiscated it. Nobody has a sense of humor anymore anyway.

By the time I pulled into my driveway the hail had

turned into light rain and the wind had picked up. Tomorrow would probably be dry and hot with ball lightning and sun dogs. I ran through the rain up onto the front porch, shook out my hair, and went inside.

"Hi honey, I'm home," I called out.

My wife appeared in the doorway to the living room wearing an oven mitt and nothing else.

"You've got a choice," she said. "Before dinner we can either compare and discuss the ideas of Freud and Jung against those of the behavioralists such as B. F. Skinner, or we can rut like animals on the carpet."

"Gee, I don't know," I said. "That's a toughie." I pursed my lips. "What was the first choice again?"

Later that evening, appetites sated, we half-dozed in front of the local evening news. Kelly was laying on the couch, her head on my lap, close enough to sleep that her breathing had turned heavy.

The Ken and Barbie onscreen, with their hundred-dollar coiffures, had already covered my shooting, and now were talking about a shooting in Rochester with barely contained joy. Probably a botched mugging they said breathlessly, and don't forget the two stabbing fatalities in Royal Oak that were probably gang related. The two anchors made sad, pouty faces and talked briefly about how awful things were, then went on to the next tragedy.

Except there aren't any gangs in Royal Oak, I thought. *And nobody gets mugged in Rochester. The problem with the media,* I observed for perhaps the hundredth time, *is that they have no obligation to get anything right. They just aren't supposed to deliberately get it wrong.* Kelly stirred in my lap.

"Are you asleep?" I said softly.

"No," she mumbled into my leg.

"Good. The last time you fell asleep with your head in my lap you left a drool pool on my leg."

"You loved it and you know it," she said softly. She lightly bit my thigh. We sat quietly for a few minutes.

"Scott called me at work and told me what happened to you two today," she said.

I nodded my head. "I thought he might've. He's a good cop."

"He was your good friend before he became a good cop. Mine too. Still is." She scratched her nose by rubbing it on my leg. "It's been so long since I've seen him that I almost forget what he looks like."

"Still ugly," I said. "You two would just fight if you got together, anyway."

"We don't fight, we bicker. There's a difference. Besides, he doesn't have a wife, he needs someone to keep him in line." After a pause, she said "Do you want to talk about it?" She looked up at me, worry in her eyes.

"No, not now. In a couple days, maybe. I'm okay, I've just got to get back into the groove."

"You're sure?"

"Yeah. Scott and I did what had to be done. No buts about it. I'll be fine. Okay?"

"Okay, if you say so. Now shut up and let me get to sleep."

"Just don't start drooling."

"Shaddap."

Chapter Three

CLEANUP

I sat in my office once again, trying to fight off the hordes of anxious, wealthy clients. Other people would say that I was just doodling on my desk calendar. My skill with a pen wasn't as good as my imagination, which I supposed was for the better in case a client got a gander at my desk top. The kind of business I did, I made a lot of money off of each client, usually, but sometimes I went a week or more between clients. It made for monotonous days.

After a while I got bored with doodling and looked at the sunlight shining on my office floor. It was divided into thin horizontal bars by the Venetian blinds installed in the window. If I used my imagination they could be my cell bars. I could be a convict waiting for them to come and take me to the electric chair. It didn't take much imagination -- I sure felt like a convict sitting in the office alone all day, nothing to do, and it wasn't even noon.

Slumped in my chair, I watched the alternating bars of light and shadow move across my floor. They would have to slide all the way to the other side of the room and up the wall before the day was over and I could go home.

At the angle they were moving, the bars looked like they just might clip the bottom edge of my filing cabinet. As I watched them inch closer and closer I made a bet with myself that they would touch, changed sides twice, then broke off the wager altogether.

"Aaaargghhh!" I cried out theatrically at the empty office, just about ready to head out for an early lunch. The only response I got was the strident, obnoxious ring of my telephone.

"Good morning, John Phault Investigation and Security Agency, John Phault speaking, how can I help you?" I took a second to breathe.

"I bet you can't say that backwards." The voice was Scott's.

"No, but I can say it in Igpay Atinlay," I replied.

"I have news," he said.

"Shoot."

"Okay, simple stuff first. The prints proved the kid was Leroy Hawkins, Red, as we suspected. Positive ID. No surprises. The other guy's a different matter, though."

"How so?"

"Well, he didn't have any ID on him, as you already knew, so we ran his prints through AFIS and came up with zilch. No state record at all. So we sent them out nationwide over the wire. Treasury, Justice, FBI, DEA, CIA, ASPCA, everybody. They all, so far, have been a big goose egg."

"But? I can hear a 'but' in your voice."

"They all came back negative, with one exception. When we faxed and e-mailed the prints and photo to everybody, we got a response back from the Justice Department in like two hours."

"Two hours? No way. That's unheard of. So who's the guy?"

He gave a snort. "Unknown. They contacted us to ask us to put a hold on the investigation." Scott paused. "They want us to hold up 'til the guys they're sending down arrive."

"Huh?"

"I thought you'd say something profound like that. Apparently they're sending over two Justice Department agents with information 'pertinent to the case' or some bullshit excuse like that. So both Fred Willis and I – he's the lead on the case – have been told to not do shit until they get here."

"What the hell? Suspend the investigation? That's not typical for the Justice Department. That's not typical for anyone. Something big must be up. I bet that message ruffled a few feathers down at the station."

"All I know is that they're sending two agents down here. They won't arrive until tomorrow morning, and they're gonna want a meeting with everybody that was involved in the shooting as soon as they get in, which basically means with you and me. I'm not even sure they want to talk to Willis, if you can believe that. Until then, I'm supposed to sit on my hands."

"When do you want me? I'm gonna have to juggle some appointments around."

Scott laughed into my ear. "Bullshit. You're probably sitting there making animals out of paperclips. When are you going to get a real job?"

"Last week I did an evaluation of a company's security system. It took me two days and I made more money than you did all month."

"Well, it's not like you need the cash, anyway," he said.

"Show up at my new, large office at about eight tomorrow morning. I'll be here. Indefinitely. Or at least until they finish the damn internal investigation on our shooting. At least I'm catching up on my paperwork, not to mention everybody else's."

"Ah, yes, I'd forgotten about how you'd gotten into policework for the excitement. And this new office, this I gotta see."

"Breathtaking, I'm telling you."

"I'll bet."

We hung up and I looked around the office, then thought of something Scott had said. I rummaged around in my desk and finally found a box of paperclips.

Scott's office was the size of a broom closet and looked like any other cop's office that I'd ever seen, except maybe that it was a little cleaner. I waded through the beat-up desks, old newspapers, and stained coffee cups in the squad room toward it. Inside I saw Scott talking to two men that probably were the Brooks Brothers, if I had to judge by their clothing. All three of them were bent over papers spread across Scott's desk. I stopped at the open doorway and knocked on the jamb. The three of them looked up, and Scott motioned me inside.

"John, I'd like you to meet Special Agents Weatherspoon and Gaines of the Justice Department." We all shook hands and Scott introduced me, telling them a little of my background.

Weatherspoon was a distinguished looking black man in his forties. Built solid, he was starting to gray at the temples and seemed in good shape. Gaines was nearly six three and skinny as a fence post, with a "Don't fuck with me I'm having a bad day" creased frown decorating his face. It looked permanent. The two of them didn't fit the "Accountants With Guns" image the feds seemed to be cultivating lately. Gaines looked like he'd be more comfortable wearing a cowboy hat and riding the range.

"I like your suits," I said. They didn't know what to make of the comment so they ignored it. Scott rolled his eyes at me.

"They were telling me a little of the reasons behind their trip here, but we just started. Why don't you guys just start from the top again?"

They nodded. "Okay," Weatherspoon said and shut the door, then walked back to the desk and picked up some papers. He waved them around absently as he talked. "Basically what we're doing here is this: Day before yesterday you sent us a picture of this man." He pulled a photo out of a manila folder he was carrying and showed it to me. It was Acne. "Anyway, we had a flag out on his file, meaning if it was inquired about we should be notified."

"What'd the guy do that had you so interested in him?" I said.

"Nothing, that is, until you came across him." He paused, and puffed himself up importantly. "His name is Gino Scarelli. He's one of the top hit men for Pietro Bufonte—allegedly. Actually, he's in charge of most of Bufonte's gambling income, but sometime several years back he discovered he had a knack for killing people. So whenever old Pietro needs someone taken care of, he's the man. He's done five that we're sure of and twice that many unconfirmed, and we can't pin a single one of 'em on him. Does the name sound familiar?"

"Scarelli? No. But Bufonte is only the top guy in organized crime in the wonderful Midwest," I said.

Scott nodded. "Based out of Detroit."

"Right," Gaines said. "Although word is that he might be moving his operation. Anyway, this Scarelli only rarely goes out on jobs now, as he's semi-retired. His latest, and last, assignment was known to us, and was in fact quite important. We found out about Scarelli being sent out a bit late, though, and we lost him, until he turned up on the fax you sent us."

I didn't ask how they'd gotten so much information about Scarelli and his assignment. They wouldn't tell me anyway, but if it wasn't wiretaps it was an informant.

"Scarelli was in Washington? What was he doing there? I thought most of these guys stayed local."

The two feds glanced at each other.

"He was local, he wasn't in D.C. He didn't like to leave the Great Lakes area."

"Then what the hell are you two guys from Washington doing here? Why didn't they send some of the local Justice Department people? Somebody once told me there's an FBI field office in Detroit."

Gaines looked down at his shoes for a moment, then spoke. "All right," he said, "I guess you guys need the whole story."

"I would hope fucking so," Scott exploded. "The guy only tried to fucking shoot me! I don't like people that're supposed to be cooperating with me blowing smoke up my ass. I've got better things to do with my time. If you want us to give you guys what help we can, treat us like adults."

"We don't normally do things like this by choice," Weatherspoon said peevishly. "It's all whether you have the need to know."

Scott and I looked at each other and rolled our eyes.

Weatherspoon had been reading too many spy novels and he wasn't even CIA.

"Gaines and I work for a special division of the Justice Department," Weatherspoon said. "The Witness Protection and Relocation Program. You've heard of it, I presume."

My eyebrows raised appreciatively. WPP was the big boy on the block when it came to protection and security. It was *the* program to be copied. Their record was legendary. "You guys don't fuck around."

"No, we don't. We can't afford to. If word gets out that the government can't protect the people that testify on its behalf, there won't *be* any people testifying on its behalf." Weatherspoon spoke grimly. "So the reason we were after Scarelli, if you haven't guessed, is that he was sent after some of our birds that have flown the coop."

"What?"

Gaines sighed and said, "Three individuals who've had dealings with Bufonte decided, with a little nudge from our side, to testify against him. So we were called in to protect them before, during, and after the trial. Bufonte is a big, big wheel, so Weatherspoon and I were called in from Washington a month ago to make sure no feathers were ruffled on the witnesses by any of the local agents. We've been working overtime on this since, making sure everything happens the way it's supposed to. Nobody's even caught wind of the grand jury yet.

"Right at the beginning, though, 'bout two weeks ago, way before we were even scheduled to go to the grand jury, something got fucked up. The three of them vanished one night, all gone, right from under our noses. Bufonte didn't find them—he'd have made sure their bodies were found quick, as examples. We didn't get it. Why would they leave our protection? We still don't know for sure. Every once in a while a witness does leave our security net, but that's only after the trial, after they've been under protection for a few years and are starting to feel safe. One day they get tired of the new identities or something and decide enough's enough. And it's pretty well known that those who do that usually end up getting whacked. In this case, the best theory that we can come up with is that maybe they felt their security had been compromised." He shrugged.

Weatherspoon took up the tale. "So, here we are, almost time for the indictments to be handed down, but no witnesses, and no ideas, no concrete evidence, as to why our witnesses vanished." He threw up his hands, the frustration of the last few weeks showing on his face. "With them we've finally got Bufonte by the balls. Without them we've got nothing."

I wasn't sure why they were being so free and forthright with their information. Maybe they just needed somebody to blow off some steam to. Maybe they thought Scott or I would give them the big break they needed. Or maybe they were just glad to talk about their troubles with fellow law enforcement people that had no interest in stabbing them in the back in hopes of a quicker promotion, a pastime pursued by a lot of feds like it was a religious edict.

"And the thing is," Gaines said, "is that we were still in secret hearings. We hadn't issued any warrants or subpoenas or indictments for Bufonte, or anyone else for that matter. We kept it so far under wraps that we were sure Bufonte couldn't know a thing about it." He looked up and saw mine and Scott's expressions and elaborated.

"Oh, sure, you can't be one hundred percent certain, but we were damn close to it this time. These witnesses weren't full-time goombahs, so they weren't even missed when we started taking care of them. And even if Bufonte did find out, which he was going to eventually anyway, so what? That's what we're here for. Regardless of what happened, we don't have any witnesses to protect anymore, and then we find out that Scarelli has been sent out to do a number on our guys. That was his assignment, as we found out. To whack our three dime droppers. And no luck blaming him, either, he didn't get the assignment until *after* our guys disappeared. So Bufonte must have found out about their testifying, but when? Another goddamn question we can't answer. So we put out a flag on Scarelli and you guys bite a week later. We had a feeling our three friends would stay in the area, since they're all metro Detroiters, so the two of us kept in close contact with the local people. The last few days we've been back in Washington trying to figure out how to keep our jobs when you guys found Scarelli for us."

"I can't believe your witnesses would stay in this area voluntarily, knowing someone would be out to dust them," I said. "Bufonte's a big man in the marvelous Midwest, but past the Rockies nobody gives a fuck about Detroit business dealings. This is the last place I'd be."

"You've forgotten how stupid some smart people can be," Scott said. "That's how we solve most of the crimes we do. Simple, stupid mistakes."

Gaines nodded. "I'll second that. So what we need from you is a detailed firsthand description of what happened in the restaurant. What Scarelli said—if anything—what he did, and also have you look at some pictures to see if any of our birds might've been in the area. They had to have been, otherwise Scarelli wouldn't have been doing what he was doing. It sounds like you interrupted him before he got to his target, but maybe you can pick a face out of your memory and pin it on one of our three missing friends. I know, it's a long shot, and I don't know how it'll help us if you do find one of 'em, but it's all we have at the moment." He rubbed his face with the palms of his hands. I suddenly noticed how dark the bags under his eyes were. "If we come up dry with you, then we'll start canvassing the other people that were in the restaurant, but that'll just as likely as not be a waste of time."

I looked at Scott. "They haven't been briefed on what happened?"

"I guess not," he replied, and I saw a familiar gleam in his eye. I'd have been willing to bet money he was thinking what I was thinking.

"You got pictures of the three guys?" I said, a silly grin on my face. Weatherspoon pulled three black and white glossies from his folder and spread them out on the desk. I went over and looked down at them. They were taken at long range but the quality was good -- surveillance photos taken by someone that knew what he was doing. I looked at them closely but I needn't have -- I saw all I needed to at first glance. I looked up at Scott and smiled and he looked up at me and smiled back.

"Bingo," I said. I held up the middle photo. "Mr. Suit, come on down."

I told the feds the whole story of what happened in the restaurant, with Scott kicking in a few comments from his perspective, as well as the info his people had dug up about Red. Gaines and Weatherspoon nodded to themselves throughout our story, thoughts unreadable behind their tense expressions.

"Did you see either of the other two at all?" Weatherspoon said hopefully. Scott and I both shook our heads.

"He probably brought this Hawkins along to make it look like a robbery instead of a hit, to throw us off the trail," Gaines said. "Confuse the locals long enough to find and hit the other two. He must've been pressed for time. Normally he never would've used someone like Hawkins."

"If we weren't there it probably would've worked," Scott said. "Most of the other people in the restaurant were panicking. They didn't know what the fuck was going on. He breezes in, blows away your man, and breezes out, and everybody thinks it's just some psycho armed robber. Maybe he even would've capped Hawkins at the scene, throw another wrench into the works. All anyone would remember is guns and blood, they don't know from faces. We all know how eyewitnesses work. Apparently so did Scarelli. Pretty good."

"If he was that good, he would have counted the customers and seen one was missing as soon as he came through the door," I said. "He also should've disguised his features just in case something went wrong and we figured out it was a hit."

"Like I said, he probably was pressed for time," Gaines said. "It might've been Hawkins' job to count the patrons. We'll never know. And one of Scarelli's trademarks is that he never wears a disguise. Any eyewitnesses suddenly get amnesia or the brakes go out on their car. There's also a little pride involved. He doesn't like to think he'll get caught, he's too good, he's been at it too long, etcetera." He shrugged his shoulders. "Like the Lieutenant said, you'd be surprised how stupid some smart people can be. At least neither one of you forgot the first rule of a gunfight -- have a gun."

He looked at Scott, but Scott was busy looking at the two remaining pictures on his desk and didn't notice.

"So," I said, "what's the mark's name?"

Weatherspoon studied the picture thoughtfully, taking a while to answer, perhaps deciding if he should.

"Arthur Polzewski, of Hamtramck," he said finally. "We'd appreciate it if you didn't put out any 'Be on the Lookouts' or other paper out on him at the moment. It'd just end up doing more harm than good. We want to handle this ourselves."

"You mean you want to cover your ass," I said. "I thought you just said these guys left because you had a leak in your department, and now you only want your people after them?"

Weatherspoon didn't like my pointing out this flaw in his reasoning, but I knew there was no way he was going to pass the ball. Not this far into the game. He'd wind up guarding check kiters in Boise.

"Maybe we've got a leak," he said, "but if we do, it's only one person. No way it could be more than that. We feel we can keep it more on the QT if it stays in the family."

I shrugged, not really caring one way or the other. Not my job anymore. Scott was looking at the pictures still, seemingly ignoring our conversation. I knew better.

"All you can do now is the same thing you've been doing," I pointed out, "only now you won't know what shooter Bufonte is sending out. What were these guys doing with him, anyway? Numbers? Drugs?"

"They worked for some computer companies," Gaines said. "They sold him software – cutting-edge stuff – and prototypes, and he sold them to rival companies. He acted as a middleman and took a hefty cut at the same time."

"Computer parts?" I said a little too loudly. "I admit that

I haven't had a badge for a few years but when I did I read quite a few briefs on Bufonte, and computer parts just don't seem his speed. Hookers or drugs maybe, but computers?"

"Nevertheless, that's the case. Our witnesses were going to testify that they sold the software and prototypes to him through his--"

"Now I know where I've seen him before," Scott interrupted. He was tapping one of the glossies on the desk violently. "I even know where you can find him."

Gaines and Weatherspoon crowded around him and looked down at the photo he'd indicated. Then they looked at each other.

"Sidney Wollsh," Gaines said. He looked at Scott. "Where?"

"The morgue." The expectant faces of the two agents fell comically.

"Fuck," Weatherspoon spat. "God--" he stopped, then looked around, embarrassed at his outburst. Apparently federal agents weren't allowed to swear anymore.

"Day before yesterday," Scott said. "We had a John Doe come in. Only reason I know is because I was attending an autopsy when they rolled him in. Shot twice in the head and let me tell you, he looks a lot better in this picture than he does now. I remember hearing that he'd been shot sitting in a car in the Hills. They ran the plates but the car had been rented with a stolen credit card or something. Looks like Scarelli hadn't lost his touch after all."

"Stolen credit cards, huh?" Gaines said. "Wasn't taking any chances." Weatherspoon snorted. "Yeah, stolen cards, but he's still in the goddamn area, letting his trail get picked up. Hell, it didn't even have to be Scarelli, one of Bufonte's men could've spotted him on the way back from stuffing his face with a Whopper and punched his ticket right then.

Surefire way to get in good with the boss. I don't suppose there were any witnesses?"

Scott just smiled at him.

"Figures. Well, we're going to want to see the body and the personal effects."

"We'll also want to see the responding officer's report and talk to the investigating detectives, if any have been assigned yet," Gaines added. Scott nodded.

"I think that's about it," Weatherspoon said. "I don't think we'll need to talk to you about anything else," he said to me, "but just in case, I'll need a number I can reach you at."

I nodded and handed him a card with my office number on it.

"And this is mine," he said, writing on the back of one of his own business cards. "The second number is my pager. Between both of them you should be able to get me twenty-four hours a day. Something important pops into your head you didn't remember before, call me."

I took the card from him and stuck it in a pocket. Weatherspoon gathered up his papers and photos and stuffed them in his folder.

"Wait here while I run these guys over to the morgue," Scott said to me. "I need to talk to you about something."

"Sure," I said. "Have fun." I nodded at the two agents and the three of them left. I sat in a chair by the door and thought. The fact that Weatherspoon and Gaines were in the Witness Protection business for the Justice Department in and of itself meant that they were probably pretty damn good agents. The fact that they were picked to care for and then spearhead the hunt for their important missing witnesses meant that they had the faith of their superiors, at least for now. But if a person was willing to change his or her entire lifestyle, and managed to track down some fake IDs, they could disappear off the face of the earth for all the luck an experienced investigator would have in finding them. And after two attempts on their lives, one of which was successful, the two remaining pigeons were going to be highly paranoid, more willing than ever to do whatever it took to keep from getting killed. Since the guy in the other picture hadn't been at the Ram's Horn as far as either Scott or I could recall, I was assuming they'd done the smart thing and split up. Three men together, even two, are a lot easier to spot than a single individual.

The feds had a handicap, though. A possible bad apple. And with the luck cops usually have, the informer would be working side by side with Weatherspoon and Gaines. I knew all about that kind of luck. After five years of working cases in the DEA, I'd had everything that could go wrong, go wrong. Short of actually dying, that is. I learned to just take the bad luck into consideration and plan for every conceivable, and a few inconceivable, screwups.

After that, I didn't do much more thinking. It was too early in the morning. I'd never liked getting up early, especially when I was in the army, and it wasn't getting any easier as I got older. I was not a morning person, not by a long shot. That I was half asleep in the chair when Scott returned twenty-five minutes later was no surprise to either of us.

"Wake up, you lazy piece of shit," he said cordially, taking a seat behind his desk.

"You're just mad because I didn't compliment your new office," I said. "I'm sorry." I cracked my eyelids and looked around briefly. "I see they did a good job of renovating it. You can't even tell where the urinals were." I looked at him, but couldn't read anything from his expression. "Was it Wollsh?"

"Yeah. Weatherspoon wasn't too pleased. He's getting a lot of heat from upstairs to find his people, he says. I've never experienced a clusterfuck of this size personally, but I can relate, and I empathize. I managed to convince him to let me put out a Be On the Lookout for the two squealers that're left. It was a little easier convincing him now that there's only two instead of three."

"So what's up?"

"Since we've known each other for so many, many years, and since you're such a close, personal friend of mine, and since you won't even deign to compliment me on my new office, and--"

"Okay, okay, Jesus Christ, what do you want?" I said. Then blinked. "'Deign'? You got a word-a-day calendar?"

"I have this acquaintance," he began, talking over me. "He was a friend of my father's, and I've known him for quite a few years. We exchange cards at Christmas, I visit occasionally on Thanksgiving, that kind of thing. To make a long story short--"

"Oh my God, come *on*."

"To make a long story short," he went on, ignoring me, "his son turned up missing a couple of days ago."

"So put his face on a milk carton and leave me out of it," I said. "Or better yet, see if you can find a cop. I've heard that they handle things like this sometimes." Then, for some unknown reason, I said, "So how old is this kid, anyway?"

"Twenty," Scott said. He saw the look on my face. "I know, I know," he said, holding up a hand, "the kid's probably off partying somewhere, or doing God knows what else. I can't even bear to think of what he might be getting pierced. But his father asked me if I could look into it. I told him I was too busy but I recommended you and said I'd have you call them. They've already filled out a Missing Person Report, but they want to do more. They're sort of freaked out."

"You want me to do a *missing persons*?" I said. "You know how much I hate missing persons. They're almost as bad as divorces, but there at least I occasionally get to follow the soon to be ex-husband into a strip club. Twenty? The kid'll probably show up in a day or two with alcohol poisoning and a new tattoo."

"I know, it's probably nothing. But the guy's a friend of mine, and he's worried. He says it's not like his son to disappear." He held up another hand as I opened my mouth. "I know," he said, "they all say that. But I have met the kid a few times, and his dad's right. It doesn't seem like something he'd do, just taking off like that. That's why I'm asking you. It doesn't have to be an exhaustive ordeal, just go through the motions if you want. It'll make him and his wife feel a lot better. The kid will probably show up before you get done asking questions."

I scowled and sighed. I really wasn't doing anything else at the moment, and finding a kid wouldn't take that much time or effort.

"Are they normal?" I said.

"Who?"

"The Mansons, these friends of yours. With the missing kid."

"As normal as you or me," Scott replied.

"That's not what I asked."

"For Christ's sake. They're in their fifties, upper middle class, live in a four bedroom house, he's an accountant, she sells insurance, one kid, no pets, three cars, cable TV, and in debt up to their eyebrows. How much more normal can you get?"

I sighed and scraped at a stain on my shoe. "Okay, okay, I'll take it," I said. "Just don't expect me to take you out for any more fancy lunches."

"Yeah, like I had a swell meal the last time you did."

Chapter Four

MEET THE FAMILY

I was heading north toward Rochester Hills later that same day. The sun was to my left and doing its damnedest to get around my visor as it set. Other than that small annoyance, I was enjoying the trip. I'd memorized the directions given to me by Mr. Phillips over the phone and so leisurely cruised my way out to the sprawling suburban growth that was Rochester Hills. Traffic was even worse than I remembered. The suburb's population had tripled in the past fifteen years and the road capacity hadn't caught up.

I passed Oakland University and in a few minutes turned into Phillips' subdivision. His house was all red brick and brown wood siding and backed up to a small patch of woods. 2500 square feet, maybe, upper middle class. Even though the house was superficially different from its neighbors, all the houses on the street looked like they were built from the same floor plan, and they probably still ran a quarter million dollars or more. Property taxes in the Hills were obscene.

I drove around two kids riding their bikes under the

watchful eye of their mother, the bikes still with training wheels, and pulled into Phillips' driveway next to a new Impala.

Frank Phillips opened the door when I rang the bell and let me into the foyer. Phillips was balding and looked older than I thought he would, but he still looked to be in decent shape. I shook his thin hand and turned down coffee. We sat on a small couch in the living room in front of a bay window. The interior of the house was decorated tastefully, the furniture stylish and in good shape. It reminded me a lot of my own house, only cleaner. I wondered briefly if they'd picked up for me.

"How do we go about this?" he said. Deep creases appeared in his forehead and I noticed his eyes were red behind his glasses. I doubted that he'd been crying, he didn't seem the type, but it was obvious he was upset about something.

"Well, I don't really know anything about what's happened yet, Scott didn't really give me any details, so why don't you tell me what you know and we'll work from there." I took out a small notebook and a pen.

"There really isn't much to it," he said. "The day before yesterday Jerry went to work like he always does. In the summer, that is. He makes what he can for college and we give him a little help. He's going to State. Anyway, when he didn't come home from work when he was supposed to, a little after six, we didn't really worry too much because we figured he was out with his friends. Or Jodi, his girlfriend. He normally tells us when he'll be out late but occasionally he forgets, so we didn't think it was any big deal. But when he didn't come home at all that night we got very worried."

"You and your wife."

"Yes. She's not home right now, she's out shopping. She

said staying around the house waiting for a call was driving her batty. I'm not holding up too well myself."

"Uh-huh," I said noncommittally, hoping he would go on with the story without trying to get me to commiserate with him. He did.

"So then the next morning we called his work, and they said that he had left for lunch the day before and never came back. The manager figured he'd gotten sick or something, and since the day after that, yesterday, was his day off, they hadn't thought to call anyone."

"Where does he work?"

"Champion Nursery on Rochester Road. He's worked there for what, four summers now? Yes, this is his fourth year. He likes the job."

"Did you call anyone else to try and locate him? His friends? His girlfriend?"

"Yes, we called his friends but they hadn't heard from him and neither had his girlfriend. In fact, she called us wondering where the hell he was because they had a date planned yesterday afternoon and he never called her."

"Has your son ever done anything like this before? Run away, disappeared?"

"No, never. He wasn't that type of kid."

"Uh-huh. Have you had any, uh, problems with him lately? Fights, arguments, even ones that didn't seem important?"

"No, no," he said, waving the idea away. "We get along fine. We had some rocky times in high school, you know, when kids think they know everything, but we get along fine now."

"How about the people he works with? Or his girlfriend?"

"Not that I know of, or that anyone's let on. He seemed

to be having a good summer, seeing his friends and his girlfriend and working."

"You said he goes to State?" Phillips nodded. "How's that going?"

"He likes it. He's on the honor roll most of the time."

"What's his major?"

"Criminal Justice."

I looked up from my notes. "Really. He want to be a cop?"

"He's leaning more toward the feds I think. Weren't you in the DEA? I think Scott mentioned that."

"Yeah. About his girlfriend. Is there a chance she could be in trouble? Pregnant?" Phillips obviously didn't like this line of questioning, and he squirmed around a bit, but he answered me without hesitating.

"Well, there's no way for me to say for sure," he said honestly, "but I doubt it. Both of them are very responsible for their ages, especially Jerry. And if she was pregnant, I'd like to think that Jerry would be able to handle the situation rationally, not run off. No, I don't think there's anything there."

"Drugs?"

Frank Phillips looked up at me in surprise, then quickly shook his head. "No, he said firmly. "He wants to be in law enforcement. He knows there's drug tests."

Parents' perspectives on their children are notoriously biased, but just listening to people talk about themselves or their family can sometimes throw light on a problem area. I listened to his responses and filed them away. It sounded like he had a good relationship with his son, but who knew? Honor roll, criminal justice major – Scott had told me that the kid didn't have a criminal record, and from what he knew of the kid he believed drugs couldn't be involved, but who really knew anybody? People had hired John Wayne Gacy to be the clown at their kid's birthday party.

"Okay," I said to him, "you'd know better than me. You haven't said anything about it, but I assume your son has a car? Has it disappeared too?"

"Yes, he does, and yes, it has. Yesterday I drove around, trying to spot it, but I didn't have any luck. It's not parked at Champion Nursery, either. I checked. I told the police but it didn't seem to matter to them. They didn't seem much interested in my missing persons report either. Except for Scott. They seemed to think Jerry was just out partying or something. He's not like that! This isn't like him at all, but they wouldn't listen. No evidence of foul play, they kept saying. 'We put it into the computer, just wait a day or two.'" He shook his head. Since I was working this case as a favor to Scott, my views on the whys and wherefores of the disappearance of a healthy twenty-year-old male from his parents' house in the middle of summer had no bearing, so I kept my thoughts to myself.

"Give me the make, model, color and license number and I can run his car through some contacts on the force to see if it's showed up anywhere."

"It's an ninety-eight Sunfire, blue, license number 425 YGG. I kept repeating it to myself all day yesterday as I looked around."

I nodded and wrote it all down in my notebook. "Any relatives that live nearby that he's close to, could be staying with?" I said. After a short pause, he shook his head no. "Okay. I'll also need a picture of your son, and the names and phone numbers, and addresses if you've got them, of his girlfriend and as many of his friends as you can think of." Maybe they'd talk to me where they wouldn't talk to his dad.

Failure Drill

Phillips nodded and left me alone in his living room for a few minutes, then returned with a photograph and some names and numbers written on a piece of paper. I took it all and looked at the photo first.

Jerry was a slender, dark haired kid with a serious face frozen in a half-smirk in the picture. He had his arm around a chesty brunette in the photo and they appeared to be sitting on the same couch my posterior was now holding down.

"Girlfriend?" I said, wiggling the picture. He nodded.

"Jodi," he said. "Her name's on the list you have." I examined the list he'd given me.

"I don't know his friends' addresses offhand," he said, "but I know they're all in the book. Ron is on Thornridge, I know that, but I don't know what number."

I looked at the names. Ron Kelly and Steve Reath. Finding out where they lived shouldn't tax my investigative faculties too much.

"He have a cell phone?" I asked.

Phillips shook his head. "There are phones at Champion and he's got a phone here. I guess he didn't want to spend the money."

I asked Phillips if his son had any credit cards but he didn't know. "I'm sorry, I'm just not coping too well," he told me. "Maybe my wife would know."

"I'll manage," I said. I stuffed the paper and the photo into the inside pocket of my jacket and stood up. "If it's okay with you, I'd like to look around his room a little. It might help me learn something about him, maybe help me find him faster. There also could be some sign of where he went. Have you looked around in his room since he's been gone?"

"No," he said. "It never occurred to me. I don't ever go

up there anyway, so I wouldn't notice if anything was missing, even. If you think it'll help, go ahead and look around, please."

He led me up the stairs to the second floor and steered me toward a half-open door.

"I'd probably just be in your way," he said, looking as nervous and uncertain as I would have if my son was missing and I was placed in the same position. "You know what to look for more than I would." He turned to leave but I stopped him.

"One more thing," I said. "It's not a pleasant thought, but . . . have you checked with any hospitals?" *Not to mention the morgue*, I thought to myself.

Phillips took off his glasses and rubbed the bridge of his nose. "Scott brought up the same question. I was going to take more time off work and call all the local hospitals, but Scott had a few spare minutes yesterday and said he checked for me. He's met Jerry quite a few times so he knew what he looked like. Thank God he came up empty. The only thing else we could do was file that damn useless report and wait, and neither I nor my wife wanted to just sit around."

"Okay, thanks. I'm just gonna look around to see if anything looks out of the ordinary. Plane tickets to Rio, etcetera." He gave a small smile at my weak attempt at humor and left me alone in his son's room.

Every time I took a case that might not have a happy ending I worried. More on some, less on others, but I couldn't help it. Missing persons cases were the worst, which is why I hated them so much and had stopped taking them. When they turned out badly, the misery the family and friends of the victim went through was unbelievable. I didn't like being the bearer of the bad news.

Against one wall of the room was a bookshelf overflowing with paperbacks, mostly older, yellowed science fiction with some newer looking mysteries. There was an X-Files poster on one wall and one of Arnold Schwarzenegger as "The Terminator" on another. The bed was wrinkled and unmade and a few clothes were scattered about on the floor. Normal for a twenty year old, at least so far. I didn't know exactly what I was looking for, but I'd know it when I found it. Maybe.

A nice oak desk that looked just a few years old was under the window on the far wall, covered with piles of magazines and opened mail. The magazines featured either guns or fast cars on their covers, and the mail contained canceled checks and statements from his bank. I wrote down the name of his bank and account number in my notebook. Leaning against the wall beside the desk was a hard-sided gun case that turned out to be locked. I hefted it and learned it wasn't empty, but it still remained locked and I didn't think vandalizing my client's son's possessions would get me in their good graces too quickly. I left it alone for the moment and went through the desk drawers. Mostly they were just full of junk, the kind of crap everyone accumulates in their desk until they get a new desk or move. The bottom left drawer contained several boxes of 12 gauge ammunition of varying types, along with a gun cleaning kit. The bottom right drawer was filled to the top with old mail that I found concealed a large collection of Penthouse magazines underneath. It took all of my iron willpower to ignore them and move on.

The bureau revealed nothing to me about the vanished kid other than he was a plain dresser and needed some new socks. A small drawer high up on the bureau above the clothes contained a large number of knives. I nosed around, pulling a few out of their sheaths and saw they were all high-quality blades by big name companies, very sharp, and had set him back a pretty penny. The only thing I could make of it all was that maybe he was a collector, but that didn't seem right either.

The only interesting things hanging in Jerry's closet were a judo as well as a karate uniform. I looked again at the trophies on his bookcase that I'd figured for bowling or baseball and saw they were from karate tournaments. Half the floor of the closet was taken up by a stack of old board games, such as Monopoly and Risk, games I could remember playing as a kid. They had a lot of dust on them, so I supposed Jerry had developed other interests. Like the Penthouses in his desk.

Against the opposite wall of the closet from the board games, in a dark corner, were several old toy rifles gathering dust, remnants of a childhood past. Between the board games and the toy guns was a brown cardboard box and a green army backpack. The box was filled with spent brass shell cases from a .45 automatic. The backpack looked empty and did little to hold my interest until I nudged it a little and saw what was underneath. There was a pistol case there on the floor, open, with a combination lock lying beside it. The lock was open and undamaged. The case was empty but the foam inside still retained the imprint of a pistol.

I knelt there a while, thinking. The conclusions I could draw from the items I'd discovered might not necessarily be the truth, but they sure were interesting. I looked at the long gun case leaning against the wall next to the desk and had a thought. After laying the case on the floor it was only a few minutes work to pick open its simple locks with a paperclip I pulled out of the desk. There was no .45 inside the case, only a gleaming black 12-gauge riot shotgun. I sat back and thought again.

Jerry Phillips was quite well armed for someone his age. Knives, a riot shotgun, and a .45 auto that so far I could only assume existed. But for the weapons, his room looked pretty typical for a college kid. Books and posters from high school and earlier gradually losing ground to older, more sophisticated tastes. All in the slightly disheveled environment most single straight males under forty call a home.

There wasn't anything else to see but I checked under the bed and mattress just in case. I covered up the empty pistol case and put everything back in its place and shut the door behind me. Phillips met me at the bottom of the stairs just as his wife came in the front door. He introduced us and I shook her hand. Under normal conditions she probably didn't look her age but now her eyes were bloodshot and had circles under them. She was short and compact and had a no-nonsense look about her.

"Did you buy anything?" Phillips asked his wife.

"It was all crap," she said tersely. She looked me over intently. "Are you the one Scott sent over to look for Jerry?" I nodded. "Are you any good at your job or did he just send you over to placate us?" she said directly. She didn't seem to be one to beat around the bush. I've always liked that.

"Both," I said honestly. "I've worked in military intelligence and the DEA, and I've worked in the private sector for a while, so I'm quite qualified to look for your son. But Scott thinks Jerry will show up soon no worse for the wear, and I'm of a mind to agree."

"You really think that?" she said, the expression on her face looking like she'd just eaten a dog turd. I guess in her opinion, my opinion wasn't good for much. It was obvious she thought there was no way her son would disappear unless there was foul play involved. That was unlikely, but her reaction was normal. I shrugged.

"It would be typical," I said, "but I don't really know enough to tell yet. I'm here to do an investigation, and that's what I'm going to do before I make up my mind one way or the other. I have to go talk to the people he works with, and his friends and girlfriend, before I can make any assumptions about why he might've disappeared. He may have a good relationship with you two, but there are things that a kid will say and do around his friends that he would never let on to his parents about."

They nodded knowingly.

"There are also things that his friends might tell me that they wouldn't tell you." I changed the subject and said, "Does Jerry own a pistol?"

"Yes, he owns a forty-five," his father replied. "Why?"

"Oh, I just saw a boxful of empty brass, that's all."

"Didn't you see the pistol case in his closet?" Mr. Phillips said.

"Yeah, but it was locked," I lied. "Could be a gun in there, could be a four-speed drill. I'd rather ask and know than just assume," I explained. Telling them that not only was their son missing but that he was also probably packing a .45 had no upside.

"What do you charge?" Mrs. Phillips said.

"Well, I was just going to treat this as a favor to Scott," I said.

"No," she said. "I don't want you taking this case seriously because you're not getting paid for it. What are your rates?"

"Forty-five bucks an hour plus expenses. But to tell you the truth, the money doesn't really make much difference in how zealous I am. I usually plod along at my own rate no matter who's pulling the strings or why."

"I'd still rather pay you," she said. I shrugged.

"So what are you going to do first?" Mr. Phillips said.

"Tomorrow morning I'll head over to this nursery and talk to the people he works with. It was the last place he was seen so that's as good a place as any to start."

"That's not entirely true," said Mrs. Phillips. I looked at her curiously.

"What do you mean?" I said.

"Well, Champion might've been the last place he was seen, but that day when I came home from work at about five I noticed that things in the refrigerator had been moved around. I'd swear to it."

"You think he came home and grabbed some food?"

She shrugged. "Maybe. I don't know. I just think that things in the fridge had been moved around, that's all."

"Okay. Well, thank you. I'll start on this tomorrow morning and I'll probably call you with questions as I look into things. If I come across anything important I'll let you know right off."

Mrs. Phillips wrote me out a check for three full days in advance and stuck it in my hand. I pocketed it and shook their hands and walked out to my car. They hadn't been as bad as I'd expected or had experienced before, but it was still early in the game. Things could change.

Chapter Five

SEEKING THE LOST

The morning dawned bright and clear, and for once that week, warm. I climbed out of bed at seven, letting Kelly lie undisturbed for the remaining fifteen minutes she had until it was time for her to get up and get ready for work. Normally she didn't work on Saturday, unlike me, but there was a big deal going on at her office about new procedures, and management had decreed that everyone had to know them by Monday.

Or what? I asked her. *The heavens will part and God will rip you a new one?* Sometimes she didn't appreciate my sense of humor.

I knocked off fifty pushups on the tile floor of the bathroom as fast as I could, immediately regretted it, then took a scalding hot shower to finish the job of waking myself up. Afterwards I put on a pair of running shoes, shorts, and a T-shirt and went on a slow four mile run.

By the time I returned and had another quick shower to wash the sweat off, breakfast was ready and on the table. Kelly was running late, as usual, and I barely had time to kiss her before she was out the door. I ate quickly and rinsed off my dishes then headed toward Rochester Hills again and Champion Nursery.

My SIG was still in the police evidence room so the techs could test fire it and see if the slugs matched rifling-wise to the ones the M.E. dug out of Scarelli and Red. It would be months, maybe years, until I got it back, so slow are the wheels of justice -- not to mention government employees. The replacement gun on my hip was a Smith and Wesson Model 65 LadySmith. It was a stainless steel .357 Magnum revolver with a satin finish and rosewood grips designed to capture the interest of females wanting a positive method of self-defense. I didn't care who it was designed for. I liked the looks of it, it concealed well, and a .357 Magnum is a .357 Magnum.

I pulled into the nursery parking lot at nine-thirty. Even at that early hour the lot was packed full of cars, but I should have expected that on a sunny Saturday. Throngs of customers milled between the rows of potted baby trees and shrubs in the fenced-in lot which covered close to four acres. There were already lines at the registers and the redshirted help was scurrying madly among the customers.

I walked up near the cashier's booth where a skinny blond guy was using a forklift to arrange pallets holding bags of topsoil. The way he was weaving the forklift in-between the oblivious customers made it obvious he'd done it a few times before. I got his attention when he paused to lower a pallet to the ground.

"Excuse me," I said loudly to be heard over the noise of the forklift's motor, which was badly in need of a tune-up.

He looked at me impatiently, probably figuring me for a hapless customer. He was in his late twenties, very thin, with sunbleached blond hair and a strawberry birthmark on his neck. Like the other Champion employees I'd seen, he had a strikingly dark tan from working outside all day every day. His name tag said KEN and below that, Assistant Manager.

"I'm looking into the disappearance of an employee of yours, Jerry Phillips," I said.

He climbed down off the forklift after shutting it off and stood in front of me, his hands stuck in the pockets of his shorts. I gave him one of my cards and told him who I was working for. He stared at my card curiously. "Yeah," he said. "His parents called yesterday, looking for him. No, I guess that was the day before," he corrected himself. "It was the police called yesterday and asked a few questions. I couldn't tell 'em anything. You working for the parents?"

I nodded.

"Huh. I never met an actual P.I. before. What do you want to know? I don't really know nothin' that'll help ya."

"Well," I began, "his parents said they were told he went out to lunch and never came back Wednesday."

"Yeah, that's what happened. I was here that day. Jerry took lunch around three, said he was going out to eat at McDonalds or someplace, left, and never came back. I figured he either got sick or got into an accident."

"Why? I mean, why did it have to be one of those two? Why no other explanation?"

"Well, because it would've had to have been something serious for him not to come back. He's solid dependable. Most dependable guy here. Been here as long as I have. Can't remember him ever missing work 'cept when he called in first. And that's almost never. That's why I figured it was something serious for him not to show up. I checked around that day with everyone who worked to see if he called in sick or told someone that he wasn't going to be working after lunch and I hadn't heard about it, but no one here knew nothing. So my guess was that he got into a car accident, the way he drives, not to mention the traffic around this town the last few years. Have you talked to his girlfriend yet?"

"No, not yet. Do you know her?"

"Yeah, he used to bring her in a lot. Me, them two, and some of the other guys here go out together sometimes after work. You seen her? Nice rack," he told me confidentially. "She don't know where he is, though?"

"No. She didn't know he was unaccounted for until he didn't show up for a date with her on Thursday afternoon. Is there a chance she could be lying, covering his tracks, just telling a story to his parents? Could he be over at her place or somewhere she knows about?" I raised my eyebrows.

"No, no way. Like I said, that ain't like him. It must be something important. Oh shit," he suddenly said, "has anybody checked the hospitals?"

I nodded, allaying his fears.

"Well, shit, I don't know what else to tell you. You might want to talk to the Beefcake Brothers over there," he said, pointing over my shoulder. "I think they talked to Jer just before he went out to lunch on Wednesday. Maybe he said somethin' to them that'll tell you where he went."

I looked to where he was pointing and saw two guys in red shirts loading a small pine tree into the bed of a pickup truck. I thanked the assistant manager, reminded him he had my card in case he thought of anything else, and walked over to the two laborers as they jumped down out of the truck, their arms covered with clay and sap.

"Hey guys," I said, and introduced myself. "I just talked to Ken about Jerry Phillips, and he said he thought that you two were the last people Jerry talked to before he left for lunch last Wednesday and never came back."

The two of them looked down at me. They looked like identical twins, about six foot four and built like professional wrestlers. They were perhaps old enough to vote, but I wouldn't have bet any money on it. At first I couldn't see any difference, however slight, in their appearance, but then I noticed the one on the left had brown eyes while his brother had blue ones.

"Yeah," Brown Eyes said. "We was loading some burning bush and cotoneaster into a trailer and he came out and gave us a hand. When we finished he said he was going out to lunch at Burger King and wanted to know if we wanted to go, or have him bring us back some food."

"But we'd just ate," Blue Eyes said, "so we didn't."

"I can't believe the two of you would've needed help," I remarked, thinking the two of them together probably tipped the scales around 500 pounds. Most of it muscle.

"Aw, hell, we had a lot a shit to load," Blue Eyes said. "'Sides, Jerry's a strong motherfucker. Don't look it because he's so skinny, but if he gets going, watch out."

"Yeah," Brown Eyes said. "One day, he was in back with a customer, like I was too, waitin' for a front-end loader to show up and dig out a white pine this guy had picked out. After waiting about ten minutes Jer got so pissed off he grabbed the wire handles of the cage around the root ball, you know what I mean? And he picked this fuckin tree *up* man, and put it on a pushcart and wheeled it up front." He looked at me and saw I didn't get it, so he stuck his thumb at the tree they had just loaded into the pickup's bed. "The tree was bigger'n that, man."

It was an evergreen of some kind with about six feet of trunk, growing out of a burlap wrapped, wire cage bound ball of dirt about two and a half feet in diameter. I guessed it would run between two and three hundred pounds, depending how much rain there'd been recently, and how much of the soil in the root ball was clay. I lowered the odds on any forcible abduction theories I might have had.

"Do you know what time this was when you last saw him?"

"Uh, just about three o'clock. We was gonna take our break when he got back, but he never showed."

"When he left, did he seem upset or anything? Nervous, worried?"

"Naw, he was in a good mood," Blue Eyes said. "We all were. We'd just found out our sales for the month were up ten percent, which means we all get a bonus, like profit sharing or whatever they call it."

"You know, something's bothering me," I said to them. "You got a guy, one of your co-workers, disappears off the face of the earth, nobody knows where he went, nobody has a clue why, he could be dead in the morgue for all you guys know, and yet nobody here, not one of you guys, has said one thing that would lead me to believe that you were in the least bit worried about him. Explain *that* to me." The two of them stared at me like the thought of something bad having happened to Jerry had never crossed their minds.

"Man, haven't you ever met Jerry?" Brown eyes said incredulously. "You must not've. He can take care of himself, I'm not worried about that. You'll see what I mean, when you meet him." The other one nodded vigorously at his brother's words.

"Okay," I said. I handed them one of my cards. "If you happen to think of anything else, or you hear from Jerry, give me a call." I thanked them and walked to my car. Once there I got in and sat unmoving for a while, thinking.

I cranked the starter until the engine caught, put the car

into gear, and pulled up alongside one of the twins as he pushed a customer's plant purchases out to her car.

"Where's the Burger King?" He jerked his head north up Rochester Road.

"'Bout half a mile up." I thanked him again and pulled out of the parking lot and onto Rochester Road. There was a strange nagging sensation, like a buzzing in my head, that started up, and it took me a minute to figure out why. Then I realized that there must've been something that I was overlooking, and my subconscious was trying to alert me to it. I didn't know what it was, or why -- for sure -- my head was buzzing, but I knew something was there. Something someone had said or done had clicked in my head, and the nagging sensation would keep on keepin' on until I figured out what it was that I'd missed.

I pulled into the parking lot of the Burger King and watched people go in and out for a while. I wasn't sure what I was doing (not an uncommon occurrence), but when in doubt my motto was Sit And Think. And maybe Eat. I didn't see Jerry's Sunfire in the parking lot but then I didn't really expect to. That would've been too easy. So I went inside and showed Jerry's picture to the counter help, but no luck. Even if Phillips had gone in and ordered food as he'd planned, the only way the harried help would've even registered his presence was if he'd done something to warrant a major amount of attention. Dropped his pants, or shot someone.

I wandered back to my car, no farther ahead than I'd been when it had all started. The little buzzer inside my brain kept going off, and it was really starting to bug me. I didn't even know why the damn thing was there.

"Goddamnit," I said, along with a few other choice words. Good thing Weatherspoon wasn't around, his ears

Failure Drill

would've turned red. I reached into the glove compartment and pulled out the picture of Phillips and stared at it a while. It wasn't telling me anything. I set it down and grabbed the piece of paper with names written on it that Frank Phillips had given me. It still said Steve Reath and Ron Kelly.

With the paper in my hand I climbed out of and locked my car, then walked over to the gas station next door. Scott's cell phone was dead, but at least he had a phone. I'd lost mine somewhere a week before, and hadn't gotten around to getting a new one yet. Remarkably the pay phone was in working order and I called information. The monotone voice on the other end of the line told me the address of the only Kelly that lived on a Thornridge Drive. I bought a map of the greater Rochester area in the gas station and headed out in my car.

Chapter Six

FINDING FRIENDS

Thornridge was a minor county road that ran east-west for about twenty miles, alternating between gravel and blacktop, about three miles north of Rochester Hills proper. As I drove north out of the Hills, I noticed the subdivisions and the yuppies seemed to disappear at roughly the same rate. A mile north of the last subdivision I saw farms and corn appear on either side of the road. Not large farms, but they were enough to remind me all was not BMWs and Cuisinarts in Oakland County.

I reached the intersection with Thornridge and stopped. On the left it was asphalt, on the right, gravel. On a hunch I turned right and followed the road for close to a mile before I saw any houses at all. To my right was mostly trees, to my left fields covered in blooming wildflowers. I checked the address on the first residence I came to and saw it was my destination. What a detective.

The Kelly property was lined with a handsome split rail fence that showed signs of recent repair. The house was large

Failure Drill

and sprawling, a tri-level set into the backside of a small hill. The builder would've called it a ranch-style home, built when the name still had some meaning. A two-story barn stood a slight distance away from the house, and behind the two structures stretched a large field bordered by the same split rail fence. Inside it grazed two brown horses. I parked in front of the house on the driveway and wandered around the side of the residence in the general direction of the horses.

Around the back of the house, standing next to the section of fence that stretched from house to barn, was who I took to be Ron Kelly. He was shirtless and sweating, wielding a small chainsaw that he was using to cut and shape timbers for the split rail fence. Several dozen nearby rails with the look of new wood attested that he'd been at it for some time.

Kelly had his blond hair in a crewcut, and from the shape he was in I figured him for current or ex-military. His upper body was muscular, but it was his legs that caught my attention. The bunched knots of his calf muscles would have intimidated most cantaloupes, and his thighs were doing reasonable imitations of tree trunks. I figured it had to be genetics, because I could work up to a thousand-pound squat and still not have calves that big.

As I walked up to him, he shut off the chainsaw, picked up the cut length of wood, and fit it into a vacant slot in the fence. He wiped his hands on his cut-off jeans and turned to look at me.

"Ron Kelly?"

He pulled up his safety glasses and wiped the sweat out of his eyes. Sawdust was stuck all over his upper body. "Yeah?" he said warily.

When he'd first turned to face me I'd seen his eyes dart

to my hands, just like a cop checking a suspect's hands to see if they're empty.

"I'm a private investigator. I've been hired by Jerry Phillips' parents to look for him. He seems to have disappeared. I was wondering if you could tell me anything about where he could be or why he might've turned up missing."

He looked at me blankly for a minute. "He's still missing?" he said finally. "Has anyone heard from him at all?"

"I take it you knew, then. No, no one's heard anything from him since Wednesday afternoon."

"His parents called me Thursday, looking for him, but I haven't seen him since last weekend. I figured he was banging the snot out of Jodi somewhere. That's his girlfriend."

"She says she hasn't seen him. At least, that's what she told his parents. I haven't had a chance to talk to her yet."

He saw where I was going. "Well, I don't know her that well, so I'm not an expert on what she'd lie about, but I know Jer, and he wouldn't disappear like this unless he was in real trouble. When did he disappear? I mean, what were the circumstances?"

I hated recounting the story, but maybe he could find the devil in the details that I'd missed. Ron stood there and chewed at his lip for a while, thinking. He didn't look pleased. While we were standing there a screen door on the side of the house opened and a man appeared.

"Goddammit, Ronald!" he bellowed. "I want that fence done this afternoon! It was supposed to be done last week." His deep voice boomed over the field and one of the horses looked up.

"Yeah, dad, I know! Jesus Christ. I'm done already,

okay?" He rolled his eyes at me, an exasperated expression on his face.

"You also got a phone call," his father yelled. "Girl named Allison."

"I'm not here," Ron yelled back. His father snorted, looked at me curiously for a second, then went back inside.

"Jesus Christ," I said. "What does your dad do for a living, pull boxcars with his teeth?"

I now knew where Ron got his legs from. His father was built like a 50 gallon drum set on two stumps. He was maybe five foot ten and had to weigh at least two-fifty, all of it muscle. If somebody lost a bet and had to shave a bear, it'd look like Ron Kelly's father.

Ron laughed. "Nope," he said.

I shook my head, then got back to the subject of Jerry Phillips. "Do you know a Steve Reath? He's supposed to be one of Jerry's friends. I was planning on talking to him."

"Know him? I'm practically the only friend he has. No, seriously, we're all real good friends. Let me go inside and clean up and I'll call him, see if he knows anything."

I couldn't think of any objections, so I nodded and followed him inside. I didn't see anyone on my way up to the second floor, but I heard a TV on somewhere in the house. Ron grabbed a towel and headed toward the bathroom, leaving me to fend for myself in his room.

On my trek through the house I'd noticed that although it was only a couple years older than the subdivision clones down the road, it was much more expensive and elaborate than they were. Most of the rooms on the ground floor had hardwood floors, and were filled with high-end furniture.

There were bookshelves built into the wall near the door, overflowing with the type of paperbacks Jerry favored.

Above a desk against the adjacent wall was a pair of expensive cross-country skis with matching poles. Next to them was a small horizontal rifle rack that held two old .22 rifles and an M-1 Garand with a Leupold scope that had to have set him back as much as the rifle. The scope was a 3.5 x 10 variable with a built-in range estimator. On the rifle that helped us win World War II? Not exactly a common combination.

The desk below the rack was about as messy as I'd expect from someone Ron's age. What caught my attention was a coffee can full of spent shotgun shells on the corner of the desk. Normally I wouldn't have paid them much attention, especially considering the somewhat rural setting of the house, but firearms and spent shells suddenly seemed to be a recurring theme. Curiouser and curiouser. I nudged a few of the spent hulls around but didn't see any .45's.

On the opposite wall, above a glass encased stereo system, was an 8 x 12 of Ron in a flashy uniform marching in unison with a number of similarly clad youths. Ron looked pretty much as he did now so I guessed the picture had been taken recently. It seemed to be from a dress parade at a military school, but I didn't recognize the uniforms. I knew the Army, Navy, and Air Force Academy uniforms from my time in the service, but this wasn't any of those.

Ron came into the room, his body wrapped in a towel and still wet from the shower. His hair was almost dry, though, which was one of the advantages of short hair. I'd always kept my hair short, but I still looked like a rock star compared to Ron. He got dressed quickly, then sat down on his bed next to a phone and dialed a number.

"Hello, is Steve there? Yeah, Lumpy, it's Ron. Yeah. Listen, it's important. When was the last you talked to or saw Sleepy?" He listened for a while. "Monday, huh? Shit.

Did his parents call --" He stopped talking and got a look on his face. "No, no one knows where the hell he is. No, Jodi hasn't heard from him either. His parents have hired a private eye to look for him, even. I shit you not. He's here right now, asking questions." I flinched at "private eye", but didn't bother to say anything. We all have our pet peeves. Ron listened for a few moments more, then glanced at me.

"I don't know, but I'm sure we'll find out." He paused. "Yeah, probably. Okay, we'll be here."

He hung up and I looked at him expectantly.

"Steve said he hasn't seen him since Monday afternoon when they went to the movies together. He said he didn't notice anything out of the ordinary, but he's on his way over so you can ask him yourself."

"What's all this Sleepy, Lumpy stuff?"

Ron smiled. "They're nicknames from high school. We all went to school together, me, Steve, Jerry, a few other guys. One day in ninth or tenth grade we were all sitting around together in class talking about – what else – sex, and the teacher called us the Seven Dwarves, looking for our Snow White. Or the nearest porno starlet equivalent. It's kind of stupid now that I look back on it, but we've been calling each other by our nicknames for so long that I don't even notice it. I'm Bashful, Steve's Lumpy, Jer is Sleepy, and another friend of ours is Grumpy. There were a couple of other kids but they moved away or dropped out of sight."

"Waitaminit," I said. "Lumpy isn't one of the Seven Dwarves. He's a character from 'Leave It To Beaver'."

"He is?" Ron shrugged. "Whatever."

I pointed to the picture on the wall. "Military academy?"

Ron looked across at the picture and a grin crept across his face. "Yeah. V.M.I. Virginia Military Institute." While I didn't recognize the uniforms, most veterans had heard of VMI, it was one of the most well-known non-governmental military academies in the country. Imagine West Point with a southern accent and an attitude.

Ron got up from the bed. "Let's go downstairs to wait for Lumpy to show up," he said. "It's cooler down there." I gave a noncommittal grunt and followed him down the stairs.

"How much experience do you have in finding missing persons?" he said in a decidedly offhand, casual manner that didn't fool me at all. I did my best not to get defensive. For some reason I found myself reacting strangely to Kelly, getting defensive at simple questions when I should've been laying back and relaxing, studying his reactions. I wasn't sure why. He wasn't nearly as massive as his father, but he had such a strong presence it was almost tangible. I had to remind myself that he was just a college kid, maybe not even old enough to buy beer in a bar, who was worried about his friend and didn't really know anything about life yet.

"You mean, what are my qualifications for finding your friend?" I clarified. I supposed it was a fair question to ask. If it was my close friend that was missing, or my wife, I'd want someone competent in charge of the investigation. "I spent five years in military intelligence with the army, and from there I went into the DEA for a while. That's the Drug Enforcement Administration," I explained.

He aimed a dirty look at me. "No shit," he said. He hadn't seemed too impressed with my mention of military intelligence, which made two of us, but he perked right up when I mentioned the DEA. He led me into the family room and I sat down at one end of a couch. He sat in another across the room from me. The two couches were angled somewhat toward a huge TV against one wall.

"I spent about five years in the DEA, then left and started my own business, which is how I came to be here." I looked around the room, impatient for Reath to show up. Hanging on one of the walls were two ancient looking sawed-off shotguns and an equally aged rifle.

"Were you stationed here in Michigan when you were with the DEA?" Apparently I had piqued his interest.

"Not really," I said. "I was in Chicago for a brief time, then Buffalo for half a second, then I got transferred to Miami, where I spent about three and a half years. All that moving around, that was one of the reasons I resigned." I kicked myself mentally, wondering why I felt I had to justify myself to a kid I didn't even know.

"You married?" He pointed at the gold band on my left hand. I smiled and nodded. I jabbed a thumb at the guns on the wall.

"What's with all the iron?" They had really intrigued me, looking like collectors items even in their sawed-off illegality.

He chuckled and walked over to contemplate the aged weapons, then turned to look at me jabbing a thumb over his shoulder at the guns. "Those are my legacy. Ron Kelly, that's a bit of an Irish name, don't you think? Actually, I'm half Irish and half Italian. How's that for a volatile combination? We talk with our hands....and spill our whiskey. Sixty years ago, my grandfather was a cop in Chicago. At the same time, my great-great uncle on the other side of the family was an enforcer for Al Capone. Robbed banks on the side. Neat, huh? Somehow they managed not to knock each other off. I forget which one of them used which of the shotguns. The rifle, that's been in the family for as long as the shotguns.

"Between those two, and my dad, who was an M.P. in Vietnam, we have quite a tradition in our family for producing men of action." He gave a quirky grin. "My dad's doing his best to see that I don't follow in the family footsteps. The family's more respectable now."

"You going along with your dad's plans for you?"

"I'm sure my chosen occupation will be far from boring," he told me, "but it probably will be legal." I heard a door open somewhere and we both turned toward the sound. Footsteps approached and a young man came into the room. "Lumpy, a.k.a. Steve Reath," Ron introduced, "meet John Phault, private dick." He said it with a smile on his face, half-jokingly, but I could tell he was trying to get a rise out of me.

I shook hands with Reath and looked him over. He seemed about the same age as Ron, with pale skin and what was known in the military world as a high-and-tight haircut. Couple inches up top with nothing on the sides or back. He had dark brown hair that didn't look good cut short, but it probably wouldn't look good any length. We all sat back down, Steve next to Ron on the couch.

"So, how qualified is he?" Steve asked Ron bluntly.

"He should do okay," Ron told him.

"Gee, thanks," I said, laughing, but more than a little pissed by their impertinence. "But I think you forgot that I'm working for the Phillips', not you. I don't need your stamp of approval." I took a couple of slow, deep breaths. *What was it about these guys that got to me?*

"Listen," Steve said. "Jerry is our friend. To us, that means everything. You wouldn't get it now, but if this thing drags out you're going to want to understand how Jerry thinks, and so you're going to have to understand us. We take our friends, and friendship, very seriously. If you're going to be the one looking for him, and it turns out he's really in bad trouble, well, you'd better make sure you know what the fuck you're doing."

Amazing, I thought. I made a mental note to kick Scott's ass the next time I saw him. "Oh?" I said to them, still outwardly unperturbed. Steve gave me a disgusted look and turned to Ron.

"I managed to get ahold of Bob before I came over," he remarked. "He'll actually be coming home on leave when he said he was, for once. He'll arrive at Metro at eleven a.m. tomorrow. I told him a little of what's going on and he reacted in typical Bob fashion."

"Bob?" I inquired.

"Grumpy," Ron explained. "He's in the 82nd Airborne and is coming home on his annual leave tomorrow."

Yippee, I thought, *another one of these guys to deal with*. I shouldn't have worried about Jerry's parents being a problem -- his friends took up the slack. Scott, watch out.

"Getting back to the business at hand," I said, gesturing at Steve, "let's talk about Jerry. You told Ron on the phone that the last time you saw him was on Monday?"

"That's right. We went to the movies at Maplewood Mall. It was his day off."

"Uh-huh," I said. "And nothing seemed to be out of the ordinary with him? Nothing seemed to be bothering him? Amiss?"

"No. And if there was, he would've told me about it, or called Ron if it was that important that he had to disappear."

"How can you be so sure?" I said. "It could've been something personal."

"Even if it was, like between him and Jodi, it wouldn't have caused him to run away. He's not like that. You don't seem to understand, we may still be young compared to you, but we've all known each other for years. Me, Ron, Grumpy, we know Jer better than anybody. Better than his parents, better than Jodi. And it is *not* like him to just disappear."

"Everyone keeps telling me that," I said. "But he's still missing." They nodded their heads in grudging agreement. "Is there any place in particular that he might be?" I said, wanting to move on. "Any place he liked to hang out?"

"Other than his house, or over here, I can't think of any place that he would be," Ron said. "But I can tell you this, if he's in hiding, he wouldn't be at any place he'd be recognized. You won't find him unless he wants to be found."

"You think so?" I thought of Weatherspoon's rogues, three supposedly intelligent older men who returned to the very area they should have avoided like the plague.

"Yes," Steve answered, no doubt in his voice.

Ah, what I wouldn't give for the certainty of youth.

"But no one's heard from him, and I haven't uncovered any reason for him to be in hiding, no evidence for any abduction, so what does that mean?"

They knew their friend a lot better than I did, maybe they could shed some light on the dark mystery of this case. The only solution I could come up with that would fit all the known facts was that he was dead, and no one had found the car or the body yet. But that assumption was counterproductive if I was trying to find a boy that was still breathing. As it stood I had very little left to look into except for maybe something Jerry's girlfriend might disclose. Of course, I was planning to check for any activity in his bank account since his time of disappearance, but that wouldn't help me in any positive way. If there was activity, it would tell me that he was still at large instead of dead, but it wouldn't tell me a damn thing about where he was or why he'd disappeared.

"That means he's either dead or in deep shit," Steve said, answering me.

I took a deep breath to steady myself. "No other explanation? Not one other reason as to why he's been missing other than because he's dead or in deep shit. You must know Jerry better than I thought." If they gave me another friends-to-the-end speech I was going to pull my hair out.

"We do," Ron said. "You need to keep in close contact with us, let us know of any developments as soon as possible."

Yeah, right.

"What you can do for me is call me if he shows up here," I said, "or if he calls either one of you, even if you guys think you can solve whatever problems he might have on your own. Even if he's okay, and it was all a big mix-up, I want to know." I fished out a card as we all stood up and handed it to Ron. "I assume from what you've told me that you'd be the first person he calls."

"Even before his parents," Ron said. Steve nodded decisively.

"Did you look around his room at home, see if he left any clue to where he went?" Steve said.

Christ, I thought, next they'll be telling me how to tie my shoes.

"Yeah," I replied. "I didn't find anything that shed any light on why he's vanished." I neglected to mention the empty gun case. I didn't want to add to their already appreciable paranoia.

"Maybe we should look," Steve said, glancing at Ron,

who nodded enthusiastically. "After all, we know him better than you do, and we've been in his room before. We might spot something that you missed." I thought it over for a while. If I said no, they might decide to go later anyway and play Young Sherlock Holmes. They'd probably notice the empty pistol case and with my luck blurt out something to Jerry's parents about it. If I went with them, I could do some damage control if they shot their mouths off. There was also the chance that there was a simple, innocent reason for that case to be empty, and they'd be there to explain it to me. They could also spot something else that I had seen but not known was unusual. Things might go a lot easier if I let them poke around in his room awhile. Maybe it would satisfy their collective curiosity and they'd let me go back to doing the job I was hired to do.

"Couldn't hurt," I said finally, lying through my teeth. "Why don't you pile into my car and I'll drive us all over."

In short order we were standing on the Phillips' porch, my finger against the doorbell. The two of them had been completely silent during the ten minute ride. I couldn't decide whether it was because they were uncomfortable in my presence or because their thoughts were being drawn to whatever horrible fate Jerry had encountered in their fevered imaginations. Whichever the case was, I was grateful for the quiet.

A bewildered Geraldine Phillips answered the door and I explained what we had in mind. She quickly let us in and took us up to Jerry's room, albeit with a frown on her face. I thanked her and shut the door gently. Then I leaned against the wall and watched the two of them go through the room. Steve found the empty pistol case immediately and showed it to Ron.

"You saw this?" Steve said to me. I nodded and he grumbled something that didn't sound nice.

"It doesn't mean anything," Ron said. "He doesn't keep it in the case anyway. He's got it in a shoulder holster he's got hanging inside here," he said, sliding clothes on the rack away from the judo uniform, "so he can get to it quickly in case of a burglar. He kept ammo in the case to weight it down in case his dad picked it up." Steve parted the folds of the uniform but there was nothing hanging from the metal rod of the hanger inside.

"He keeps a loaded gun where it could be found by his mother putting clothes away?" I said.

"No," Ron explained to me patiently, "he keeps it empty, and keeps the loaded mags in here." He opened the top right drawer of the desk, but there were no magazines inside. The two of them looked at each other, and I could almost hear them thinking. "Besides," Ron said absently as he thought about the missing gun and mags, "his mom folds his clothes and puts them on his bed and Jerry puts them away in his closet, or dresser."

Damn, I guess they did know him pretty well.

"Well now," Steve said to himself, his eyes stuck on the pistol case.

"How bad of a burglary problem could you have in this area anyway?" I said aloud, my mind on other things. Steve and Ron exchanged a look that said they shared a secret I wasn't privy to.

Ron gazed at the empty case again and put his hands on his hips, a grim expression on his face.

Here we go. "What?" I said.

"What this means is," he said, "is that whatever Jerry got himself involved in, he felt he needed a gun. And he does *not* overreact."

"There's no other place the pistol could be?" I said. They shook their heads, confirming my own fears. "Great." Ron busily chewed at his lip.

"If he felt he needed a gun," Steve enunciated slowly, staring at the carpet while he thought, "then he needed a gun. He is not one to *not* take firearms seriously. Especially the illegal carrying of one. None of us are."

All of which meant absolutely nothing to me. Who knew what these guys considered appropriate behavior. Even if they were twice as competent with firearms as the average police officer—not a difficult feat, unfortunately, although most citizens wouldn't believe that—I had a twenty-year-old roaming the streets illegally packing a .45 automatic. And I still didn't know why.

The two of them went over the rest of the room quickly, but nothing else seemed out of place to them. Now that they had what they considered concrete evidence that their friend was in bad trouble they stopped with the smart-ass comments and began to look worried.

I reassured Mrs. Phillips on the way out and drove the two of them back to Ron's house. I thanked them for their help and assured them that I would indeed let them know if I turned up anything on Jerry. I didn't really care if they believed me. As I pulled out of Ron's driveway I could see the two of them in my rearview mirror, heads together, talking intently.

Chapter Seven

PAPERWORK

My office mail was as thrilling as usual, so I dropped all of it unopened into the circular file and sank into my chair. Leaning back, I ran my fingers through my hair and tried to organize my brainwaves.

I reviewed what I had so far. Jerry Phillips, twenty-year-old white male, leading a seemingly calm and complacent life, suddenly shows up missing. No advance warning, if everyone was to be believed—and I doubted that they were *all* lying—and not a trace of him since. Thirty-six hours gone. Everyone I talked to who knew him said this behavior wasn't like him; he wouldn't just run off. Nevertheless, I had one missing boy. If he was ten years old, I could only come up with one solution: abduction. But he was twenty, all grown up, and where was his car if he was abducted? No body, no car, no ransom note.

Then there were his friends. Just from their attitudes and physical appearance I was pretty sure I could rule out drugs as a reason behind Jerry's disappearance. They didn't seem the type to disappear for several days on a crack binge.

Vigorously enjoying their Second Amendment rights, they were convinced he was either "dead or in deep shit". Eloquent but not very helpful. They seemed to be taking his disappearance more seriously than anybody else. They probably knew Jerry better than anybody, perhaps even better than his parents did, but I didn't know if I was convinced by their predictions of impending doom for Jerry. They could just be pessimists. Pessimists barely of legal drinking age that were fond of guns. What a wonderful combination. The whole situation was getting weirder by the minute.

I sat and thought for a while longer, then reached for the phone. It rang just as my hand touched it.

"John, it's Scott." He sounded like his scowl was back in permanent residence again.

"Hey. I was just about to call you."

"Oh? Well, I just called to tell you a date's been set for the departmental investigatory hearing on our shooting."

"Already? Christ, whatever happened to red tape?" I hated post-shooting hearings. I'd had to go through three in the DEA, twice as the shooter and once as a witness. Presidential debates had nothing on them when it came to bullshit and double-talk.

Scott sighed. "Quit your damn whining. It's my hearing, not yours. I don't like these things any more than you do, and it's not until next Monday, the twenty-eighth. Nine a.m. in Room 2B at the Sheriff's Department."

I wrote the information down on my desk calendar.

"You don't *have* to come and give testimony as an involved party, but considering the outcome of this hearing will be used by the Oakland County Prosecutor to decide if he's going to charge me and you with murder, I thought you might want to be there."

"Yeah, yeah, I'll be there," I said. "With my lawyer."

"Christ, you're high maintenance. Are you ever going to give me a break?"

"The day you get a wife," I told him. "Kelly keeps me young. You need someone to wipe that scowl off your face sometimes."

He grumbled. "What were you going to call me about?" he asked. In the background I could hear the hustle and bustle of his office.

"Well, I'm running down that missing Phillips kid for you, and I need you to check on a few names for me." I heard rustling as he grabbed paper.

"Okay, shoot."

I gave him what info I had on Steve and Ron, and he repeated it all when I was done to see if he'd written it down right.

"These guys are only twenty, twenty-one right now, so you might have to check with your juvenile people to get any records they might have, if they have any," I told him. "Also, see if you can find anything on a friend of theirs named Bob. That's all I know about him, no last name, but he did go to high school with them and is in the army now." I heard him scribbling some more. It was probably a shot in the dark, but if I didn't look into the backgrounds of Jerry's friends, Murphy's Law said that they would be the ones that had kidnapped, raped, and murdered him.

"Okay, I got it. You got any ideas on where this kid might be?"

"Not really. This is a weird one. From what I've found out about him, you were right, he's the last person you'd expect to do something like this, vanish without a trace, but he's gone anyway and is probably packing a forty-five for company."

"*What?* Oh, great," Scott grumbled. "You didn't tell his parents, did you?"

I assured him I had not.

"Do you want me to put out a BOL on him on top of the missing person's report? Another kid with a gun I don't need," he said.

I thought about it for a second. "Nah," I said. "I want to gnaw on it for a while yet. Something's funny about the whole set-up, I can't put my finger on it yet, but if I work on it long enough maybe I'll see the light. Besides, I'd hate to stick him for life with a concealed weapons conviction."

"All right, but if you need anything, let me know."

"You know it. Hey," I said, a thought occurring to me, "what's the word from the Justice Department? How's their manhunt going?"

"I haven't heard word one. They tend to keep to themselves unless they need something. But I would've heard something if they'd found one of their pigeons. Dead or alive. Which means they haven't."

We made some more small talk and then said goodbye, and I sat back in my chair. I rested there for a few moments, then bent over with a grunt and retrieved a thick manual from one of my desk drawers.

The tome was the latest manual on new types of electronic security systems, my supposed specialty. I sat there and read it for close to an hour, trying to keep my lips from moving and silently wishing that I remembered more from my computer and electrical classes in college. It was getting to be so I couldn't do any type of job without running into computers, and I didn't like the damn things. I was enmeshed in a thrilling chapter detailing the workings of the latest motion sensors when the phone rang and I grabbed it with relief.

"J. Phault Security and Investigation," I said, the consummate professional.

"Yeah, I need to talk to John Phault." He was middle aged, smoked too much, and was probably overweight if I had to judge him by his voice.

"Yes, can I help you?"

"Name's Garrity, I'm calling on behalf of Lieutenant Copley about some information you requested."

"What's the matter with Scott? He too busy?" I quipped.

"No, he figured I could get the information quicker than he could. I was just transferred under him, before that I spent ten years in Juvie, school liaison programs and so on. I'm doing this as a favor to the Lou."

"Okay," I said, "thanks for the help. What've you got?"

"Well, not too much, really. Both Steve Reath and Ron Kelly went to Adams High School in Rochester and graduated with this Jerry Phillips kid the Lieutenant said you're looking for. Neither of them has a record, but Kelly was suspected of complicity in the destruction of school property."

"What was he suspected of doing?"

"Oh, he did it all right, the only problem was nobody could prove it. Their senior year, the school decided to stop its open-campus policy for lunch, and put up a new guard shack complete with gate to help enforce the policy. Needless to say, this didn't go over too well with the kids, especially the seniors who'd been going out to lunch for two years already. It was a big thing to them, and you know how kids can get over trivial shit. All their parents, of course, were ecstatic. No more chances for car wrecks when little Johnny goes out for lunch."

"What did Kelly do, drive through the gate with a car?"

"No," Garrity said in a serious voice. "We can't prove it

was him, but *someone* blew it up. With homemade plastic explosive," he said slowly, and let that sink in. "Way more than what he needed, according to the ATF, but shit, I coulda told you that. They found the damn door in the middle of the street about two hundred yards away, bent like a pretzel. The blast knocked out windows all over the place—the school, the two cars in the parking lot, hell, even in houses across the street. Took 'em a couple days for them to clean up all the glass. By the time the school had the money to get the gatehouse replaced, the school year was over and the seniors had graduated. ATF was crawling all over the school for a week. I forget how many pounds of explosive they thought were used."

"Jesus," I said. "What evidence did you have against him?"

"Nothing solid, really. We never had enough for a search warrant. Mostly it was all hearsay and rumors that wouldn't stand up in court. You know – somebody said *this*, somebody heard *that*. That and the fact that Kelly, the day the school reopened, wore a T-shirt to school that said 'There Are Very Few Personal Problems That Can't Be Solved By A Suitable Application Of High Explosives' all across the front of it, the smart ass." Garrity laughed in spite of himself, and it turned into his version of a smoker's hack. "ATF tried for months to get something on him, they figured he was half an idiot since he used way too much explosive for the job, got the mix wrong or something, but I'm pretty convinced that was a statement, not an accident. Kelly's not dumb. But anyway, the ATF got nowhere. Nothing. He refused to take a polygraph, I remember that. I also checked the yearbook for any Bobs, but I couldn't find anything until I looked up the bombing. Then I couldn't believe I'd forgotten about him."

"You know who he is?"

"Oh yeah. His name's Robert Grinnand." He spelled it for me. "He graduated with the rest of them from Adams. I remember him because I investigated an assault charge against him when he was sixteen. And another when he was eighteen. Chances are it was him and Kelly together that blew up the fence."

"What's the story?" I said.

"Well, on the first assault charge, when he was sixteen, he was a sophomore at Adams. First year playing ball at the big school. Anyway, one of their traditions over there has been that during Homecoming Week, all the senior football players go after the sophomore football players. They use baby powder, baby oil, shaving cream, whatever makes a mess. Generally they make a pit out of the place for a week, but the administration's never been able to stop the practice."

"Nice tradition," I said.

"Yeah, well, you know kids, what can you do? Anyway, one day during Homecoming Week our friend Bob is walking down the hallway and gets jumped on by five seniors bearing gifts."

"Five?" I interrupted. "Not exactly a fair fight, you ask me."

Garrity paused for a second. I could hear him breathing, the air chugging in and out of his lungs sounding like a train in the old west laboring to get up to speed.

"No, it wasn't," he said with what sounded like a smile. "When it was all over two of the seniors were in the hospital in temporary serious condition and the other three would've made good poster children for the Red Cross. Grinnand ended up with a sprained thumb, if I remember correctly." I heard him chuckle. "And don't you know, three of the seniors tried to press assault charges against him but it never made it past the preliminary hearing. The prosecutor figured there'd be no way he'd ever get a conviction, that five seniors on one sophomore got what they had coming."

"What about the other incident?"

"Nothing much there," he said. "When Grinnand was a junior, one of his wrestling teammates got pissed at him for some reason and put him into a headlock at the lunch table. He got a broken nose for his trouble. The kid tried to press charges, but there were four hundred witnesses in the lunch room that said Grinnand was only defending himself."

"The boy sounds like he's trouble waiting for a place to happen," I said.

"No, that's not it," Garrity said. "I talked with him a few times at length, once after the first incident, and he's a very smart, personable young man. He just doesn't like to be messed with, and has a natural talent for defending himself." I heard Garrity sigh. "You ever met those people, oh, shit, I don't know how to describe 'em—I want to say driven, or intense, but that's not it. Not all of it, leastways. I met a lot of people like Bob in the 'Nam, the same personality I mean. Those people were all mostly Special Forces, I guess. Not my deal at all. In fact, I recall Grinnand was going to go into the army when he graduated. I don't know if he did, but it's been two and a half years since that last incident. If he was still in the area I'd have heard about it. If he did go into the military, he'd have done well."

"He did. Airborne, or so I'm told. He's coming home on leave tomorrow and I may be talking to him. I just wanted to know what to expect. What does he look like?" I asked.

"Grinnand? He's blond, about five-ten, built like Mike Tyson in fighting trim. And his jaw's about the size of Texas. Hard to miss."

Failure Drill

I thanked him, got his number in case I had any more questions later, and hung up.

Great, I thought. I'd told Scott there would be weird people involved in this. Little did I know how right I'd been. Homemade plastic explosive. Great. I picked up the phone and dialed a number.

"Mrs. Phillips?" I said when a female voice answered.

"Yes?"

"It's John Phault. I need to ask you a few questions. Have you heard from your son at all? I know you said you'd contact me if you did, but I just wanted to make sure."

"No, dammit, I haven't heard anything at all. Have you found out anything?"

"I've found out a great many things," I said, fishing my notebook out and laying it on the desk in front of me, "but I'm not sure what it all means." I was an expert at doubletalk. Working for the government will do that to you. "Mrs. Phillips, in your son's room I saw the name of his bank and account number. Can you tell me exactly where the branch he goes to is located?"

"Oh, Christ, I don't know. It's the National Bank of Detroit, you know. I think he goes to the one right over here on the corner. Why do you want to know?"

She didn't sound too good, her voice was real shaky, but at least she hadn't broken down yet. Then again, maybe she had.

"Well, I'm assuming your son's still alive, because I don't have any reason to assume otherwise." A calming, supportive presence, that's me. "So, since he's alive, he'll need money. Does he have a checking account or a savings account there?"

"Checking account, I think."

"How about a money card? Or any credit cards?"

"He doesn't have any credit cards, but he does have an ATM card for his checking account."

"Okay, good," I said reassuringly. "I'll have Lieutenant Copley check with the bank to see if your son has used his money card or withdrawn any money since he's disappeared."

"Why don't you do it yourself? We're paying you, not Scott." She sounded a little indignant, which was a good sign that she hadn't yet given up the ghost.

"Do you know how much trouble it is to open a new checking account?" I said, trying to put her at ease. "Or to close one? Imagine how much red tape I'll have to swim through to get confidential info like what I want. Scott, with his badge, will be able to cut through a lot of it, hopefully. Finding your son quick is what this is all about, isn't it?"

"I'm sorry," she said, sounding like she meant it. "I'm just so afraid and upset that I'm snapping at everybody. I don't mean to be such a bitch. I'll hope you'll forgive me."

"I understand. I'm doing everything I can to find your son," I assured her. "Trust me on that." After a few more platitudes I hung up.

I called the department, but Scott was in a meeting and wouldn't be available for forty-five minutes. I left a message for him to call me and then steeled myself for what I was about to do next.

Chapter Eight

OFFICE POLITICS

An hour and fifteen minutes later my ear was sore and I had a good start on a migraine. I was calling every hotel, motel, YMCA, or other business or institution in the metro Detroit area where a person could stay overnight, asking for Mr. Phillips' room. After a few short calls I'd determined that all desk clerks sounded the same. Even the females.

I tried every place I could think of, without luck. I talked to quite a few Mr. Phillips', but none of them was the one I wanted. I gave up, put down the phone, and picked up my technical manual. After ten minutes my vision was blurred and my eyes kept trying to cross. I put the manual back in the desk, rubbed my eyes, and looked out the window. The day had dawned sunny and warm, but from what the people outside were wearing I assumed that it had cooled down. I could see the leaves fluttering on the maples planted in the grassy boulevard on Big Beaver. I was glad I'd brought my leather jacket upstairs with me. The phone rang again as I was staring out the window.

"Hello, John Ph --" I began.

Scott interrupted me. "You think I've got nothing better to do than converse with you via Ma Bell? I've got four pounds of paperwork on my desk."

"Quit your whining," I said. "That's what you get for sticking me with this case. And speaking of the which, I have a favor to ask." I told him what I needed, and gave him the bank name and account number.

"Aw, come on," he said, "you know I hate banks with a passion, ever since that one lost my balance. I had to threaten to arrest that bitch for embezzlement before she'd get off her ass and find what they did with my account."

I smiled at my empty office. Scott had been enraged for a month after that debacle.

"Poor baby," I said, still smiling. "Shoot a teller if you have to. Gimmee a call if you find out anything." I hung up before he could protest any further.

The bank's info might help, but probably not very much. If Jerry had used his ATM card it would take Scott at least half a day to find out about it, so Jerry would be long gone. It would be too much to hope that he would stay in one spot and keep using the same teller machine or bank. He seemed smarter than that. Even if the information proved worthless in finding Jerry, though, it would tell me one thing; it would tell me that he was still alive. Or at least had been, up to that point in time.

I popped open the center drawer of my desk and pulled out a book my wife had given me for my birthday six months before. I hadn't gotten around to reading it yet, but the building was empty and quiet. Come to think of it, the only person I'd seen on the way up to my office had been the old security guard in the lobby. The muted noise of traffic below was the only sound and I lost track of time as I read.

Failure Drill

I battled it out until five o'clock, then closed the book. Five o'clock was when my office closed, at least according to the yellow pages. I'd been leaving early the past couple of weeks and had been feeling guilty, so I'd promised myself I'd stay all day even though it was Saturday, and do my penance on a day I normally would be at home.

I waited until the second hand on my watch hit the twelve and then packed it in. I put on my jacket and locked up my office, then headed toward the elevators. There didn't seem to be a soul in the building -- I'd bet even the cleaning crews had the day off. I thought about Kelly at home and wished I'd picked another day to act responsibly.

I hummed to myself as the car dropped on well-greased cables, trying to drown out the Muzak coming from hidden speakers. Whoever composed an easy-listening version of Zeppelin's *Kashmir* deserves a special place in Hell. The car glided to a stop and its doors opened silently on the lobby. A skinny man in a dark overcoat had been waiting for the elevator, and I almost bumped into him getting off.

"Excuse me," I said, and moved to step around him. Something slammed into my stomach, and I felt a sharp pain. I looked down to see the black handle of a knife sticking out of my midsection. The man in the overcoat had a hand on it, trying to pull it out, but it wouldn't budge. It took me a second to react, to figure out just what the hell was going on, and then I hit him in the throat with my right forearm. The blow caused him to backpedal into the lobby, cutting short his attempts to free the knife.

He made a gagging sound and tried to hit me in the face with a weak right hook. I smacked it away and hit him hard in the solar plexus with my right, then swung a low, hard left under his right arm into his ribs. He grunted and swung hard at me again with his right.

I ducked below his punch almost in time and took a blow to the top of my head that normally would've dazed me, but my heart was pumping so much high-octane adrenaline into my arteries that I didn't feel a thing. I used his own momentum from the punch to turn and ram him face first against the wall. As he rebounded I took his head in both my hands and smacked it hard back into the marble veneer twice before he sent me reeling with a backhand that came out of nowhere.

Back off the wall he came at me, the blood smear on his forehead a bright red arc. I regained my balance just in time and came in under his punch, hitting him with my shoulder and bicep across the chest. His legs went out from under him and he landed flat on his back, his head thumping against the floor with a dull thud.

As he sat up from the fall, slightly dazed, I kicked him as hard as I could in the middle of his forehead with my heel. His head bounced hard off the tile floor of the lobby, the sound reminding me of the time I dropped a coconut on the concrete floor of my garage.

I managed finally to pull my gun out and point it at him, but he wasn't moving and the spreading pool of blood matting his hair told me he wasn't going to for a while, either.

I looked around the lobby, the muzzle of my gun following my gaze, and a dark sedan idling outside the lobby doors that I hadn't noticed before took off with a squeal of rubber. There was a conspicuous absence in the security guard department, and I believe that he probably would've taken at least a slight interest in the commotion my new friend and I had made. Then I saw the foot sticking out from behind the lobby's information desk.

The adrenaline high was beginning to wear off, and my

hands started to shake. I put my gun away and leaned against the wall, drawing in a deep shuddering breath, then gasped as I felt something stab into my skin. I looked down and saw the knife handle still sticking out of my leather jacket. I grabbed the handle and pulled, needing to wiggle it back and forth before it came free. It was a skinny stiletto type, with about a four inch blade. I looked at it in disgust and threw it down.

I unzipped my jacket, then pulled out the hardcover book that I had stuck in my waistband, a habit acquired in my college days when I had to walk across campus to class during winter and wanted to keep both my hands warm. Who could afford gloves? The book, from my wife, was a 50th Anniversary edition of The Hobbit, with a rune-covered gold binding and nearly 400 beautiful, heavy-weight, gilt-edged pages.

Under the title on the cover was a three-quarter-inch wide cut that went through to the back, angling upward. I looked at my T-shirt and saw a corresponding rip in it just above my navel. Lifting my shirt, I saw a quarter-inch wide cut in my skin that was maybe the same depth. I might need one stitch, or two. The back of the book was smeared with blood, and a bit of it had soaked into the top of my underwear. Without the book the knife would have bit deep into my liver. If he'd hit me a few inches to one side or the other he'd have missed the book entirely. I looked at the knife on the floor with its four inch blade and then at the book in my hand.

"Bilbo Baggins, I love you," I said, my voice coming out like a croak.

I'd been in firefights and had had to pull my gun on people more times than I wanted to remember while in the DEA, but I had *never* been in a hand-to-hand fight for my own life. Sure, I'd been trained for it, but I'd never actually had to use the skills I'd been taught. The brutality of hand-to-hand was a far cry from the antiseptic distance involved in shooting someone. I found I didn't like it, not in the least. Then again, I was glad I was the one with the shakes instead of the one on the floor with blood coming out of my head.

I knelt next to the guy on the floor and pressed my fingers against his neck, the muzzle of my Smith & Wesson against the tip of his nose just in case. My blood was still pounding in my ears and that made it hard to find a pulse, but with all of his bleeding he wasn't going to have that strong of a pulse anyway. I held my hand on his neck for over a minute, but if he had a pulse I couldn't find it. I thought about CPR, another skill I'd learned but never had to use, but I didn't have much interest in reviving this victim and one peek at his different-sized pupils told me trying to revive him wouldn't do much good anyway.

I stood up and walked over to the lobby desk, which served as the security guard's station on the weekend. He was lying on his back partway under the desk, a stain on the lower left side of his chest discoloring the light blue of his uniform. One look at his pale skin and the awkward way he was lying and I knew a pulse check would be a waste of time, but I checked anyway.

From the amount of blood he had lost I could assume that his heart had stopped rather quickly. A red swipe on his sleeve showed where his assailant, and mine, had wiped off the murder weapon before coming to find me.

The guard's face drew me. He was old and had more than a little grey, probably a retired cop. I hadn't noticed him much while he was here, and didn't even know his name. If he'd made more than ten dollars an hour I would've been surprised.

I picked up the phone on the desk and called Scott. Luckily for me he answered. He showed up less than ten minutes later, tires smoking, followed immediately by two squad cars and two ambulances, their lights going but sirens quiet. By that time I'd collected a three member gawking team. They gabbled among themselves and stared at the bodies. I ignored them for the most part, other than to tell them to stay away from the bodies and to assure them that yes, I had in fact called the police.

"What, no sirens?" I said tiredly as Scott stopped in front of me. A pair of Troy P.D. officers busied themselves with each body, and two paramedics entered the lobby carrying a lot of emergency first aid equipment.

"The watch commander's on his way over right now," Scott told the Troy uniforms. They'd heard as much on the radio, and nodded. They eyed Scott surreptitiously, not sure why a Sheriff's Department Lieutenant was involved, much less on the scene first, but didn't ask any questions. I'm sure they thought they'd be better off not knowing. They stared at me as well, wondering exactly who I was to garner such special treatment, before busying themselves with the two bodies. Under normal circumstances I would've been on the floor in cuffs – Scott must have spoken to someone with a lot of clout.

One of the paramedics knelt over the guard and futilely checked for a pulse. After a few seconds he gave up.

"The knife that did that is over there on the floor," I said, pointing, "but it looks like he cleaned the blood off of it before he came after me." I motioned at the blood stain on the guard's sleeve.

The paramedic nodded, mumbled something about a

cold-blooded bastard and moved off to assist his partner who was examining my assailant.

Normal procedure for Michigan EMT's and paramedics whenever they rolled up on a body was to perform CPR, no matter how dead the person obviously was. The law and their rulebook said that unless someone is declared legally dead at the scene by the M.E., they have to try and revive them, with very few exceptions -- decapitation being at the top of the list. Less lawsuits from grieving family members that way, I imagine.

"He made his move when I went to step off the elevator," I said to Scott and the two uniforms not poking the body. I gave them what description I could of the car that took off when the bad guy went down, not that it would do any good. I also theorized that there was in all probability a third person involved, who was up on my floor at one point and had somehow let my assailant know when I was coming down. If he did know. Maybe he *had* been waiting for the elevator, to take it up to my office. That was a sobering thought.

I showed the book to Scott and he examined the gash through the middle of it. "I got a little scratch, but that's all," I told him.

"It's better to be lucky than good," he said absently, his eyes skipping over everything in the lobby.

The uniforms examined the book and then set it on the lobby desk, later to be stuck in a plastic evidence bag by one of the crime scene techs. The younger of the two uniforms standing by us went to shoo away the gawkers after ascertaining that none of them were witnesses.

"That's what you said when I won the lottery," I replied tiredly. Coming down off an adrenaline high was a real bitch. We walked over to where the two paramedics were hunched over my attacker's body. One of them looked up as we approached.

"He's about three quarts low," he said with a smile. He'd been at the job long enough to pick up a cop's sick sense of humor, I guess. "The back of his head is cracked wide open. Even if he hadn't bled to death, my guess is that he would've needed help to tie his shoelaces from now on with this cranial damage."

"I can see the shoeprint," the other paramedic said, marveling. He looked up at me. "Lions could've used you last week when they needed that fifty-yard field goal." I don't know what kind of look I had on my face, but he went pale and immediately bent back to his job.

The two paramedics began packing up their life saving equipment in preparation for the arrival of the Medical Examiner and the crime scene technicians. Nothing they hadn't done a dozen times before.

"Know who he is?" Scott said.

I looked down at him for a long time, the blood, the knife. Amazing. A move here, a move there, and bang, you're dead. Or you're not.

"Nope," I said. "Haven't the faintest idea."

"Or why he came after you?"

"Can't help you there either. But from the way he worked it, he's done this before. Maybe a pro. I didn't see the knife at all until it was in me. Or rather, in the book."

"But why go to the stomach," Scott asked, "if he's a professional? A wound like that won't kill you quickly, if at all. If he wanted you dead, why didn't he go for your throat or eye?"

"I've heard of it. It's kind of a technique. He probably was told to kill me by someone else, since I don't recognize him at all. He therefore doesn't know me or my habits too well, so there's a chance that I might be quick enough to dodge a jab to my head."

I was amazed at how calmly I was talking about an attempt on my life not twenty minutes old. "So he goes for a quick, short, concealable stab to the body," I said, "which pains and disorients the victim and would slow down anyone enough for the attacker to stab him again in the throat or eye." I hoped talking about the attack like it was a classroom example would put distance between it and myself. It wasn't working too well. "I saw a stiff in the DEA that had been killed like that. One hole in the stomach, one in the eye. If it's done right, it's safe, quick, and quiet."

"Why not just use a gun? With a silencer, it'd be just as quiet. Anyone knows that you can make a silencer from four dollars worth of crap from any hardware store."

"How the fuck do I know? Maybe a knife's his trademark. Maybe he doesn't like guns. Maybe his religion forbids shooting people on Saturdays. I don't really give a fuck." I ran a shaky hand through my hair as Scott put a hand on my shoulder.

"The number one question, though, is who's sending bad guys after you? A *Hit Man*. If we're going to assume that's what this guy here is. Who have you pissed off lately?"

"Nobody. Business has been dead." No one even noticed the pun.

"How about old enemies? Ones you made while you were a fed?"

"I don't think so, but --" I shrugged.

"Once we find out who this guy is, we'll know better," Scott said. "Any ID on the guy?" he asked the uniforms as they stood around waiting for the watch commander and the M.E.'s people to arrive. They weren't supposed to disturb the bodies once they'd determined the people were

Failure Drill

dead, not until the crime scene pictures were taken, but checking for ID was second nature for with them.

"No, nothing," one of them replied. "Not even a wallet."

"It's looking more and more like a pro job," Scott said, looking at me.

"I guess I'd better check with my friends at the Don't Expect Anything, see if they've reopened any old cases that I worked on, anything like that. The idea of having a bullseye on my back is *not* a comforting thought."

We both looked outside as the M.E.'s meatwagon pulled up, along with a TV news crew. The circus had arrived. I looked back down at my expired assailant.

"What did I do now?" I asked him.

Chapter Nine

WALKING WOUNDED

I sat in the extra chair in Scott's office and looked at him over the desk. It was after midnight and I felt like a stepped-on bag of cheese. I had a plastic bag filled with ice in my hand and was alternating it between the lump on my head and my sore jaw. Actually, it wasn't ice in the bag anymore, it was more like cool water. Four hours before it'd been ice.

My head where I'd been slugged and my jaw where I'd been backhanded had begun to hurt just after the M.E.'s people had shown up. Shortly thereafter Scott had escorted me out the back way, away from the news crews, to the Troy Police Department building about half a mile down Big Beaver from my office. I'd called Kelly from there, telling her not to wait up. I didn't have to explain why; when I'd called she'd been watching a live newscast from the lobby of my office building. Since then I'd been answering questions, from everyone between Troy detectives to county homicide dicks to a couple clowns from the Prosecutor's office. It was amazing how many people thought they had to get involved. Or how many wanted to, to grab their share of the limelight. Scott hung around more or less just as an interested party—I'd called him in, but it was Troy's show.

Everybody interviewing me felt obliged to ask the same questions over and over, just like all their heroes did on the TV cop shows. With the amount of time I was spending with area detectives, not to mention paramedics, I was going to have to add a lot of names to my Christmas card list.

The last of the coffee-breathed note-takers and recorder-toters had finally left me alone, deciding for the moment that I wouldn't be charged with anything, so Scott and I retired to his office for a little peace and quiet. I felt like I'd been violated. I supposed it would've been a lot worse if Scott hadn't been there acting like a guardian angel. Most cops seemed to get an almost sexual pleasure from asking a person the same questions over and over and over. Some of them like to see people flinch, too, so I knew that without Scott there they would've been whispering First Degree Murder in my ear just to see the reaction it would get.

I set the bag of lukewarm water on the floor next to my chair and tilted my head back. The discolored ceiling tiles were interesting, but I found the inside of my eyelids to have much more draw.

"You might as well go home now," Scott was saying. "I'm going to have to stay here and fill out paperwork for the next six days because you felt you had to call me in on a shooting that wasn't even in my fucking jurisdiction, but that's no reason to keep you up any longer."

"Troy's in Oakland County," I pointed out.

"Try telling them that. Besides, city supersedes county, you know that."

"I told you you needed to work on being sweet and loveable," I mumbled. I pried open my eyes and gave him a smile.

He was scowling at the papers on his desk, trying to intimidate them into disappearing. It wasn't working. I slowly stood up and stretched, feeling the two stitches in my stomach pull. The crime lab guys had taken pictures of my jacket and shirt as well as the cut in my stomach before and after it had been stitched. And even though I was only in the emergency room for a record time of twenty-three minutes, most likely because there were half a dozen uniformed cops staring down everybody in the place, the detective in charge from Troy felt it necessary to take a statement not only from the doctor that stitched me up but also from the nurse that admitted me and filed my paperwork.

I'd soaked and scrubbed my jacket and shirt in a bathroom sink at the station, effectively removing all the blood. I was surprised they hadn't confiscated them as evidence. There wasn't anything I could do about the cuts in my clothes, and for some reason that really annoyed me. It had been my favorite jacket. At least I was still around to wear it.

"Call me when you find out who the guy was," I said. The crime lab crew, who Scott knew personally, told him they would put a rush on the prints they'd taken from the dead guy at the scene. So far there had been no word back.

"I'll call you the minute I hear anything," Scott assured me. His forehead wrinkled as he looked up at me. "Are you sure you don't want any police protection? I can't swing anything official, since no one knows what the hell is going on, but I know some guys around here that would do it solely as a favor to me plus fifteen bucks an hour."

I shook my head. "All I need right now is a ride back to my car," I said.

Failure Drill

Twenty-five minutes later I found myself being dropped off in the parking lot next to my car. The two uniforms in the squad car watched, amused, as I crawled around the car and checked under the hood for a bomb. I wouldn't necessarily recognize a bomb as such, but I'd notice anything that looked out of place. Like something not covered in rust.

Everything looked kosher so I climbed in and started my car, flinching, and drove off with a wave to the officers. I could've been showing signs of paranoia, but if the guy was a professional he might've wanted an ace in the hole in case he missed me at the elevators.

I'd been up over seventeen hours, with over a third of that time spent being hassled by cops, and all I wanted to do was go to sleep. Once home I locked the front door behind me, then went around the ground floor making sure all of the windows and doors were locked. It was only then that I began the long climb up the stairs toward my bedroom and sweet oblivion.

Kelly had tried staying awake until I returned but had finally nodded off while sitting up, propped against a mound of pillows, the bedside lamp on. As soon as I sat on the bed she woke up and looked around blearily.

"Are you okay?" she said, blinking her eyes.

I began pulling off my clothes. "Yeah."

I should've said more, reassured her, but I was so damn tired my eyes weren't focusing properly.

"What happened?

I grabbed a pillow from the mound and flopped onto it. "I'm too tired to think," I said. "I'll tell you all about it tomorrow." *I don't want to talk about it* was the unspoken message.

I laid there with my eyes closed. I'd probably succeeded

only in making her mad. She was looking for reassurance, but instead I'd brushed her off.

After about a minute I heard her huff and toss the pillows around. The light went out, and the bed shook as she laid back down. I thought I'd fall asleep immediately, but sleep wasn't quick in coming. I lay next to Kelly, my eyes open in the dark, listening to the rapid breathing that told me she was awake too. Finally I rolled over, away from her, closed my eyes, and tried to will myself into unconsciousness.

The next thing I knew the phone was clanging beside my ear. Waking up was like crawling out of a deep, dark, comfortable hole into harsh sunlight. The luminous hands on my watch said five after three. Groaning, I picked up the phone and grunted into the receiver.

"John, it's Scott. I just got word from the A.F.I.S. operator." AFIS was the Automated Fingerprint Identification System used by all Michigan police departments. The system was about ten years old and could be amazingly fast compared to digging for print cards by hand. "They've ID'd our guy."

"Couldn't you have waited to call me in the morning?" I mumbled. Kelly shifted in her sleep and groaned. *What the hell was the AFIS operator doing at work at this time of night?*

"You told me to call you when I found out," he said. "Besides, if I have to be awake doing the paperwork on the guy *you* killed and felt you had to tell me about, you should be awake too. According to this printout, the guy you killed is one Frederick Pellicek, also known as, get this, Freddie the Knife."

"Charming," I said, my head in the palm of my hand. "Christ, it sounds like I'm in a bad B-movie."

"You are. It's called your life. Here's the fun part though.

I called around. Ol' Mack the Knife was last known to be employed by one Mr. Pietro Bufonte."

I sat up straighter, silent for a while, letting what Scott had said sink slowly into my sleep-dazed mind.

"Does he ever freelance," I said, "or do favors?"

"Not according to the file I've got here. Although it's always possible. According to this, the only buttons he's pushed since we've become aware of him are the ones fingered by Bufonte first. A very loyal employee."

"Isn't that special," I mumbled. "But the sixty-four-thousand-dollar question is this—why? Why the hell would Bufonte want me dead? Because I wasted Scarelli? That's the only reason I can think of why he'd be pissed at me, but it doesn't make sense."

"You're right. He'd figure it was business, bad luck that his boy got hit. He wouldn't take it personal. He'd never have survived in the business if he did. I asked you before, who have you pissed off lately?"

"Nobody. I can't think of any case I've handled in the past year where anyone like Bufonte would've been involved or even remotely interested. It was mostly all alarm installations and consultations about security set-ups."

"How about when you were in the DEA?"

"No. I was always just one person in the group that was involved, and none of the operations I went on involved Bufonte. Hell, I wasn't even in this state, remember? I got a few inter- and intra-agency memos on his suspected smuggling and distribution activities, but that's it."

The little buzzer inside my brain started to go off again, telling me I was overlooking something obvious.

"You know," I said, "if it is Bufonte, and he's pissed off that I shot Scarelli, he probably knows you're involved too. You might want to start watching your back."

"Yeah, I thought of that too," Scott said. He didn't sound too pleased.

Normally, the fact that Scott was a cop would be enough to protect him, but if Bufonte was wired up enough to go after me, he wasn't being rational, so who knew how he'd view Scott's role in all this. Whatever *this* was.

"Hell, it could be for something completely unrelated, totally different," I said, trying to sound upbeat. "There's even a chance that I wasn't the target at all, that I was just in the wrong place at the wrong time." Neither of us believed that, but seeing as we were both stumped I said goodbye and hung up.

Kelly said something unintelligible and rolled away from me. I laid back in bed and stared at the ceiling, trying to get my tired eyes to close. That little something, whatever it was that was bugging me, buzzed away at the back of my mind all night. I slept fitfully until six, then crawled out of bed, took a long hot shower, and called Scott. The bored dispatcher I talked to said the lieutenant had gone home to sleep an hour earlier. I left a message for him to call me when he came in and hung up. If I'd called him at home he would've shot me.

I brewed myself a strong pot of coffee and sat down with a cup of it in the recliner in my family room. I sipped it slowly as I sat and pondered my next move in locating Jerry Phillips.

I could always call and visit the girlfriend, to see if she was hiding him or knew where he was, but the possibilities there were limited. If I knew anything about people, and I believed I knew a little about Jerry Phillips, he wouldn't be there. I could wait for the information from Jerry's bank, but that could take God knew how long, depending on how difficult the branch manager wanted to be. My tired mind kept running around in circles and I rubbed at my eyes futilely. Whatever sleep I'd had was already vanished in a mass of blurry eyes and sore joints.

I tossed the remnants of my coffee into the sink and exchanged my robe for some street clothes. I left a note for Kelly on the table saying I was out working and didn't know when I'd be back. She'd be pissed, but I had other things on my mind more important and she'd just have to understand. People wanted me dead, and I wanted to know why. I felt bad, leaving without even having talked to her, but my leaving while she was still asleep solved more problems than it created. The next time I saw her I'd tell her everything.

As I walked out the door I heard the buzzer on Kelly's alarm clock go off.

Chapter Ten

DAZED AND CONFUSED

I drove aimlessly for the better part of an hour. My subconscious, however, took over, and shortly I found myself turning into the parking lot of the Burger King where Jerry Phillips was last reported to be heading.

I rolled through the drive-thru and grabbed a biscuit and coffee, then pulled into a space and left the motor running, mouth in gear and brain in neutral. The early morning breakfast crowd in front of me filed through like parts on a conveyor belt.

Why am I here? Because it was the place where all the lights and buzzers had begun to go off in my head. Maybe returning would trigger something in my memory. At least that was the idea.

I sat there for quite a while, my mind moving in circles. Either there was some information I was missing, or I wasn't putting the puzzle together the right way, because nothing wanted to click into place for me.

"Jeeeezus Christ," I said, and opened my door to climb out.

In my rearview mirror I'd spotted a pay phone at the gas station on the corner. I was almost to it before I realized it was the same one I'd used the day before.

"No wonder I can't figure out what's bugging me," I muttered. "I'm going senile." I wasn't sure why I wanted to use the phone, maybe just out of sheer frustration. I hit the buttons violently, hoping to break the damn thing. No such luck. In what was probably a futile attempt, I was trying Scott at his office. If he was there, I was going to have to ask his supervisor to put him up for sainthood.

After two rings, he answered.

"What, are you trying to earn frequent caller points?" he said. "The guys here are gonna think you're sweet on me. I called your house a few minutes ago but you weren't there. The person that was wasn't too happy. What's up now?"

"You tell me," I said. "I'm sitting in the parking lot of a Burger King on Rochester Road. Ever since I came here yesterday there've been bells going off in my head and I don't know why. It's driving me crazy."

"Where on Rochester Road?" he said. "Rochester?"

"Yeah. Well, the Hills, I think, technically."

"What are you doing there in the first place?"

"What, are you writing a column? It's the last place Jerry Phillips was seen headed. Why?" I heard him rustling papers.

"It's also the last place Sidney Wollsh was seen, alive or otherwise."

"Who?"

"Weatherspoon's guy. The one shot in the head."

"When was he killed?" I said, listening closely. Things were starting to click together in my head.

"Let me think," he said. "Wednesday. Last Wednesday afternoon."

I sucked in my breath and clicked my teeth together in a nervous paradiddle. I might actually earn my money on this case.

"What is it?" he asked.

"Jerry Phillips was last seen heading for lunch here at three o'clock Wednesday afternoon," I said. There was silence at his end for a while as he digested the information.

"Do you think maybe he witnessed it? Jesus, what are the fucking chances?"

"That's what I'm thinking, all right. And that either they grabbed him, in which case we'll never find the body, or he got away and is in hiding. Since his forty-five has disappeared along with him, I've got to assume he got away and is hiding somewhere, scared shitless. His friends were right, dead or in deep shit," I said more to myself than to Scott. *I'll be damned. Score one for them.* "You've checked the morgue recently, haven't you?"

"Yeah, and he's not there. So chances are that if he saw the hit the hitter doesn't know it."

"Or couldn't catch him," I said. "You'd be surprised how fast you can run when someone with a gun is behind you. Well, he either saw Jerry or Jerry thought he did, because he has vanished, but good. I have had absolutely no luck in finding this twinkie. I thought I was starting to slip. But if the mob's after him, well, hey -- that's a different story. You haven't heard anything definite from your people or Weatherspoon's about whether the hitter was Scarelli, have you?"

"Nobody knows nuthin'" he told me. "If anybody knows who pushed his button they're not telling. Hell, we can't even find anybody to question. Scarelli was carrying a forty-five and that ain't what killed Wollsh, so --" he cut himself off. "Shit," he said. "Give me your number and I'll call you back in five minutes."

"What's up?"

"Just give me the damn number. I'll get back to you." I did and he hung up. Four long minutes later the phone rang.

"Yeah," I said, massaging the back of my neck.

"Johnny Secco and Robert Gantz, two known Bufonte associates, were found knifed to death on the playground of Oakridge Elementary School in Royal Oak early Wednesday evening." I heard papers rustling. "They were found just after seven by a lady walking her dog, I guess."

"How come I didn't hear about this on the news?"

"You did. They called it a gang-related homicide because no one knew what to make of it. Dicks thought maybe the two of them had messed up on a job and Bufonte had them iced for their trouble, but that didn't seem quite right. Nobody I talked to even thought to connect it with that hit in the parking lot. I guess 'cause it was across town in a different city, and neither one of the damn crime scenes are inside the jurisdiction of the D.P.D. major crime guys, no one wanted to use any brain power on it."

"You'd think the FBI would've noticed something. I've heard they don't like the mob. Could somebody be keeping it quiet?"

"It wasn't covered up. Not really. But it's the same game as usual. Publicity. You know that S.O.P. for any law enforcement agency is to only publicize murders and violent crime when somebody's up for reelection. Or when we want a bigger budget for the department."

"And you think it's related to Phillips?"

"Maybe. It's a hefty coincidence, everybody getting wasted on the same day and none of the deaths related. What do you think?"

"I have this feeling that Phillips is somehow involved, but I don't think I want to know how. How were they stabbed?" I said, morbid curiosity overcoming me. Or maybe I wanted to know because I'd just recently evaded a knife of my own.

"You wondering if Freddie the Knife warmed up on them before he came for you? Let me think. When I spoke to the M.E., I remember him saying that the cuts were made by a single-edged, probably serrated blade at least three inches long. It was unusual because he'd never seen anything but stilettos or icepicks used on hits, which is sure as hell what this looked like. Two grown men in a playground in the middle of the day?" Scott paused. "Are you thinking what I'm thinking?"

"That the kid got 'em? It's a stretch, even for this case. I wouldn't consider it, normally, but it fits here. Jesus, just think if he did do it. Twenty years old and in a knife fight with mob muscle. Surprised the fuck outta them, I'll bet. They probably weren't expecting a fight, that's what gave him an edge."

"Pretty professional job when you look at it. The two stiffs were both armed with revolvers. At least, they think they were. One of 'em just had an empty holster under his arm. There weren't any cars parked nearby whose owners couldn't be found, so the main line of thought was that somebody drove the two of them there. That's why one of the theories floating around was that they were whacked for unsatisfactory job performance. Another guy they trusted drove them to the schoolyard on a pretense, middle of the day, who'd suspect anything, and BLAM! you're fired, literally. Maybe the reason nobody suspected them for the hit at the Burger King was that the gun found on one of the guys was a thirty-eight, and from the looks of the holster the other guy's missing gun was a revolver too. Wollsh was killed with a three-eighty auto. Silenced, I'll bet. If it wasn't for that little fact, I'm sure someone around here would've connected these two incidents. Figured that Bufonte had these two guys whack Wollsh, then had somebody else whack these guys, and *magic!* -- nobody to tie him to the crime." He let out a long breath.

"Since we know now that that's probably not the case, my guess is that the three-eighty was in the car that we didn't find, and there was a third guy, a driver, that bolted when he saw Phillips drop his two friends. You thinking they followed the kid to the school?"

"I don't know what to think." I said. "Maybe the kid got lucky. He had to've been flying on adrenaline. The two of them must've been overconfident and tried to intimidate him into getting in the car with them, instead of just taking him out on the spot, probably because it was too public for them. From what I know of Phillips and his friends he'd probably carry at least a knife for protection under normal circumstances." I told Scott about Jerry's friends and their peculiar habits.

"Well, it seems like you've got everything satisfactorily fucked up," Scott observed.

"You gave me this damn case."

"Well, you're going to get some help now, so sit back and relax."

"No, don't," I said quickly. "Don't put anybody on this. Not yet."

"What, are you kidding me?" he said. "It's procedure. With what I suspect is going on, I'd think you'd want the help."

"Fuck procedure," I said. "Give me a day or two to find him. You gave me this case, let me see it through. By the time I explain everything to the investigating detectives the kid's likely to be dead. I could be wrong, anyway. Both of us could be. And Royal Oak's got people working Secco and Gantz already. Just don't share any of my theories with them yet."

"You need the help, now."

"Don't tell me what I need, you know I hate that. They'd only get in my way, besides. Hell, we don't even know for sure what's going on, remember? It could be just a weird set of coincidences. If the shit hits the fan and it comes back around to you, that's the excuse you can use. In the meantime, let me go after him alone." I waited expectantly on my end of the line, hoping he'd go for the deal. I heard a sigh.

"Okay," he said finally. "I'll keep my guys out of this, but I want to tell the feds. It was their witness that got wasted, after all. They'll be too busy trying to catch up to you to tell any of my superiors what's going on. Hell, they'll want to keep it in the family anyway, not get embarrassed."

"Try and hold off for as long as you can," I said.

He snorted. "What have you got in mind to do next?"

"How the hell should I know?" I said. "I'm making this up as I go along."

We'd talked in circles around what was almost the clincher, the reason we suspected Jerry had witnessed something. The attempt on my life. Neither of us believed in coincidence, and Freddie "the Knife" Pellicek had shown up at too convenient a time for me not to believe it was tied in with the case.

If the guys in black shirts were after Jerry, they sure as hell didn't want me mucking around trying to find him, throwing a wrench into the works. Especially if I did find him first. It was an uneven race anyway, with the bad guys having a good four day head start on me, at least when it came to knowing the reason why Jerry had disappeared. But they always liked the odds in their favor, and I guess they figured the risk of killing me was worth the chance I might find Jerry first. Who was I, anyway? Just another shmuck.

A big question on my mind, though, was how they came to know I was on the case at all. Scott wouldn't have told anyone, and I couldn't imagine Jerry's friends or family accidentally mentioning to their mobster friends how they'd hired a detective to find him. My best guess was that they'd been watching either the Phillips house or Champion Nursery, seen me asking questions, copied down my plate number, and found out exactly who I was and what I was doing. Why they didn't just let me go about my business of locating Jerry was an intriguing question. They could've let me find him where they couldn't and then killed him. There had to be a logical answer to that problem, but I didn't have enough facts in my possession to figure it out. Yet.

I started to walk back to my car and was halfway there before I noticed the man leaning against it. Instinctively I went for my pistol, then relaxed when I saw who it was.

"A bit early for you to be up and about, isn't it?" I said, annoyed.

Ron Kelly shrugged. He wore faded jeans and a ripped, paint-splattered T-shirt. I didn't really feel like dealing with him or his idiosyncratic friends so early in the morning, but despite my mood I forced myself to be civil.

"I was on my way into work and stopped in here for breakfast," he said. "I saw you on the phone. What are you doing out here and who could you be calling on a pay phone at this hour of the morning?"

"Nosy bastard, aren't you?" I said. So much for civil. "I don't really think it's any of your damn concern. Now, if you'll excuse me," I said with exaggerated politeness, motioning him away from the car door. He didn't move.

"You look like shit," he said. He peered a little closer at my face. "You've been in a fight," he observed matter-of-factly. "I really think you should tell me what's going on."

"I'm not interested in what you think," I snapped. "If there are any developments concerning your friend, I'll let you know. But now I have to go." He looked at me closely for a second.

"You're lying," he said simply.

I sighed. I was not having a good week. "Shouldn't you be getting to work?"

"Fuck work," he said. "I was willing to let you do your thing before, but now with this," he pointed at the bruise on my jaw, "I'm going to be a pain in the ass until you tell me what's going on. Do you normally go for your gun when you see someone leaning on your car? Fill me in, or I'm going to be your fucking shadow. People are going to think we're engaged." He smiled. "Hell, you shouldn't be upset. You look like you could use a good bodyguard. What's the other guy look like?"

I stood there and stared at him, my mouth open. Jesus, what next? All I needed now was some smart-ass barely out of his teens, his mind full of TV and trying to act tough, following me around, playing cops and robbers.

"Listen, dammit," I said, poking him in the chest hard with a finger. "I'm trying to do a job here. I don't know you, and I'm not a baby-sitter. I don't need you fucking up my day trying to act tough. You've been watching too much NYPD Blue. I appreciate your concern for your friend, and if any news comes up on him I'll let you know, but until then get the fuck out of my life."

"You listen, fucker," he said, stabbing me in the chest

with his finger. "Jerry's my friend. That means a lot. It means almost everything. And if I think he's in trouble, it means that I'm going to do everything in my power to find him and help him, even if I have to risk my own life doing it. Because he'd do the same for me. Do _not_ patronize me! I'm not a little kid." His chest was heaving with emotion and the veins in his neck were sticking out.

If I got into a fistfight in the parking lot of a Burger King it would ruin my whole day, so I decided not to flatten him no matter how appealing the idea might be. Besides, I wasn't completely sure I'd be the one standing when it was all over. I had more experience, but he had ten years and twenty pounds of muscle on me.

"Listen," I said softly, but with an edge to my voice. "I know you're upset, but this isn't the movies, it's the real world. Something you've just begun to experience. You're out of your depth."

"Horseshit," he said.

So much for reason. Time for Plan B. I grabbed him by his shirtfront.

"What're you going to do? You going to beat my ass 'cause I won't take you along? How's that going to help your friend? Do you even *know* what it's like out there?" I jerked my head back at the real world. "You don't have the first clue how things work. You think you're going to be Clint Eastwood, turn the town upside down? Maybe Jerry is in trouble. What's that to you? You think you're going to grab a gun and go on an adventure?" I got in his face and spat the words out, trying to get his attention, get him to think. I still hadn't gotten even a flicker behind his eyes.

"Have you ever even seen anyone die? Not a dead person, someone actually dying right in front of you, and both of you knowing it but you can't do anything about it?

This isn't make-believe. You do something out here, it's forever." I was off on a tangent now, but couldn't seem to stop. "Do you even have an inkling how your life would change if you had to shoot someone?"

"Yes," he said tonelessly.

I stopped my ranting and stared at him. Something in his voice got to me.

He stood before me, stock still, and looked me in the eyes as he spoke. "I shot a man twice in the chest and as he lay there on the floor in front of me I shot him once in the head and he died."

"Bullshit," I said, but there was a hint of uncertainty in my voice that even I noticed. I'd seen the look in his eye, but I just couldn't let myself believe that he was doing anything other than trying to save face.

He spoke through clenched teeth. "I was seventeen when I came home for lunch one day and saw a strange car in the driveway. I didn't recognize the car, so I went into the barn and got one of my father's pistols. I walked through the front door and found a burglar busy dismantling the stereo in our living room. Most burglaries occur during the day, when people are at work. You probably know that, but I didn't. Not then.

"He went for a gun in his waistband and I shot him, twice. That fuckin' guy lay on the floor of my house swearing at me, yelling at me to call an ambulance, saying how he was going to sue my ass off, that he was gonna *own* my house before he was done. I don't doubt it, as fucked-up as the world's gotten. So I shot him in the head. Fuck the courts, they probably would've convicted me of attempted murder for shooting a guy trying to pull a gun on me in my own house. Because I made no attempt to retreat, or whatever the bullshit law is in this state. And say he'd lived with the two bullets in him, and actually got convicted and sent to jail, how long do you think he'd get? Ten years? Less? Minus time off for good behavior. After trying to kill me. In *my* house. Think about it.

"So I wrapped his body in an old saddle blanket and carried him over my shoulder way back into the woods behind our property. I got rid of his gun and mine, cleaned the blood off the carpet in the living room as best I could, burned the blanket I'd wrapped him in, and put back all the things he'd moved. I took his car and drove it a couple miles into Pontiac and abandoned it. I left the keys in so hopefully it would be stolen. It was, I checked back the next day. Four weeks later someone found the body and called the police. They came around and questioned everybody in the neighborhood, including my parents, but of course they didn't know anything. The case is probably still listed as unsolved and if you try to prove any of this you'll have no shred of evidence and I'll sue you for slander and win." He put his face close to mine.

"I know this isn't television," he said. "I had roommates knifing each other at VMI because the pressure was so intense. One of my friends from VMI got in a car accident last year. Last I heard he was doing real good learning how to talk again. I may be only twenty years old, but if you think I can't handle anything you dish out you're wrong. The same goes for my friends. So either bring me into this case or look forward to seeing me in your rearview mirror twenty-four hours a day."

We stood there staring at each other for a long time. He'd worked up a sweat during his outburst, but now just stood quiet and motionless, breathing loudly through his nose.

It was painfully obvious that it would be far more trouble

to try to get rid of Ron than to take him along. I knew I'd be able to ditch him later, but I could just see him showing up again and again, most likely at the most inopportune times. "If I say yes," I told him, "you're going to be quiet when I tell you, move when I say move, and generally do your best to be no more irritating than a pimple that won't pop."

"Listen," he said. "I may be just an annoying over-muscled jarhead barely out of his teens to you, but I know enough to know I don't know a damn thing about how to find Jerry. If I did, I'd be out doing it, not here bowing and scraping."

This is bowing and scraping? Well, I was glad to hear he at least had some slight grip on reality. Not that I had any more ideas on how to find Jerry than he did.

"Okay," I said finally. I shoved a thumb at my car. "Get in." He looked at it distastefully.

"Let's take mine," he said. "I'd rather not be riding in something that needs a push to get into second gear. Besides," he said, as if reading my mind, "if we meet up with the people that did that to your face, wouldn't you rather my car got trashed than yours? They'd go after the driver first, anyways." I stood there and eyed him for a long time, keys in hand, then followed him over to his car.

I shouldn't be doing this, I really shouldn't be doing this, I kept telling myself. *I should ditch this kid, beat the shit out of him if I have to, but I should scram. That would be the smartest thing to do.* It was what my brain said was the best option. But my guts were saying something else. There was something to Ron. I couldn't quite explain it. Maybe it wouldn't be a debacle. Stranger things had happened.

"It looks like an unmarked police car," I said. "Old school." He was standing next to a late model dark blue

Dodge Diplomat with wide tires and heavy duty bumpers. The car was showroom immaculate inside and out.

"It used to be one," he explained. "*Beverly Hills Cop*-era Detroit Police cruiser. I got it for a steal because it had a lot of miles on it and major body damage. I redid everything on it except the frame." He unlocked my door and I climbed into the passenger seat.

"Well," he said, after sliding behind the steering wheel, "where to, boss?" He rested his palms on the wheel and looked at me.

"Do you know where Jerry went to grade school?" I asked him, grabbing onto the thread of an idea.

"What does that have to do with anything?"

"Listen chief," I said, "I'm letting you play Robin to my Batman 'cause I think it'll be more trouble to get rid of you than not, but don't start with me. I've been doing this a lot longer than you. Now, once again, do you know where Jerry went to grade school?" He looked at me for a second, trying hard not to get angry.

"No," he said finally, "not exactly. Somewhere in Royal Oak, I think. He moved here from there about eight years ago."

Maybe I should have been surprised, but I wasn't. Everything was coming together, like pieces in a puzzle.

"Well, onward James," I said to my impromptu driver, "on to Royal Oak."

Ron gave me a dirty look, and opened his mouth to ask another question, but after a second thought better of it. He turned the key and the engine growled to life, shaking the whole car. I could feel the wax in my ears vibrating loose. As it idled, the engine made the same "WUBWUBWUB" sound I associated with hot rods as well as junkers that needed new mufflers, a sound I could feel in my bones as much as hear with my ears.

I was pressed back into the seat as he whipped the car onto the road with a chirp of rubber. Ron weaved us in and out of the early morning traffic with ease, the automobile responding immediately to his every command.

"This thing is an industrial sized vibrator," I said, trying to keep my teeth from clicking together.

"Once you get above seventy it smoothes out and feels like you're riding on glass," he said.

"My car may be a dog compared to this beast," I said, "but I bet it gets better gas mileage."

He grinned. "As long as there's a gas station every third block," he said, "I have no problems."

Chapter Eleven

SCHOOLYARD BLUES

"Well, this is cute."

We were sitting in front of a medium-sized, two story school that looked like it had been built in the fifties. Its windows were closed and its doors were locked, but in less than a month the kiddies would be back and it would be busy and loud again.

"Like I said before, this is all very nice and cute, but what the hell are we doing here?" Ron was a bit on edge, annoyed at having to drive me through most of Royal Oak before we found the school.

"Shut up, I'm thinking," I said.

"And for that we needed to come here? Is it that hard for you?" I gave him a sharp look and he raised his eyebrows at me, feigning innocence.

"I wanted to come here and think," I explained, "because this is the last spot I can place Jerry at. Maybe."

"When do you think he was here?"

"Last Wednesday afternoon," I said, and climbed out of the car. I started walking toward a playground I saw behind a row of trees to one side of the school. The trees were growing between some houses and the playground, an attempt at peace and quiet by some past residents. The car door opened before I got too far away.

"How do you know he was here?" I heard Ron yell out behind me. I ignored him and kept on walking toward a swingset. "Hey!" I reached the swings and sat down on one as he came up behind me. He stuck his hands in his pockets and looked at me intently, waiting for an answer.

I dug the toe of my shoe into the dirt as I pondered what to do next. I respected Ron's earnestness to find his friend, and I hoped that I would find Jerry safe and sound, but if I told Ron everything I knew or suspected I'd have a lot more problems than I did now. The only way I could get away with telling him nothing was if I ditched him, and that didn't look like it was going to happen. I decided on the middle road, telling him the cold, hard facts. Just not all of them. It would keep him satisfied and yet keep him from doing something stupid and potentially dangerous. Hopefully.

"It's not definite," I reminded him, "but I'm pretty sure Jerry was here Wednesday afternoon. I'm not sure why he came here, maybe he was just in the area at the time and thought here'd be a good place to stop."

"What was he doing in Royal Oak in the first place, when he was supposed to be working?" he interrupted me to say. I squinted up at him.

"He was being followed, maybe chased, by at least two men. I don't know how, I don't know why," I lied, "but they caught up to him here. Unless I'm completely wrong about this whole thing."

"And?"

"And now there are two more bodies in the Oakland

County Morgue. Stabbed to death with a serrated knife. Sharp. Four inch blade. Sound familiar? If Jerry killed them, and right now I'm thinking he did, he got very lucky. These guys were professionals, by their appearance."

"Huh? But -- I mean, how come I didn't hear about this on the news?"

"The cops kept it quiet because they didn't know what to make of it."

"And you don't know why these guys were after Jerry?"

"Not yet. I'm hoping that when I find that out it'll tell me something about where he could be."

"How do you know all of this? And what do you mean, professional, the guys were professionals?"

Oops, a little too much information there, should've kept my big mouth shut.

"I mean, these guys had guns on 'em," I told him. "They weren't dairy farmers. And I told you before, I have a friend on the Sheriff's Department, that's how I get my information."

"After he killed those two guys is when he came home and grabbed his forty-five, I'd bet," Ron said. "It's what I would've done." He shook his head disbelievingly. "He always carried a knife. We all do. At work he's got to cut a lot of things, burlap, rope, shit like that. He's got a three and a half inch Spyderco knife with a serrated blade. It's got a thumbhole in the blade so you can open it with one hand. And I bet he did. It saved his ass." He cocked his head. "If he killed them, why'd he go home and grab his gun?"

"I don't know," I told him. It was almost the truth.

He shook his head again. "A couple of times when we got drunk we talked about if we had to kill someone, whether it would be harder doing it or harder living with yourself afterwards." His voice faded off.

"It's harder afterwards," I said, my mind flashing back to a few adrenaline-filled moments I'd had.

"I know," he reminded me. "That's what I told him."

"You told Jerry about your burglar?" I said disbelievingly.

"Any of them would've done the same thing," he said. "They're my friends, they talked with me about it a lot. Bob always shook his head at us, though."

"Why?"

"Why? Because if Bob had to kill someone, made his mind up that it had to be done, it wouldn't bother him. Before or after. He'd just do it."

"Swell. I can't wait to bring him home to meet mom and dad," I said sarcastically. I was tired beyond belief of Ron and his friendly suburban psychopaths, and it wasn't even noon yet.

"He'll like that," Ron replied. He looked at his watch. "I'm going to have to pick him up at the airport pretty soon."

"What? I have shit to do," I said. "You want to drive me, you go where I say. I don't have time to screw around at the airport with you."

"Don't worry, you're not going."

I blinked at him, dumbfounded. "You're going to abandon me here, after all the shit I just had to listen to? Unbelievable." Was he a flake or just an asshole? It wasn't going to be fun finding out. And, really, I only had myself to blame. Idiot.

"Don't wet your pants," he said. "I'm gonna get you a ride." He looked at the ground, then squinted up at me. "You got a cell phone I can use?" he asked. "I left mine at home." Seeing my openmouthed, venomous glare he looked around and saw a gas station.

Failure Drill

I got up off the swing and walked beside him toward the gas station, trying very hard to control my urge to throttle him.

"So," he said, "the big question is, who is trying to kill Jerry, and why? And you're clueless about the whole thing."

"So far," I said. "Hopefully I'll know more soon."

"Like what?"

"Like whether Jerry has used his ATM card since he's disappeared. That might help us, it might not. All we can do now, though, is wait until the info arrives, unless you've got some treasured secret about Jerry you'd like to share with me but haven't found just the right opportunity for."

He made a face. "I hate waiting."

"Tell me about it. You're young still, though, you'll get better at it."

"You're not telling me everything," Ron said slowly, thinking, "but I guess it's better than nothing. In your place I'd probably do the same thing. You don't know me, don't know what you should and shouldn't tell me. That's okay, you'll find out. Just make sure your keeping me in the dark doesn't hurt Jerry."

I looked at him and decided I was definitely underestimating him.

There was a working pay phone at the gas station. Ron dropped in change and punched in a number. While he waited for the other end to be picked up, I looked in awe at the massive amount of traffic filling the streets around us. Didn't they know it was Sunday when nobody was supposed to be out of bed before eleven a.m.?

"Is Steve there, please?" he said. "Well, could you wake him up, then? It's important. Yes, I know what time it is." He rolled his eyes at me. A few seconds later I heard a voice on the line.

"Steve. Steve! Wake your ass up," Ron yelled. "I need you to meet me somewhere." He gave Steve the short version of everything I'd told him and he had told me in the past hour. "But I have to go pick up Grumpy, so it's your turn to watch and play chauffeur." He listened for a few seconds. "No, we're in my car. Yeah, I know he can drive himself, but I think it's a good idea if we stay close. He won't tell me, but from the bruises on his face it looks like whoever's after Jer doesn't want any competition."

Ron was either a lucky guesser or damn close to psychic. Even if he and his friends were a pain in the ass, they were on target when it came to putting two and two together. Pretty soon I'd have to throw them more meat to fill up my skeleton of a story about Jerry's disappearance, unless I wanted more hassles. But I was pissed at myself for getting tangled up with them in the first place. I should've smacked myself upside the head. It's also what I should've done to Ron, instead of letting him play Junior Achiever. *God, if the guys from the DEA saw me now I'd never live it down.*

If there was another attempt on my life, I'd probably end up having to cover my tagalong's ass as he stood there frozen. And then I'd have to explain to the authorities why the kids were hanging around me, when I suspected I was in danger. Lawsuit city.

"Why can't Steve pick your friend up?" I asked him.

Ron grinned. "He could, but Bob has issues with his driving." He hung up, fed more change into the machine and dialed a second number. He leaned against the light pole the phone booth was bolted to and looked at me. "Here we go," he said with a twinkle in his eye.

"Yes, can I speak to Mario please," he said into the receiver. He waited a few moments. "Mario. It's Ron Kelly."

Failure Drill

I heard a loud voice start bellowing. Ron pulled the receiver away from his ear slightly.

"Yeah, I know I was supposed to be there ten minutes ago." He paused and the angry voice on the other end started up again. "I know, I know," Ron was saying. "Listen, Mario, will you listen? Shut up, godammit! I have to take some time off. It's important. I don't know how long, maybe a few days, at most a week." Ron pulled the phone away from his ear again and I heard Italian profanity that probably would've offended me had I understood it.

Ron yelled into the phone. "If you want to fire me, fire me then, godammit! I *have* to take this time off!" He paused. "Yeah, a few days to a week." He stopped and listened for a second. "If I'm not back in a week you won't have to fire me, I'll be dead." Mario stopped his yelling. I could hear his voice, at a moderate volume, as he asked Ron something.

"Yes, it's fucking serious. No it's not family, it's a friend." He paused. "No, it's not Bob, do you think he'd need my help to get out of anything? Jerry. Yeah. Okay. If I don't come in to work next Monday, fire me." He hung up.

"Jesus," he exclaimed. "Fuckin' Italians."

"You would've had to pick up Bob anyway today," I said. "What excuse were you going to use then?"

He shrugged. "I do my best work under pressure. Sick mom, maybe. Mario would've liked that. Talk about your stereotypical Italian. Sheesh. He could've been an extra in The Godfather." Ron shook his head. "Well, I guess stereotypes exist for a reason, right?"

We walked back to the car. I left him standing there and went over to the swings again and sat in one. It was so low that if I put my feet flat on the ground my knees almost came up to my chest. I liked the feeling I got sitting there. It made me feel young again. I was starting to wish I could go home and curl up into a fetal ball under my bedcovers. Mommy could come in and tell me it was all just a bad dream. Except if I went home now and got into bed my wife would take a baseball bat to my knees. I looked down at the ground and saw I'd scraped a three-inch-deep furrow into the dirt with my heel.

"I need a drink," I said to no one in particular. I looked up and saw Ron talking to Steve, who'd parked an old, beat up and rusty RX-7 next to Ron's Dodge. I watched them talk for a short time, Ron occasionally gesturing in my direction, then Ron got into his car and drove off. Steve crossed his arms and leaned against his car patiently.

After a while I stood up and brushed the wrinkles out of my pants. I looked down at the line I had made in the dirt for a few seconds, then smoothed it out with my foot.

"Where to, boss?" Steve said as I walked up to him.

"My office," I said. "I'm not accomplishing anything here so I might as well not accomplish anything there where at least people can reach me." He nodded and opened the driver's side door, got in, and reached over to open the door on my side. I waited for him to clear some junk off of my seat before I sat down. He tossed the stuff, bags from McDonalds and Burger King and two paperback books, into the back of the car where they could be with more of their kind. He pulled out into traffic and headed toward my office as I directed him, shifting with all the smoothness of an epileptic in mid-fit.

"Just learning how to drive a stick?" I inquired casually.

"Everybody's a critic," he snapped. "I drive jerky. Everybody's told me. Learn to live with it." He shifted again and I rebounded off my seat cushions. By the time we pulled into the lot of my building I was nursing a respectable headache.

Failure Drill

What was I doing with my life that was so bad God felt he had to punish me like this?

The building was even emptier than it had been the day before. The dead security guard had been replaced by the security company and now a fresh-faced kid manned the lobby desk instead of an ex-cop, probably looking to get some job experience that would look good on a resume. He watched, bored, as Steve and I walked across the lobby. I wondered if he knew the fate of his predecessor.

"What floor?" Steve said as we strode toward the elevators.

"Sixth," I answered. I walked right past the elevators and pushed open the stairwell door. I turned to look at Steve, who'd paused at the elevator call buttons.

"Broken?" he asked, sticking a thumb at the elevator.

"Nope," I said, and continued holding open the door. He stood there looking at me for a few seconds, then slowly crossed the floor. Standing just outside the doorway, he gazed up the stairwell for a second, then turned back to me. His eyes focused on my jaw where it was swollen and discolored. He eyed the elevators again.

"Uh-huh," he said, and went first up the stairs. He reached into his windbreaker and adjusted something under his left arm, dropped his hand, then thought better of it and put his hand back. He set his feet down softly on each step, and kept his eyes always on the next tier up. I stayed four steps behind him, hands in my pockets, whistling soundlessly.

Chapter Twelve

SMELLS LIKE TEEN SPIRIT

My office was exactly as I remembered leaving it: no warnings in blood across the windows, no trip wires attached to bombs in front of my door, no unmarked brown packages stuffed with dead fish. I was almost disappointed.

The message light on my answering machine stared at me unblinkingly as I circled the desk and sat down in my chair. Steve sat on the small couch against the wall, apparently preferring it to the customer's chair in front of my desk. He stretched his legs out, then let his gaze wander about my humble abode.

"Not bad," he said, "but they probably screw you on the rent because of the stylish decor." He said "stylish" like it was a dirty word. Maybe it was.

"More than you know," I said. We sat and looked at each other for several long minutes. He shrugged his shoulders under his windbreaker.

"Shoulder holster uncomfortable?" I said.

"Yep," he replied.

We stared at each other for a few minutes more. I faintly

heard the cars going by outside, their engines growing slightly louder then fading as they passed by six stories below. The sun came out from behind a cloud briefly, warming my neck and brightening the office. Before long it was behind another cloud and the warmth on my neck faded. Steve stretched out on the couch, laying his head on the arm and closing his eyes.

"Care to tell me about it?" I said.

"Nope," he said without opening his eyes. He shifted on the couch once and was still. Staring at him on my couch, I wondered, if our places were reversed, whether I would say anything to me or not. Doubtful. I pulled open a drawer and retrieved my technical manual.

I sat there and read the manual for half an hour, with Steve sleeping or pretending to sleep on the couch, before the phone rang. It was Scott.

"What's the news?" I said.

"Well, I finally got the information you wanted from the bank," he said. "Talk about pulling teeth. I forgot it was the weekend, but you'd think these people were defending the secrets of the free world. I called the bank manager at home, though, and finally got some results after I threatened physical violence."

"That was tolerant of you."

"She didn't think so. But I did get what I think you wanted. Phillips apparently used his ATM card at two-fourteen p.m. on the seventeenth."

"That would be Thursday, three days ago," I said, writing on my calendar.

"I can tell you're a detective," Scott said. "You figured that one out right away."

"How much money did he take out?"

"Two hundred and fifty, which is the daily max for his

account. Looks like he plans to stay bye-bye for a while. Or didn't want to keep using his card. And what's the next question you're supposed to ask?"

"Where did he use it?" I said in a childlike singsong voice, playing along. Steve opened one eye and looked at me for a second, then closed it and went back into his coma.

"At the National Bank of Detroit branch at thirty-three forty-seven Woodward Avenue, right in the heart of beautiful Royal Oak. Almost." I sat up a little.

"What cross-street is that by?" I said.

"How the hell am I supposed to know?" Scott said. "Am I a phone book?"

"You were on a prominent stake-out resulting in newspaper-grade arrests right around there. That's better than a phone book when it comes to addresses. Now, where is that?"

"Somewhere near Thirteen Mile," he grumbled.

"Thank you," I said. "Talk about pulling teeth."

"One more thing," he said. "They got Polzewski this morning."

"Who?" I said.

"Polzewski. Arthur Polzewski. The guy in the suit at Ram's Horn. Christ, you're bad with names. He was cut in half by a shotgun early this morning at a Stop and Rob in Pontiac. It was made to look like he got in the way of a stickup attempt. Just like before."

"That leaves just one out of the three. I bet Weatherspoon is sweating."

"That's an understatement. He called me to confirm that it was Polzewski that got hit. Since I'm one of the few people outside of Justice that he's confided in, I think he just called to talk to someone with a sympathetic ear. He's got everybody and their brother mobilized over at the Fed Building, looking for that last guy."

"If he doesn't get to that guy first I wouldn't bet on his promotion chances," I said. "That is, if he doesn't get canned." I'd heard about the turnovers in Justice and the FBI when a job went awry. The same thing had happened in the Secret Service after Kennedy got shot, and to a smaller extent after Hinckley, even though nobody really did anything wrong there. I'd never had to worry about that, though. With all the agents that got burned out, not to mention killed, in the years I worked for the DEA, they had enough trouble trying to persuade veterans to stay on. I had less than five years in when I quit, and I was considered an old hand. Unless an agent shot his superior or himself his supervisor would do cartwheels to keep him on. Things might be different now, but I knew agents that had gotten drunk and shot out streetlights in downtown Miami with their issued Glocks and they'd never even received a written reprimand.

"Have you had any luck in finding Phillips?" Scott said.

"No," I said petulantly. "It's easier to find someone that's kidnapped by the Red Brigade than somebody halfway intelligent that's disappeared voluntarily. If he doesn't want to be found, there's no telling the inconvenience he'll put up with. Sleeping in storm sewers, abandoned buildings, you name it. He can get to money any time he wants with his card, too."

"And the bank says he's got over a grand in his account. That could last him a long, long time," Scott said.

"Super," I said. I looked at Steve, who had his eyes open and was watching me.

"If Jer grabbed his forty-five," Steve mused, "he may not be interested in hiding."

"Hold on a minute, Scott," I said, and cupped a hand over the mouthpiece. "What are you talking about?" I said.

Steve sat up and clasped his hands together between his knees. "What I'm talking about is that I know Jerry," he explained. "He may not be the frightened rabbit you think he is. If he knew someone was after him, instead of running blindly, not knowing when they'd catch up to him, he might try to choose the spot where they caught up to him. Give himself the high ground, so to speak. He already took two guys out with just a knife. Maybe he feels he can do the same or better with a gun. It's what I'd do in his place." He spread his hands and shrugged.

Dear God, I thought, *are these guys for real? Somebody pinch me.*

"I have the strong feeling, though," he continued, "that you're still not telling us everything. I think you know who's after him and why. As long as you don't endanger Jer by not telling us, I'm not gonna call you on it, but until I know the whole story I'm just taking shots in the dark when it comes to guesstimating what Jer'll do."

I stared at him for a few seconds. "What's your major?" I asked him finally.

"Criminal Justice."

"You too. I should've guessed. Okay, let's put that college education to the test. Why would Jerry be at Woodward and Thirteen Mile?" I asked him.

Steve sat there for a second and thought, staring at his clasped hands.

"Eddie's Gun Shop and Range?" he replied quizzically.

Bingo. I took my hand off the mouthpiece. "Scott?" I said. "I might have something. I'll give you a call if it pans out." I hung up before he could say a word and grabbed my coat.

I followed Steve down the stairs and in a few short minutes was gritting my teeth in anticipation of him putting the RX-7 in gear. I sat quiet in the passenger seat and watched the upper-middle-class houses of Birmingham slide by. As we angled onto Woodward the restrained affluence of Birmingham slowly disappeared and a slightly seedier side of Woodward began to show its face. Southbound toward Detroit, Woodward became just another strip. Discount car audio stores, pawn shops, fast food joints, massage parlors, and invariably a motel called The Dunes – Woodward had it all, stretching from Detroit northwest through ten cities over twenty-five miles before ending in the depressed heart of downtown Pontiac.

We drove on Woodward for less than five minutes before I saw the bank. I pointed it out to Steve and he slowed down enough to swing into its deserted parking lot. I'd told him about Jerry using the Automatic Teller Machine on Thursday and it put him in a better mood to actually have some sort of lead on his friend. Steve drove the car slowly past the semi-enclosed booth containing the money machine. We both stared at it as if it was going to tell us where Jerry was. I didn't see Jerry's car in the lot, but then I hadn't expected to. He hadn't been stupid yet.

Less than a mile down the road Steve pulled into a turn-around in the boulevard and angled into the diagonal spaces in front of the gun shop. There was a large sign on the door, done in highly visible hunter's orange. We both read it.

Firearms MUST be unloaded and in locked cases before entering.

CCW permits NOT valid.

I looked at that last sentence and then at Steve. He looked back at me. I held the door open for him and we went in.

One wall of the establishment was covered with an array of gun cases and holsters, leather and synthetic. A long glassed-in case, which also served as a counter, ran the length of the opposite wall. The latest in handgun technology was laid out on cloth covered shelves inside, oiled and gleaming. A rack ran along the wall behind the counter, where shotguns, rifles, and muzzleloaders all pointed their bores at the ceiling. Splitting the rack in two was a small, thick paned window that looked out onto a pistol range. I saw the door that led onto the range at the far end of the counter. The inside of the window was covered with a fine, grey layer of spent gunpowder.

A few customers wandered here and there through the store, rummaging through items on floor displays or peeking through the glass of the counter at the handguns on exhibit. They ignored the dull pops emanating from behind the rack of long guns. At first I couldn't figure out what was making the noises, then I realized that someone was firing on the range behind the "soundproof" wall.

We walked up the aisle along the glass counter toward two of the help, who were discussing something fervently. I stopped in front of them, noticing a security camera bolted to the ceiling above us. Its blank eye stared at me as one of the salespeople cut short his argument about Benelli shotguns and headed our way.

"Can I help you gentlemen?" he said. He had dark hair and a droopy mustache, and his arms under his polo shirt were lean and muscular. Both he and his partner wore pistols on their hips, not flagrantly displayed but visible to anyone who looked. I'd been in the store a few times before, and every time I'd noticed that all the employees were armed. To the best of my knowledge, no one had ever gotten up the nerve to rob the place while it was open. I hoped Steve didn't start shrugging his shoulders again.

"Yes," I said. I pulled out a card and let him stare at it a while. Then I showed him the picture I had of Jerry.

"We're looking for this young man here," I said, laying the picture on the glass countertop and tapping it with my finger. The salesman picked up the photo and looked at it closely. He ignored the dull pops from the range on the other side of the wall behind him.

"I think he was here on Thursday," I continued. "About two-thirty, give or take. I was hoping you could tell me if I'm right."

The man shook his head. "I had Thursday off," he said. He looked at the other counterman who was hovering nearby. "Ted?"

Ted came over and took the picture and stared at it. Then he looked at my embossed business card, which was still sitting on the counter.

"Who's he?" he said, nodding at Steve. I opened my mouth to answer, but wasn't quick enough.

"I'm Gumby, dammit," I heard from behind my right shoulder in a distinctly Jewish accent. I turned and looked at Steve. He gazed back at me, his hands clasped in front of his body and a deceivingly innocent look on his face. When I turned back to Ted I saw he was smiling.

"Well then," he said to me, "you must be Pokey. Yeah, I saw him here on Thursday."

I almost broke a tooth grinding my jaws together to keep from blurting out a stream of questions at him.

Instead, I took a deep breath and said, "Do you remember if he bought anything?"

"I'll say he bought something," Ted said. "He asked if we had any forty-five Hydra-Shoks. I'd just unpacked a shipment of them, so I knew we did. He bought four boxes. It's not often you see someone buying that many Hydra-Shoks all at once. One box is usually it, it's not exactly plinkin' ammo."

I knew what he meant. Federal Hydra-Shoks were premium-grade street-proven hollowpoints and cost about sixty cents a round, retail. Four twenty-round boxes would run Jerry over fifty dollars, more than four times as much as the same amount of practice ammo.

"Did he buy anything else?" I said.

"Shit yeah. He bought a couple of Wilson magazines. For a Colt forty-five. He also bought some thirty-eight special Silvertips and an inside-the-pants holster. If I remember correctly, the holster was for a revolver, a snubnose. He paid for it all in cash, a big wad of bills. Pretty stupid if you ask me. I wouldn't be caught dead carrying that much cash on me, and I sure as hell wouldn't pull it all out at once." He shrugged. "For a second I wondered if he was a drug dealer up from beautiful downtown Motown, but he just didn't have the look. Besides, most dopers go after the big black mean lookin' guns that take long mags, buy a lot of cheap ammo, and never practice, so they can't hit shit. 'Cept maybe some lady's kid playing on a porch across the street."

"Ain't that the truth," the other employee chimed in. "But they steal their guns, they don't buy 'em."

"Do you remember anything else?" I prodded him.

"I don't --" he began, then stopped. "Oh yeah. He had a shoulder bag with him. Black. Nylon, I think. He stuck everything he bought into it as he was going out the door. When he first came in with it I thought he was going to heist the place, you know, shoulder bag, day's growth of beard, bloodshot eyes. That's why I remember him, I thought we had a live one." He shrugged again and crossed his arms.

"Do you remember his mannerisms at all when he was in here?" I said. "Did he seem worried or upset? Did he appear to be injured at all?" Ted shrugged. He seemed to be good at it.

"Not that I remember," he said. "Which I guess means that I didn't see anything out of the ordinary. Why are you guys looking for him, anyway? He rob a bank or something?" He grinned at his joke.

"No," I said, "nothing that simple." I retrieved the picture and stuck it back in my pocket. "If he happens to come back could you please give him this number to call?" I asked, pointing at the office number on my card. "It's important." I thanked them for their cooperation and headed for the door, Steve in tow.

"Where did Jerry get a thirty-eight?" Steve asked me as he unlocked the car door. "He doesn't own one." Once inside the car he reached across and unlocked my door. I opened the door and squeezed my frame down into the small car's seat.

"One of the dead goons at the school had an empty holster," I said.

Steve nodded. "Well, we know one thing for sure," he said as we sat there.

"And what's that?" I said. I found the appropriate lever and reclined the seat a bit more.

"That he's not running scared," Steve said. "Not at all. He's armed for bear and ready to rock and roll. Dammit!"

he said, striking the steering wheel. "I wish I knew where the hell he is! I feel like we're just spinning our wheels, following a cold trail."

I could argue that Jerry was probably scared out of his skin, that's why all the firepower, but what use would that be? "All we can do is wait for something to stick its head up," I said. "He'll surface sooner or later, don't worry." I looked at him sideways. "I'm surprised he hasn't contacted you, if you're all such good friends. I would think that'd be the first thing he did."

Steve shook his head. "I don't know why he hasn't," he said. "Maybe he doesn't want to get us involved. Maybe he thinks he can handle it alone." He shook his head some more.

"He knows us," Steve continued. "He knows that as soon as we found out he was in trouble we'd start looking for him. He would *know* that." He emphasized the point by hitting the wheel again. "I don't know, maybe he's left us some clue that we haven't got, didn't find. Something." He gripped the steering wheel tightly, a sour look on his face, but seemed to have finished.

"Well," I said, "I appreciate your and Ron's help, but I don't really think you need to shadow me any more today. Why don't you take me back to my car. I've got a few calls to make back at my office, and a few return calls to wait for, but other than that. . ." I spread my hands. Steve stared at a point in space and scowled.

"I don't like it," he said, "but it seems like the most logical thing to do. I'd rather not leave you alone, though. If you get bumped off, we'll be in trouble. I hate to admit it, but you do have more experience and more contacts in this line of work."

"Gee," I said, "coming from you, that's quite a compliment."

He smiled. "You know what I mean," he continued. "Someone already tried to dim your lights once. At least, I assume that someone did, and that it's related to Jer's case. For all I know you could've run into a door." He frowned at me.

"Someday maybe I'll tell you all of my secrets, Grasshopper," I said. "Until then you can get by with doing what I say. And now I say drive me back to my car." I looked at him with an innocent smile on my face.

"Christ, everybody's a comedian," he said, and cranked the starter until the engine caught. "Would you happen to know where your car is?" It was his turn to raise his eyebrows innocently.

Chapter Thirteen

CONNECTIONS

Steve dropped me off at the Burger King, but only after the obligatory promise to contact him or Ron if anything new came up. I got a few funny looks as I crabwalked around my car and checked under its hood for any surprises, but that didn't bother me. I'd stopped caring about what people thought of me sometime in college.

My office was as crowded as usual. Dust motes glinted in the sunlight streaming through the window, spinning and swirling in minuscule air currents. I sat down in my chair and watched hundreds of new motes join their compatriots in flight. It was then that I noticed the message light on my answering machine was flashing. I hit the Play button and sat back.

"Mr. Phault," a voice came on, "this is Geraldine Phillips. I was wondering if there's any news about my son. I know you said you'd call us if there was, but you can understand if I'm a bit worried. It's been four days since anybody's seen him. Please, if you find out anything, let us know. Even if it's bad news, that's better than not knowing."

Failure Drill

She paused for a second, then seemed to decide not to say any more and hung up. I was trying to decide if I should call her when the machine beeped and a second message began playing.

"Mr. Phault?" The voice was young, soft, definitely female, and a bit tenuous. "My name is Jodi Shippley. I'm Jerry Phillips' girlfriend. I got your number from Mrs. Phillips. I -- I'm really worried about Jerry. I thought at first that he wasn't in trouble, but if he was he'd call me. Then I thought that if he was in trouble, he wouldn't be able to call me. I -- I guess I don't know what I thought. What to think. Please, call me if you know where he is, or if you've heard from him." She left her number and offered a mumbled goodbye. I listened to a dial tone for a few seconds until the machine cut it off.

I leaned my elbows on the desk and steepled my fingers in front of me. I couldn't believe I'd forgotten how much I hated missing persons cases. I blinked my eyes a few times and squeezed the bridge of my nose between two fingers.

I sighed, trying to extend my period of self-pity just a few more seconds, then picked up the phone. I punched in a number and listened to it ring.

"Kang Distributing," a sedate voice answered.

"Could I please speak to Charlie Kang?" I inquired.

"I'm sorry, there's no one here by that name," the voice answered in a polite monotone.

"Of course there isn't," I agreed. "In fact, I dialed this number specifically because I knew no one named Charlie Kang would be there. How 'bout you do me a favor, though? If, perchance, someone should drop by and mention that his name is Charlie Kang, would you tell him I've called? My name is John Phault." He hung up without saying a word. I shook my head, put the phone back in its cradle, and waited. Seven minutes later the phone rang.

"John Phault," I said.

"I see that you haven't lost your sense of humor," the man on the other end said, without any introduction.

"I see that your help hasn't gotten any brighter," I replied. "Are you recruiting out of the soup kitchens now?"

He snorted derisively. "To what do I owe this honor?" he said. "How long has it been? Four years?"

"Three," I said. We sat in silence for a moment I finally said, "I assume you're still in the business?"

"As I recall," he said, "you were working for the people with initials. In Florida, of all places."

"For the DEA," I said, "not ATF or FBI. And that's done with now, I've been out for close to two years."

"That's interesting," he commented. "Perhaps you could tell me why there is a little red light blinking on the box next to my phone, then." A tap, I realized. He was talking about a tap. Someone was tapping my phone. Or maybe . . . .

"Do our new friends like what I say or are they more interested in what you think?" I said to him.

"I just got off the phone with some business partners," he said. "I had a green light then." *Shit*, I thought. *My* phone was tapped.

"Let me call you from another line," I said. "Give me the number you're at."

"Why?" he said. "Then our friends will have my private number and all I'll have is you."

"Goddammit!" I said. "I wouldn't have called if it wasn't important." He thought it over silently for a few seconds then gave me the number. He was probably curious, and knew he could get a new unlisted number in a matter of hours if he had to. I locked up my office and went down the corridor where there was a pay phone in an alcove. It wasn't too private but at least it wasn't tapped. I hoped.

"Kang Distributing," Charlie answered.

"Do we have a green light?" I said. There was a pause as he checked.

"Yes," he said. "Who are your friends?"

"Who knows?" I said. "Everybody likes me. Now, you never answered my question. Are you still in business?" I knew from past experience Charlie had a talent for avoiding the subject.

"What? Oh, that. Yes, I do still dabble in that area. From time to time." It was my turn to snort derisively. He ignored it. We both knew that if he was still in, he was in all the way. Charlie was never one to dabble in anything.

"Well, at least something's going right," I said. "I need some information."

"What do I get in return?" he said.

"That depends on what you find out."

"I don't work that way, and you know it," he said sharply.

"Listen," I cut in "aren't you even curious as to why my phone is tapped? Or are you all business? I need to find out why Pietro Bufonte is trying to have me killed." He shut up and listened. "I'm pretty sure I know why," I continued, "and I'm pretty sure that it's him. But I need to know for sure before I can act. I wouldn't want to provoke any of the wrong people."

"If it's Bufonte, you already have," he said. He tsked. "What did you do?" He almost sounded.... amused. Bastard.

"If you still have your connections, you can find that out too." He grunted noncommittally. He wanted to play games with me, try to see if I'd lost my edge. I knew how his mind worked, though. "That's all I wanted. If I'm still around later, I'll find some way to pay you back."

"I know," he said. "You always were good on your word." He paused and sighed. "I don't want to waste my time," he went on, "so don't go getting blown away til after we're even. You're in it deep, boy, if you're right about this."

"No doubt," I said. "I should've stayed in the army."

"You and me both. But I'd still be dogging your ass on the road marches."

"In your dreams, Johnny Socko," I said. "You were too busy trying to scam on the bar sluts interested in a bit of Asian weenie." He laughed and we sat and remembered for a bit. Distance and time, for a brief moment, had no meaning.

I'd met Charlie six months into my enlistment, about the same time I was discovering that the U.S. military wasn't all its television ads played it up to be. One night while we were relaxing at a bar four sailors tried to engage in a little Japan-bashing at the personal level, Charlie's head being their intended target. Charlie and I explained to them as politely as we could, using beer bottles and barstools as teaching aids, that he was of Chinese, not Japanese, descent. Charlie had to spend an inordinate amount of time demonstrating to an especially difficult sailor, using a pool cue, how he was first and foremost an American. I dragged him out of the back door just ahead of the cops, and the incident cemented our friendship. After he got out of the service Charlie decided that he would go into the family business of "import/export" after all. We hadn't kept in very close contact since the military, our careers not exactly lending an aura of disclosure to our infrequent conversations, but both of us remembered that night in the bar.

"I'll see what I can do," he said finally.

Failure Drill

"Thanks," I said, and hung up.

I lifted the receiver again, put in change, and punched in a new number. It seemed like a day to renew old acquaintances. The number I dialed was a more familiar one, but one that I hadn't called in quite a while. A strange nostalgic feeling swept over me quickly as the phone rang on the other end. I briefly wished I hadn't made some of the choices in my life that I had, but quickly pushed that thought out of my head.

"Group Six," the pleasant female voice said.

"William Magruder, please," I said. She put me on hold and I listened to electronic humming for a while. She didn't bother asking my business; the line I'd called in on was unlisted. That and my knowing the name of an agent guaranteed me no questions asked, in case I was a skittery informant.

"Yeah."

"Bill," I said. "Who is this?" I could hear him mentally shuffling through the possibilities as he tried to place my voice.

"John?" he said tentatively.

"Right again."

"It's been quite a while," he said. "Eight months?"

"Jesus, has it been that long?" I said. I could almost see him sitting there nodding his big bearded face. His body matched his face, large and hairy, and it had earned him the nickname "Bear" in our group of agents. His deep voice didn't hurt the image, either. When he told someone to freeze in his bullhorn voice, they did. He'd been transferred to Detroit shortly after I'd quit in Miami, and I'd tried without much luck to keep in touch.

"Actually," I went on, "I'm surprised I caught you at your desk. Was it luck or skill?"

He laughed, a deep rumble sounded like storm clouds gathering. "It wasn't luck," he said. "I'm a chairborne ranger for the next month and a half. Have been for four months already."

"Why? Did you molest the SAC's daughter again?"

"No, not that. What it was, we had a house clearing party on the west side and you-know-who forgot to wear his vest. A shitbag taught me the error of my ways."

"How bad?" I said.

"Well, I'm still here to talk about it, aren't I? The truth is, I almost bought it. This punk popped out from behind a sofa and shot me in the chest four times. Just my luck, the day I forget to bring my vest I run into cocaine's answer to Wyatt Earp." I winced on my side of the connection. "Luckily, all he had was a snubnose thirty-eight. I still ended up spending eight hours on the table, though. One of the slugs cracked a vertebrae, later the wound got infected, all sorts of fun shit. Can't complain, though," he said. "Could be dead."

"What happened to the perp?"

"Bertha ate him. I saw to that before I hit the floor." Bertha was the sawed-off 12-gauge pump that Bill took with him on raids. It wasn't regulation, but with the hazards we put up with the bosses sometimes allowed us a little leniency. "Not to mention the fact that everybody else there felt they should empty their guns into the guy as he lay there twitching. But enough about me," Bill said. "What's happening with you? How's your little business doing?"

"It's got its ups and downs," I said.

"Any excitement? Or did your wife outlaw any more of that once you left here?"

"Actually," I said slowly, "that's what I've called about. I need a favor." I knew he wasn't going to turn me down, but it was only proper to be polite about it. When I'd first joined the DEA, I went with him and two other veteran agents on a raid to a suspected dealer's house in one of the many shitty areas of Miami. The end result had Bill standing over the dead dealer, his pistol empty, as another wastoid drew down on him. Which is where I came in and saved the day. I hit the second guy on the head with the butt of a shotgun I'd just found. My adrenaline was flowing so freely and my blood was pumping so hard I don't even remember feeling the impact of seasoned wood against skull, but it took fifty-six stitches to close up the guy's head so I must've connected.

The empty pistol was enough to convince Bill that he needed a different method of defense, one that didn't require emptying his gun to drop a 130-pound Puerto Rican high on crack. Hence Bertha, named in honor of his first wife. Since then Bill had said that if I ever needed a favor all I had to do was ask. So now I did.

"I need you to access all the info you have on Pietro Bufonte, and send it hard copy to me," I said.

"That's a lot of paper," he observed. "What's up?"

"Someone wants me dead and chances are it's him. I need everything I can get that might give me an edge."

"What the fuck have you been doing?" he said, astounded.

"I wish I could tell you," I said. There were a lot of ways he could've taken my response, not all of them good. He didn't press it.

"Right now it's all guesswork on my part," I told him, sidestepping.

"How can you be so sure it's him, then?"

"A few things, the most important of which is Freddie the Knife Pellicek. Last known to be working for Mr. Pietro

Bufonte, he tried to stick a knife in me yesterday. I tried to put his head through the floor of my office building's lobby. I had more luck than he did." I paused, then asked, "Can you get me what I need?" He didn't need to point out that most, if not all, of the information I was asking for I wasn't legally entitled to. Even if you've filed a Freedom of Information Act request, you can't look at information in any active investigations. But I wasn't just anybody.

"You know I can," he said without hesitation. "Freddie the Knife? Seriously?"

"Yeah, you like that? Also, make sure that nobody else knows what you're doing over there for me. Especially the boys over in Justice. I know you share the same database now, and they might have a flag on the file. I don't want it public knowledge that I asked for this file."

"Remind me never to have you save my life again." He sighed. "I don't know, I can't promise anything. Everything's computerized now, and I type with two fingers. One of the new guys here misspent his childhood as a hacker, maybe he can tell me how to get around a flag. Whatever happens, I'll do my best." He coughed twice, like someone who was getting over the flu. Or someone recovering from lead poisoning in his chest. I grimaced just thinking about it. "Now, where do you want me to send the stuff if and when I get it? Neither your house or office can be very secure right now, if he really has a hit out on you."

"Tell me something I don't know. I'm squeezing my cheeks together as we speak." I thought for a few seconds. "Remember the last place we ate out together?" I said.

"Uh -- yeah," he said. "You mean that palace royale?"

"Exactly," I said. "Can you meet me there tomorrow morning at, uh, ten?"

"Probably. If I can't I'll call."

"Good," I replied. "I guess that's it, then. One more thing, though. What the hell are you doing in the office on a Sunday afternoon? Even you aren't that dedicated."

"Justice never sleeps," he said. "That, and I haven't been out of the house since I came home from the hospital, except to go to physical therapy. I was going stir crazy. I wasn't even doing any work, just sitting here soaking up the atmosphere."

"Man, why didn't you have someone call me when you got shot? I would've visited. I owe you. I'd even admit to liking you."

He heaved a deep sigh. "It's not your war anymore, John," he said. There wasn't anything I could say to that, so we said goodbye to each other and I hung up.

I walked back to my office and sat in my chair and thought for a while. Bill's comment about neither my office nor my home being safe had gotten to me. I swiveled around in my chair and looked out the window. I was on the sixth floor, with the closest building that would make a good sniper's roost over a quarter of a mile away, but still I was getting a tingle between my shoulder blades as I sat in the chair, like someone was sighting in a rifle on me. Unlikely. Hell, even the sun was on my side, reflecting off the window at such an angle as to make a clear shot almost impossible. Knowing all that, I did the only logical thing I could in such a situation. I got up, lowered the venetian blinds, and tilted them so that only thin strips of daylight showed.

For some reason, and the thought made me worry for myself briefly, I wasn't taking the idea of a contract on myself seriously. I knew that I was in trouble, but the actual idea that someone wanted *me, specifically,* dead hadn't hit home yet. Not really. It was like I was watching the events of my life unfold on a TV show. They were interesting but not too realistic. I supposed if another person tried to kill me I'd start taking things more seriously, though. Or die.

I called home but there wasn't an answer. It seemed strange, especially -- I looked at my watch -- at two-thirty on a Sunday afternoon. Kelly was probably out shopping again, though, ready to tear me a new asshole when she came home, for not telling her where I went and for not staying long enough that morning to say goodbye. Surprising that she hadn't left a nasty message on my office answering machine. I wasn't looking forward to my come-uppance, but I had other things a bit more pressing on my mind and the thought of one of her tirades didn't have the same effect on me that it normally would have.

The phone rang and I picked it up, figuring it was Kelly, back from the mall and ready to castrate me.

"John Phault Investigations," I said cordially, almost hoping it was a telephone solicitor. I braced myself for an onslaught of verbal abuse, all the more dreaded because I would deserve it.

"John, it's Scott," he said in a rush. "I just got word that your wife was just taken to Beaumont receiving."

"What? *What*? What happened? What happened to her?" She was in the hospital? My heart had stopped and I couldn't breathe.

"Calm down, I don't know, I just found about it myself. You know everything I do. I heard it from one of my sergeants that she was en route to the hospital from your house in an ambulance. He heard the call over the radio and recognized the name from me talking about you. There were two deputies on the scene, I'll be able to find out what happened from them, they're heading to the hospital now."

"What the fuck were two deputies doing at my house?" I yelled. I was out of breath, my hand clammy on the receiver as I clutched it next to my ear. I'd somehow risen halfway out of my chair, but I couldn't remember moving.

"I don't know," Scott said emphatically. "I'm going to see the uniforms at the hospital, meet me there. I'm on my way." He hung up, and I stood there with the phone in my hand for several seconds.

Oh shit, I thought. *You dumb motherfucker. You think you're so damn smart, it never occurred to you that they might go to your house when you weren't there, or maybe even try to get at you through your wife. You were so damn cocky, feeling so invulnerable, sitting up here in your roost with a gun on your hip, playing John Wayne.*

I slammed the receiver down, feeling it crack in my hand. I didn't bother locking my door as I slammed it behind me. I ran down the stairs because I couldn't stand to wait for the elevator. The only reason I took the time to check my car for wires was because I wasn't going to be cheated of any revenge. I wasn't thinking clearly, if at all, and as the adrenaline triggered by the call wore off and I saw I was doing twenty-five over the limit, I began to realize I had to calm down.

I took my foot off the pedal a little and drew in a few deep breaths. As the grip around my heart eased off I was left with a worried, hollow little feeling inside of me. I tried to tell myself that maybe it wasn't what I thought, that maybe Kelly had just slipped and taken a bad fall and it wasn't anything serious, but I just couldn't buy it. I didn't believe in accidents any more than I believed in coincidence. My mind rocketed back and forth between anger and worry. *Please, God, let her be okay.*

Chapter Fourteen

ENTER THE STORM

I swung into the parking lot outside the emergency entrance and screeched into a space. I was out of the car and halfway to the building before the engine had stopped. As the glass and metal doors slid open I saw that the emergency room was barely half full. Remarkably, only two people were bleeding on the floor. I grabbed a rotund nurse's arm as she strode past at Mach Four. She had to windmill her free arm to keep from falling over.

"Sir," she said in a strident, professional voice, "if you take a seat, someone will be right—"

"Shut up," I told her. "I need to find out where—never mind." I let her go and she gave me a dirty look. Through the windows of some double doors that led into a long white corridor I saw Scott talking to two men in brown.

The nurse tried to tell me that I wasn't allowed to go where I was going, but I ignored her and pushed through the double doors. She was right behind me all the way, getting angrier and louder, until she saw I was headed toward the two deputies. Then she faded into the background.

The two uniforms were arguing furiously with Scott, along with a fourth person I didn't recognize. The two cops saw me first and motioned to Scott, who had his back to me. He turned just as I got there and made calming motions with his hands when he saw the look on my face. Whatever they'd been arguing about was overridden by my presence.

"Whoa there, John," he said. "Keep the horsepower under control. Everything is all right."

"*What* everything?" I demanded. "Where's Kelly? What happened?" The two cops studied me, and gauged my reactions. One was young and skinny, and barely looked twenty. The other one was older and obviously more experienced. A scowling young man was standing next to the gray-haired older cop, his arms crossed. I ignored them all and focused my attention on Scott.

"I want you to calm down," Scott said firmly. "I want you thinking clearly." He raised his eyebrows and gazed piercingly at me. I took a couple deep breaths and tried to shake the pounding in my ears.

"All right," Scott said. "That's better. Now, I want you to listen carefully. Bufonte—his men—went to your house." He saw the look on my face. "Yeah, you fucked up, you should've thought of that. I should've too. It doesn't matter now. She's okay." His reassurances didn't make me feel any better, but I'd save the anger and recriminations for later.

"Tell me what happened," I said icily. I was trying to keep my feelings in check, trying not to explode. I wanted everything to slow down so I could take things one at a time, but the world wasn't cooperating. It never did.

"Well, about an hour and a half ago, it seems—" Scott started, then looked at the young man standing beside him.

"I'd better let you tell it," he said to him. "You were the one there. I haven't heard the whole story yet anyway."

"Who the fuck are you?" I said to him. He uncrossed his massive arms and let them hang loosely at his sides. I figured it out at the same time that he spoke.

"Bob Grinnand," he said. "Nice to meet you, too." The younger cop shot him a look and jabbed a finger at him.

"Listen shithead, you just better watch your mouth. You've already given us enough trouble. One more crack and I'll cuff ya, take you outside, and pepper spray your ass!" Bob just stared at him with no expression on his face. The older cop turned his head toward his partner.

"Shut up," he said out of the corner of his mouth. The young officer opened his mouth to speak but shut it when he saw the expression on the older cop's face. I guessed, correctly as it turned out, that the younger was a rookie.

Now that I knew who I was looking at, I recognized Bob from the description of him I'd been given. He was wearing a red rugby shirt and faded blue jeans. Although he was a few inches shorter than me, I'd bet he outweighed me by a good twenty-five pounds, all of it muscle. Popeye would've envied his forearms.

"Sorry," I said reflexively. "But what the fuck were you doing at my house?"

Bob took a deep breath before he spoke. His voice wasn't deep, but it had an odd rumble behind it, like the sound of an avalanche in the distance. If I had heard it on the telephone I might've thought he was a heavy smoker.

"Ron picked me up from the airport and told me about everything. I decided that I wanted to talk to you. There was no answer at your office and I didn't want to talk to your machine, so I decided to drop by your house to see if you were there."

"How did you get his address?" Scott said.

"I looked it up in the phone book," Bob replied, like it was the stupidest question he'd heard all year. "Only one Phault in there." Scott looked at me, the question in his eyes.

"I never got around to getting an unlisted number," I explained. "I'm an idiot." Scott shook his head.

"There was no answer when I called but I decided to drop by anyway," Bob continued as if we hadn't interrupted. "So I rented a cab." Scott interrupted him again.

"Where's your car?" he said. A cop's habits die hard.

"Fort Bragg," Bob sighed, loudly, then continued once again. "So I took the cab to your house. Once I figured out I was at the right address I let the cab take off and went up to the door. If you weren't home I figured I would wait. How late could you be out on a Sunday?

"I was going to ring the bell, but I heard shouting inside. I didn't know if it was you fighting with your wife or what, so I went around to a window to check first." He stopped then and rubbed his eyes.

"There were two guys inside," he continued, "and a lady I assumed was your wife. They were all in the middle of your living room, near the front door. One guy was in his forties, dark hair, overcoat. He had a pistol in his hand but it wasn't pointing at anything in particular, he was just holding it at his side while he argued with the other guy. The other guy was about thirty, brown hair, in good shape." Bob had been looking at the floor as he recited the details, but now he paused and looked straight at me. He kept looking me in the eyes as he continued with the story and didn't move his eyes from my face until he was done.

"The younger guy had just smacked your wife, or hit her," he said. "I don't know, I didn't see it. All I saw was her lying face down on the floor in front of him. He was trying to pick her up and bend her over the coffee table." He saw I understood what he meant and didn't go into any more detail.

"The older guy was arguing with him, saying they were just supposed to wait for you and didn't have time for this. I could hear them pretty well through the window," he explained. "The younger guy wasn't listening. I decided that I should make the acquaintance of these two gentlemen, and in a minute or so I found an unlocked window on the side of your house that led into a bathroom."

"I cut the screen, went through the window, and opened the bathroom door. From there I could see the young guy had his pants around his ankles, was on his knees behind your wife and trying to do the same to her pants. She was out of it, I figured unconscious. The older guy was behind him, his back to me, not trying to stop the guy but still saying he should cut it out, they were there to do a job."

I found I was grinding my molars together and forced myself to stop. I also forced myself to keep looking Bob straight in the eyes. His steel grey eyes never wavered from mine as he told his tale. He was trying to keep a detached tone to his presentation, but I could tell he was fighting back a lot of strong emotions. Even with all the chemical distractions racing through my own body there was no denying the almost tangible force of Bob's personality. It felt like standing next to a bomb you knew was armed.

"The rest of it," Scott prodded him.

"I proceeded to introduce myself to the two gentlemen and kindly persuaded them to stop." He smiled wanly. The smile didn't reach his eyes.

"No bullshit," I said, and his smile vanished. "The whole

thing. I want to hear it." He considered for a second and then nodded.

"I slammed the older guy headfirst into a wall and he went out cold. The younger guy got his pants on and we started dancing."

"English," I growled.

"He came at me barehanded," Bob said. He had a far away look on his face. "I guess he had a gun, but apparently he didn't think he'd need it, or didn't want to make any noise. He was really fast, but—" Bob shook his head. I noticed then a small mouse under one of his eyes. Other than that, he looked none the worse for wear.

"Where is he now?" I said. My head swam with visions of revenge and death and dismemberment.

"He had a cardiac arrest en route to the hospital," Scott said, "due to complications from his injuries. The paramedics tried to bring him back, but he was too fucked up."

"Goddammit!" I swore. Now I would be cheated of inflicting any harm on him personally. "God!" I spun around in a circle, fists clenched in impotent rage.

"The older guy must've come to while I was busy with his friend," Bob said, "'cause when I looked around later he was gone. Adrenaline rush, tunnel vision. Sorry." He said it like he was giving me a recipe.

I closed my eyes slowly and squeezed my temples. Inside, I knew I should be glad that nothing serious had happened to Kelly, but I had so much wanted to exact my own biblical vengeance on the men responsible that I felt cheated.

The older cop said to Scott, "I was going to put out a BOL on the guy, with the description he gave us earlier, but I thought I should check with you first, since this whole thing is so screwed up. We can update it later with a name if he can pick the guy out of a mugbook. No chance for prints, Mr. Grinnand here said they were both wearing gloves." Scott ran a hand through his hair and shook his head.

"If this guy made it back home, he'll be buried so deep we won't see him for the next month. And then he'll have four people saying he was somewhere else at the time. We don't really have anything on him but B and E, anyway. There were no specific threats overheard. I assume you checked the neighborhood?"

The cop nodded. "Didn't find a thing," he responded. "Two other units were called to help out. Right now they should still be checking with the neighbors to see if they saw anything, but you know the chances of that." Both Scott and I nodded.

"You'll probably want to look at the body to see if you can identify the guy," Scott said. "They stuck him in one of the vacant examining rooms for us instead of wheeling him down to the cooler right away."

I slowly nodded my head. "Before I do anything I want to see Kelly. Where is she?" Scott pointed the way and I walked beside him down the corridor. Bob was behind us, and the two cops walked behind him. The rookie was either very pissed at the way he was being treated or very constipated, judging from the look on his face. I didn't care either way.

"The doctor that treated her said she has a mild concussion," Scott said. "He got done looking at her and assigned her a room just before I showed up. She was hit in the left temple, but the X-rays didn't show any fractures, so she's lucky. A little harder and the guy might've killed her." We stopped and waited for an elevator to arrive, and when one did we rode it up to the third floor.

"Too bad he's dead," I said through clenched teeth. "I wanted to have a private discussion with him about dispensing pain."

"Right now she's mildly sedated," Scott went on as if he hadn't heard me. "They say they'll want to keep her under observation for twenty-four hours." We rounded the corner of a nurses station and stopped at a door to a private room. I slowly pushed the door open and went in. Scott stayed out in the hall with Bob and the uniforms.

Kelly was lying on her side in the bed, sleeping peacefully under sedation. In the dim light I saw she was wearing a light blue paper gown, which combined with the serene look on her face made her look like a little girl again. A little girl with a white gauze bandage over one temple. I stepped back until I found a wall and leaned against it, drawing in a deep, shuddering breath, then another. My whole body was shaking and I couldn't stop it.

There was my wife, the woman I loved, that I had known for six years, the person I wanted to spend the rest of my life with, lying wounded in a hospital bed because of me. I felt a piece of myself, way deep inside, turn hard and cold and shrink down to next to nothing. It was my fault. No getting around that, even though I knew that it was other people who'd done the harm to her.

That my own shortcomings were responsible for my wife being in the hospital was no easy thing to admit to myself; not two hours earlier I'd been thinking how it didn't seem real that people were out to get me. My perspective on that situation had been radically altered, permanently. I finally saw how serious things were. My opponents were undoubtedly serious men, it was only right for me to be serious about them. But in attacking my wife they'd made one mistake—not only had they made my predicament plain for me to finally see, they had turned this conflict into something *personal*. I didn't care if it was only "business as usual" for them. Not with my wife in the hospital, chance the only reason she was still alive and unmolested.

I wasn't sure how long I stayed in that dim room, just watching her, but I left the room a different person.

Back out in the hall, the rookie cop and Bob were squaring off, the cop throwing threats in Bob's direction. Scott was stuck acting as an unwilling referee. The rookie looked like he was about to lose control. Bob was smiling warmly. The older cop was in the background, whistling silently. Apparently he'd had enough with getting involved and was sitting the next round out.

"What the fuck is the problem now?" I said tiredly.

"You didn't hear the rest of the story," Scott explained. He made a sweeping motion with his hand at Bob, signaling him to continue. Bob gave us a wry expression but went on.

"I called nine-one-one after . . . everything, asking for an ambulance. The Keystone Kop got there first."

"Listen, dirtbag," the rookie said, jabbing a finger, "one more word out of you and you're going to be a week getting out of the hospital."

"You tried that already," Bob said calmly. He looked at me. "He called me *dirtbag*," he said, amazed. He smiled happily. "Can you believe it?"

"Listen," I cut in sharply, speaking to the older cop. I looked at his nameplate. "Randolph? Why don't you tell it. You seem to be the only one not . . . involved here." Bob was smiling good naturedly, not a care in the world. So far he was living up to his advance press.

Randolph raised his head and took a step to get into the circle the rest of us had formed. He sucked at an imaginary piece of food stuck between his teeth for a second before he spoke.

"We arrived on the scene approximately three minutes after the call was placed," he said in a voice that could've been taken from any one of a dozen cop shows on TV. Apparently he had a lot of experience testifying in court. "Mr. Grinnand had apparently unlocked the front door and he yelled for us to enter as we arrived on the porch. We went in cautiously, Billy in front." Billy was apparently the rookie.

"We found Mr. Grinnand on the couch with Mrs. Phault, as it turns out examining her and supporting her neck which he thought was injured, and we also saw the recently deceased intruder on the floor, at this time bleeding profusely and moaning. Billy -- Deputy Paxton -- was a little torqued up and misinterpreted the situation. He took his baton out and instructed Mr. Grinnand to assume the position against the nearest wall. Mr. Grinnand told Deputy Paxton to blow it out his ass, that he was the person who called nine-eleven in the first place. I believe he also mentioned something about where Billy could stick his baton. Deputy Paxton then proceeded to try and force Mr. Grinnand into assuming the appropriate position for cuffing. Mr. Grinnand relieved Deputy Paxton of his baton and smacked him in the ass with it." I tried to hide the grin on my face from Paxton, but I wasn't quick enough. He saw it and turned red from a mixture of anger and embarrassment.

"Where the hell were you while all this was going on?" Scott inquired of Randolph.

"I thought I saw fresh blood coming out of Mrs. Phault's ear when Mr. Grinnand was standing up to . . . interact with my partner, so I turned my attention to her first. I didn't realize how quickly the situation would escalate. When I was reassured that Mrs. Phault was in no immediate danger, I turned my attention back to these two." He gestured with his thumb. "Mr. Grinnand tossed me Deputy Paxton's baton and asked me to intervene. I told Billy to examine the injured man

and as he did I got a short explanation of what happened from Mr. Grinnand.

"Deputy Paxton recovered a thirty-eight revolver from the injured man, as well as a folding knife. The ambulance arrived shortly thereafter and took Mrs. Phault and the now dead suspect, who had no identification on his person. The man died of cardiac arrest in the ambulance, all attempts at resuscitation failing. I got that from Turner, he was there working on the guy, you've probably met him on a few calls." Scott nodded. "After the ambulance left, two more units arrived, and I had them first patrol the neighborhood for the missing wounded guy and then when no one had any luck, start interviewing the neighbors for any eyewitnesses. It was then that we got word to meet you here, Lieutenant." Randolph tilted his head back, ready for whatever praise or chastisement Scott might level at him.

"Oh, yes," he continued, "right before Mr. Grinnand was going to climb into our patrol car to come over here he turned this over to me." He reached behind his back and handed Scott a Browning Hi-Power, still cocked and locked, undoubtedly loaded. Scott, after staring disbelievingly at the pistol for a few seconds, took it and held it muzzle down at his side.

"I was afraid if Wild Bill Hickok here saw me carrying it," Bob explained, eyeing Paxton "he'd try to perforate me first and read me my rights later." He looked at Scott. "I'll want it back."

Scott couldn't decide whether to be angry or amused. He settled on slightly stunned. "I don't suppose you have a CCW?" he inquired rhetorically. Bob kept a steady gaze on him and didn't blink. "No, I didn't think so. I won't even ask if it's registered." He stuck the pistol in his jacket pocket.

"Son of a bitch," Paxton muttered.

"Deputy Paxton," Scott turned to address him, squaring his shoulders, the full weight of his rank in his voice. "You need to learn how to read a situation or you'll be dead in under a year, and that is one thing I do *not* want. Our job is public service, and as such it is our responsibility to treat everyone we come across as they treat us or better, or failing that, at least be polite to them as you beat them into submission. You didn't do anything *wrong*, but you didn't quite set the department up as a shining example of excellence and professionalism, now did you? How many days have you been on the street, did you say? Fourteen?"

"Fifteen." Paxton was examining the tips of his shoes very intently. No wonder Randolph wasn't covering his ass. Randolph wasn't sure yet in his own mind whether or not Paxton was cut out for the job.

"Right. I suggest that you follow your partner's example. You know the way it's supposed to be, he knows the way it *is*. He's supposed to be teaching you that." Scott aimed a sharp look in Randolph's direction. "You should also learn how to use your baton correctly." Scott's voice was an icy mist. "Is that understood?"

"Yes sir." Paxton stood there stiffly.

"Good. Randolph, when you finish your paperwork, turn it in to me. I'll handle this from here." Scott gave me a brief glance. Randolph opened his mouth but Scott cut him off. "I know what SOP is," he said firmly. "If you get any flak you should refer all questions to me, understood?" Randolph nodded his head, still puzzled.

"Should we escort Mr. Grinnand downtown to look at any mugbooks? Or to enroll him in one?" Randolph said.

"I'll handle that later, after I've had a talk with him," Scott said coldly. "You've got your hands full tonight with a lot of paperwork and more; I'll take this from here." Randolph and Scott exchanged a glance over Paxton's head, and Randolph nodded. The two deputies excused themselves and walked rapidly down the hall. Scott pressed the heel of his hand against his forehead for a second, then turned to Bob.

"You." Scott said it like it was a four letter word. "If I weren't so involved with this case I'd string you up by the balls. Assaulting a police officer, carrying a concealed weapon, probably a few others I don't know about yet -- I could put you away for three years, easy. Probably more. The cell doors would be smacking you on the ass before you even figured out what was going on." He held up his thumb and forefinger an eighth of an inch apart. "I'm this close to putting you away," he warned him.

He glared at Bob. I'd seen Scott do that before. The dressing down was designed to instill the fear of God into youthful offenders, make them malleable putty in Scott's hands. I looked at Bob to see the effect Scott's words were having. None, as far as I could tell. Malleable putty. Yeah, right.

"Cut the horseshit," Bob told him. "I'm not a kid. We both know you're not going to press any charges. No prosecutor would take this to court and expect to win, which means they wouldn't take it to court. I was alarmed, and the dead guy had a gun, not to mention the fact that he was in the process of *raping* somebody when I beat him to death.

Women jurors? Fuck, they'd introduce me to their daughters. And I'm not about to plea bargain this out like an ignorant douchebag. Why don't you give us both a break and treat me like someone who knows the score. I do, you just don't know it yet." They looked at each other, neither one giving any ground.

Finally, without taking his eyes off Bob, Scott said, "How about trying to identify the body."

"Fine," I said. I watched, and Scott was the first one to break off his stare. "This way." He led Bob and I back downstairs toward the emergency waiting room. We strode through, ignoring the suffering people sitting and standing, waiting for their pain to be eased, through another set of double doors into a wide hallway. Scott led us into a room through a door marked Examination Room B.

Chapter Fifteen

POETIC JUSTICE

The room was about twenty feet square, painted and tiled in off-white and blue. There were three examining tables in the middle of the room, with a cluster of equipment around each one as well as wheeled screens. Against one wall there was a stretcher holding a body covered with a white sheet. We headed toward it.

"Hey, you're not supposed to be in here." A young resident in his mid-twenties was busy at a storage cabinet against one wall. He put down what looked like a bundle of gauze and strode toward us, the tails of his unbuttoned white lab coat fluttering behind him.

Scott flashed him his badge and pointed at the body. "That's ours," he said. The guy nodded vigorously and moved with us over to the stretcher.

"Going to have to move him soon," he said. "He can't stay in this room for long. We use it in the evenings when things start to get hairy in the ER." He came up alongside the stretcher and rolled the sheet down to the corpse's waist.

"I was there when the paramedics brought him in," the

resident said. "They got him beatin' and breathin' for a while, but it was a lost cause. His ribs were caved in, probably punctured a lung or two. Have to wait for the autopsy to find out for sure. Did somebody go after him with a baseball bat or what?"

I wasn't really paying attention to what the young doc was saying, I was more interested in the man on the table. His shirt had been cut away by the medics trying to revive him, and there were red dots between two of his ribs where he'd been injected, probably with adrenaline or epinephrine, in a fruitless attempt to restart his heart.

The man had light brown hair and at one time might've been considered handsome. Not any more. The features of his face were contorted and sunken, so much so that it would've been hard to identify him as my brother. Most of the blood had been wiped away, but that didn't help much. It just made the damage more obvious.

"Jesus Christ," I said. "What did you do to him?"

The eager resident took it upon himself to elaborate for me. "You can't tell about internal injuries," he said, "but on the outside he looks like road pizza. His nose is broken, probably his left cheekbone too. This here on the side of his neck is from some sort of blunt trauma. Also, the elbow of his right arm seems to have been broken with a large amount of force." He pointed out the details with a pen he'd drawn from a pocket, like he was pointing out highlights on a map. He moved from head to toe and missed nothing, acting like a professor teaching a lab class he truly enjoyed. Close Combat Injuries 101. I wondered if he wanted to be a pathologist when he grew up.

"Two, maybe three of his ribs are broken," he went on, "and I think his sternum is fractured, but that could have been from the CPR. See those red marks? Almost looks like knuckles. I suppose all this damage could have resulted from a single impact, the ribs are cracked all around the sternum, but that would have been one hell of a hit. That could be what ultimately killed him, if I had to guess. Massive shock to the heart muscle can stop it like a clock." He moved the pen and pulled the sheet down further, showing where the corpse's pantleg had been cut open by the paramedics. "His right knee seems to have been broken laterally. You can see the bone from the compound fracture sticking out of the epidermis here." Scott wasn't looking anymore, but I wasn't going to let it bother me. I reminded myself that this guy was interrupted in his efforts to remove my wife's pants while she was unconscious, and after the rape he was going to lie in wait to kill me in my own house. That made looking at his wreck of a body a lot easier. Bob, as I should've expected, was looking on impassively.

"That seems to be about it," the resident joked. "I've seen guys worked over before, but whoever did this was a lot better at it."

"Why didn't you just shoot him?" I said. "You had a gun."

"So did he," Bob said. "He came flying at me and popped me in the face before I even saw the punch." He paused. "He must not've ever fought someone who knew what they were doing. I moved into him, and I think that's the only thing that kept me from getting my throat crushed. He wasn't expecting that." He looked at his huge left forearm and from the red mark there I guessed he must have blocked a second punch. He shook his head again. "Talk about not expecting it, I slopped two wild Hollywood punches into him that shouldn't have come close and managed to break his nose. When he came back in I managed to get my shit together, stepped inside again, and joint-locked him. I wasn't even trying to break his elbow. I don't even think he felt it. He tried to thumb my eye and that's when I took his knee out, I kicked *that* as hard as I fucking could, then I hammered him in the chest. He went down flopping and never got back up. I didn't mean to kill him but he must've had weak bones or something, I couldn't have been hitting him that hard." I looked at his hugely muscled arms but stayed silent.

"How long were you two going at it?" Scott said, staring at the dead man and blinking erratically. His voice was strained.

"I don't know." Bob considered the question. "Eight seconds?" Scott stared at him in disbelief. Bob scowled. "It's a no-win situation, isn't it?" the young man said. "If I'd shot him you'd probably try to bone me for carrying a concealed weapon. Christ. What a fuckin' world." Shaking his head again, he pushed through the door. Scott motioned to the resident and he covered the body again. We went back out into the corridor. Bob was standing there, hands in his front pockets.

"Give him his gun back," I said. Scott snapped his head around and opened his mouth but I cut him off.

"Do it," I said sharply. We traded withering glances. "Do it," I said again. Scott stared at me, then looked at Bob. "This isn't just me anymore," I told him. "They brought my wife and him into this." I stuck a thumb at Bob. "He's bought his way into this party, his ticket's laying in there on the table. You don't want him here? So what. If it wasn't for him, Kelly and I would probably both be dead. That bastard in there was going to rape Kelly," I growled. "He was going to rape Kelly and then shoot her and then shoot me. You've known Kelly for as long as I have, goddammit! I don't care if you don't like it,

I don't care if *I* don't like it, he gets that fucking gun back."

"Fuck," Scott said, but handed over the Browning to Bob, who quickly concealed it at the small of his back. "This is getting out of hand. I don't think I can keep this under wraps. You know how many bodies have piled up in the last week? Stevie Wonder could see a pattern. Scarelli, RedMan, Polzewski, Wollsh, Secco, Gantz, Pellicek, and now that guy." He jerked his arm at the examination room's door. "And it's not going to stop here. As soon as I turn in Randolph's incident report, the shit is going to hit the fan, and I'll be in front of the Sheriff listening to a bunch of questions I can't answer without digging myself in deeper."

"I need some more time," I said. "Keep everybody off my back for as long as you can." I started walking down the hall.

"Shit, the only reason the dicks aren't here asking you a lot of difficult questions is that I was supposed to call them and haven't yet." He and Bob started down the hall after me. "I'm gonna have to call them, unless I want to get fired. What am I supposed to tell them, genius? And where the fuck are we going? You know," he went on, not waiting for me to answer, "this can't end well. I'm fucked. We're both fucked. Christ, do you know how many people are dead?" he repeated himself.

"I want to see Kelly again," I said. As we passed through the emergency room again, I turned to Scott. "You know exactly what to say. Nothing. Not a damn thing. You don't know anything that someone else doesn't know you know, and then make them drag it out of you. Now, see if you can find me the doctor that's taking care of her." Shutting off his brain and gutting it out on pure friendship, he nodded and veered off, leaving just Bob behind me. He missed me at the elevators but sped up and caught me a short distance before Kelly's room.

"I need to talk to you as soon as you're available," he said. "Privately." I nodded curtly and pushed into Kelly's room.

She was still in the same position, but as I entered she stirred and opened her eyes. I stopped in my tracks and smiled faintly.

"Hi, baby," I said gently.

"Hi," she replied in a soft voice. I almost asked her if she was all right before I realized what a stupid question it was. I compromised.

"How are you?" I said.

"That's a stupid question," she replied. "My head feels like an acupuncture experiment. How do you think I am? I'm scared and I'm angry. Why the hell didn't you tell me you were in trouble? I answer a knock on the door and the next thing I know I wake up in an ambulance with one of the guys that knocked on the door bleeding to death beside me. I had to find out from Scott what was going on, dammit!"

I moved my mouth and made a few garbled noises before I could speak. "It was a mistake," I said. "A stupid mistake. It never occurred to me that they would . . . . I -- I wasn't thinking, I guess." *Well, I guess that makes it all right then,* I swore at myself. What can a person do when he fucks up and there's no one there to whisper in his ear that it's all gonna be fine. Hell, it was only your wife's *life* you almost ended.

A harried looking grey-haired man pushed into the room, Scott in tow. He glanced at me briefly, then studied Kelly's chart.

"Well?" he said impatiently, looking from Scott to me. "What is it you want?" I resisted the urge to smack him.

"How long does she have to be here?" I said.

"Well," he said, crossing his hands in front of his paunch, "we could let her go now, but I wouldn't recommend it. She took a nasty bump on the head, and our usual procedure in a case like this is to keep the patient under observation for twenty-four hours in case of complications. Blows to the head sometimes do unpredictable things.

"If you'd like to go home early tomorrow, though," he said to Kelly, "and nothing untoward develops with your injury, I don't see any problem."

That was all I wanted to know so I thanked him and Scott ushered him out of the room.

I sat on the edge of the bed and took Kelly's hand in mine. "You know I'm not good at this," I said, meaning both explaining and apologizing. She nodded her head and smiled sort of sadly. My heart did a loop and I wondered how a putz like myself had ever managed to find and marry someone as wonderful as her. I bent down and kissed her lightly. Kelly's lips were warm and dry. Her eyes looked wet, but mine probably did too.

"How are you?" I said. "Are you still doped up?"

She shook her head. I took out my pistol and held it up in front of her.

"You know how to use this," I said. It wasn't a question. I'd made her practice with all of my firearms, just in case. It made good sense while I was in the DEA, because every once in a great while a drug dealer would forget he was in a business and take something personal, somehow get an agent's home address and go hunting. Someone had tried to follow me home from the office more than once. Miami, even long after the "coke rush" years, had still been a little like Dodge City. Kelly knew how to handle a gun, took the training seriously, and hoped to God she never had to use one for real. I laid the Smith & Wesson in her palm.

"If anybody comes through that door and tries to do you harm," I said, "kill them. Worry about it later. That goes for after you get out of here, too. Scott," I turned to look at him. He was shaking his head and frowning. "Scott is going to have a cop outside this door until you get out of here. Aren't you, Scott?" I turned back to look at her, not waiting for him to respond.

"I'm going to be busy trying to find these guys," I told her. "If when you get out of here this thing still isn't over, I'll send you to stay with your father or somebody." She nodded silently. The gun in her hand disappeared beneath the sheet.

"There are also going to be a lot of cops in here, county and otherwise, asking a lot of questions," I told her.

"Since that guy hit me on the head, I can't seem to remember a damn thing," my brilliant wife said. I smiled slightly, touched her cheek with the back of my hand, then stood up to go. The back of my hand tingled all the way to the door.

"When this is all over I am going to bitch at you like you wouldn't believe," Kelly called to me. Her eyes moved to my right. "It's nice seeing you again, Scott," she called softly from across the bed. Scott turned halfway back toward her, an uncertain look on his face. Looking at the floor in front of his feet he gave a halfhearted smile and then followed me out. He muttered "Shit," then something else I couldn't hear. Bob was leaning against the far wall of the corridor when we came out. He looked up when we appeared but didn't move.

"I want someone in front of her door tonight," I said to Scott. "I don't care if it's Paxton, just get somebody. It was

Mafia guys, one got away, she can identify him, that should be enough for your superiors to justify the manpower expenditure, even though they won't be able to find me to ask questions. I know I'm asking a lot, Scott, but if I live through this somehow I'll make it up to you. Maybe I'll take you out and get you laid. I could introduce you to my wife's sister, she just got divorced."

"I'll make a call," Scott said. "There'll be someone on her door." He was more subdued now. Maybe he finally realized just how deep in it we all were, riding the events of our lives out like a stalled plane, waiting for the crash, wondering who'd survive.

"I'll call you if I get any leads," I said which we both knew was a lie. If I got any leads I'd be too busy following them to call. And I knew if I fed him any more information he'd have to funnel it straight to his bosses. He nodded at me anyway. I left Scott in front of the door and walked over to Bob. "Well?" I said, a trifle impatiently. "What's the story?" He casually looked over my shoulder to where Scott had found a hospital phone.

"Not here," he said. "You'll make a scene." He led me unwillingly down the hall away from Scott until we found a men's bathroom. Inside, he leaned against a sink on one side of the small tiled washroom. I leaned against the opposite wall. "The guy I slammed into the wall of your house?" he said. "The one that got away? Well, he didn't."

"What?" I said. I took my weight off the wall and my hands out of my pockets.

"Ron has him. At his house, I would imagine," he said.

"What?" I said again. I couldn't seem to understand what I was hearing. "What the fuck are you talking about?"

"He was still there after I dropped the young guy. More or less out of it. I figured you'd might want to talk to him without the police or any lawyers around, so I had Ron take him. The guy kept going in and out of consciousness so he wasn't hard to manage."

"Ron?" I said stupidly.

"Yeah. I didn't take a cab to your house, Ron drove me straight from the airport. When he saw me go around the back of your house he was sitting in his car in the street and didn't know what the fuck was going on. He came up to your front door but by then the older guy was out cold and I was busy with the other guy. We loaded him into the trunk of Ron's car and he took off about two minutes before I called for an ambulance. I guess nobody looks out their windows anymore, me and Ron weren't exactly being subtle."

"Why didn't you tell me any of this before?" I demanded.

"We had company before," he replied. "Besides, the guy isn't going anywhere."

"'C'mon," I said, grabbing his arm and propelling him through the bathroom door. In two quick steps I'd passed him. "Ron's house?"

In a second he was beside me. "Yeah," was all he said.

Neither of us spoke as I led the way to my car and got in. On the way we passed Scott, who was still on the phone and would stay at Kelly's door until he could get another cop on the job. Bob slid in beside me and gave the car's interior a cursory glance. I didn't bother checking the car for bombs. There was too much foot traffic, cops included, going in and out of the emergency room doors for anyone to have wired my car unnoticed. Besides, Bufonte probably hadn't heard yet that the last guys he'd sent had failed. I ground the starter until it caught and pulled out of the lot as fast as my engine would allow. After I'd been driving for five minutes in silence I hit a red light, and I took a good long look at Bob. He noticed my stare and looked back.

"Thanks for what you did," I said. It wasn't easy to say it, not because I wasn't appreciative but because things weren't working out the way I'd planned. It happened that way a lot. You'd think I'd be used to it by now. Bob just shrugged, which for some reason really annoyed me. The light changed and I stepped on it.

"You're acting like this doesn't bother you," I said. "Which we both know is a crock of shit. Or do you beat people to death a lot?"

"No, I don't," he said. "This is the first person I've ever killed. Sure, it's affecting me. What would you like me to do, complain? Homey don't play that. Who would I go crying to, anyway? Mommy? She'd hold my hand and pat my shoulder and tell me to wake the fuck up, it's the real world out there. It's done, and nothing's going to change that." He paused, and looked down at the floor between his feet. "I'm in the 82nd Airborne right now, and in a few months I'll be heading to Ranger School, then the plan is Special Forces. I knew when I chose my path in life that this was likely, hell, probably, going to happen, so I made sure that I didn't let my emotions get in the way. It's what I've always wanted to do, and I will be *extremely* good at it."

"Killing," I said. He cocked his head and thought about saying something, but instead just nodded. I stared at him, shaking my head and trying to compare last weekend with this one. Not even close. "Don't get so choked up," I told him sourly.

"Listen," he said, trying to keep his voice even, "I don't talk about my feelings much, it's pointless. And acting like I'm horrified at what I did isn't a game I play. I'm actually pretty proud of what I did, that and the clean technique I used when I took that motherfucker apart. I was too busy to get scared when it was happening, but if it'll make you feel better I did get the shakes a little afterward. Your *wife* doesn't have any complaints, I'll bet." I shot him a sharp look but he wasn't even looking in my direction.

"Ron told me a little about you," he went on. "That you were in the DEA. Did you ever kill anybody?"

"Yes," I admitted.

"And did talking about it help you?" he said.

"Not me. It helped a couple of people I know," I replied.

"Well, I'm not one of those people," he said. "It would be stupid for me to pretend I'm anything else but what I am. Life's too short. I figured you could relate to what I'm saying, being in the DEA and all. I hear they're not prone to romanticizing." We sat in silence again. I was managing to hit most of the lights when they were green, for which I was grateful.

"There's an easier way to get to Ron's house," Bob said beside me.

"I'm stopping off at my house first," I said. He grunted in reply.

I wasn't thinking too far ahead, on purpose. Instead I concentrated on one thing at a time. Right now I was going to my house to rearm myself. After that I'd worry about what came next.

Chapter Sixteen

LOGISTICS

The party was over at my house. All that was left from the crowd was tire tracks all over the front lawn and candy wrappers in the driveway. The neighbors probably were in fits, trying to figure out what had happened. Surprisingly, whoever had left my house last had remembered to lock my front door. I unlocked it and went in with Bob in tow. The furniture in my living room was moved around, not much but just enough for me to notice. There were a couple of cigarette butts on the coffee table next to the couch. Bob hadn't said anything about either of the intruders smoking, and he didn't seem one to miss details, so I had to assume they were a present from the police.

The carpet in my living room had at one time been tan and needed a lot of vacuuming to keep the dirt out. It was past saving. The pile was dark with footprints from the front door clear across to the far wall, plus a few more butts that hadn't made it to the coffee table. There were several dark stains in the middle of the room that weren't from dirt. I also noticed a few dark speckles on the off-white wall opposite me. Bob hadn't been lying when he'd said he didn't like rapists. He'd hit the guy hard enough to splatter blood on my walls.

I went upstairs and into our bedroom. Memories of happier times flooded into my head, but I pushed them away and kept to the task at hand. Striding across the room I opened the door to the closet and pulled out a large, hard sided case and laid it on the bed. I spun the combination locks on either side of the handle and popped the latches. There were four pistols inside, and one blank space where my Sig fit. The Smith & Wesson Kelly now had usually stayed in the bedside table.

I wasn't much of a gun collector, but through the years I'd spent in the DEA I'd bought what I thought I needed. I picked out two pistols and laid them on the bed, closed the case and spun the locks, then replaced it in the closet. I went to my chest of drawers and pulled open the bottom drawer. Bob watched while I tossed a box of cartridges and two holsters onto the bed. There was a mirror on the wall above the chest of drawers, but I studiously avoided looking in it.

The big gun on the bed was a full-size Smith and Wesson .45 automatic, bought on a whim less than a year before. I'd already left the DEA when I bought it, but I'd put a lot of rounds through it since to keep my skills sharp. I shrugged on the shoulder holster for it. The holster held two extra magazines for the gun under one armpit, opposite of the pistol, and I popped the snaps and tossed the two mags on the bed along with the one I ejected from the pistol.

Bob watched me fill the three magazines with leftover DEA issue Federal Hydra-Shoks, put the two back under my arm, and slip the third one into the pistol. It looked like he wanted to say something, but didn't.

I chambered a round, ejected the magazine and topped

it off with another round, then slammed it back home in the gun. Once the gun was strapped into its holster, I started to shrug under its weight but caught myself. Bob stuck his hands in his pockets as I loaded the second gun, a Colt Lightweight Officer's Model, from the same box. I stuck it behind my right hip in the holster I'd dug out for it. Compared to the small Sig I was used to carrying it felt like I was armed for a foray into Iraq. It reminded me of the old days raiding crack houses. I grabbed a blue windbreaker from the back of the closet and shrugged it on.

"Okay," I said. "Let's go." I followed Bob down the stairs and out to the car, locking the house behind me. Although visions of vengeance were dancing in my head, I knew that the most intelligent thing I could do was try to get some answers from the guy Bob had grabbed.

I kept thinking Bufonte would try to get out of the situation, since it kept dragging him deeper and deeper, but who knew what he was thinking? How many men had he lost now, six? I couldn't let myself believe he'd give up yet. It would be too dangerous to my health. But now maybe I'd be able to get some solid answers.

I kept the image of Kelly in her hospital bed out of my mind. If I thought of her like that for too long, I would have brought along a baseball bat to help with the questioning, which wouldn't be the best avenue for success. As it was, I almost turned back four times to get that bat.

Chapter Seventeen

THE BARN

Steve's RX-7 was parked next to Ron's Dodge at the end of the driveway, near the barn. I pulled up beside their cars, shut off my engine and got out, hearing Bob slowly climb out of the car behind me. I noticed that my car wasn't visible from the road. All the better. I stared at the sun for a while as it headed toward the horizon. There were still several hours of daylight left, and the sun felt warm on my face and neck. I gazed westward for several minutes, until Steve and Ron emerged silently from the barn. I studied them for a moment, wondering what weird fate had brought us together. Would they have what it took; would *I* have what it took to get through this? Or would Kelly be a young widow?

I walked toward the wide, dark door of the barn. Steve and Ron turned and I followed them in. The first floor of the barn was half concrete. An old Jeep decayed in one corner, next to a cluttered workbench and a stained sink. The other half of the first floor was a foot lower and contained roped off stables. The stalls were empty, the horses out roaming the field where it was quiet.

Steve and Ron went up stairs that descended from the center of the ceiling. The stairs were made of unfinished pine and didn't have a handrail. I stared at them blankly, then went up. Bob brought up the rear, breathing softly.

The second floor was all bare walls and unfinished wood, with steel beams at regular intervals coming through the floor and supporting the ceiling about five feet above our heads. Naked bulbs hanging from bare wires provided harsh light. It was to one of the beams that he was tied.

He looked like the stereotypical Hollywood Mafia goon, and if the circumstances weren't so serious I might've laughed. Handsome, he was in his forties, with black wavy hair and a five o'clock shadow so dark it looked drawn on. His eyes glowered at me under thick eyebrows that merged above his nose. There was a small dark smear of dried blood near his left ear. I guess it helped, really. Most of the time the bad guys just looked like regular people.

The boys had him sitting on the floor, his back to one of the I-beams and his legs splayed out in front of him. I circled around behind him and saw that his hands were manacled with a pair of cheap handcuffs. The cuffs should hold him, but even if they didn't, there was no way he'd get out of the barn through all four of us. Alive, anyway.

I walked back around in front of him and squatted down near his face. He looked at me with a mixture of anger and uncertainty. There wasn't any fear, though. Not yet. All he'd seen so far had been a bunch of kids with guns and I'm sure he'd seen that before. His small paunch moved in and out as we stared at each other.

I didn't see any hint of recognition in his eyes, which

meant it had been a blind hit. They'd probably just been told to kill the first guy through the front door of my house fitting a general description. It was both good and bad news. Either the people out to get me were unorganized, and didn't have access to my picture, or they were being rushed and hadn't had time to get one to the triggermen. I was betting on the latter.

Bufonte was organized, but I might be putting enough pressure on him to make him hurry and make mistakes. If so, he must know something that I didn't, for as far as I could tell I wasn't any closer to finding Jerry Phillips than I had been the day I took the case. The only problem was that if it was a blind hit, the guy in front of me probably wouldn't know diddly. I'd find out soon enough.

He finally got tired of me staring and let anger get the better of him. "Okay, so who the fuck are you?" he said.

"You first," I replied. I heard movement behind me and a wallet landed on the floor next to my foot. I turned and looked at Steve and Ron, who were sitting on folding chairs against one wall with Bob.

"Jacket pocket," Ron said.

I picked up the wallet and opened it. Inside there was a driver's license made out to one Donald Valenti, plus several credit cards in the same name. There was a little cash and a little clutter, but nothing that gave me any more of an edge. I tossed the wallet back over my shoulder and heard someone catch it.

"Donny, Donny, Donny," I said, shaking my head. I snagged the last folding chair and sat on it backwards, resting my elbows on the back. "You're getting too old for this business. Didn't your mother ever tell you not to take your wallet with you on a hit? Not very smart." The chances of a low budget Mafia goon having a fake driver license with collateral pieces of ID in the same name so good it could fool me were exactly zero.

"Fuck you," he said quietly.

"But then," I continued, "at your age, if you're still doing grunt work instead of sitting behind an oak desk ordering other people around, it must mean that you're a regular fuck-up." Actually, the truth was older men made better hitters, being more proven, stable, and less prone to emotional outbursts, but my object was to piss him off, not impress him with my knowledge of human nature.

"And now you've really fucked up," I said. "Your partner's lying in the morgue looking like an extra from Dawn of the Dead and you get your clock cleaned by a kid. Now you're handcuffed to a barn in the middle of Yuppieville USA, talking to the guy you were supposed to off." He'd been looking away as I picked at him, until I let go who I was. Then his head whipped around and he looked at me with new interest.

"What's the mob coming to?" I went on, and shook my head theatrically. Then I perked up and smiled at him. "But you're lucky -- Congress just designated today 'Give a Dumb Dago a Break Day'. All you have to do is give me a little information, and you're outta here." I gave him my best buddy smile, but like I figured, he didn't go for the deal.

"Blow it out your ass," he said.

"Now, that's not very nice," I said, "or very smart, considering the alternative." I got in his face and said very slowly and calmly, "If you don't talk to me you're dead." I'd like to say I surprised myself when I said it, that I was flying by the seat of my pants and it just snuck out, but in all honesty I had a good idea where this all was going to end.

"If I do I'm dead anyway," he said. "Unless you're

dumber than you look, you know that too." He was right, of course, and we both knew it. If anybody in his organization found out that he'd talked, and they would, he'd be done away with rather messily. Nobody likes a squealer. But I was going to kill him whether he told me anything or not.

I don't know when I'd made that decision, but it didn't really surprise me to see it there in front of me. Maybe my mind had been made up to kill him for a while and I just hadn't been ready or willing to admit it to myself. I'd never planned to kill someone, or much less gone ahead with killing someone in cold blood, but I tried to tell myself that my options, as I saw them, were limited. Not only would Bufonte still want me dead, but if I let Valenti go it would only increase Bufonte's available manpower by one. One that knew exactly what I and all my young associates looked like.

I could consider all of my available information and best guesses and tell myself that I had a legitimate, logical reason for deciding to kill him, but deep inside I knew it was because he'd entered my home, without hesitation, with no other purpose than to kill me. I could not allow that to stand. A rash decision? Maybe. I was in a rash mood and wanted to stay that way. Rash felt safer than calm. Action safer than thinking.

I heard someone get up behind me, and turned around to see Ron going down the stairs. I looked at Steve and Bob questioningly. I didn't think that any of them would lose it, not so early, but then I didn't really know them. At all. I tried not to think about what would happen if they wanted to let Valenti live. I tried not to think about what the actions of the next few minutes would mean to the rest of my life. I shut out the fact that I was planning to commit murder in front of a bunch of strangers.

Steve was looking nervous as hell, and held up a finger at me, signaling me to give Ron a minute. I gave them a disgusted look but wiped it off my face before I turned back to Valenti. He was looking at us, wondering what was going on. I was wondering too.

"Well, that's our problem then," I said. I stood up, turned the chair around, and sat in it normally. I leaned back and crossed my legs and looked at him. He was beginning to sweat, and not just because it was warm in the room. I'd made sure I was close to him, my knees a foot to one side of his head, to make him more uncomfortable and invade his space. It was working, but he wasn't the only one sweating, and the room was getting a little rank.

"My problem," I said, "is to convince you that it will be in your best interest to tell us what you know. My questions are simple, really. Let's start with an easy one. Let's try . . . who hired you to kill me?"

"Fuck off," he said. He looked back and forth between me and the boys, uncertain what was coming next. He wasn't the only one.

I wasn't sure what my next approach would be. The most obvious would be to physically beat him, a time honored method of obtaining information. A seasoned inquisitor could produce unbearable pain through beatings without killing the victim. The only trouble with that was that I'd never done anything like it before, and I was afraid that once I got started hitting him I'd get carried away and kill him before he got around to answering my questions. Maybe before I got around to asking any.

I had to hand it to Valenti, though. He was showing some nerve. He hadn't even asked where the college kids fit in. Then again, in the predicament he was in, did it matter who they were?

I heard a noise and saw Ron come up the stairs with an olive drab ammo can in his hands. I got up and went over to Steve and Bob, who'd stood up. Bob took the can from Ron and cracked the seal on it. Inside was an old Ruger *.22* pistol and a box of ammo. I looked at Bob with a suspicion of what he intended. He looked back at me, face blank, and I sensed that he was waiting for approval, or at least permission. I didn't think I would like whatever happened next, but I wasn't there to do things I liked.

"Don't kill him," I murmured. He nodded, then took the gun and box of shells out of the can and set it down. He checked the magazine of the automatic, saw it was already loaded, then slapped it back into place and chambered a round. He held the automatic low against his leg in his right hand, the brick of .22's in his left.

Bob walked over to Valenti, who looked at his expressionless face and immediately started to sweat faster. Heart racing, I sat down in Bob's chair and leaned forward, my hands clasped and my elbows on my knees. My palms were slick with sweat.

Quickly, so that Valenti didn't have time to react, Bob straddled his legs and sat on them. Valenti tried to squirm out from under him but he couldn't move. Bob's butt was resting just forward of Valenti's ankles, and he used his knees and feet to lock Valenti's legs together.

"What the fuck is this?" Valenti shouted, trying to wiggle his legs. They may as well have been set in concrete. He took one look at Bob's face and stopped squirming.

Bob set the box of .22's down by his knee. While Valenti was watching him do that, he placed the muzzle of the Ruger against Valenti's right thigh, just above the knee, and pulled the trigger. The pistol's report was drowned out by Valenti's bloodcurdling yell. He couldn't move his legs, try as he might, but he strained against the beam with all his strength. I jumped a little at the yell, not expecting it, but then I hadn't been expecting the gun to go off. At least not yet. Ron jumped a little at the scream, and his face paled, but he recovered his composure quickly and made his face hard. Steve, on the other hand, shot to his feet, a shocked look on his face. I don't know, maybe he had thought the gun was only for show.

"That's to show you I mean business," Bob said as the blood pumped slowly out of Valenti's thigh. Valenti choked back a sob and grimaced in pain, tears rolling down his cheeks.

"You noticed I avoided the kneecap," Bob was saying. "And any major arteries. I also tried to avoid the bone. It'll heal faster that way, and there's a good chance you'll be able to walk normally some day." I got up and stood behind Bob on shaky knees. He didn't seem to mind the blood that was staining his jeans, but I couldn't be so single minded and had to keep checking my shoes to make sure I didn't step in it.

I glanced at Steve, whose mouth was working like he wanted to say something. Pale, he looked from Bob to me and back to Bob. All of the emotions wracking his mind and body were tearing through mine as well, and probably Ron's, but Steve couldn't hide it. Maybe he hadn't thought the whole thing through to its logical conclusion. As for what was going through Bob's head, I didn't have a clue.

"You see," Bob went on, "I was planning on having John here ask you some questions. For every wrong answer, I put another hole in your leg. Right through the meat. If I have to, I'll work my way up one leg and down the other. And luckily," he held up the box of ammo with an ugly smile,

"I've got these, so I can reload if I have to. Hopefully that won't be necessary. It's up to you, though."

Steve licked his lips, looking queasy, and sat back down.

"You fuckin' bastard," Valenti spit out. He sucked in a runner trailing from his lip and spat a wad onto Bob's shirt. Bob looked up at me, his face expressionless.

"Who do you work for, Donny?" I said, looking at his sweaty face. He looked up at me, then back at Bob.

"Fuck you both," he said, leaning into Bob's face. Bob shot him again a little higher up on his thigh without even a blink. Valenti's yell turned into a moan that made me clench my teeth. His head bent down and saliva strings trailed from his lips onto his shirt.

"Fuckin' bastards," he panted. He repeated it over and over to himself. The blood was spreading on the floor beneath his thigh, a lot of blood. The .22's were probably going all the way through his leg into the floor.

"I don't want him bleeding to death," I told Bob. I felt disconnected, somehow, with what was going on in front of me, like I was being operated by remote control.

"If he loses too much blood I'll put pressure on his femoral artery, and if that's not enough I'll use a tourniquet," Bob said to me flatly, like he was giving me the recipe for turkey pot pie.

Steve stood back up, and jerked his head at me. He and I had a whispered conference with Ron at the bottom of the stairs.

"What the fuck are we doing here?" Steve asked through clenched teeth, the corners of his mouth white. He looked back and forth between Ron and I.

"We're trying to find out what the fuck is going on," Ron growled at him. The three of us glared at each other, emotions high.

"Like this?" Steve said, incredulous.

"You got a better idea?" Ron replied. "You think any of us want to be here? It's a fucking nightmare." He looked at me. "Cops ever find a car belonging to him near your house?" He jerked his head toward Valenti.

The question surprised me. "No. Nobody's said anything."

"Because we didn't move it. Or see it. Which means there was probably another guy, a wheel man. I thought someone tried to follow us out of there, but I lost him so quick I can't be sure."

"You sure you lost him?"

"You forget what I drive?" Ron said. Losing somebody didn't have a lot to do with horsepower, but he did have a point.

"He see your plate?"

Ron shook his head. "I don't know. I don't think so, but…." He looked at Steve. "We have to assume he did. Which means we're in this up to our eyeballs." He paused, glancing over at Valenti before speaking again.

"This guy may know where Jerry is, or why he's missing," Ron went on. "We don't even know if Jerry is still alive, *he* might be getting tortured somewhere. Even if he doesn't know that, this guy knows *something*, and it's not like he's an innocent bystander. This guy'd kill all of us in a fucking heartbeat if he could, and you know it."

Steve's mouth grew pinched, and his nostrils flared. "I know," he spat. "But . . . . this isn't the way," he said finally.

"It shouldn't be," I said. "But it's what we've got. Right now it's *all* we've got."

I could hear the air moving in and out of Steve's nose as he glared at me, Ron, the floor, and Valenti, still slumped over and in a daze. Finally, he nodded, and we headed back up. Bob was staring furiously in our direction, wondering just what the hell was going on. I flicked my hand at him to continue, and Bob turned to Valenti, who might not have even noticed our minute meeting. He was having trouble seeing past the pain.

"You'll notice I missed your femur again," Bob said. "I'm really being very considerate. I think that the least you could do is answer this man's questions. They're not that hard." Valenti raised his head, his lips pulled back in an ugly rictus.

"Go to hell," he hissed. "Go to fucking hell!"

Bob stared at him silently for a second. "There's always that possibility," he said, and shot him again. The bullet punctured his thigh halfway between knee and groin. Valenti let out a long wail that was hideous to hear. I was getting sick watching him, and I looked at Steve and Ron to see what they were doing, or maybe just so that I didn't have to look at Valenti any more. They were both pale and sweating and sitting uncomfortably in their chairs.

The muscles in Bob's jaw clenched and he glanced at me. He wasn't enjoying it any more than the rest of us, or at least I wanted to think so, but he wasn't willing to give up just yet. He swallowed once and got back to business.

"That's good," he said to Valenti. "Make some noise, it'll make you feel better. Don't worry about disturbing the neighbors, they can't hear you. And when you're done, you can get back to answering some of our--"

"What the fuck is this!" we all heard. I spun around, hand on my gun butt, and saw Ron's father on the stairs, a small automatic in his hand. Another glance and I saw that it wasn't a small automatic, it just looked small in his meaty paw of a hand.

"Dad!" Ron bounced out of his chair and rushed over to his father, who was staring at the spectacle before him, the gun in his hand forgotten. The two of them held a hurried, whispered conference, with Ron doing most of the talking. I watched the sequence of expressions on his father's face changing from shock to amazement to anger and then I saw his face go hard, a familiar sight in the company I'd been keeping lately.

His father looked from me to Bob to Valenti, his expression now unreadable. He looked back at me and I met his stare. We stood there and looked at each other, two men thrust into circumstances they didn't want to be in. If he wanted to stop us I didn't think I'd be able to dissuade him through argument. My bet was that Ron's blockheadedness was inherited. And getting physical with him was *not* an option. Hell, the only way I'd be able to physically stop him would be to shoot him in the head repeatedly with a large caliber weapon. Or hit him with a car. As I considered my predicament I drifted back into focus in time to see him nod his head at me, so slightly I almost missed it, tuck the pistol into his pants, and head back down the stairs. As I let out my breath, a small part of me briefly wished he'd stopped us, but that was the part of me that hadn't seen Kelly lying on a hospital bed with a bandage on her temple.

The sweet copper smell of blood filled the room, along with the rank smell of nervous bodies. Valenti's upper body had fallen forward, his arms taut as he pulled against the handcuffs, his chest heaving. He was close to passing out, and for a second I thought he had, but then I heard his quiet sobbing.

Bob turned back to Valenti as Ron's father left. He looked down at the .22 in his hand as if he'd forgotten it was there. He squeezed the grip in renewed determination and pressed the muzzle against Valenti's thigh again, a few inches higher up than before. At the touch Valenti's head jerked up.

"Donald," Bob said quietly. His voice had an edge of exhaustion to it. I probably would've sounded the same if I'd tried to speak.

"Donald," Bob said again. He pushed on the gun. Valenti's eyes, vague from the pain, focused with some effort on Bob's face. "I'm going to keep shooting you until you tell us what we want to know or until you die. There are no other options. No one knows you're here. No one is going to save you. The cavalry is not going to come. The cavalry only saves the good guys, anyway. I was the cavalry, and now you're here. I'm going to keep shooting you and you're going to keep bleeding on me until the situation changes. The process will continue until you talk or until you die." Bob sighed and pressed the gun harder into his leg.

"Make my job easier," Bob spoke. If I hadn't known better, I would've thought he was pleading with Valenti. I guess, in a way, he was.

"Fuck you," Valenti spat. His eyes blazed briefly with hate then faded back into his vague, pained expression. The muscles stood out like golfballs on the sides of Bob's jaw once more and his finger tightened on the trigger. The crack made us all jump. Valenti let out a strangled cry. More blood streamed out of his leg, joining the pool on the floor.

"Shit," Valenti hissed, then passed out, his head slumped and his chin resting on his chest. I smelled something acrid and looked down to see a dark stain spreading across Valenti's crotch. It was suddenly very close inside the room. Too close.

"Jesus," I heard Ron say, his voice gluey.

"Wrap something around his leg and don't let any of that piss get in his wounds," I said, trying to make some order out of the whole mess. Bob had straightened up and was standing over Valenti, the pistol dangling loose in his hand. Steve and Ron were still sitting in their chairs, white faced and stiff-backed. "Move!" I half shouted when they didn't respond. Steve and Ron stood up quickly and scrambled down the stairs after the supplies we needed. Bob walked slowly over to the now vacant chairs and sat down. He set the pistol down on the chair beside him and ran shaking hands through his short hair.

"Are you gonna make it?" I said a little roughly, projecting my own doubts onto him.

He turned his head quickly and glared at me, the muscles in his jaw clenched, then his gaze softened and he glanced down at his hands. "That which does not kill us makes us stronger," he quoted, staring at his hands. "Some shit, huh?" He took a deep breath and sat upright. His eyes moved from Valenti back to me. "I'll make it."

"Good," I said. I turned and went down the stairs as fast as I could without tripping.

Ron's father was standing in the doorway of the barn, looking out over the field, his arms crossed over his barrel chest. The pistol he'd brought upstairs, a Beretta, was still stuck in his waistband. I stood beside him, concentrating on breathing normally. I sucked in the evening air through my nostrils, trying without much luck to get rid of the smell of blood.

The shadows were getting long as the sun went down. The sun's rays turned the prairie grass crimson behind the barn, making the whole scene look ridiculously like a landscape painting, the cheap kind found in cut-rate hotel rooms. I stood inside the barn's shadow and watched two sparrows chase each other across the field. They veered up at the far end to avoid a grazing horse, did a loop, and the chaser became the chased.

"I went through something like this when I was in 'Nam," I heard from beside me. I looked at him and saw he was also staring out at the field.

"But that was in wartime," he continued, "and it wasn't my wife. Or my son," he added after a pause. He turned to me and looked me over for a second, then stuck out a hand. "George," he said.

"John," I said, and shook his hand. We watched as Steve and Ron came out of the house carrying a leather belt and some towels. They passed us without saying a word and went into the barn.

"Those are the good towels," George said. "His mother is going to kill him." He looked at me, the incongruity of his statement hitting both of us. I might have laughed, but I was in no mood for laughter, so I shook my head.

"They're so young," I said.

"Age is relative," he said. "It's relative to your experience. The more you get, the older you are, no matter what date is on your driver license. Hell, I was younger than them when I went to Vietnam."

"That's a great theory," I responded, "but your son's in there helping to torture someone."

"Someone who not five hours ago was ready to off you and your wife," he said. "Who, I'm told, is in the hospital right now."

I watched the sparrows loop and twirl above the field. The horse stopped its single-minded pursuit of food for a second and watched them, then gave a snort and went back to grazing.

"I know what I have to do," I said, "and I'll do it. But it sure as hell ain't easy."

"Son," he said, "you are one dumb sonovabitch if you thought life was easy. You're young, but you ain't that young. Stop feeling sorry for yourself, go back up there, find out or don't find out what you need to know, then kill the bastard and get him off my property." George turned his back on me and started up the driveway. There wasn't any reason for me to stand there any longer, so I went back upstairs.

Chapter Eighteen

.22 QUESTIONS

Most of the blood around Valenti's legs had been cleaned up, and the towels tossed into a corner. The dark stains on them blended with the shadows. The belt had been cinched tight around Valenti's thigh and had stopped the bleeding as far as I could tell. Valenti was conscious once again, leaning back against the post and staring at the ceiling with glazed eyes.

The three of them were standing by their chairs and talking quietly. They looked like I felt. As I came up they made room for me.

"This isn't going to happen," Ron was saying. "He's made his choices and he's not going to talk, not this way."

"He'll die from blood loss before he talks," Bob said softly. Steve nodded and looked at me. The others did too.

"I agree," I murmured. "Well, I'm open to suggestions. Anybody got any ideas?"

"Yeah," Ron said. "I think I do. It might work, then again it might not, but we won't know until I try and we're not going to get anything this way."

"What?" I said.

"Just play along," he said, sucking in a breath and squaring his shoulders, trying to brace himself for what was coming.

I almost stopped him, not wanting any more surprises, but I was running out of options and steam. *Hell*, I realized suddenly in a crystal clear moment of comprehension, *I'm not even the captain of this ship anymore, I'm just the navigator.* When the hell did that happen?

Ron held out his hand and Bob set the pistol in it. Ron walked over and knelt on top of Valenti's legs like Bob had done. I stood beside him, wondering what game we were playing now.

"Donny," Ron said. "Donny!" He snapped his fingers in front of Valenti's nose a few times, then tapped him on the cheek. Slowly Valenti's eyes focused and he looked at Ron.

"Howya doin', Donny?" Ron said.

"Fuck you." It was barely audible.

"That's good, keep that spirit up! You don't have any worries, you know that pretty soon you'll be dead from the blood loss. One, two more shots, and we'll all fade to black before your very eyes. Bufonte will throw you a big funeral, everybody will be there, crying and drinking Dago red. They'll all be saying what a loyal guy you were." Ron shook his head in mock admiration.

"I know how it is, Donny, I'm Italian myself. Don't look it, do I? Blond hair and all, that is." He ran his fingers through his hair. "Actually, I'm half Italian on my father's side, but that's enough. He taught me the way things are, just like the way your dad taught you, I'm sure. So, we both know how things are going to end up here, right? Right?" He leaned forward to stare at Valenti.

"Right," Valenti croaked.

"Right," Ron said. "The only problem is, we're not going to kill you. Even if you don't talk. Isn't that nice of us? C'mon, don't you think it's nice of us?" He wasn't able to provoke a response from Valenti, probably because he didn't believe a word Ron was saying. I wondered what Ron was up to.

"We've decided that if you really don't want to tell us anything, we're not going to kill you," Ron continued. He was watching Valenti closely.

"Oh, I know what you're thinking," Ron said. "You're thinking, 'They want to make it look like they tortured me until I talked, then let me go.' The only problem with that is that Bufonte will kill you anyway. Seeing as how you took a lot of pain and lasted a while before talking, he'll probably be nice and kill you quick, too. The problem is, we won't be any farther ahead." Valenti was too far gone to be getting all of the details, but he got the main points. He was paying more attention now, trying to see what Ron was leading up to.

"So your question is," Ron said, "is 'What's the catch?' The catch is this. You tell us what we want to know and we let you go without inflicting any more damage. Maybe you can run far enough to be safe. Maybe not. But you'll live to fight another day. You don't tell us what we want to know and I blow your dick off. With a little luck and some compresses, you shouldn't lose much more blood. I know some first aid. We take you, dump you on Bufonte's doorstep, and see what happens. You know what's gonna happen, don't you? One look and Bufonte will know you've talked. Hell, point a gun at his dick and I guarantee you he'd be singing six verses of Gospel to anyone who'd listen.

"Normally, he'd straight out kill you for squealing, as an example and for the principle of it, but that wouldn't be much of a surprise for anybody. This time, though, he's got a chance to make a bigger impression. Why kill you, when you'd just be a greasy-haired, one-legged guinea who has to piss sitting down? Hell, he'll let you live just to serve as an example to all his other potential squealers. Who loves their dicks more than the Italians? You'd be an example of living hell for them. Maybe he'll make it the new punishment for squealers.

"'Look at this guy,' Bufonte'd say. 'This is what happens when you rat. You end up having to piss like a woman and hobble around in a walker.' Hell, you're the perfect incentive to keep someone from squealing. 'Don't forget Donny' they'd say. 'You squeal and you'll end up just like him, havin' to squat to pee'." He grabbed Valenti's chin in his free hand and leaned close.

"Your family will love it," Ron said. "Especially your wife." Valenti's eyes blazed and he tore his chin out of Ron's grasp. In doing so, he moved his leg a little, bringing a short gasp from him as well as a little blood from his thigh. Ron placed the muzzle of the gun firmly against the crotch of Valenti's pants.

"You ever play Good Cop, Bad Cop?" Ron said. He jerked his head at Bob, who was standing with me and Steve. "He's the good cop," Ron said. He waited for the message to sink in, watching Valenti's eyes move to Bob and then back. Ron leaned in closer. "What's it going to be, *paisan?*" he whispered.

Ron's was a weak argument, we all knew it. If Valenti had been in a normal state of mind he wouldn't have even listened to what Ron was saying. He would know that we were going to kill him no matter how loud he sang. Now, however, it was a different story. Ron had him worried about having to live without his equipment for the rest of his life, a frightening thought for any man, and Valenti had lost sight of the overall picture. Plus, he was about three quarts low, not the best situation to be in when clear thinking is a must.

As the four of us stared at Valenti expectantly, he raised his haggard face to stare at me.

"What do you want to know?" Valenti's voice was choked with phlegm. Ron looked up at me. I throttled back my excitement and said slowly, "Who do you work for?" It sounded like an obvious question to both me and the boys, but I'd learned through the years that even the simplest questions can get unanticipated answers.

"Don't tell me you don't know," Valenti said in a tired voice, resting the back of his head against the beam, his eyes closed. I could see the pulse beating weakly in his neck.

"Answer it," I snapped.

"Bufonte," he said. "Pietro Bufonte."

"And he ordered you and your dead friend to come to my house, rape my wife, and kill us both?" He shook his head and coughed, the jolt to his leg making him wince.

"No," he said. "We were supposed to go to your house and do you and anybody else there, just for good measure. We got a description of you. It was a rush job, otherwise we would've had more information, maybe a picture. If you weren't there we were supposed to play it by ear. You weren't, and I was for leaving and coming back later—pose as cops, ask to come in, you know the routine—but Bobby pushed his way in."

"Bobby's the dead kid?" I said.

"Yeah. Young and full of himself. He goes in and decides he might as well have his way with your wife before you came home. It wasn't my idea, it just—"

"Save it, you're breaking my heart. Bobby's renting

space on a slab right now and looks like drunk pre-med students have been experimenting on him." I changed the topic, more for my sake than anything. If I thought about Bobby and my wife I might lose it. "So, Bufonte talked to you and told you to do the hit?" I probed.

"No," Valenti said. "He doesn't get involved with the dirty stuff anymore. He always sends out his orders through Kellogg. Less chance of getting nailed by the feds that way."

"Who's Kellogg?" I said.

"He's his guy, his right hand man." Valenti wanted to go to sleep, or more likely pass out, but I wouldn't let him.

"And he's the one that told you to kill me?" I pushed.

"Yeah." He paused and thought about what I was asking. "I know what you're thinking," he said, "but that ain't it. Kellogg only tells people to do what Mr. Bufonte tells him to tell them. He's real loyal."

"You don't know what I'm thinking," I said.

"Kellogg isn't a very Italian name," I heard Steve say from behind me.

"Haven't you heard?" I said without turning around. "The mob's an equal opportunity employer now. Isn't that right, Donny?" I smiled at him. "That is," I continued, "as long as you're white and stupid. Let's try another one." I searched my memory. "Do you know," I reached for the names, "a Johnny Secco and Robert Gantz?"

"Yeah, yeah, I know 'em," he said. "What does that have to do with this?"

"Who are they?" I said, ignoring his question.

"They work for Bufonte," he said. "They're errand boys and muscle, working their way up."

"When was the last time you saw them?"

"Geez, I don't know," he whined. Ron shifted his weight on top of Valenti's legs and he grimaced in pain. "Uh-they-uh-dammit, I don't know," he said. "Sometime last week, I guess. I don't know."

"What were they doing the last time you saw them?" I said. "Think. It doesn't really matter when it was." He closed his eyes and concentrated.

"They were—they were—okay, yeah, the last time I saw them was Wednesday morning. I remember 'cause I had waffles for breakfast just before and I only have waffles on Wednesdays."

"Save me your daily meal plan," I said. "What were they doing?"

"Kellogg dragged them off into a corner and talked to them for a while, then they split. I don't know where they went. That's all I know, I swear."

"Do you know Frederick Pellicek—Freddie the Knife?" I felt ridiculous just saying it.

"Never heard of him. Wait—yeah, he does work for Mr. Bufonte once in a great while. Basic grunt work. Real moron."

"Uh huh," I said. "Now, what's Bobby's last name?"

"Fuck you," he said. "You're so smart, figure it out for yourself."

I repeated my request. "What's Bobby's last name?"

"How the fuck does that make any difference?" he said, then groaned as Ron squeezed his bullet riddled leg.

"It doesn't matter why it makes any difference," I said. "You're not here to ask questions. You gave up that right when you fucked up your hit, you sloppy motherfucker. That's twice you guys have tried and missed. Christ, even the Mafia can't find decent help these days. Now," I said, trying to get myself under control, "what's Bobby's last name?"

"Fuck you," he said. He was tired of playing games.

"Fine, I got what I needed anyway." I motioned to Ron. "Blow his dick off," I said. "He broke the deal." I turned to go.

"Waitaminit!" Valenti screamed. Apparently he wasn't ready to give up the ghost—or anything else—quite yet. I turned back and squatted in front of him.

"It's Cross," he said frantically. "Bobby Cross. Robert."

"Good boy," I said. He looked relieved. "I suppose it would be too much to ask for you to know why you were supposed to kill me?"

"No, no, I don't know. I don't even know who you are, what you do. Kellogg just told us to ice you, he didn't care how, just get it done, quick."

"I believe you, Donny," I said. "I don't know why, maybe it's 'cause you seem so sincere."

"Fuck you," he said tiredly.

I was weary of the game, more tired than I could ever remember being, and yet I was full of rage, too, thinking of my wife. I moved my face closer to his. "How does it feel to pull the trigger on someone, Donny?" I said. "Someone whose only crime was knowing too much, or because he wouldn't take any of your boss' shit? You kill a lot of people? You must have, if you're still around at your age. Have you ever pulled the trigger on a woman, Donny? Huh? How do you do it, give her a quick feel and a kiss, put the gun to her head and say sorry, that's the biz sweetheart as you blow her brains out?" Valenti wasn't looking at me, he was staring into space, trying to ignore me.

"Are you married, Donald?" I said innocently. "I'm sure you are." He jerked his eyes away from my gaze and didn't say anything, but I knew. "That's great, Don," I said. "Do you love your wife? Do you come home after a hard day's work, she fixes you dinner and asks how was work, and you say fine, today I had to blow some hooker's brains out 'cause she was going to turn snitch, but it's okay, I didn't get any on my shoes. Pass the butter, honey." I was throwing my anger at him, blowing off the frustration at the first target I had that wasn't dead. Valenti surged at me, straining against the cuffs.

"Fuck you, you motherfucker! Fuck you! You keep my wife outta this, you goddamn prick! Who the fuck are you, anyway? You think you know me? You think you know anything? Fuck you!" He sank back against the beam, sobbing.

"Uh huh," I said. I looked at Ron. "Kill him and dump the body," I said and stood up. Valenti snapped his head around.

"Wait--!" he began, then the .22 bullet went through his left eye socket and into his brain. His body slowly slumped sideways toward the floor until his arms, still locked around the beam, stopped the movement, his head inches from the floor. More blood came out of his body.

Ron stood up, looking with disgust at what we were left with. He shook his head, then turned away and came over to where I was standing with Steve and Bob. The tension in the room was palpable, but if they'd made it that far they would go the distance, whatever it would be. They looked at the body for a while silently, then turned their eyes to me.

"Take his body somewhere and dump it," I said. "Somewhere it'll be found quickly."

"Why do you want it found at all?" Ron said.

"I want to send a message," I said. They knew exactly what I meant. "You better make that pistol disappear, too. Permanently." Ron looked down at the gun still in his hand. He nodded.

"Did we have to kill him?" Steve asked quietly.

"Steve," I said as gently as I could, "if he and his partner didn't manage to kill me neither one of them would have left my house alive. Far as I'm concerned they both committed suicide, he just took longer to die."

"Why do you care about Johnny Secco and Robert Gantz?" Bob said. "Wait, before that, who are they? And who the hell is Freddie the Knife?"

I'd expected the questions, or similar ones, for some time now. After what all of us had been through together, I figured I could, should, tell them the truth. All of it. I owed them that much.

Chapter Nineteen

WAR FOOTING

"The U.S. Justice Department, " I said, after explaining to them just who Pietro Bufonte was, "was ready to pop the cork on Bufonte's organization a couple weeks ago. Everything was all set to go. Then, the three star witnesses, under care of the Witness Protection Program, up and disappear. No one knows why, for sure, even now. They just rabbitted."

"I thought those Witness guys were the best in the protection business," Steve said. "Why'd the three guys split? Their disappearing doesn't make any sense, " he reasoned, "unless they thought they were in danger."

"We'll find out sooner or later," I said. "Maybe one of their guards was on the take and they found out in time." I shrugged. "Anyway, one day last week, one of the three vanished witnesses gets a little hungry and goes out for a quick bite to eat at lunchtime. This was last Wednesday. He went to a Burger King over here on Rochester Road." The three of them exchanged looks.

"Somehow, Bufonte located him. Whether he was spotted by chance, or Bufonte's men knew where he was hiding out and were waiting for the chance to do him, it doesn't matter. His guys, Secco and Gantz, took care of the problem. My guess is that they were following Polzewski—that's the dead guy—and thought BK would be the best place to make the hit. Crowded, lot of people going in and out, no one knows or sees anything. Well, it just so happens that Jerry decided to go out to lunch on Wednesday. Out to Burger King. That Burger King. I'm just guessing, but I'd bet he either saw the hit itself or saw enough to figure out what happened. The only trouble is that Secco and Gantz saw that he saw." Jerry and I could have a long talk about our luck. If we ever met.

"Oopsie." It came from Bob.

"Oopsie is right. I'm still guessing but from the bits and pieces I've gathered it appears that Jerry drove to Oakridge Elementary School in Royal Oak, God knows why. I'd bet that he went to the school because he saw he was being followed and didn't want to go home If he was smart he'd have figured that if he drove to a police station, the guys following him would just disappear. That is, until they showed up at his house one night, seeing as they had his license number. The school must've been the first thing that popped into his head, and since he'd gone there he knew the layout."

"It's the middle of the summer," Steve observed. "School's out." He thought about it for a few seconds, then smiled and looked at me.

"Apparently Jerry was thinking the same thing," I said. "My bet is he walked out onto that playground and Secco and Gantz followed him, thinking he was just some dumb, scared kid. Up until today that's what I would've thought too."

"And now?" Bob said.

"Now I know different," I said. "If Jerry is anything like the three of you, chances are that he wasn't the dumb, scared kid Secco and Gantz thought he was. He has some balls doing what he did, I'll tell you. Either way, Secco and Gantz are now dead, from wounds inflicted by a serrated knife."

"It's no luck he had that on him," Steve said. "We can't get CCW's until we turn twenty-one, but sometimes a knife works just as well."

"Well, he's very fucking lucky it wasn't used on him," I said. "His skill with a knife wasn't what killed Secco and Gantz, it was their overconfidence. But it doesn't matter anymore, he's in it for good, now. From the school he went home, grabbed his forty-five and some food, probably some clothes too if he was thinking, and is now the Invisible Man. One of the two guys he killed had an empty holster, and when Jerry went to the range in Royal Oak he got some thirty-eight ammo, so the bet is that now he has two pistols. You all know about our trip to the range, don't you?" They nodded their heads.

"Who's Freddie the Knife?" Ron asked.

"He's a new friend I met on an elevator Saturday," I said. "In my office building. He was looking for on-the-spot organ donations, step right up, no waiting."

"Is that how you got the bruise?" Ron asked.

I nodded. "I got lucky," I said. "He wasn't that good at his job, but then I'm not used to people trying to kill me, either. There must be a shortage of professionals in this town, or they were in a rush, because there's no way I should still be breathing. I'd hate to think they were only sending second stringers after me 'cause that's all they thought they needed."

"Are we going to talk to him, too?" Steve asked, his

voice a mix of emotions. Everyone eyed me covertly, as much to see how I'd react to the question as to hear my response. With a hell of a lot of effort, I kept any trace of emotion off my face. Up to now we'd all been avoiding looking at Valenti, but now each of us snuck a glance at him. His condition hadn't changed.

"No," I said coldly. "I caved his head in." The three of them nodded to themselves.

"So that's twice they've tried to kill you?" Steve said. "Jesus. They must want you pretty badly."

"It's not me they want," I said, "it's Jerry. He can ID Bufonte's men as the ones that took out Polzewski, and if the feds get hold of them they'll interrogate them until they roll over on Bufonte or their brains turn to mush, whichever comes first. They *will* extract a penalty for their three witnesses. Bufonte doesn't want me, a wild card, in there fucking things up and finding the kid first, although with the luck I've been having I'll never find Jerry." *Alive, that is.*

"Well it's about time we heard the whole story," Ron said. "Why didn't you tell us all this before?"

"Look at it from my point of view," I said. "I'm looking for a kid, a simple missing person's case, and then suddenly I've got Freddie the Fucking Knife trying to carve me up in an elevator. I find out the mob's trying to kill me and/or the kid I'm looking for, and then you guys come along, a bunch of college kids for Christ's sake, packing heat, and expect me to take you seriously and let you into my confidence, treat you like you know your asses from a hole in the ground. Yeah, right.

"Things have changed now, and I don't like it, I don't think you guys should be involved, but I owe Bob, and the rest of you too, now. We're *all* in it. Deep. And I'm coming to realize that your age doesn't have a hell of a lot to do with this. Or anything."

"It never did," Bob said.

"Well, Jerry really stepped in it," Ron said. "But I'm still pissed he hasn't called us yet. That just doesn't make sense."

I shrugged. "Maybe he doesn't want to get you involved. Or maybe he's just not thinking. Think about it. He's what, twenty? None of you are even old enough to fucking buy a beer, and he's on the run from the *Mafia*," I emphasized the word. "He's witnessed a murder, he can't go home because they know where he lives or will shortly, he probably figures he can't go to the police because there's bound to be a leak—he's watched enough TV to believe that, whether or not it's true—in which case he's dead. He's got limited amounts of cash, and no experience with being away from home other than college. Actually, he's done pretty well for himself so far. He managed to kill two armed wiseguys with a knife, no one's spotted him or his car, and he's still alive. I mean, I don't *know* he's still alive, but if he wasn't they wouldn't keep trying to kill me. I hope. Soon, though, he's going to realize he can't keep running forever. Running gets old, and he's been doing it for four days already. That's a hell of a long time when you're looking over your shoulder. Chances are he'll try to contact someone soon. If he's smart, and I'm betting he is, he'll presume that some sort of authorities have been called. He may even be thinking that they're working with you guys, since you know him best. If you're as close as you say, he'll probably call you before he calls his parents or the cops. And he'll be hoping that whatever authority is involved will have figured out why he had to disappear and that by the time he does that, you know all or at least some of the story, so you'll be armed and ready to help him. Hell, knowing you guys, even if he had disappeared without any evidence of foul play, you'd still be locked and loaded."

"And so?" Ron said, crossing his arms over his chest.

"And so we keep trying to find him before anyone else does. Unless he makes the evening news by getting in a shootout, a phone call here should be the first time we hear from him. We'll keep someone by the phone, since he'll probably call here before he calls anyplace else, right? Meanwhile, I can hunt down whatever leads I can find."

"If he calls?" Steve said.

"If I'm not here, keep it short. And don't let him say where he is. Tell him your phone is bugged if you have to."

"Why?"

"Because it probably is. My office phone is, probably my home, too. I don't have the equipment to check for sure." Actually, the chance that Ron's phone was bugged already was slim to none, but better safe than sorry. If I didn't find Jerry soon, and these guys kept tagging along, his phone would be tapped, no doubt about it, sooner or later. Weatherspoon would be on my trail, along with the homicide dicks from half a dozen jurisdictions. Or I had to assume they were. I couldn't know how close behind me they were running, although Scott would do his best to be obstinate and uncommunicative, but I knew one thing -- they wouldn't be far behind.

"Then how did you find out your office was bugged?" Steve asked. "And who bugged it?"

"I was talking to someone who has his office lines monitored, and a red light came on when I got on the line. I don't know who's bugging me. I doubt it's Bufonte. Even though it's the digital age, bugging isn't the mob's style. They leave that to the feds." If it was Weatherspoon who had the tap on my phone, it had to've been done illegally.

He didn't have probable cause yet to get a legal one. If that was the case, and he was the one tapping my phone, illegally, he must really be feeling the heat. "If it's Weatherspoon, one of the guys from Justice that I've been dealing with, he's had all of his people working triple-time trying to find the three vanished witnesses. With all of the deaths of mob people in the past few days the chance of his people not picking up a pattern is slim. My name is going to pop up on a lot of those reports."

"So?" Ron said. "How would you get tied in with this in his mind anyway?"

I explained to them the incident between myself, Scott, RedMan, and Scarelli. Their eyes widened as they listened.

"But back to the phone tap. Since Weatherspoon may have a leak in his department, he would have only selected people listening to me on the phone, and not want to make any moves until he knows something for sure. He wants Bufonte, but not bad enough to lose his job. Maybe he figures I'll get faster results than he will so he's leaving me alone for now. Shit, I don't know. There are too many pieces missing for me to make any sort of educated guess."

"Why don't we just do Bufonte?" Bob said in half jest. "It would solve all of our problems." I couldn't help but smile—somehow, I knew that was coming.

"Well, for one," I said, "I don't know where he is. And anyway, we don't have enough people or firepower."

"Don't bet on that last one," Ron said with a slight smile on his face. Since we were only joking, ha ha, I let that one lie. I hadn't forgotten about the exploding gatehouse anecdote. What a childhood.

"Other than it being illegal," I said, expecting the disparaging looks that followed, "I don't want to make any moves against anyone until I find Jerry. I'm picking up the federal file on Bufonte tomorrow, maybe that will tell us something new." I noticed I was saying "us" instead of "me."

"So basically we just wait to get shot at," Steve said in a pissy tone.

"Beats last summer," Ron remarked.

"You're not targets yet," I said, "and I want to keep it that way for as long as I can. For as long as you let me. I don't want to be responsible for any of you catching a bullet, but I know you won't wait by the sidelines, and there's no way I can make you."

"What, do you wanna live forever?" Bob said to Steve.

"We're on you like glue, Jack," Ron said. "You're our best chance for getting Jerry. If we can't go after Bufonte we'll just wait for him to send more people after you. Maybe we can win by attrition. We've got the youth and the guns, but you've got the contacts and the experience. We're just going to have to make sure nothing happens to you for as long as we can. Think of us as your guardian angels."

Christ, I thought. *What a clusterfuck.*

I looked at Valenti half slumped over, the dark red blood congealing on the floor. If I was very, very lucky -- big if -- then maybe I wouldn't get myself, Steve, Ron, and Jerry killed. The only problem was I had never been lucky before. Well, just that once. *Too late to worry about that now.* For some reason I wasn't worried about Bob. I had the feeling that whether or not he died at a young age would have nothing to do with any decisions I'd make. I looked at Valenti again. It was getting easier.

"Where the hell did you get the idea to do that?" I asked Bob, looking at Valenti's leg.

"An episode of *Miami Vice*," he said. "One of G. Gordon

Liddy's henchmen was torturing Bob Balaban like that. Crockett of course shot him numerous times."

"*Miami Vice*," I said disbelievingly.

"Yeah. Highly underrated show. You really should watch more TV," he said, a faint trace of humor in his voice. "You'd be surprised at what you can pick up."

"TV," I said.

"Yep," Bob said, and smiled, then looked at Valenti. His smile vanished. He took the keys from Ron and unlocked the cuffs binding Valenti's pale wrists. Valenti's face thudded into the floor. Bob picked him up under the arms and Ron grabbed his legs and together they carried him to the stairs.

"Bob," I said. He stopped on the top step and looked at me. "Try not to kill anyone while you're gone, huh?" He looked at me for a second, his face blank, then I saw a small smile touch his lips. Then he and Ron moved down the stairs with the body and disappeared from view. For a brief moment I wondered if I was perhaps going crazy, but then realized that if I was, I'd be having a lot more fun. A few seconds later I heard the rough cough of an engine, probably the Jeep. It idled for about a minute and then moved away. In a little while I couldn't hear it anymore.

"Help me clean this mess up," I said to Steve, gesturing at the blood and urine on the floor. I could only hope Valenti believed in safe sex, I was all out of rubber gloves. "Whatever we can't burn needs to get soaked in bleach."

"Okay," he said. "I'll get some more rags." He went down the stairs and I was left alone in the barn, feeling drained and scummy. There were two windows in the wall opposite the stairs that I hadn't noticed before, and I wandered over. After I pushed aside the curtain I saw I was on the opposite side of the barn from the house, and all there was to look at was scrub brush and trees. A quarter mile away I saw the signs of an imminent subdivision, promising to make the future view from the window even bleaker.

"Progress never stands still," I said to myself, not making much sense and not liking the sound of my voice. The window was open a crack and as a soft breeze blew on me I realized I was dripping with sweat. I shrugged off my jacket and draped it over my shoulder. I didn't think any of the boys would get upset at the sight of my gun.

I heard steps on the stairs and half turned, my fingers lightly on the grip of my Smith & Wesson. Steve's head and shoulders appeared above the level of the floor, his head turned to where he expected me to be.

"Here," I said. I moved over to where he was and took some of the rags he had. Along with the rags he'd brought bleach and a canister of Comet and after ten minutes we'd pretty much removed all the traces of Valenti. There was still a dark stain left, but the odor was gone and it looked like a dozen other stains on the floor. The only problem was the several small fresh holes in the wood floor.

I followed Steve down the stairs with the dirty rags in my hands and dumped them into a fifty gallon drum that had grey-black ashes covering its bottom. Steve took a disgusting looking jar off the workbench and dribbled what smelled like turpentine over the rags, then lit the works with a strike-anywhere match. The fire was weak and the smoke acrid, but in a few short minutes the rags became just more ashes at the bottom of the drum. Even with all that a forensics team should have no trouble proving Valenti had been there, but if even one person showed up at Ron's we were in serious trouble.

"Valenti who?" Steve said to himself, satisfied. We washed our hands and arms in the sink next to the workbench with a bar of black pumice soap that was older than I was. I slipped on my jacket again and wandered out of the barn door and sat on the trunk of my car. Steve joined me.

"Well. . . shit," I said. Steve nodded, understanding completely. He was wearing a dark blue T-shirt under a red windbreaker, with faded jeans and well worn high top basketball shoes. Dark rings of sweat were drying under his arms, and he shivered. I'm not sure it had anything to do with the temperature.

"Do this a lot?" he asked, sounding totally exhausted.

"Do what?"

"Orchestrate the systematic torturing of organized crime hit men using innocent young college students as your lackeys. And on a Sunday, too."

"Oh, that," I said. "I've been trying to cut down."

We sat there for quite a while, looking at nothing in particular, until the Jeep crunched onto the gravel driveway. I got off the trunk and stood up as the Jeep pulled past me into the barn and cut its lights. Bob and Ron climbed out and shut their doors, then pulled closed the large barn door, concealing the Jeep. When they were done they came and stood in front of me. It was getting dark enough so that if I wasn't looking, I wouldn't have seen the smeared blood on their shirts.

"Done," Ron said. "They should find the body sometime early tomorrow morning, when it gets light. We got rid of the Ruger too."

"Not in the same place as the body, I hope," I said. I didn't think they were that stupid, but my heart jumped a little anyway.

Bob shot me a disgusted look. "Yeah, and we left both our prints all over it too," he said sarcastically.

I sighed and ran a hand through my hair, surprised that

I hadn't lost any since yesterday, and winced when my fingers touched the lump on top of my head. I'd forgotten about my souvenir from Freddie.

"You're going to have to replace the floor up there," I told Ron. He nodded. "I'm hungry," I said to no one in particular. I hadn't had anything to eat since the biscuit for breakfast. Looking at the three of them I could see I wasn't alone. "You guys got any food?"

"My dad's probably making dinner right now," Ron said. "Probably enough for all of us." I blinked at that, then nodded.

"I'm gonna want to go home first to get rid of these clothes, grab some stuff," Bob said.

"Bloody clothes go into plastic bags, then bring the bag here to burn," I told them.

They all nodded. "Drop me?" Bob asked Steve.

"Yeah," Steve said. "I gotta grab some stuff from home anyway." Bob started towards the RX-7, Steve turning to follow. "We'll be back," Steve said to Ron and I. They drove off and I trudged toward the house after Ron.

"Make sure you wash out the Jeep in the morning," I told Ron. "Bloodstains aren't good luck for anyone."

Chapter Twenty

DINNER LA STRANGE

The kitchen was filled with a delicious aroma that got my saliva flowing. George, who was fiddling with some bowls, grunted when we came in but otherwise ignored us. Not that we had much to talk about anyway. I noticed the pistol he'd had earlier laying on the kitchen counter, out of the way but within easy reach.

"Chili," Ron observed from the aroma. He pointed. "The bathroom's over there if you want to get cleaned up. I'm gonna go shower and change upstairs."

I flicked on the light in the bathroom, took off my jacket, and laid my shoulder rig on the counter next to the sink. I splashed some water on my face, smoothed back my hair, and washed my hands with a small pink bar of soap. My reflection in the mirror above the sink was haggard and questioning. I didn't have any answers so I shut off the light and went back into the kitchen, jacket and shoulder rig dangling from my left hand.

The smell of cooking food was stronger now. A covered pot was bubbling noisily on top of the stove and George was busily chopping greens and throwing them into a large bowl. Salad, maybe. Upstairs I heard water running.

"If you want a drink, there's beer in the fridge," he said. It was Labatt's, and cold, and the bottle was empty surprisingly fast considering beer wasn't one of my favorite beverages. I reached for another but stopped myself. I was still a target, and after a second beer a third would taste even better. Although there was probably more firepower in the house than in some National Guard armories, I grabbed a Diet Coke instead and sat down in a wooden chair beside an oval table just to one side of the kitchen. I hung my jacket and shoulder rig unobtrusively on the back of the chair and watched George move his bulk around the kitchen, his hands moving rapidly as he prepared dinner.

"Need any help?" I asked politely.

"Nope," he said. "You'd just get in the way."

He was right. Considering the speed he was moving about the kitchen, I'd be standing in the wrong place and get accidentally bodyslammed into the refrigerator. He finished adding ingredients to the salad and tossed the contents of the bowl quickly. He checked the pot on the stove, nodded, and turned a knob.

"You married?" I asked. He peered at me around a cupboard as his hands fiddled with something.

"Yeah," he said.

"Where is she?"

"We had a disagreement yesterday," he said. "She went to her sister's to cool down."

"Oh," I said, feeling like a jerk.

"Yeah," he said. "She told me I was an asshole and I disagreed." He smiled at me. "Happens a lot." He brought the bowl of salad over and set it in the middle of the table. "It was good timing, actually. She's had enough excitement from me, she didn't need this." He set out placemats, plates, bowls, napkins, and silverware, then sat down across the table from me. Amazingly, even after all I'd seen, I still had an appetite, and I sat there and listened to my stomach growl as we waited for the others to arrive.

"So what do you do for a living now?" I was trying to fill up the silence with some words.

"This and that," he replied, in a tone that told me I'd get nothing more out of him. I'd had quite enough of questioning people, so I shut up.

Ron came down the stairs and into the kitchen quietly. He looked at his father's back, winked at me, and started to lift the lid off the chili pot.

"Leave the damn chili alone, Ronald," George said without turning around. It was his turn to wink at me. Apparently they'd done the routine before. It was normal enough behavior unless you knew about the hour and a half we'd all just gone through. God, had it only been an hour and a half? It felt like a lifetime.

Ron had changed into a grey T-shirt and olive drab fatigue pants. Tightly laced Nike high tops covered his feet. His blond flattop was clean and level again and still slightly damp. Under one arm he was carrying a large cardboard box that he set on the cushions of a couch in the family room which was off to one side of the room I was in, the three rooms forming an L. The family room was where I'd talked to Ron and Steve earlier in the week, when my life was still normal.

"Bob and Steve eating?" George asked.

"Yeah, they should be back pretty soon," Ron said.

He sat on the couch next to the box and began removing items. First was a small pistol case from which he took a short barreled .357 magnum revolver. From a box of ammunition he filled two speedloaders and then loaded the gun. He put the .357 in a holster and stuck it in his pants behind his right hip, covering it with his shirt. The two speedloaders went into two separate cargo pockets in his pants, one against each of his thighs. His father watched without comment, his face expressionless. George looked at me briefly, then turned away and studied his cuticles. He got up abruptly and went back into the kitchen to fiddle with the chili and anything else he could find. Leading a life of danger and excitement was one thing, watching your children do it apparently was another.

Bob and Steve came through the kitchen without a word and went into the family room, both with gym bags in their hands. They set the bags on the couch next to Ron, then all three of them came and sat around the table.

That I had a appetite at all after what I'd gone through surprised me more than anything. Maybe I was just glad to be alive. I ate more than I usually did, but the four of them made me seem anorexic. I hadn't seen so much food eaten so fast since college. Nobody said much during the meal, which was fine with me. When the feeding frenzy was over, I sat with the three of them in the family room, bloated, while George did the dishes in the kitchen.

Bob unzipped the gym bag he'd brought in with him and dumped the contents on the couch. Among other things, there was a stainless steel Smith & Wesson .44 Magnum with a four inch barrel in a shoulder rig. With smooth, precise movements, Bob loaded the revolver and two speedloaders with ammunition. Setting all that aside, he took a spare magazine for his Browning Hi-Power, which I assumed was still concealed on his person, and loaded it.

"Planning on taking on the whole Zulu nation?" I asked conversationally.

Failure Drill

Steve, sitting next to Bob, had taken out several large double-column pistol magazines and began loading them. I soon learned they went with the Taurus nine-millimeter still under his arm in the shoulder rig.

"There are four things you can never have too much of," Bob said. He ticked them off on his fingers. "Sleep, food, sex, or spare ammo."

"You guys have seen too may movies " I said. "Do any of you even know how to shoot? Or more importantly, *when* to shoot?"

"Well," Ron said, "Steve is probably the worst shot here, and he can run an El Presidente in under ten and a half seconds with that Taurus, out of that shoulder rig."

I was impressed, and I guess it showed on my face from their reactions. Not just with the respectable time Steve had on probably the most internationally recognized combat pistol drill, but that they even knew *what* an El Presidente was. I hadn't heard of it until the DEA Academy. Anything around ten seconds for the El Presidente was respectable, anything under eight, from concealment and using an out of the box gun, was damned near amazing. My best was nine flat, using my DEA-issued Glock.

"Kiss my ass," Steve retorted. "You're not any closer to Bob's best time than I am." I raised my eyebrows and looked to Bob, but he declined to comment. I motioned at the .44 sitting on the table in front of him.

"You do it with that?" I inquired, doubting it. Not just because of the blast and kick of the .44, but more so because the El Presidente requires a combat reload, and even with speedloaders revolvers take almost three times longer to reload than automatics. My bet was he had used the Browning, cocked and locked. Bob smiled and hefted the .44 in its holster in response to my question.

"Only six shots," he explained, "and it kicks like a bitch, but if I hit you you *will* go down."

"As well as the person standing behind me," I said, "when the round overpenetrates."

"Not with the loads I'm using." He could see that didn't satisfy me, but he just shrugged. "As long as I get to make my 'Most Powerful Handgun in the World' speech before this is all over," he said with another smile, "I'll be happy."

"Your what?" I said.

"You know, from the movie? *Dirty Harry*? 'This is a .44 Magnum, the most powerful handgun in the world, and could blow your head *cleeeeeean* off.'" He smiled at me. I stared at him, my mouth open.

"I don't know which it is," I finally managed to get out. "You guys are either insane or retarded. I just don't get you." They'd just participated in the torture and execution of a man, and it didn't seem to bother them as much as it did me. Calling that strange was a major understatement.

Ron looked at me intently. "You don't, do you?" he said quietly.

"When I was your age I was drinking beer, chasing trim, drinking beer, trying to get laid, getting laid, and drinking beer. The only people I knew even remotely similar to you, with your point of view, were Vietnam vets. Hell, I don't know that many people like you now, and that's after working in the DEA. And those people have sure as hell seen a lot more shit than you have."

Steve, toying with the placemat in front of him, spoke. "Let me see if I can explain it," he said. "For whatever reason, maybe just because none of our parents got divorced and they raised us right, we all grew up with a pretty strict moral code. Principles, I guess you'd call them. Right and Wrong. Most people used to have 'em, I guess, but the way our society's going down the shitter, finding someone principled today ain't easy. And Right and Wrong, hell, every TV show you watch, every movie you see, every confrontation in every supermarket parking lot after a fender bender involves one of those two words. They're the original basis for our laws. They're the basis for our society, *any* society

"Everything you do, or don't do, is Right, or Wrong. Whichever one it is you know clearly, or would if you took the time to examine your actions, an idea a lot of people are completely unfamiliar with. Nowadays it's money or power they follow, or some other shit. Even those people that usually do the right thing, they're not doing it because it's what they *should* do, they're doing it out of habit, or to stay out of trouble."

"Rather cynical viewpoint, don't you think?" I said. He looked at me like I was stupid, and I almost got upset, until I realized that I really was interested in their perspective on the world, as stupid as it seemed to be discussing philosophies of life with people barely old enough to vote. Maybe because I had a beer in me. Maybe because it kept my mind off of what we'd just done.

"But it was different for us. Maybe that was because we were such a close knit group, I don't know. It sounds corny, but basically we wanted to be the good guys."

"There's nothing wrong with that," I said. "Hell, your 'Right and Wrong', that's just good and bad, and no one wants to be thought of as a bad guy."

"Not really," Ron said. "Here, look." He leaned forward and began using his hands to punctuate his words. "Good and Bad are very close to Right and Wrong, but they have legalistic overtones. If a man murders my mother, which is wrong as well as bad, I could take him to court. Good. If he got off on a technicality, I would take it upon myself to kill him. Killing him would not be good, so to speak, and it's definitely not legal, but it would be Right. Do you see what I mean? Or, instead of taking him to court, I could kill him outright. That would still be bad, but it wouldn't necessarily be Wrong."

"So you believe in eye-for-an-eye justice," I said.

"There's no such thing as justice," Steve said. "Well, that's not quite true, but the word has been twisted around by our court system, so that now they can say 'Justice has been served' when they screw up what's supposed to happen to bad guys in court but usually doesn't. 'Justice' should mean doing the Right thing, but that's not what those people think. 'Justice is blind', what a pile of shit."

"You got something in mind that works better?" I said.

"How about revenge?" Ron said. "Revenge is the purest, oldest motive there is. It's human. Nothing to be ashamed of, but that's not what the media would like you to believe. Treat others as they treat you, that's what's Right, and punish them if they go astray." He pointed a finger at me. "You know as well as I do that rehabilitation doesn't work. On a rare occasion it might, but that's people rehabilitating themselves, nobody does it for them. What's left? You got it -- Retribution." He raised his voice to a falsetto and waved his hands. "But the death penalty doesn't work, studies have shown that it's not a deterrent," he mocked. "Two things. First, you kill a scumbag that murdered somebody else, it'll sure as hell deter him from killing anybody else. He'll be dead. Second, I think I could make the point that nowhere in this country do we even *have* the death penalty.

"How long does it take, usually, for people to get executed after they're convicted? Ten years, Fifteen? After their seven hundred appeals have run out, and they haven't died of old age, then maybe we'll kill them. ***That's*** not the death penalty! I say three years, and a limited number of appeals, all of which have to show cause for their existence and not be frivolous. After that, *ZAP!* And, I like the electric chair. It's the most horrible form of execution ever devised. Well, except for crucifixion, but they're never going to bring *that* back. Nobody'll ever let relatives of the deceased be the ones that flick the switch, so the least we can do for them is to send the guy to hell in the worst way possible short of torture."

I sat and digested all of that for a while. "You're not saying a hell of a lot," I said to Bob. He was just sitting there, watching and listening.

"They talk too much," he said quietly.

"As far as he's concerned this is all patently obvious," Ron explained.

"So murder is bad, in and of itself, but under certain circumstances it's the Right thing to do," I said, following their reasoning. "That's pretty simpleminded, don't you think?" What I thought didn't matter, the point of the exercise was to find out what made them tick. And keep my mind occupied with things other than a bloody barn.

"No!" Steve practically shouted. "Simple, not simpleminded. People think, huh, right and wrong, is that it? But think about it, what else is there? *What else is there?* Early in high school, around age sixteen or so when we first began to talk about this kind of stuff, we gradually became aware of how the world really was outside of school. And we realized that it wasn't going to be easy to keep to our values. And if you don't live up to your values, why even have them? We figured early on that to keep our values against the onslaught of this shitty society we'd have to become hard."

"Hard?"

"Yes, hard. Hard of heart, hard of body, hard of mind. 'That which doesn't kill us makes us stronger.' Nietzsche said that, and we adopted it as our own rule of life."

Ron threw a thumb at Bob. "He can do anything he fucking wants, he's a fucking machine." He turned to look at Bob. "When did you get your black belt?"

Bob, who'd been examining his cuticles intently, glanced up. "Which one?"

Ron looked at me. "You see what I'm talking about? Karate," he told Bob.

"Seventeen, almost eighteen," Bob said.

"Oh, I thought that was the one you got first," Ron said to him.

"No, that was judo."

I squinted at him. "You have two black belts?"

"Yeah."

"How old were—"

"Fifteen."

We looked at each other for a while. I stared, once again, at his huge arms. "How good *was* the guy you killed at my house?" I said finally, studying his black eye.

Bob chose his words carefully. "If he hadn't been so overconfident it would have gotten real ugly." I could tell he didn't want to talk about it any more.

Ron snorted. "Some of us need more help than others," he flipped the bird at Bob, "so we chose occupations that would put us in contact with people that thought the same way we did."

"All little boys like playing cops and robbers," I deliberately goaded them.

"Sure, go ahead and make fun," Steve said. "But we're not playing. I joined the Reserves when I was sixteen," Steve went on. "My parents weren't sure why I wanted to do it, but they gave their permission anyway. I was the youngest one in my company in basic, but I worked my ass off and got second in my graduating class. Now, once I get my criminal justice degree I'll go into some sort of law enforcement career."

"Unless you get arrested for carrying a concealed weapon first," I commented. He ignored me.

"I got in shape from sports in high school," Ron said. "When I graduated I went to VMI to work on my mindset."

"VMI? For your mindset?" To me that sounded like joining the Army to work on your tan.

"Freshman year at VMI is as hard, physically, as Basic in the Army. Mentally and emotionally it's worse. Remember I told you I had roommates stabbing each other the stress got so bad? Over an unmade bed! I'm tired of it though, I've learned all they've got to teach me, and their teaching staff isn't exactly Ivy League. Not to mention I miss these boneheads, so I've been trying to get into State."

"How about you?" I asked Bob. "What's the plan after Airborne?"

"Ranger School. Already got a slot. And as soon as I make rank I'll be getting into Special Forces," he said. "Do that for a while, see if that's what I want or whether I'll want to move on."

"You don't just 'get' into SF," I said. "Very few people, *very* few, ever make it. There's no guarantee you'll even make it through Ranger school." In my life I'd known or worked with a few Special Forces veterans, and most of them had told me that physically Ranger School was tougher than the Special Forces 'Q' course.

All three of them treated me with identical looks that

told me they suspected I might be slightly retarded and just hid it well.

"Well, shit, you've met Bob," Ron said. "What do you think?"

I looked over and saw Bob was regarding me with just the hint of a smile on his lips.

"You guys," I said, shaking my head and avoiding answering the question, "you guys are something else. Have you ever heard the term 'adrenaline junkie'? You're still playing cops and robbers."

"Like you, when you joined the DEA?" Ron shot back. I looked at him, at them. "You aren't as hard as you think you are."

Ron smiled evilly. "Maybe not, but we're harder than you think we are. And you don't know us as well as you think."

"We don't fight with each other," Steve said. "We bicker a lot—"

"Some," interjected Ron.

"Shut up," Steve said, and smiled. "But we don't fight. Our value systems are consistent enough so that we wouldn't do anything the others wouldn't approve of, at least for the most part. They say you should never room with a friend in college, because you'll end up enemies. I say if that's true, you weren't much of a friend to begin with, or you didn't know the person well enough to call them a friend. All of us have spent a lot of time together, as roommates or otherwise, and we're still together. We know how each other think, at least about the important stuff. Hell, I know these guys better than I know my own parents."

Ron leaned forward and put on a serious expression. "To us, friendship and friends are everything. It goes along with right and wrong, and honor. None of us make friends very easily. Real friends, that is. For most people, what they call friends are merely acquaintances. You've been with us, you see how we'd do anything to help one another. That's a friend."

"Who's Damon and who's Pythias?" I said, vaguely remembering some of my mythology. They apparently knew what I was referring to, because I was rewarded with big smiles and nodding heads. At least they were learning something in college.

Ron gestured widely, swinging his arm in a circle. "Grumpy, Steve, Jerry, these are my friends. If I had to, I would risk my life, kill or die for them, as long as it didn't violate my personal code of right and wrong. They would do the same for me. We don't screw each other over, because it would be like screwing over ourselves, a violation of everything we believe in. That's why I told you at the beginning of all this that I was going to help you find Jerry, whether you wanted me to or not."

"Because it would only be Right," I said. "He'd do it for you. And if he's been harmed—"

"Or killed," Ron continued for me, his eyes intense with that thought, "it would be Wrong. Not to mention piss us off. And—"

"And being who you are you would have to right that Wrong," I finished for him. "That's an awfully heavy responsibility, especially considering the consequences."

Ron sat back and nodded emphatically. "Shit happens. So, do you 'get' us now?"

I gave him a thoughtful smile. "I get more than you think," I said. "Whether I think you're *right* . . . ." I tilted my head to the side. "I'm a lot older than you guys and I'm still learning about myself. About how I view Right and Wrong, not to mention a bunch of other things. This past week has made me reevaluate a lot of my thinking. It gets pretty complicated."

"Not complicated," Steve said to me, "that's the problem a lot of people have. It's not complicated, it's simple. Everything is simple, people just stick in a lot of crap that confuses the issue. They let the problem get complicated by mushing together a group of simple issues that should be decided separately and then trying to solve them all at once. A lot of the problem too is that too many people don't have a consistent value system. There's a quote from a movie, I wish I could remember which one, where one character angry with another says 'Everything just isn't right or wrong.' The second character replies, 'What else is there?' Now that's beautiful in its clarity and truth. What else is there? Most people don't understand that."

"Finding a consistent value system and then sticking to it is a lot harder than you think," I said. "It's more effort than what most people want to put out. It has a tendency to produce a lot of conflict in your life."

Ron spread his hands. "None of us expect to live very long lives," he said nonchalantly. We sat there in silence for a while.

"You're lucky," Bob said finally. "Usually people only get the full lecture when we're really drunk." I looked over at him, and he stared back at me. I finally nodded at him.

"So boss, what's next?" Steve inquired. I noticed for the first time that all three of them were wearing almost identical hightop basketball shoes.

"What's with the shoes?" I said. "Was there a sale at Footlocker that I missed?"

Bob looked at one of his feet. "Hightops are comfortable to move around in," he said, "and they won't slip off your heels if you have to run. Combat boots won't slip, but they're a bit heavy and conspicuous. Idea is to leave as few things as possible to chance."

Ron wiggled his feet. "Nikes," he said. "Most comfortable things I ever wore on my feet."

"You going to answer the question?" Steve asked me.

They had it thought out down to their footwear, for Christ's sake. On second thought, why was I even surprised? "If I had any answers, I'd be glad to give them to you," I told him. "*You* know him better than I do, can't you think of anyplace else he might be? Unless you can, all I can suggest is waiting for him to call or for more people to try and kill me. There's a few other small details I can check up on, but I doubt that they'll lead anywhere." I heard a phone ring somewhere in the house. Halfway through the second ring it stopped. A few seconds later George came into the family room.

"Ronald," he said, "get the damn phone, it's for you. Girl named Jodi."

"I'm not here," Ron said automatically. "Waitaminit," he said after a second, "I don't know any Jodi."

"What about Jerry's girlfriend?" I said.

"Oh yeah." He stood up. "She probably wants to know about Jer. What should I tell her?"

I thought a second. "Hell, I don't know, you guys know her better than I do. Tell her enough to keep her off my back at least. Worst comes to worst, just plead ignorance."

"An easy task," Bob remarked. Ron flipped him off with practiced ease and left the room, followed by his father. I sank back in thought, trying to think of where their friend could be. Bob produced a wicked looking knife from somewhere and started whittling his fingernails, his brow furrowed in thought.

"What's with Ron and his girlfriends?" I said after a few minutes of silence.

"Ron doesn't have girlfriends," Steve explained. "He meets a girl and screws her until he gets tired of her, then moves on to the next one. *Mobile semen receptacles* I believe is his current preferred term. He's usually got two or three in reserve."

"So he's the romantic type," I said.

"All a female is is a life support system for a pussy," I heard Ron say from behind me. He came into the room and sat down next to Steve, on the couch opposite the one Bob and I were on. "With very few exceptions."

"Miss Ogyny is on the phone," Bob said to him. "It's for you." Ron flipped him off.

"Charming," I remarked. "My wife'd love you. What'd Jodi have to say?"

"She wasn't happy with the info I had for her, or the lack of it I should say, but there's not anything else for her to do but take it."

"Jennifer," Bob and Steve said simultaneously. Startled, they looked at each other.

"What?" Ron and I said together.

"Jennifer," Steve said again, looking expectantly at Ron.

"What, that bitch?" Ron said. "What about her?" Suddenly, comprehension blossomed in his eyes. "Oh shit—of course!"

"What?" I said again.

"It's a girl, a friend, that we all know. Have known, for a few years. Jer, too. Ron even dated her for a while." Steve jerked a thumb at him.

"Til she found out the truth and dumped him," Bob said, beaming. "You think Jerry might be with her?" I asked.

"Maybe," Steve said. "I didn't think of it before, 'cause

she's up at Michigan State for summer term, but yeah, it's a pretty good bet. They're pretty close."

"East Lansing is a safe distance away," I said. "At least he might think so. Maybe he figures that only you guys would know about her, so he could just sit back and wait for you to show up. It could also explain why we can't find his car. If he's parked on campus, eighty miles away, where only campus cops roam...." I was getting excited. I finally had a lead that might pan out. Maybe I was overreacting, but I was entitled.

"Speaking of State," Steve said, "he could be up there with his boss, too."

"You just lost me," I said. Ron was nodding.

"Yeah, that'd be a even safer bet," Steve was saying to himself. He looked up at me and explained. "Jerry's got a maintenance job up at school when he's there. Mows the grass and shit like that. His boss is some sort of war hero. Handful of tours in 'Nam, some bronze stars, half a dozen purple hearts. LRRP," he told me, pronouncing it "lurp". It meant Long Rage Reconnaissance Patrol, the guys who went out behind the lines in small teams, taking only what they could carry with them, looking for somebody to shoot or something to blow up. "Yeah, Jer could be staying with him," Steve said excitedly.

"Sounds good," I said. "But you guys sure are shitty when it comes to thinking of this stuff. I should've been told this three days ago, goddammit." The three of them looked nearly appropriately reticent, but I couldn't stay upset. The thought of actually finding Jerry had my spirits up. "Do you know his name," I asked "or where we can call him? Or Jennifer?" Steve shook his head.

"No, I don't," he said "All I know is his first name, Richard, and where on campus he works. Jenny we can call but him we're gonna have to see in person. And really, should we even call her? If he's there, he won't let her tell anyone over the phone. At least I wouldn't. Visions of phone taps'll be dancing in his head, he's seen enough movies about cops and the mob. And even if we dig up zip, the trip shouldn't take more than three and a half or four hours, max, round trip." He was probably right. Jerry getting on the phone anywhere he was staying was a very slim possibility.

"Road trip," Bob said.

"Seeing as it's our best bet, our only bet at the moment, you wanna go tomorrow morning?" Steve said.

"I have to go see someone tomorrow at ten," I said, "but we can go straight from there."

"We can take my car," Ron said.

"The Bluesmobile," Steve said admiringly. He looked at me. "You might as well sleep over here tonight. We're going to." He motioned at Bob and himself. "Safety in numbers."

I nodded. Hell, I'd rather be where I could keep an eye on them anyway. "I didn't particularly feel like sleeping in an empty house that's already been a target once," I said. "First, though, I've got some business to take care of."

"What?" Ron asked.

"I want to go see my wife." I walked over to the kitchen table and shrugged on the shoulder rig I'd left slung over the chair.

"My turn to baby-sit," Steve said, standing up. I didn't bother arguing with him. I knew how useless it would be.

"Who gets first watch tonight?" Bob asked Ron.

"First watch?" I asked him. "The chances of them trying for me again this early, much less connecting me to you, is slim."

Failure Drill

"I know, but I'd rather have someone on watch than not. It comes from my own deep seated feelings of paranoia."

I pulled on my blue jacket and smiled ruefully. "I can relate." I said. I headed for the door, Steve bringing up the rear.

"And tomorrow," I heard Bob say behind me, talking to Ron, "we can go see Jenny."

"Bitch," Ron said.

Chapter Twenty-One

VISITING HOURS

I walked down the hospital corridor with Steve, our steps echoing softly. We'd managed to avoid any nurses, and I guess that was better than if they'd seen and tried to stop me because it was past visiting hours. I was in no mood to argue with anyone. I'd reached Unprovoked Head-Smacking stage about twelve hours earlier.

"I've been thinking," Steve was saying. "Don't you think you ought to get a bulletproof vest?"

I smiled and tapped the blue jacket I had on. "What do you think this is?" I said. "It's the unmarked version of the jacket I used to wear on raids. The others all say FEDERAL AGENT on the front and back in big yellow block letters. I managed to liberate this from the company stores shortly before I left. It'll stop up to a three-fifty-seven."

"Too bad you didn't get a couple extra," he said wistfully.

We turned a corner and in front of us was a man sitting in a chair, chewing gum. He was wearing blue jeans, a brown T-shirt and a blue baseball jacket. His brown hair was cut short and receding from his forehead, turning grey as it did so. He'd been looking in our direction as we turned the corner and was sitting slightly forward, a hand under his jacket above his right hip. After he stared at Steve and I for a second, he relaxed and leaned back.

"When you're done visiting your wife," he said to me, "the lieutenant wants you to call him."

"Who am I?" I asked him. I'd never seen him before in my life and wanted to know how he knew who I was.

"John Phault," he said.

"How do you know?"

"The lieutenant described you to me before I came on. He also said you'd look like shit and probably be wearing a blue jacket." I looked down at the jacket I had on and fingered the kevlar. I hadn't been wearing it the last time Scott had seen me.

"I bet he did at that," I said after a second. I started to push open the door to Kelly's room.

"Who's he?" the guard said, pointing at Steve.

"William Wonka," Steve said cheerfully, putting out a hand. "But you can call me Bill." I definitely didn't want to hear the rest of their conversation so I entered Kelly's room and closed the door.

The lights were off but there was a small nightlight in one corner that illuminated the room enough for me to see her on the bed. I softly picked up a chair at the end of the bed and set it down close to where her head was on the pillows. A dozen red roses were on the table next to her bed. The card said they were from Scott and that he wished her well.

I hadn't sent her any flowers I'd had her assailants killed instead. I'm not sure which she would've preferred, given the choice. I sat in the chair and took one of her hands in both of mine. She stirred and half-opened her eyes and looked at me.

"That's not fair," she said. "You keep coming either when I'm half doped up or half asleep. I can't get worked up enough to yell at you like you deserve."

"That was the idea," I said. "Don' t worry, I'm sure you'll find time for it later."

We sat there for some time in the dark, me at least hoping that I'd be around later for her to yell at. Even though I knew her better than anyone, most of the time I couldn't tell what my wife had on her mind—most of the time. I sure as hell couldn't tell what she was thinking about lying in that hospital bed. I wanted to ask her, ask what she thought of everything that had happened, find out whether she approved of my actions, but I didn't. Maybe I was afraid of what she'd say, of her disapproval, of a situation where I wouldn't do anything different if I had it to do all over again. So, instead, we sat there holding hands—both of us silent, thinking our own thoughts.

Her voice finally broke the silence. "Scott says tomorrow when I go home either he or one of his men will guard me."

"I won't be there," I explained, or tried to. "I'm trying to get this all taken care of. I wouldn't be very good company anyway," I said weakly.

I listened to her slow breathing. Part of what I said was true, but that wasn't the main reason I wanted to be apart from her until it was all settled. There were going to be a lot of tough things that I'd have to do before it was over, and if Kelly was around I didn't think I'd be able to go through with everything I'd have to in order to survive. She brought out too much nice in me.

"I know," she finally said softly. "You never were when things like this used to happen. Well," she corrected herself, "not things like *this*, but I thought we were done with this kind of life."

"So did I," I said. "So did I."

"If not, why have we been trying to get pregnant?" She let the question hang in the air.

"We've had this conversation before," I told her. "The stress bothered both of us, but it was harder on you because you were at home, worrying, while I was out working. But I said 'I do', which means I can't have you a nervous wreck all the time. But you knew I was going into a career like this when we got married. And I can't not respond when I should. I can't do that. I'm doing what I have to right now, and when it's over our life will go back to more or less normal. It's the way I am. I can't be any way else. I couldn't live with myself if I didn't stand up and fight for what I think is right, you know?" I wasn't being very eloquent, but she knew what I meant.

Kelly lay on her bed and looked up at me. Her eyes gleamed faintly in the dim light as she blinked rapidly and gave me a little nod.

I bent down and kissed her lightly on the forehead, then straightened, still holding her hand. I sat there for a long time, images flashing through my mind, drifting through other times and places, until I realized her breathing had slowed and become more regular. I laid her hand gently back on her stomach, put the chair back quietly, and went back out into the world, feeling every bit the shithead I was.

The cop was still sitting in his chair, his jaws moving rhythmically as he chewed his gum. Steve was a few feet down the corridor, leaning on a wall.

"Where's the phone?" I said. The cop jerked a thumb down the hall. "The lieutenant at home or the office?" I asked him.

"Office."

I used my credit card on the pay phone down the hall and after being transferred around for a couple minutes Scott picked up the other end.

"Yeah," he said.

"Still have to work on those manners a bit, Scott," I said.

"John! Where the hell are you?"

"At the hospital. You wanted to talk to me?"

"I've been calling you at home and the office for a couple hours now. Where the hell you been?"

"Out skinnydipping," I said. "What's up?"

"Pontiac P.D. pulled a guy out of a ditch about a half hour ago," he said. "He matches Grinnand's description of the guy that got away at your house."

"Really." So much for him being found tomorrow morning. I'd have to talk to Ron and Bob.

"Yeah, really," Scott said. "He'd also been shot about eight times in the leg with a twenty-two. Once in the eye, too."

"Really," I said again. Scott paused, and I could swear the phone got colder.

"Tell me you didn't have anything to do with it," he said.

"I didn't have anything to do with it," I said, not making any effort to sound sincere.

"That's what I thought," he said after a second. His voice changed. "You know, you're in way over your fucking head, buddy. I don't know what's gotten into you. This is a fucking missing person's case, for the love of Christ," he said, worry and pleading under his anger.

"You need anything while I'm at the *hospital?*" I asked him. "Visiting my *wife?*"

I could hear him breathing heavily into my ear. Several times he started to say something, then stopped. "Shit," he said finally. "You're going to go balls to the wall on this one, aren't you? Well, as it so happens, Weatherspoon found out about the dead guy, and the attempt on your life at your office building, and *very* badly wants to talk to you. He finds it very curious that you've run into so many of Bufonte's men lately. I guess half the dead guys are people he wanted to pull in and question about his hot-footed witnesses."

"Imagine that " I said.

"He wanted to know if I knew where you've been hiding. Apparently he's been ringing your phone off the hook, too. I didn't know where you were, of course. Not that I would've told him. Not that you deserve my loyalty, either, asshole. He also wanted to know if I had any clues as to why one of Bufonte's men was found dead, apparently tortured, in the bottom of a ditch on the border of Pontiac. Some guy had a flat and saw the body when he was changing his tire, I guess. Weatherspoon's got more than half a brain in his head, he'll start figuring this shit out. And he knows more than he's willing to tell me in any case, probably trying to catch me in a lie, fucking feeb."

"Thanks," I said. "I think, I hope I'm getting close."

"I hope so, he said. "You're not a cat, you don't have nine lives. And, I'm beginning to get a lot of heat from the people who count. In case you hadn't noticed, a substantial number of bodies have been piling up the last couple of days. When the brass gets here in the morning, I'm going to have to answer a lot of questions. My delaying tactics have just about run their course."

"One or two days," I said. "Leave word on my office machine if anything comes up, but don't get too specific 'cause it's bugged."

"Wh—" he began, then stopped. "Forget it. I don't want to know." I heard him sigh. "Watch your back," he said.

"I don't have enough mirrors " I said, and hung up.

"Back to Bashful's?" Steve asked.

"Not yet. I want to grab some stuff from my house first," I replied. He grunted.

My house felt empty and cold, even worse than on a return from a long trip. Empty and cold was better than filled with people with guns waiting for me, but it still felt like I was a visitor in my own house. The gun in my hand didn't help me feel any more at home.

With my steps echoing through the rooms, I grabbed a few toiletries out of the bathroom and a couple pairs of underwear out of the dresser along with a few changes of clothes. I looked around once, slowly, then locked up the house and got back in the car with Steve.

"Feel strange sneaking in and out of your own house?" Steve said.

"Yeah. "

"Bet you want this over with even more than we do, huh?"

I didn't bother answering him. It was a stupid question.

Ron stepped out of a shadowed alcove in the foyer as we came through the front door and nodded at us once. He had a 12-gauge pump shotgun cradled in his arms.

"Everybody sleeping?" Steve asked.

"Or trying to," Ron said.

"Where am I?" I asked.

"There's two couches in the family room," Ron said. "Bob's got one." I nodded.

"If all you guys are planning to escort me to MSU

tomorrow, who's going to man the phones for the four or five hours we're gone?" I inquired.

"My dad doesn't work normal hours," Ron said, "so he's off tomorrow and said he'd stick around all day. I've already talked to him about it."

"Will Jerry talk to your father if he calls?"

"You mean, would he trust my dad enough to tell him anything? You tell me, you've met my dad."

"Okay, I withdraw the question," I said.

After saying goodnight to Ron and Steve I tiptoed quietly into the family room. A pillow and blanket were already on the vacant couch. As I silently passed him on the couch, Bob opened one eye halfway, looked at me, shifted his body a little, then closed his eye and appeared to go back to sleep. I stripped down to my pants, set my hardware on the floor below my pillow, and laid on the couch. I lay there for a while, trying to think coherent thoughts, but worries about Kelly and thoughts of revenge kept my mind wandering.

That night I had nightmares for the first time since I'd left the DEA. At first they were of Valenti, blood dripping from his eye, chasing me, and of what would've happened to my wife had Bob not intervened, but later they turned to unfocused feelings of intense dread. My dreams didn't exactly require a degree in psychology to decipher. I woke up once, a little before three by my watch, covered in sweat, and couldn't get back to sleep for a long time. Apparently I wasn't required to pull guard duty, because the next time I opened my eyes the sun was shining through the windows of the kitchen.

I looked over and saw Bob gliding through the slow motion movements of *T'ai Chi Chuan* in the middle of the family room. He was dressed only in a pair of shorts, and the slabs of muscle on his body tensed and relaxed as he slid through the movements. His face was blank as he did his form, warming up and stretching out his body, the image of concentration.

I hadn't seen anybody do T'ai Chi in a while, the only sounds in the room his rhythmic breathing. It was relaxing just to watch him. At last he finished and stood there unmoving, taking slow, deep breaths.

"I take it no one forced their way in and killed me last night," I said.

"Due no doubt to the impenetrable security force you have amassed around you," he said.

"That or blind luck," I replied. I sat up on the couch and put my feet on the floor.

"That, too," Bob said. He dropped into what drill sergeants fondly call the front leaning rest position and began to knock out pushups at a disgustingly high rate of speed. When he hit seventy-five I stopped counting. Shortly thereafter he stopped and stood, breathing hard and ragged but by no means exhausted. He went over to his gym bag at the end of the couch and pulled out some clothes and shampoo. "I'm gonna take a shower," he said, and left me alone in the room. I looked at my watch and saw it was five minutes before eight. I stood up and stretched, still in my now stylishly wrinkled pants. Ron came into the kitchen and took some orange juice out of the refrigerator and set it on the counter. He looked fresh and clean and recently showered.

"Is there an empty shower anywhere around?" I asked.

"I would hope so. We've only got about thirty-eight in this goddamned house," he said. He led me through several hallways and rooms into a bathroom filled with gleaming porcelain. I'd taken the little Colt with me and set it next to the sink, a constant reminder of the predicament I was in. Taking a pistol into the shower -- ridiculous? Paranoid? All I know is that it's better to have a gun and not need it than need a gun and not have it.

In less than half an hour I was showered, shaved, and feeling relatively human again. I'd put on an old pair of faded jeans and a red T-shirt. It was supposed to be sunny and hot, and the sun was already glaringly bright through the small square pebbled glass window in the bathroom. Wearing the blue kevlar jacket was going to be a real chore.

I went back into the kitchen. Bob and Ron were puttering around fixing makeshift breakfasts for themselves. I grabbed a large glass of orange juice and a warm bagel and sat down at the table. Bob and Ron had most of their armament laid out on the tablecloth, and it looked like a centerfold for *Guns & Ammo*.

"Where's Steve?" I said, looking around.

"Shower," Bob said around a mouthful of toast. "Takes forever." He sat down at the table across from me and chewed. The muscles in his law popped in and out.

"How 'bout your dad?"

"Feeding the horses," Ron replied.

I grunted and ate my bagel. Ron came to the table and sat down to my right. He had a can of Diet Coke in one hand and a slice of pizza in the other.

"All of you guys don't need to go to State," I said pleasantly. "I managed to get by without any help for quite a while before you guys came along."

"Steve knows what Jer's boss looks like," Bob said. "None of the rest of us do. Of the three of us, Jenny knows me the best. That is, knows me and will talk to me," he added, kicking Ron's chair. Ron picked a pepperoni off the slice of pizza and ate it, ignoring him. "And finally, Ron's car is the best we've got. It goes fast and is pretty good sized."

"More metal between you and the rest of the world," Ron said.

"And no one but Ron drives Ron's car," Bob finished.

Ron nodded and ate some more pizza. Bob eyed him with a disgusted look on his face.

"How can you eat that shit this early in the morning?" he said. "My ass is still burning from that chili last night." At that I smiled inwardly. At least I wasn't the only one who'd had problems with the chili.

"Stomach of Iron," Ron said. "Nerves of Steel."

"Brain of Stone," Bob finished for him.

Ron took a big bite of the pizza slice and, looking at Bob, chewed for a while with his mouth wide open.

Road tripping with the three of them armed to the teeth. What a stellar idea. We'd be as inconspicuous as Michael Jackson.

"Who do you have to meet at ten?" Bob asked. He sipped some orange juice.

"A friend in the DEA," I said. "He's getting me some information on Bufonte. I doubt it'll help much, if any, but I'd rather have it than not—just in case."

"I don't remember, did you say you were in the DEA in Detroit?" Ron gulped his soda.

"For about two seconds," I said. "Mostly I worked south Florida. Dade, Broward County, the Glades, Miami proper, I worked the whole area. This was about eight years ago and things were still hot, although nothing like they were in the eighties. Still, half our informants got whacked and a large percentage of the agents were either on the take or flipping out from the stress."

"You tell your wife that?" Bob asked.

"She figured it out real quick on her own. After work I used to come home and sit in front of the TV like a vegetable, trying to relax. In the five years I was in, of the ten guys in my group, one got shot and disabled, one was shot and killed, and another had to see a shrink every other day to keep it together. The rest drank. I would've too, if I hadn't had Kelly behind me."

"How do you know this DEA guy up here?" Bob slurped at his orange juice loudly and Ron shot him an annoyed look.

"He was one of the agents I worked with in Florida. Not long after I quit, Bill—that's his name—was transferred to Detroit."

"How long have you been doing what you do now?" Ron asked. He furrowed his brow and said, "What exactly *do* you do?"

I smiled. "I quit the feds about three years back and set up shop here. I do a little PI work, divorces, workman's comp cases, but I specialize and do most of my business with security systems. Businesses call me up and I look over their place and their alarm if they have one, and decide what kind of alarm system would best suit their needs. Alarm companies do it too, but they're a little more interested in selling their most expensive systems than in installing the most appropriate one, however much it may or may not cost. I get a straight consulting fee for exactly that purpose, to assure my clients that I'm recommending what I believe is the best system for them, regardless of cost. I get most of my business through referrals."

"Make much money?" Bob asked.

"Enough that with what I make I can cover my office's rent and the utilities at home and the gas I burn driving back and forth. Maybe a little more than that, I guess."

"How the hell do you manage?" Ron asked. "Your wife make mucho bucks?"

"I won three and a half million dollars in the Florida State Lottery about three and a half years ago," I explained.

"Ahh," Bob said. "I'm beginning to see why you quit your job."

"Yeah. Kelly works, but only because she wants to. She'd be bored as hell sitting at home all day."

"This is gonna sound stupid," Ron said, "but why in the hell do you drive a Cavalier? With no extras or anything. It's not even a Z24."

"My house is paid off," I said, "as well as both our cars. I've got fifty thousand dollars in the bank. My wife buys all the clothes she wants, and we have the finest furniture money can buy, considering what we like. I've got an entertainment system in my family room that can take the roof off, with a TV large enough to use as a drive-in screen. A fancy car just wasn't a priority."

"How much do you clear after taxes?" Bob inquired.

"Ninety-seven thousand, four hundred twenty-two dollars and seventy-five cents a year, for twenty years. So far I've received a grand total of three lottery checks. Not to mention the eighty grand or so my wife and I gross every year."

"Jesus," Ron said.

"Tends to take the pressure off a bit, doesn't it?" Bob said.

"Yeah," I agreed. "It's not a fortune, but we're investing it in mutual funds and real estate, so hopefully someday it will be. We'll never need Social Security, that's for sure, and if I can ever manage to impregnate Kelly our kids'll be able to afford any college that accepts them. I'd probably have stayed with the DEA if I was single, but the stress was tearing me and Kelly apart. Hell, I'm still young. I like what I do now but I don't know if I want to do it the rest of my life. The money gives me the chance to step back and look over everything without being hassled."

"Until now," Bob pointed out.

"Until now," I echoed. I looked at my watch. Nine after nine. Steve came into the kitchen and started poking around. His eyes were a little bloodshot. I thought maybe he might've had a rough night, but he didn't volunteer anything so I didn't ask. Ron told him about my winning the lottery and he immediately asked for some money.

"Ha," I said. "I'm supposed to meet Bill at ten at a McDonalds in Dearborn Heights," I told them. "If all of you are planning on going to State, you might as well come with me. From there we can hop on Ninety-Six and take it straight to Lansing and save at least an hour of back-and-forth." They looked at me somewhat blankly, not moving. I stood up and looked at them. "So get your butts in gear," I finished.

They were ready in short order, as I suspected they would be, all crew cuts, hightops, fatigue pants, and baggy jackets to cover the heavy metal. Dress for success.

We piled into Ron's car. At the roar of the Diplomat's overpowered engine George waved noncommittally from the barn where he was doing something with or to the horses. He didn't seem too happy to see us all leaving together. I didn't blame him. The last time we were all together we'd tortured and killed a man in his barn. Maybe today we could rape some nuns and pile their corpses in the field behind his house for a bonfire.

"What kind of engine you got in this thing?" I asked Ron as we sat there. There were a lot of aftermarket gauges on his dash, but after speedometer, odometer, and tachometer, everything else was Greek to me.

"It's a big block V-8," Ron said enthusiastically.

"Here we go again," mumbled Steve.

"Had any work done on it?" I had to ask.

Ron was off and running. "Yeah! I had it bored forty over, and put in a heavy duty transmission to handle the extra power. I've got a racing cam in it, Hooker headers and a Holley carb. New rings, rods, you name it. Had to chain down the block. High flow muffler and pipes, Splitfire plugs, you name it. I had nitrous in it for a while, but not now. Too much hassle. I even thought of going for higher specs on it, real high compression, but then I would've had to run it on avgas or alcohol all the time, and you know how much that would cost."

"I have no idea what you just said," I told him.

"It goes *really* fast," he explained in terms I could understand. "Four hundred and fifty horsepower, more if I run avgas in it."

"Avgas? You mean jet fuel?"

"No," he explained. "Jet fuel is actually a type of diesel. I'm talking avgas, aviation gas, what they use for prop—propeller—engines, like Cessnas and stuff. Turbo Blue is a low grade, and it runs about one hundred thirty-six octane. High grade runs about one-sixty. I've got a drum of it in the barn, I used it to fill this baby up this morning. Four bucks a gallon, but I get over twenty more horse, not to mention slightly better mileage."

"I don't even know how to change my oil," I said to no one in particular. I noticed that we still hadn't moved, that I was still staring at the barn where I caught glimpses of George as he moved around.

Failure Drill

"How's your dad going to hear the phone ringing if he's out playing with the horses?"

"There's an extension in the barn," Ron said. He hung his arm out the window, Steve beside him riding shotgun. I was behind Steve and Bob was beside me, all of us one big happy family. The sun was already warm through the car's windshield and we rolled down the car windows to keep comfortable. None of us thought it wise to remove our jackets.

"You waiting for something in particular?" I said to Ron. "The opening theme song or something? *Drive*."

Chapter Twenty-Two

FAST FOOD

The McDonalds where I was to meet Bill was off Telegraph in Dearborn Heights, so we avoided sidestreets and stoplights for most of the way. Music was playing on the radio at what I'm sure they considered background noise level, which meant it was loud. An intense feeling of nostalgia washed over me, taking me back to my college and high school years when I rode around in cars with my friends listening to rock 'n roll.

At four minutes to ten we pulled into the parking lot of the McDonalds, which was nearly empty. Too late for breakfast and too early for lunch.

"Stay in the car," I told them. "You can see through the windows okay. If anybody walks through the door with a rocket launcher let me know. Beep the horn or something. Then get down."

Bill was sitting in a booth in one corner, his back to the wall. A cane stood next to him and I eyed it covertly.

"I don't need it too much anymore," he said, following my gaze. "But it makes it easier to beat back the horny coeds." With smiles on our faces we shook hands and I sat down opposite him. He eyed the familiar lines of my blue jacket but didn't say anything. I looked around the restaurant and saw Steve just sitting down at a table, his back to me and seemingly oblivious to everything around him. I sighed and looked back at Bill.

He had dark hair and curly eyebrows and was thick as a fireplug from his neck to the tip of his little toe. If he let it, someday his body would turn to fat, but as yet it still had a long way to go. He slid a plain manila folder across the table at me. I stared at it for a bit and then turned it rightside up and opened the flap.

"It's Anthony Quinn," I said. "But somebody really gave him a sloppy facelift." The photo was of Bufonte getting out of a car, and was slightly out of focus like most surveillance photos taken by cops were. I studied it for a while and then moved on.

Next was a somewhat detailed biography of Bufonte, which included date and place of birth—Cleveland—past criminal record, known aliases, known companions, residential address, place of business, and a whole lot of other information that was pretty much useless to me. I noted the address of his home, and also that of the restaurant he owned and probably did business out of, and ignored the rest. There was a lengthy synopsis of our government's attempts over the years to throw a net over him. I started to read it but decided it wasn't worth my time. I took the shortcut.

"So, what's the story on him?" I looked at Bill closely. "What cookie jars does he have his fingers in?" I knew Bill. He would've read the file out of curiosity if nothing else.

"Quite a few, actually," Bill said. "He likes to dabble. He started out as muscle for the Corsini family in the fifties, then quickly realized he had the smarts to make it on his own. He latched onto a couple of dreamers in the Corsini's organization and set up shop. At first no one took him seriously and the Corsinis tried to force him out, but suddenly a large percentage of them were dead. He recruited anyone he thought could do the job, not just family or Italians, and pretty soon the Corsinis were just a bad aftertaste in his mouth as he went about running their business."

"Which is what?"

"Gambling, hookers, racketeering, extortion, a little of this and a little of that. He was one of the first from the old school to see the future in drugs, and thanks to him his people control about eighty percent of the grass and coke that gets shipped to Detroit. Allegedly. At least until a few years ago. Now he's having some problems with enterprising small businessmen, but they'll get the message soon enough."

"What's he like, personally?" I asked. "I remember you saying you'd done a few cases where he or his people were implicated. What's he like?"

"He's a very simple man, actually. He does what he likes and he does what he wants and he does what he has to. He's killed, and people remember that. Very straightforward. If you cross him on a deal you get popped. If you treat him right he treats you right. Very predictable."

"Does he run it all himself or does he delegate?" I asked. "I was under the impression that he had sort of a right-hand man."

"Reginald Kellogg," Bill said. "There's a picture in there somewhere of him." I shuffled through the papers looking for it.

"The best way to describe Kellogg is like a ivy-league mobster," Bill continued, "Very up-and-coming." I found the picture and pulled it out. Kellogg was an average looking middle-aged white male, nothing special. Brown hair and thin eyebrows, and a vague resemblance to a young Dean Stockwell. I studied him thoughtfully. The Detroit Mafia seemed to be a veritable library of Hollywood look-alikes. I wondered when Brando would make his appearance.

"How much of the show does Kellogg run?" I asked. "I mean, is Bufonte semi-retired or is he still in charge and just orders everybody around through Kellogg?" If I had to go balls to the wall at some point in the near future, I wanted to be killing the right people.

"He's still pretty active as far as I know. He's not ready to retire yet."

"And you've never been able to get anything to stick on either of them?"

"Me? You mean the F.B.I. He's their darling, they'd love to get something on him. A lot of his little people have been nabbed, but big Mr. B. is clean. Hell, he even makes it easy for us if we did have anything on him. He's always at his restaurant for lunch from about eleven to one every day. Same booth even, I'm told."

"Isn't he afraid a routine will make it easy for someone to whack him?"

"With his security? The president should be so well protected."

"Anybody can kill anybody," I said.

"Go ahead and try," Bill responded. "Just make sure you sign over your lottery checks to me first." I smiled and pocketed the two pictures and the bio. I glanced out the window and saw Ron and Bob sitting patiently in the car, in a spot not too far away from the front door with an unrestricted view of me. Steve was still studiously ignoring Bill and me. I slid the manila folder back across the table.

"Well, I owe you, now, " I said. "Hopefully I'll live long enough to pay back the favor." We threw wry smiles at each other. "So, anything new happening?"

"They're building us a new building," he told me.

"Oh?"

"Yeah, about two blocks from where we are now in the Federal Building. It's gonna say Drug Enforcement Administration right across the front door, so all the dealers will know just where to go to photograph all our undercovers."

"Oh no," I said. That had been enough of a problem in the Federal Building, but at least there there were a dozen other federal bureaucracies to provide natural cover for agents going in and out. "Well, at least now you'll have your own underground garage, so you won't have to walk through the street people to get to your car."

"No we won't, that would make too much sense. You forget I work for the federal government. We're still going to be using the same old parking garage."

"Shit."

"Yeah, tell me about it. Now, if I want to go to court in the Federal Building, or see an Assistant U.S. Attorney to go over stuff for trial, I won't be able to just load the paperwork on a cart and take an elevator down to their offices or to a courtroom. Now I'll have to go out and get my G-car, double-park it in front of our new building, load my files into it, drive the two blocks over to the Fed Building and double-park while I tote all the files up to the proper room, then go back down to park the car back in the lot and *then* walk back to the Fed Building."

"You say that like it's a bad thing," I said, grinning. He rolled his eyes at me and shook his head as I stood up.

"Keep that jacket on and you should do okay," he told me. "It's supposed to get hot today but smelly pits are better than the alternative." And someone once said there were no wise men left.

I said goodbye and walked away, Steve somewhere behind me. Outside as I walked toward the car I looked through the windows and saw Bill moving slowly toward the exit. Leaning heavily on the cane.

"Did you get anything we can use?" Ron said as I got back into the car. Steve slid in beside him. I took out the photographs and they passed them around.

"Bufonte and Kellogg," I said, pointing out who was who.

"Did you find out where we can dust them?" Bob asked. He looked at me with half a smile on his face, eyebrows raised innocently.

"I know where we can find them," I said. "Whacking them is another thing altogether. Plus, I'm sure that isn't our best bet at the moment."

"What do you mean?" Ron protested. "We whack them, or at least Bufonte, and the heat is off Jerry."

"And on us," Steve said.

Bob, I'm pretty sure, was only half serious. Ron, on the other hand . . . . "Something about this ain't right," I said. "This isn't the way organized crime usually works, no matter what happened in *The Godfather*. There are way too many dead people laying around. Have any of you read the papers in the last couple days? This thing is page one, all the dead mob guys, dumbass reporters think there's some sort of turf war going on, calling for police investigation. Increased scrutiny is the one thing the Mafia doesn't want, but they would know that'd be exactly what they'd get. It doesn't make any sense. I want to find Jerry and see what he has to say before I decide how to deal with Bufonte."

"Unless he finds Jerry first."

"Which would solve some of my problems," I said. "With Jerry out of the way, they'd probably lose interest in me. Probably." I saw them looking at me. "But then," I continued, "I'd probably end up doing something stupid like going after Bufonte myself for idiotic reasons like guilt and honor and revenge."

"*Revenge is a dish best served cold*," Bob recited, "but let's hope it doesn't come to that." He smiled. "I might need more than my one week of leave."

"Sheeee-it," Ron drawled. He started up the car and we were out of the parking lot with a squeal of rubber.

"Onward and upward to higher education," Steve said sarcastically, miming taking a drag on a joint.

After only a few minutes on Telegraph we hit the expressway and headed west. Past what little traffic there was in the city at ten forty-five on a Monday morning, we settled down for the seventy-five minute trip to East Lansing. The sun was shining bright behind us, warming my neck through the rear window. We had all four windows rolled down halfway and the wind was tossing my hair. If the boys had any hair longer than an inch it would've been doing the same.

The speed limit went from fifty-five to sixty-five as we left the more built-up areas, and I watched the needle start to climb on the speedometer.

"Keep it down under light speed, Ronald," I said. "I don't want a statie pulling us over and finding out we've got enough artillery in the car to overthrow El Salvador."

"How's seventy?" he said. "Five over."

"Fine," I said. I felt like a parent, or a teacher taking kids on a field trip. I also felt that the Diplomat actually ran smoother the faster we went. Even with the four of us in the car, that monster thing Ron had under the hood wasn't straining.

The Aerosmith song playing on the radio ended and a classic song by Bruce Springsteen came on. The reaction was immediate.

"Get this goddamn ex-hippie whining-about-all-the-troubles-I've-never-had-because-I've-been-rich-my-entire-adult-life prick off the fucking radio!" Bob exploded beside me.

"Don't sugarcoat it Bob," I said, "tell us how you really feel."

"I've got a box of tapes under my seat," Ron volunteered.

"Well then, how 'bout some actual music?" Bob replied. Ron reached under his seat with one hand while watching the road. He fished out a tape, glanced at it to make sure it was what he wanted, and stuck it into an after-market tape player underneath the dash.

A horrendous grinding shrieking noise blasted from a speaker right behind my head. I jerked away, glanced at the speaker, then at Bob. He had a pained look on his face.

"What the fuck is this crap?" Bob said. It sounded like the sound effects track to the Texas Chainsaw Massacre. Steve didn't seem to care about the music one way or the other.

"Anthrax," Ron replied.

"Take it out and put in something good," Bob said.

"Up yours," Ron told him. He glanced back at us. "It's my car and we're going to listen to whatever I want to fucking listen to or we're not going to listen to anything at all." Bob tapped Steve on the shoulder and jerked his head toward the dash. Steve punched the eject button on the player and handed Bob the tape. Bob tossed it out his window.

"Hey!" Ron yelled.

"I'll pay you back later," Bob told Ron. "You have a guest, or three, and you were being impolite," he explained, sounding damn near like an English butler. To Steve he said, "See if you can find anything good in there." Steve reached under the seat by Ron's legs and pulled out the box full of tapes. He began to dig through it. Ron sulked in the front seat next to him. Bob winked at me and I smiled, then leaned back and stared out the window, privately wondering if I'd make it through the day without shooting one or all of them.

A few minutes later I noticed Ron looking steadily in the rearview mirror. He looked at his side mirror, at the rearview mirror again, then at me.

Shit, I thought. *Just my luck.*

Chapter Twenty-Three

UNWELCOME GUESTS

"What." I said. It wasn't a question.

"I think someone's following us," Ron said. Bob looked up. Steve took his head out of the box. To their credit, they didn't turn around and rubberneck. To mine, neither did I.

"What is it?" I inquired leisurely.

"A grey Ford. Two people in it."

"You sure?"

"Yeah. It's been about two or three cars back since we left McDonalds. I lost sight of it for a while when we first got on Ninety-Six, but I spotted it again a couple of minutes ago."

"You spotted it only *after* we left McDonalds? Not before?"

"No, why? Oh, I get it." Not driving, I'd paid minimal attention to who might be behind us, so I had to trust Ron. But the fact that we hadn't been followed until after I'd met with Bill had disturbing connotations. I'd used a safe phone to call him. Either Bill's hacker wasn't careful enough and set off an alarm that went to the Justice Department, or Bill had called them himself. I had a hard time believing the second. I was assuming they were feds. Probably some of Weatherspoon's boys. If they'd been Bufonte's men, they probably would've tried whacking me right there at McDonalds. They seemed to have a penchant for fast-food establishments. Why they only showed up after McDonalds could maybe be due to some sloppy hacking, but I doubted if I'd ever know for sure. Maybe Ron just hadn't noticed them before.

"Bufonte's guys?" Ron asked. His face showed a mixture of fear and excitement. Steve was grimfaced and nervous. Bob was grinning so fiercely I thought his head would crack.

"I don't think so," I said. "Probably just feds eager for a lead. But there's no way to know for sure unless we stop and strike up a conversation." Steve stopped fiddling with the box of tapes. He withdrew one and set the box down on the floor. I turned sideways slightly and saw the Ford about a hundred yards back in our lane. There were two cars between us.

If they were Bufonte's men, they would want to make a move on us, sooner or later. Preferably -- for them -- sooner. Unless they were hoping to wait until we'd led them to Jerry and get five for the price of one. If they were Weatherspoon's men, they wouldn't care if we knew they were following us or not, and would be on our bumper if that was what was required. Either option was unacceptable. If we came upon Jerry I didn't want any uninvited guests tagging along. Bufonte's guys would pop him, and try for the rest of us just for practice, and the feds would stick him in protective custody. I couldn't allow that, seeing as they probably had a leak.

"What do you want me to do?" Ron said. He was gripping the wheel tightly in both hands.

"Four hundred and fifty horse?" I asked him. I watched him in the rearview mirror as he nodded. I dug around in the seat until I found both ends of a seat belt. I clicked them together and pulled it tight.

"Lose 'em," I said. One corner of Ron's mouth slowly curved up in a mean smile. He glided gently into the left lane and punched it. The engine roared and the skin on my face tried to crawl around to the back of my head. I watched the needle on the speedometer move from seventy to one hundred in what seemed like two seconds.

"Boy, you sure can tell the difference in acceleration with four people in the car," Bob said to Ron over the buffeting wind.

"Yeah, it's almost sluggish," Ron replied. "Sort of ass-heavy or something." I couldn't tell if they were serious or not.

"Roll 'em down," I said. "Minimize flying glass if there's any shooting." We rolled down our windows the rest of the way and locked any doors that weren't. Auto glass, except for the type used in the front windshield, rarely stops pistol bullets, and glass shards thrown around by an impacting slug can be as dangerous as an actual bullet. A car door, however, sandwiched with a layer of glass in the center, will stop most handgun and shotgun rounds.

I thought about something else. "Stick that box of tapes under the seat, Steve, we don't want it flying around." Evasive moves at high speed turned any loose object in a car into a projectile weapon. As Steve complied, I turned and saw the Ford pull into the left lane behind us, rapidly gaining the ground it had lost. They didn't have a stock engine either.

"Oh, you think you're bad?" Ron said to the car's reflection in his rearview mirror.

Steve looked at me and Bob in the backseat and smiled, a little nervous still but with more confidence showing on his face. He took the tape he was holding and fed it into the player and turned up the volume. There were a few seconds of hissing dead air and then an unmistakable set of guitar chords roared out of the speaker behind me and knifed into my brain.

Stranglehold, by Ted Nugent. Old school rock, the kind that got better the louder it was played. Steve had the volume knob just halfway to top end and my brain was already vibrating loose. The speakers weren't stock either.

"Great Gonzos," I said to myself. Bob's grin was so wide it looked painful.

"Fuck yeah!" he yelled. "Uncle Tedly!"

"Wang Dang Sweet Poontang!" Ron answered with a yell of his own.

At ninety-seven miles per hour, we were coming up so fast on the cars in the left lane they didn't have time to move over. Ron didn't seem to worry about it. With his face set in a mask of concentration, he slewed the Diplomat around the other cars like he was in a slalom and they were standing still. His hands were at nine and three o'clock on the wheel, the proper position for high speed maneuvering as taught by all my precision driving instructors. A hopeful sign. I prayed he knew what he was doing.

The Ford was being more careful, but it was still there behind us, about seventy-five yards back. I took out the Smith & Wesson and held it in both hands between my legs. Bob did the same with his .44. Without taking his eyes off the road, Ron pulled his .357 out of its holster and wedged it under his thigh. He reached over and turned up *Stranglehold* as far as the knob would turn. It felt like Ted was standing inside my head and screaming at the top of his

Failure Drill

lungs. If there was going to be any shooting I wondered if I'd even hear it.

We were rapidly closing on two cars that were traveling side by side, blocking both lanes and doing close to the speed limit. Beyond them the highway curved up and away to the left, clear for over a mile. The Diplomat's speedometer was hovering near ninety-five. My heart rate had it beat.

Ron laid his fist on the horn as we came up behind the car on the left. I couldn't hear it above the music. He twisted the wheel and suddenly we were passing the car on the shoulder, two wheels on asphalt and the other two spewing gravel. I got a brief glimpse of a woman's terrified face inside a blue Escort as we hurtled by, then she was gone.

Ron yanked the wheel again and with a bump and a squeal we were back on the road. With the car in the exact center of the road, the dotted white lines vanishing under us, he put the pedal to the floor. The car surged forward like it had been standing still and kept accelerating way beyond my hopes and fears. Watching the needle on the speedometer was like watching the second hand on a clock. It kept moving forward, forward, and nothing could stop it. When it hit one-thirty I stopped looking but I could tell it didn't stop moving. The wind screamed past my ears. If the engine was laboring at all, I couldn't hear it over the music and the wind.

"GOD I LOVE THIS CAR!" yelled Ron.

Bob whooped loudly beside me. Actually, it was more of a primal scream. I looked over at him. The veins in his neck were bulging and his left hand was gripping the strap above the window, the muscles in his forearm bunched like cables.

"*One express elevator to Hell!*" he screamed. "*Going dooown!*" I barely heard him.

I looked back over my left shoulder. The two cars that we'd just passed were half a mile back. I could just make out the Ford behind them, trying to go around, but the driver apparently wasn't willing to risk driving on the shoulder at such speeds.

"Feds," I said silently, relieved. Technically I said it in a normal speaking voice, but it was lost in the din. Meanwhile, Ted was busy screaming into my ear:

"*If a house gets in my way baby, you know I'll burn it down!*"

We hurtled along the center of the blacktop, barely touching the ground. I came to the realization that at those speeds, you didn't drive a car, you aimed it. We flew over the top of a hill and saw the road for the next mile in front of us, before it curved to the right and disappeared behind some trees. There was one car a quarter of a mile ahead of us and a small cluster just rounding the bend but otherwise the road was empty. Along the side of the pavement near the curve there was a green rectangle, a sign for an exit. I couldn't read it from that distance but that didn't matter. The actual exit I guessed was some distance past the turn, out of sight. I leaned forward and yelled in Ron's ear.

"Take that exit up there," I bellowed, "and hide the car somewhere." He nodded. As we rounded the first gentle turn the Ford dropped from our sight. I felt the car speed up for the straightaway and braved a look at the speedometer. I saw the needle swing past 140 and keep climbing. Jesus Christ. If I'd noticed before that the speedometer on the Dodge went up to one-sixty I might not have been so willing to ride in it.

The car between us and the exit sign went by in a dark

blur. I didn't worry about it other than to hope it wasn't a cop. Not that a cop would've caught us, or even tried.

Stranglehold had reached a comparatively mellow point, and Ted was hissing:

"Sometimes you want to get higher, and
  Sometimes you gotta start low.
  Some people think they're gonna die someday,
  I got news, you never got to go."

I looked over and saw Bob mouthing the lyrics. He grinned at me and winked.

The second turn, designed to be gentle at normal highway speeds, was way too sharp for us, even after Ron slowed to a stately one-thirty. The Diplomat's wide tires squealed as we hit the turn and the back end started to slide out. My heart leapt into my mouth, and I had visions of us rolling, catapulting across into the oncoming lanes, turning into an incandescent fireball, the combined impact speed in excess of two hundred miles an hour.

Before the back end slid past the point of no return, Ron did the only thing to do. He performed the correct technique, the proper course of action, the thing that almost gave me a heart attack. He accelerated.

The Diplomat's engine roared, its weight shifted backward, and the rear tires stopped sliding and bit. We rocketed around the rest of the curve onto another straightaway, coming up quickly on the exit ramp. More quickly than Ron expected. He had to stand on the brakes to keep us from sailing through the intersection, but miraculously the wheels didn't lock up and there was only a slight chirp of rubber to signal our stop.

Ron turned right on the red light, cutting off a Chevy van, sped across the road on a diagonal and drove for a hundred feet on the wrong side of the yellow line before turning into a Shell station. He circled around the side of the building, narrowly missing a girl coming out of the restroom, and ended up idling behind the station with the nose of the Dodge sticking out just far enough for us to see the end of the freeway exit ramp. The gasoline sloshing back and forth in the Diplomat's tank was surprisingly loud. I pulled my legs out of the floorboards and tried unsuccessfully to keep them from shaking.

"Adrenaline rush, adrenaline rush," Bob chattered, bouncing up and down in his seat, an idiotic grin on his face. For him, this was nothing but fun.

We sat there for maybe three minutes, until it was safe to assume the guys in the Ford hadn't seen us leave the highway and were now vainly searching somewhere up ahead. The unique odor of overheated brake pads wafted up through the car. It made me harken back to my days in the DEA. Steve uncurled his fingers from the armrest and Ron, with some difficulty, let go of the wheel.

"I have to go to the bathroom," Steve said. I felt lucky that I hadn't already.

I became aware that I could hear again, albeit with a loud ringing in my ears. I looked over at the tape player.

"What, only one song on the tape?" I said. I knew I was just imagining the quaver in my voice.

"Yeah," Ron said in a garbled voice. He cleared his throat. "Don't you think it deserves a tape of its own?" He reached over and ejected the tape and tossed it into the box.

"Hang here for a few minutes," I said. "Let those guys

Failure Drill

in the Ford get a little more lost. I'm pretty sure they were feds, the way they were driving, but I'm not too worried either way. If they show up here they'll be outgunned and outmanned." Of course, once the two guys in the Ford realized they'd lost us and that we'd probably taken an exit behind them, they'd either check the previous few exits for us or wait us out somewhere down the highway. There was also the chance that they'd put two and two together and figured out that we were heading to Michigan State. They also might have done their homework and found out about Jenny. It was a near impossible long shot, but I didn't want to take the chance that someone would find Jerry before me. Finding him was becoming an obsession of mine.

I reholstered my pistol and looked around. The overgrown field behind the gas station didn't hold any surprises.

"All right," I said. "Three minutes to take a leak or whatever, then back here."

"What's the rush?" Steve asked.

"I don't want those guys putting two and two together and then waiting to surprise us when we knock on Jenny's door," I explained. I looked at my watch. "Two and a half minutes." They gave me dirty looks and we all climbed out of the car. I hit Bob on the shoulder and he quickly put the .44 away, a sheepish look on his face.

It was more like five minutes, but by then we all had happy bladders and a large supply of junk food. Ron pulled out of the gas station and cruised onto the long downslope of the on-ramp to 96 as I stuffed my face full of Salsa Rio Doritos.

As we curved closer to the highway proper, I noticed we were across from a very new and expensive Jeep Grand Cherokee. It was maroon with gold trim, and kept getting closer to us as the on-ramp merged with the Interstate. Ron kept glancing at the Cherokee.

"If this butthead doesn't move over . . . . " he said threateningly. There was a car in front of and behind the Cherokee, but there was room for it to move into the left lane. The driver seemed determined not to. I couldn't see who was inside because all the windows were darkened.

"Shit!" Ron said. I looked just as we reached the end of the on-ramp, and the right side of our car dropped an inch as the tires went from asphalt to gravel. The driver of the Caddy behind the Cherokee put on his brakes and dropped back sharply, more out of self-preservation than anything else, swerving into the left lane.

The adrenaline which had begun to leave my bloodstream now flooded back hard enough to make my heart slam in my chest. I noticed a line of posts topped with reflectors in front of us, starting about fifty yards in front of our bumper. Ron saw them too.

"Shit," he said again, hit the brakes and swung the car to the left. The rear of the Cherokee filled our windshield. I heard a squealing noise and smelled burning rubber, then we were safely in the lane about ten feet behind the Jeep. Its brake lights came on.

"Shit," Ron said a third time. He threw a quick glance over his shoulder at me. "What do you want me to do?"

"Better stop," I said. "I don't want them giving our license number to the cops, or worse, have them follow us all the way to Lansing."

"Shit," Ron said one final time. We slowed down as the Cherokee did and stopped behind it on the shoulder, hazard lights blinking. Three guys got out of the Cherokee and looked at us. We looked back.

"This should be interesting," I said.

Failure Drill

The three guys couldn't have weighed more than seven hundred pounds altogether, but they were short; not one of them was over six-six. Ron, of course, bounced out of the car and began yelling at them.

"Geez, we're never gonna get there," Steve said. The three of us got out of the car. I leaned against the passenger side with my forearms resting on the roof and watched.

"You're supposed to fuckin' yield when someone's trying to get on the fuckin' freeway," Ron yelled at the driver, in his face. He towered over Ron, had him by at least five inches, and outweighed him by fifty pounds. He was wearing a grey Michigan State sweatshirt with the sleeves cut off to show his muscles. His artificially faded jeans were artistically ripped at the knees and patched with pieces of blue bandanna. His high-tops were left stylishly unlaced. He had a dangly silver earring in his left ear and short hair, and was making an attempt at growing a goatee. Gargoyle sunglasses completed the look. The two guys with him were dressed just as spiffily.

"It's Bill, Biff, and Bart Campus," Bob said to me over the roof of the Dodge.

"Captains of Fashion," I agreed.

"I've got the fucking right of way," the driver was yelling at Ron. "It's your fucking responsibility to get onto the road, not mine! You should've stopped if you couldn't merge!"

The driver's two buddies, one white and one black, crossed their arms and tried to look mean. They looked like ugly bookends. They were huge, but they had babyfaces. Or maybe it was just age, college students were looking younger and younger to me every year.

"I didn't think the Spartans had pre-season training so early," I said to Bob, munching on Doritos I'd snagged out of the back seat. He shrugged.

"Have you ever fucking heard of common fucking courtesy?" Ron yelled up at him. The driver, probably an offensive lineman, looked about ready to hit Ron. Bob stepped up beside him. The driver looked down at Bob, angry already and now annoyed at the intrusion.

"Nice sunglasses," Bob said politely. The driver shot him a murderous glare that was pure Eastwood. I clasped my hands together and looked at Bob for his reaction. He had none. I was enjoying it all in a wary sort of way, still coasting on adrenaline.

"Nice earring," Bob said in the same pleasant voice. Cars whooshed by occasionally. I noticed Steve was watching the road for the Ford, instead of Bob doing his version of *The Good, The Bad, and The Ugly*. I slid around the front of the Dodge to see what damage had been done.

The left corner of the Diplomat was slightly scraped, and matched the right corner of the Cherokee's rear bumper. In addition, there was a black streak of burned-on tire rubber just in front of the Cherokee's bumper. All in all, the damage was negligible, not that Ron or the driver of the Cherokee had bothered to look yet.

As I was examining the damage the driver's two buddies stood and glared at me with their arms crossed in front of their large chests. They weren't glaring as much now, though, as they had been right after they got out of the car. They couldn't figure out why the four of us weren't impressed or more worried by their size.

"Who the fuck are you?" the driver said, turning his attention to Bob. He was probably half a foot taller than Bob, and considerably wider, but it still seemed to me like Bob was looking down at him.

"Jiminy Glick," Bob replied. "Nice hair. What is that, mousse?" He reached up a hand as if to touch it. The driver smacked the hand away, ignoring Bob's grin, and turned his attention once more to Ron, maybe because he was easier to figure out. He moved closer to him, trying to intimidate Ron with his bulk, but it didn't work. I wet my thumb and rubbed hard at the black streak on the Cherokee's maroon quarter-panel. With a little effort, I managed to take some off. The driver's two buddies weren't watching me any more, they were watching him. They now looked puzzled more than anything else.

"The damage isn't that bad," I said. "Just a few dents and scratches on the bumper. The rubber here even rubs off." The driver threw me a look that intimated I should fuck right off.

"It was your fuckin' fault," he said to Ron. "My insurance --" Bob cut him off.

"Why don't you call it even and give it a rest. Both of you were to blame—" he smacked Ron, who was about to object, on the back of the head, "and both of you received about the same amount of damage."

The driver looked daggers at Bob, looked seriously at him for the first time. This wasn't going the way he'd expected, not at all. He curled his lips to bitch at Bob.

Bob slid his hands up his thighs and stuck them into the front pockets of his jeans. The move made his jacket gape open, and the .44 in its shoulder holster was clearly visible. All the color went out of the behemoth's face when he saw it.

"Please," Bob said, stone-faced. The driver took off his sunglasses and looked at Ron, Steve, and I. He probably noticed that we were wearing jackets, too. Then he took a good look at Ron's car, the former police cruiser. His two friends were statues.

"We're in a bit of a hurry," I explained.

"Uh huh," the driver said. He folded up his sunglasses and stuck them in a pocket. "You're probably right," he said. He climbed woodenly back into the Cherokee with his two friends, slowly and carefully so as not to further upset us, and pulled back out onto the freeway as soon as it was clear.

The four of us got back into the Dodge and Ron started it up.

"Never, *ever* flash a gun!" I yelled at Bob, exceedingly pissed at him. "The first time someone should know you're armed is when they're looking at the muzzle."

Bob didn't like me yelling at him, but he didn't offer anything in his own defense. I leaned forward over the front seat and put my lips close to Ron's ear.

"Drive the speed limit the rest of the way and do nothing else to upset me or I will shoot you in the back of the head," I told him.

Ron didn't say a word.

Chapter Twenty-Four

NEW GUY ON CAMPUS

We drove along Grand River Avenue and the retail strip that formed the northern boundary of MSU's campus. I hadn't been back in quite a few years and a lot of things had changed. They always did.

"Who first, Jenny or Jer's boss?" Ron said over his shoulder. I looked to Steve, since he was the only one of us who knew both of them.

"Let's try his boss first," he said. He gave Ron a few directions and we hooked a left onto campus, heading south.

"Been a few years since I've been here," I said.

"Go to school here?" Ron asked.

"No, to parties during my younger, unmarried years," I replied. Bob smiled.

"Maybe the beaches are open," Ron said, and brightened up immediately.

"Yeah," Steve joined in.

"You got a lake on campus?" I said. "When did they put that in? No wonder your tuition is so high."

"No, not a lake. You'll see."

"We don't really have time to go splashing around," I said, a bit annoyed.

"You'll see," Steve said again.

We cruised south through campus, obeying the twenty-five mile-per-hour limit. There were a few people walking around, but they were nothing compared to the forty-thousand-plus students that arrived in the fall. The sidewalks then made claustrophobics yearn for rush-hour in Manhattan.

We pulled up to a light and idled. A big dormitory sat to our left. The Red Cedar River, which bisected campus running east to west, meandered by the dorm. On the grassy expanse between the dorm and the river were dozens of glistening, young bronzed bodies in stylishly small swimwear. Most of them were female.

Ron lazily trailed an arm out his open window and pointed. "Beaches," he said. I looked again.

I was working on a theory about how bikinis were getting smaller every year and I saw nothing to disprove it. I checked carefully though, just to make sure. "I should come up here more often, the campus is really beautiful," I said, and adjusted my jeans.

Bob thought that was hilarious and laughed and laughed until Ron double-parked and Steve nodded and said, "That's him."

I looked at where he'd nodded and saw a lean, middle-aged man wrestling a green beast of a riding mower around a tree.

"Okay," I said. "Can't you find a parking space?"

"On this campus? Are you kidding?" Ron scoffed like a French waiter. "They deliberately have too few parking spaces. It's the way they generated three million extra dollars last year, through parking ticket fines. Seriously, three million. I'm not making that up."

"Well, see what you can do," I said, and got out of the car and started walking. Bob and Steve appeared on either side of me.

"The goddamn Keystone Kops on parade," I mumbled to myself.

As the man drove the mower in a circle around the tree, a great cloud of dust floated up around him, covering his clothes with a layer of grey. When he saw us coming purposefully toward him he shut down the rattling engine and waited for the blades to stop spinning.

"What can I do for you guys?" he said after the mower stopped backfiring. He coughed and futilely waved at the dust.

"Do you know a kid named Jerry Phillips?" I asked him, wanting to make sure we had the right guy.

"Yeah," he said, "I know him. Who are you and why do you care?" He said it politely but I could tell he wasn't going to tell us a damn thing whether he knew about Jerry or not, not unless he was happy with our answer. He ran a hand through his hair, now dingy grey with dust. I noticed that his forearms were covered with round, pink and white hairless lumpy scars.

"We're looking for him and we thought he might've come to see you," I said. "He got himself into some trouble that we're trying to get him out of. Have you seen him recently? Last few days?"

"What kind of trouble?" he said. He inspected the considerable amount of dirt under his fingernails with a surprising degree of interest. A ragged scar trailed from just below his left ear, disappearing under his collar.

"Real trouble," Steve said. "Some people are trying to find him that he doesn't want to be found by."

"And who are you?" he said to Steve. He looked back and forth between Steve and Bob, finally resting his eyes on Bob, whom he studied thoughtfully.

"We're his friends," Steve said, motioning at Bob and himself.

"Now, if what you say is true, about Jerry being in trouble," the man said slowly, "how do I know that you're his friends instead of the other people looking for him that he doesn't want to be found by?" I glanced at Steve and saw he was getting quite aggravated.

"Well shit, we knew enough to come here to ask you, didn't we?" Steve asked him shortly.

"I'm not too hard to find," was the reply. Steve gathered himself to make another outburst.

"He is definitely not a morning person," Bob said. "He likes spicy, really spicy food. And if you have any food at all he will find some way to mooch it. He could mooch food from an Ethiopian."

The man nodded and chuckled. The cords in his lean arms moved as he absently played with his belt buckle, a nice bronze piece embossed with the Marine Corps' anchor and globe.

"Yeah, you know him all right," he said with a grin. "I swear I took that boy to raise. You'd think he never got fed at home. Food from an Ethiopian. Haw." He chuckled to himself.

"Do you know where he is?" Steve asked.

"Nope," he replied with a smile. "Haven't seen him since school let out in June."

Steve rolled his eyes at me. I grinned in sympathy -- I wanted to strangle the guy too.

"If you do happen to see him," I said more politely than I felt, "would you tell him that Bashful would *really* like to talk to him? Please?"

"Bashful?" He let the word roll around in his mouth.

"Yeah, it's a nickname," I said. We turned to go.

"How badly will he need help if he shows up?" he asked, his tone serious.

I frowned. "Very badly," I said, the implication in my voice.

He frowned back. "How bad of trouble could a college kid like Jer be in?" he said out loud, more to himself than any of us.

"If Jerry shows up at your house," Bob said, "you'd better get him to us fast. Either that or set up claymores in your yard."

"Boy, you're talkin' out your ass 'cause your mouth knows better. I--"

"Grey Ford," Steve said softly. Bob's hand darted inside his jacket and he half turned. Jerry's boss got a good look inside Bob's jacket and became quiet. His eyes quickly scanned the area.

"Where," I said, looking with great interest at my shoes. A lot of profanity I wanted to use ran through my head but remained unspoken.

"Over to the right," Steve said. I turned my head slightly and saw the Ford out of the corner of my eye. They'd found an open metered space and pulled into it, the two men inside the car sitting quietly.

"Bob, wander around the far side of that building and come up on their passenger side. We'll be joining you shortly, but don't feel you have to wait for us if anything untoward happens. I'm betting that they're feds but don't *you* bet on it." He smiled at me and walked off to our left, looking neither right nor left, disappearing behind a very old, very ugly red brick building.

"Feds, huh? Bet you guys have been having fun," the mower said. He stuck out his hand. "Richard Anderson," he said. I shook his hand.

"John Phault," I said.

Anderson's eyes kept scanning the area, flicking back over the Ford behind me every few seconds. I stood there and stared at nothing for a while, then nodded at the scars on Anderson's arms.

"Agent Orange?" I asked. I'd seen similar scars on guys I'd worked with. The scars looked like someone had put out a lit cigar by pressing it into their flesh. I was told that was what happened when you walked through undergrowth still wet with the powerful defoliant. In the sweet ignorance of youth I stupidly asked one such guy I knew why he didn't go around the sprayed area, or just wait until it dried. As I was only a young fool that didn't know anything, he tempered his response and merely stated, "Because people with guns were chasing me, stupid."

"Yep," Anderson replied. I stood there for a while more.

"If they're feds, even if we ditch them now they'll find their way back to you eventually," I told him. "They'll have three questions they'll ask you in a hundred different ways."

"A bunch of accountants with guns don't really scare me all that much," he said, smiling.

I looked at the emblem on his belt buckle again. "They'll threaten you with the IRS and God knows what else if they think you know where Jerry is and aren't talking," I warned him.

"Paper cuts always hurt like a bitch," he told me, "but they're never life threatening." He paused. "Do me a favor and let me know how this all turns out." I had to grin at him. No wonder Jerry liked this guy.

Figuring enough time had passed, I tapped Steve on the arm and we turned away. "Head toward our car," I told him, "and let Ron know what's happening if he hasn't figured it out already. Keep your eyes open for any other uninvited guests." He nodded and I veered off from him toward the Ford, which was parked about a hundred feet behind the Diplomat.

I walked in the general direction of the two men in the grey sedan, but not in a direct line straight at them. I wanted them wondering where I was going until the last possible moment. If they were feds, they'd pretend not to see me even if I was barfing on their hood.

When I was about fifteen feet from the front of their car, Bob appeared out of thin air along the Ford's passenger side and pressed the muzzle of his .44 against the passenger's ear.

"Hi!" I heard him say cheerfully. "This is a forty-four magnum in your ear, the most powerful handgun in the world, and will blow a man's -- that's you -- head clean off -- unh unh, keep looking straight ahead," he said as the driver turned his head to look at him, finally realizing something was seriously wrong. "And keep your hands in plain sight. Thanks for your cooperation."

They did as they were told, maybe because they were still in doubt as to their assailant's level of sanity. That made three of us. I reached the driver's door and peered in, standing slightly behind the driver like a good cop so if Bob had to shoot I wouldn't get hit by the bullet after it went through the man's head. It also put them at a disadvantage, having to crane their necks up and back just to look at me. One look at the two guys told me all I needed to know. Feds.

"And what have we here, me boyos?" I said in my best Irish brogue. "Are ye doin' a bit o peepin', now then? Aye, tis a nasty beezness, seetin' in a car ohl day an' watchin' theengs ohcurrin." I tsked a couple times. "If ya might kindly take out some aye-deentification and hand it over ta meeself -- slowly now, lad, no hurry. Aye, that's a baye."

The man in the passenger seat handed his wallet to the driver, who gave it to me with his own. Up close, I could see that they were both young, maybe late twenties at best, with near matching dark blue suits and Princeton cuts. They looked like fraternity brothers all dressed up for a job interview.

The wallets told me they were Matthew Harding and Joseph Campbell, aged 26 and 28 years respectively. They also both worked for the Justice Department.

"Aye, now, tis worse than I feared," I said. "They're preppy commandos after our argyle socks." Neither of them found me very funny. Maybe they were thinking about all the foot-pounds of energy Bob still held near their heads.

"We are --" the driver began in an angry voice.

"Save it," I said. I reached over the steering column, and Campbell darted his hand out to protect the keys in the ignition. I grabbed hold of the transmission lever and with a jerk snapped it off close to the column. I tossed the lever in the gutter.

"Sorry," I said, "but we're very private people. Maybe if you'd called first. We could have done lunch." Both of them gaped openmouthed at me. The driver moved his hand around vaguely where the lever had been. If he couldn't get the car into Drive he'd have a hard time following us. At least, that was my plan.

I motioned to Bob and he made the revolver disappear as he came around the front of the car. Very original and abusive profanity came from inside the still car, but neither of them got out. Both of them had enough common sense to realize they'd lost the toss, and exiting their vehicle wouldn't improve their situation any. I walked with Bob back to our car.

"That was the worst accent I've ever heard," he said. "What was it, Australian?"

"At least mine were original lines," I said. "You took yours from an old movie."

"An old, *classic* movie," he replied. "If the lines work, stick with 'em."

"You forgot to squint when you said them, though," I pointed out. "Clint would be upset."

Steve and Ron stood on either side of the Dodge as we approached, hands out of sight underneath their jackets, and they climbed in after we did.

"Onward, James," I said to Ron, and waved my hand for him to get the car rolling, pleased with myself. Without turning around he flipped me off. Bob elaborated to them about our little encounter group at the Ford. He'd handled himself well back there, and now he told the story as it happened, not bothering to embellish on the truth.

I thought about Anderson, ex-Marine Corps Vietnam vet, now mowing lawns for a living. I mumbled something about society's ingratitude.

"You've got to be kidding," Ron said to me. "You feel sorry for him? Jerry told me he makes fifty-five grand a year, not including overtime, with five weeks of paid vacation a year. *That's* why our tuition's so high."

"How come you're so down on these Justice guys?" Bob asked me. "I seem to remember something about you working for the federal government at some point."

"For the DEA, not the FBI or Marshals or any of those

other guys," I said indignantly. "You want to know why I'm so down on them, the FBI especially? We've got a saying in the DEA, it goes 'DEA makes the cases, FBI makes the headlines'. The FBI is practically ten times the size of the DEA in manpower, yet the DEA makes more arrests than all other federal agencies combined, *including* the FBI. But whenever there's a bust by a federal agency on TV, it's always the FBI, right? That's because they're always the ones who call the press. They're one big PR machine, meanwhile we're busy arresting people." I was on a roll now, warming to the subject. "Next time you see a story on TV about feds making a drug bust, see if they mention the DEA. I'll bet you they don't. But they'll be there, everybody's supposed to call them for any kind of federal bust involving drugs. The same goes for any kind of case involving bombs, the BATF, Alcohol, Tobacco, and Firearms, is supposed to be called, and usually is. But the FBI'll take most if not all of the credit, sure as shit. The DEA doesn't feel its main purpose in life should be to curry favorable public opinion, so calling the press ain't real high on the list of priorities when a bust goes down."

"Sorry I asked," Bob said.

"What about the ATF guys, what're they like?" Steve asked me.

"Of the couple hundred ATF agents I met and worked with in my five years with the DEA, I'd say roughly five percent of them could find their ass with both hands and a flashlight."

"That's what I thought," Steve said.

It's not the organization's fault, per se," I went on, "it's just that ninety percent of what the ATF does is harass gun owners that *have* registered their legally owned weapons, because those people are easier to find than the criminals who buy their illegal guns on the black market. So what kind of people do you think would be attracted to that kind of job? Nobody that you'd ever want in a position of authority, that's for sure."

There was a parking lot across from Jenny's dorm that actually contained a few empty spaces. Ron pulled into one and cut the engine.

"I take it you're not going to go in and say hello to your lost love?" Bob said to him. Ron looked at him silently. "I didn't think so," Bob said with a smile. The three of us got out of the car and crossed the street towards the dorm.

Chapter Twenty-Five

DORM LIFE

"What dorm is this again?" I glanced upward.

"Tsk, tsk, tsk," Steve said. "They are not referred to as dorms anymore. They're residence halls. It's a very important difference."

I smiled with the corner of my mouth. "That's what I thought," I said. "I was thinking about it intently one afternoon, while watching a daytime drama on TV and listening to the sanitation engineers outside collecting my processed consumables."

"Glad you've got it straight," Steve replied.

There was a directory of the residents in the lobby in a glass case on the wall. Steve quickly found Jenny's name and we headed for the stairs, not necessarily out of choice this time. I didn't see any elevators, at least for public use. The dorm looked pretty old. I looked to Bob and saw he wore a grim face.

"What's the matter?" I asked. "Did you have a falling out with Jenny too?"

"No," he said. "It's not that. I hate stairwells."

"What?" I asked. We stopped before the fire door to the stairwell. Bob smiled sheepishly.

"We used to play with paintguns in houses under construction in my subdivision," Steve explained. "Hunt each other with those guns that shoot paintballs, you know, trying to use proper room clearing techniques." He gestured at Bob. "He always used to get nailed on the stairwells."

I smiled. "It's good to be afraid of something," I said to Bob. "Trust me -- elevators are worse." I slapped him on the back. "You go first."

He gave me a dirty look and pushed open the door with his left hand. His right was inside his jacket on the .44. The stairwell was wide and well lit, with large landings at and between each floor. I could only assume that this made moving the furniture easier for the parents come spring and fall.

We went slowly up to the fourth floor, Bob in front and Steve behind, pausing at each landing to check the next flight up. On the fourth floor we went down a hall and around a corner and Bob knocked on a door.

"Who is it?" a sweet voice asked from inside.

"Lumpy, Grumpy, and Dumpy," Bob said.

"Dumpy?" I said. "Thanks a lot."

The door opened and Jenny appeared. Somehow I managed to keep my tongue in my mouth.

She was a light-skinned blonde wearing a tight white midriff-baring T-shirt and baggy shorts that proclaimed MSU across front and rear. The T-shirt was tight because she was what my old roommate in college used to call topheavy. Overabundantly so, and it appeared to my untrained eyes that she'd neglected to put on a bra that morning. Her flat stomach and toned legs said she worked out regularly.

God I missed college.

Once I got finished looking at her I looked into the room and saw there was a large loft covering the back half of the room, a desk near the door, as well as several portraits of half-naked muscular males occupying the left-over space on the walls.

Her face lit up when she saw Bob and Steve, then got anxious and worried when she glanced down. I guess she saw the lump in Bob's jacket and knew what it meant. It didn't show that much, but considering who her friends were I'd bet she knew what to look for.

"What's the matter?" she asked warily.

"Have you seen Jerry lately?" Steve said in answer to her question.

"No, why? What's the matter?" Her eyes dropped and rested on the lump under Steve's jacket. Her lips were thin lines as they pressed together with worry.

"He's in real trouble. We thought he might've come here."

"No, I haven't seen him in over a month. Why would he come here? What's wrong with his house?"

When she said that she hadn't seen him, my positive attitude bit the dust. I don't know why I was disappointed, I should've expected it -- or worse -- with the luck I'd been having.

"It's too much trouble to explain now," Bob said. "Plus, we're in sort of a hurry to get back home. We don't know the whole story, anyway. Let's just say he pissed off the wrong people."

"Who's he?" she said suspiciously, pointing at me. Her eyes examined my jacket and didn't come away happy.

"He's a private investigator," Bob said.

"A private investigator! What --"

Failure Drill

"Don't worry about it now," Bob cut in, putting a hand on her shoulder. "You know it won't do you or anybody else any good to worry about it."

"What kind of wrong people are these that he's pissed off that I don't have to worry about?" she demanded.

Bob looked down and awkwardly kicked a toe at the ugly carpet. "The mob, probably," he told her.

An exhalation of shock and dismay sprang from her lips involuntarily, and her hands flew to her hips, in preparation for a tirade.

"Just do me a favor," Bob said rapidly, before she could start up. "If Jer calls or shows up, let him know we were here looking for him. Have him call Ron's house. Will you do that?" From the look on her face I couldn't tell whether she wanted to cry or yell.

"You guys show up here unannounced, carrying guns, all freaked out with worry over Jerry, ask me where he is, but then don't expect me to want some answers to some questions? What the fuck?"

This is Bob freaked out with worry? I thought.

"Will you do it?" Bob asked her. "Please. We don't have any extra time."

"It's important." Steve stressed each syllable. She reluctantly nodded.

"I'll tell him," she said. "But if I don't hear from him, I'd better hear from one of you assholes so I know what's going on."

I smiled -- I could guess why Ron had broken up with her, she had a mind of her own and probably refused to put up with his crap.

"Do you still have the pistol we bought for you?" Bob said.

"Are you kidding?" she replied. "With all the rapes on campus last year?"

"Good. Don't go paranoid, but it might be a good idea to keep it close. If we thought to check with you, there's a small chance, maybe one in a thousand, that the people after him will, too. Not to mention the feds."

"The feds?"

"Don't ask," I told her.

She was literally dying to ask some pointed questions, but instead she just bit her tongue and tried to look unperturbed. As she glanced back and forth between Bob and Steve, I saw a sudden look of enlightenment come across her face, like a light bulb had popped on over her head.

"You guys are really loving this, aren't you?" she said. "Whatever it is. This is what you've been hoping for all your lives. A chance to prove yourselves."

Bob didn't answer her at first, I could see he was trying to decide what to say. Hell, I'd only known them a week and I could see she was right on the money.

"Don't forget to have him call," he said finally. "We've got to go." Bending down, he kissed her lightly on the cheek. He backed out of the room and she smiled ruefully and gently closed the door.

"Shit," was the only thing Bob could think of to say. We started walking back towards the stairs.

"Do you know Ron's definition of the difference between a slut and a bitch?" Steve asked me with a smile. I shook my head.

"A slut gives it to everybody," he told me, "and a bitch gives it to everybody but you."

"Figures," I said. I snuck a glance back at Jenny's door, pondering what 'everybody' might mean. Steve reached the stairwell door first and held it open, making a sweeping motion with his free arm.

"You first, Mr. Paranoid," he said to Bob. Bob shot him a dirty look and went through the doorway, his hand on the gun butt under his jacket. I followed right behind him.

As Bob stepped onto the small landing, we heard a soft rustle and a dark-haired man in an overcoat came around the corner and stepped onto the landing below us, pulling out a sawed-off double-barreled shotgun.

As the identity of the object in his hands registered on my brain, and I started to reach for my gun, I knew I was going to be too slow. My arm felt like it was moving through molasses as I watched the muzzle of the shotgun rise to point at me. This was going to be it, the instant of my death, and somehow I felt cheated. All my preparation and then I get ambushed before I even find Jerry.

Suddenly Bob's .44 Magnum exploded beside my head. The gunman below us fired just as the heavy slug hit him in the right side of the chest and spun him around. The sawed-off sounded like a nuclear blast in the stairwell, not that I could hear out of my left ear anyway.

I stumbled back from the blast, disoriented, and then Bob grunted and lurched against me. What little balance I had left was lost. My right hand, which would've been the one closest to the railing, was inside my jacket gripping the pistol I'd attempted to draw in a futile effort to save my life, and I couldn't do anything to stop my forward momentum.

As I twisted my already horizontal body sideways to more absorb the impact of the fall, I saw another man appear on the landing above us, holding an identical sawed-off. Steve, his gun already out, stepped onto our landing and shot him in the stomach. The man doubled over and his shotgun went off with another ear-deafening blast.

I caromed down the stairs, banging my head hard enough to see stars, doing a backward somersault in the process, until I landed with a thump and a grunt on the body of the first gunman. *Death by Three Stooges*, I thought dazedly. *Nyuk nyuk nyuk.*

I looked up, blinking, to see Steve and Bob firing into the second gunman's body as it tumbled down the stairs toward them. They didn't wait for it, instead they rushed down to me just as I got into an approximately upright position on top of the bloody gunman. A lot of blood was running down the left side of Bob's face and down his left sleeve. Steve's jeans where they covered his shins were shredded and bloody and he was limping. Bob grabbed me with his left hand and hoisted me up with a grimace. The stairwell was clouded with gunsmoke and the smell of spent gunpowder and blood.

"Move!" I tried to yell. It came out more like a gasp. "They probably had a spotter to tell them when we were heading for the stairs, and I've had enough fun for one day!"

We heard a cough and looked down to see the first gunman clawing at the wall, trying to right himself. His fingers left crimson streaks on the blood-spattered wall. Bob shot him in the head and we ran and stumbled down the rest of the stairs to the lobby, the two of them with their guns out, supporting me with their free hands. The knock on the head I took had caused me to lose all coordination in my limbs.

Bob kicked open the stairwell door to the lobby and went through it gun first. He had my collar in an iron grip and dragged me stumbling along behind him. Steve limped along behind us.

We went through the lobby in a stumbling jog, guns out

and covered in blood. The girl behind the desk screamed and hid, and most of the other people in the lobby dived for cover. As we went by I yanked down on a fire alarm on the wall. It started shrieking immediately.

Through the glass and aluminum doors and outside, and I was getting some of my muscle control back. We ran towards the parking lot, dodging the cars in the street. Halfway to the car I saw Ron with his revolver in his hand, standing behind the open driver's door.

"What?" he yelled. "What the fuck's going on?"

"Start the car!" I screamed at him. I was gasping and sweating from the adrenaline pumping through my bloodstream. So were Bob and Steve. There was a cold spot between my shoulder blades where I imagined the next bullet would hit unless we made tracks, and fast.

We piled into the car and Ron took off with a squeal of rubber. He didn't bother to back out of the parking space, he just drove straight over the curb and grass, ignoring the pedestrians and fishtailing onto the road. By then I'd determined I hadn't been shot, and was searching the road behind us for signs of a tail.

On curvy campus roads designed for a hair-raising maximum possible speed of 35 mph Ron kept the needle above 50 in an impressive display of driving skill, narrowly missing several dozen students as we put distance between us and the blood covered stairwell.

"Where are we going?" Ron yelled as we left campus and hit East Lansing.

"A hospital," I said, looking at Bob, whose face and arm were covered in sticky blood, his chest heaving. Steve had his head leaned back on the seat, his teeth gritted together against the pain. *Shit, wait a minute, hospitals have to report gunshot wounds, and you aren't carrying a badge anymore, buddy. And with our luck we'll go to the same hospital they take the two guys in the stairwell to and get nabbed by the local cops for murder until proven otherwise.*

"No, wait," I corrected myself. "A hospital won't be safe, not this soon."

"Where then?"

"Flint," I said, thinking fast. "I know a doctor there that'll help us and won't report the gunshot wounds. Keep this thing under the speed limit!" I snapped at Ron as he put on a new burst of speed now that he had a definite destination. "We don't need to attract any more attention. And watch the road behind us. I don't want any more surprises."

I took off my jacket and threw it on the floor. The back of it was covered in blood, that of the first shotgun-wielding hitman whom I'd landed on. I noticed that somewhere along the way I'd lost a shoe.

With a relatively clean rag I found under Ron's seat I wiped the blood off Bob's face as well as I could. About a dozen shotgun pellets, small ones, had struck him in the left side of his head. There were two red furrows in the skin above his eyebrow, curving around the corner of his skull, and his hair was matted with blood, but the pellets didn't appear to have hit anything major. His eye was undamaged, thank God. The bleeding had been profuse but was already slowing. I pulled back his jacket to look at the wound in his shoulder. He'd been hit by another half dozen or so pellets in his large deltoid muscle and bicep, but the pellets hadn't gone very deep. They also appeared to have entered his body at a different angle than the ones that had hit his head.

"Ricochets, maybe," I said. "Off the wall of the stairwell. You're lucky." He grinned at me. His teeth were stained pink with blood. It was a gruesome sight.

"Rock and Roll," he said.

Seeing Bob was more or less back to normal I leaned over the seat to check on Steve. He had what was left of his jeans pulled up and was examining his legs which were covered in blood from the knees down.

"How bad is it?" I said, grimacing in sympathy. I handed him the rag and he swabbed at his shins.

"Not too bad," he said, his jaw clenched tight. "Looks worse than it is, I think. I caught some pellets in my legs. Birdshot, looks like, those dumb fucks. I think most of the pattern went right between my legs. Nothing fatal. Hurts like a bitch, though." He eased his pants back down and leaned back against the seat, pain on his face.

"Your ear's bleeding," Bob said to me, his voice gluey. He hawked and spat a pink wad of phlegm out the window.

"From your forty-four," I said. "Went off right next to my ear."

"You're shouting," he pointed out.

"No shit." I was still shaking with adrenaline.

"What the fuck happened?" Ron demanded. I saw that we'd made it to I-69 already and were heading east. The speedometer needle hovered right at 65, the posted limit.

"What happened was I'd be dead if it wasn't for Mr. Reflexes, Wyatt Earp here," I said, poking a thumb at Bob, who'd opened the cylinder of his .44 and was extracting four spent cases. He replaced them with fresh rounds from a speedloader he pulled from his pocket.

"Ambush," Steve said. "In a stairway. Two guys with twelve-gauges, sawed-off. We were damn lucky."

"Is Jenny okay?" Ron asked worriedly.

"She's fine," Steve told him.

"They screwed up on their timing," I said. "They should've popped out at the same time, and one of them was a second too slow. Even then Bob nailed the first one before he got his gun up, before the second one turned the corner. If they'd done it right, and Bob had normal reflexes, probably all of us would've died even if we'd managed to get one of them. That stairway was like shooting the proverbial fish in the barrel."

"How did they find us?" Steve said from between his clenched teeth.

"I don't know," I said, upset and wired and angry. "They must've been behind the feds, and when we lost the feds we lost them. They probably followed the feds for lack of anything better to do, not wanting to go back empty-handed. When Campbell and Harding found us again, so did they. I never thought to look for a second car following us, but still, they must've been pretty good for us not to have spotted them, especially driving on campus."

"Not good enough," Bob said, and smiled. His teeth were still pink.

"No, not good enough," I said. I sounded strange, but I told myself it was because I had only one good ear to hear myself with.

Chapter Twenty-Six

ANY PORT IN A STORM

Ron kept to the speed limit and in just about forty minutes we hit Flint. The sweat and blood had dried on us and we made quite a pretty sight. All our hardware was away but we kept a keen eye out for unwanted tailgaters.

Steve and Bob had been pretty quiet for most of the trip, not enjoying the pain after the adrenaline rush wore off. My ear was aching as well. I told Ron which exit to take off the freeway and, after five minutes and a couple turns, we were in an older, well-kept neighborhood.

"Where are we going?" Ron asked.

"My father-in-law's," I told him. "He is -- was -- a doctor. Retired."

"Surgeon?" Bob asked.

"What?"

"SURGEON?"

"Gynecologist," I said.

"Now there's a man I can respect," Ron said.

Every once in a while Steve would shake his head, pinch

his nose, work his jaw up and down. "My ears are still ringing," he complained.

We glided to a stop in front of a medium sized, two story red brick house with white trim house and an immaculate lawn. We all got stiffly out of the car and waited while Ron opened the trunk and pulled out the shotgun I'd seen him with the night before. It seemed like a year ago. He held it down along his leg and I led our procession up to the porch.

My father-in-law was actually home. I was pleasantly surprised. He stood there and stared at us for a second, his mouth open.

"Hi, Lloyd," I said. "Can we come in? You leave us standing out here too long and the neighbors might talk."

"Ub," he said, hesitated a second, then backed into the living room. The four of us followed him in and Ron shut the door behind us, locking it.

"This should be an interesting story," my father-in-law said after he got his mouth working, crossing his arms in front of his bony chest.

"I don't really have the energy to tell it," I said truthfully. I did manage to work up enough energy to introduce him to everybody, then lapsed back into exhausted silence. My mother-in-law came into the room.

"Who is it dear?" she said. If I ever got the chance to meet Santa's wife, I was sure that she'd look just like my mother-in-law. Fluffy white hair, usually pulled back into a big bun, rosy cheeks, not to mention the fact that she was the nicest person anyone would ever want to meet. When she saw me she smiled handsomely. When she saw the others, the smile turned a bit puzzled. When she saw the blood and the shotgun her face went grey and rigid and she about-faced out of the room.

"Thirty-six years married to a doctor, you'd think she'd get used to the sight of blood," Lloyd said with a grin. "C'mon." He took us into the kitchen and sat us in the chairs there. Ron stayed by the front door with the shotgun, looking out the windows.

"I don't know what instruments or supplies, if any, I have in the house, but I'll see what I can find," my father-in-law said.

"Thanks, Lloyd," I said. He nodded and left the room. In about five minutes he was back with an assortment of items wrapped in a towel, which he spread out on the kitchen table.

"Who's first?" he said. I pointed to Bob. Bob took off his jacket and shoulder holster with a little help. His T-shirt was stuck to his skin with the dried blood, and Lloyd had to cut it off.

Lloyd took some clean cotton rags, soaked them in warm water, and gently wiped off Bob's shoulder. The entry wounds from the pellets were puffed up red dots in his skin. He wiped Bob's head, getting everything I'd missed. Bob's hair was short enough most of the blood came out easily.

"I don't have any anesthetic," he said, "but the wounds that aren't grazes don't look too deep, so I shouldn't have to do a lot of poking around." He directed a questioning look at Bob.

"Go for it," Bob said, grinding his teeth together.

My father-in-law took the fancy medical equivalent of tweezers and began to work on Bob. Occasionally he needed a little help from a scalpel to get at pellets just under the skin of Bob's head. Bob's face started to bleed again, and Lloyd wiped at it intermittently. Bob took it all without a sound, although I could see from his varied expressions that it didn't feel good.

Lloyd held up something between the tines of the tweezers.

"Copper-plated shot, number four I'd say," he said. "Good rabbit load. I don't suppose you guys had a hunting accident. Or two." None of us answered him, so he went back to working on Bob, mumbling to himself. He made a small pile of bloody pellets on the towel, talking to the room as he did.

"Haven't done anything like this in a long time," he said. "Not since I was a resident and had to take my turn in the Emergency Room. Of course, back then, there wasn't nearly the carnage you see today, but I can tell you from experience if there's something longer than it is wide some kid'll manage to poke himself in the eye with it. And don't even get me started on seatbelts."

Every once in a while Bob would grunt as Lloyd probed for a deep pellet, but other than that we all kept silent. When Lloyd was done taking pellets out of Bob's head he moved on to his shoulder.

"These pellets here aren't very deep," he commented. "How far away were you from the gun when it went off?"

"About ten feet," Bob said. Lloyd looked up, startled. He turned quickly to me.

"I know you'll tell me what the hell is going on here," Lloyd said, "sooner or later, and I'm not going to press. But I want to hear, with my own ears, right now, that my daughter isn't involved in all this."

"It has to do with my business," I told him. That, at least, was partially true. Lloyd wasn't too happy with the situation, but there wasn't anything he could do to change it, so he went back to work on Bob.

"Is there a chance these ricocheted and hit you?" he asked Bob.

"Yeah," Bob said, "that's probably what happened. Off the wall to my left. You got any beer?"

"I don't know. There might be one or two in the icebox. I --"

"I'll check," I said. I got up and went over to the refrigerator. When I opened it and bent down to look inside, a tiny copperplated pellet fell out of my hair and bounced on the floor. It looked a lot like the BB's I used to shoot out of my air rifle when I was a kid, only slightly smaller. I stared at it a while and then grabbed the only two beers inside.

"Ricochets," I said to Bob, and handed him a beer. I stuck the other one at Steve but he shook his head, so I cracked it open and took a long swallow. The cold liquid felt good on my throat.

My father-in-law finished pulling out the pellets he could get to in Bob's arm and took some suturing thread and a small, curved needle. He stitched up the two grooves above Bob's eyebrow, slowly at first, then quicker as the moves came back to him. Every time I saw it done I was amazed at the tiny knots doctors could produce.

With a gauze pad and first aid tape he covered the wounds on the side of Bob's head. "I can bandage up the other holes in your head," Lloyd said, "but the bandage might obstruct the vision in your left eye."

"Forget it then," Bob said. "Just do the arm." In a few short minutes Bob's shoulder and upper arm were tightly wrapped in white gauze and tape. He moved the arm around a little, to check its mobility, then nodded.

"Who's next?" My father-in-law turned to face Steve and I. Steve pointed to me. Lloyd slid his chair over to me and looked at the side of my head.

"What happened to you? Your hair is singed. What's that, a powderburn?"

"A large caliber pistol went off very close to my ear," I said, looking straight at Bob. He shrugged and drank some beer with his good arm. I did the same, trying not to move my head as my father-in-law swabbed the dried blood from my ear and neck.

Lloyd wet down one end of the Q-Tip and very gently worked his way inside my ear. He had to be very careful and it took a long time for him to clear away enough dried blood to see what was what. I've experienced things that felt better. He peered into my ear with the help of a penlight older than me.

"You've probably got a ruptured eardrum," he said. "If so, there's not much I can really do now. Half the time they heal by themselves. Unless you want a real thorough examination, and I can't give you that here, the best I can do is clean your ear out and disinfect it."

"Do what you can right now," I said. "Later on I'll have it looked at at a hospital."

"For the next few days you've got to keep it dry, or it will get infected," Lloyd warned. "Trust me, you don't want that. I'll give you something to help fight infections, but seriously, you've got to keep it as dry as you can."

"I'm not planning on going for any swims."

"We're you planning on getting into a gunfight today?"

He had a point.

After swabbing out my ear for a while with hydrogen peroxide, he turned my head to the side and squirted something warm in it to clean it out. I couldn't really hear out of that ear, and every once in a while a sharp pain would go lancing through my skull, but all in all I felt rather lucky to be experiencing *any* sensation. Lloyd wiped off the side of my head with a clean rag and stuck a wadded piece of cotton inside my ear. I pointed out the bump on the back of my head and he probed it with his fingers, making me yelp. After examining it for a second he reached over and handed me two aspirin and patted me on the shoulder. Doctor humor.

"Take those pants and shoes off," Lloyd said to Steve, "and put your legs up on a chair."

I stood up and slid my chair over to him, then walked back into the living room where Ron stood by the window with the shotgun over his shoulder. I handed him the half empty beer.

"Thanks," he said. He emptied the can in one long swallow and handed it back to me. I grinned and he grinned back. I'd stared death in the eye once again and lived to tell the tale. It shouldn't take a brush with the reality of my own mortality to make me appreciate the small things in life, like an ice cold can of beer, but that's the way it was. Like the song said, you don't know what you got 'til it's gone.

I gave Ron a long, hard look. "You guys did good out there."

"I can understand if you're surprised," he said, "but I'm not." He paused, then added, "Although we're a little disappointed in *your* performance."

I stared at him for what seemed a long time, mouth open, as he frowned at me. Then, finally, the corner of his mouth twitched.

"Oh you motherfucker," I said, as he exploded in laughter. "You rotten, miserable bastard." I went back into the kitchen and set the empty on the table next to Bob's. The laughter faded away and then I heard a loud belch from the front room.

"Ron's always been a class act," Steve said, then hissed as my father-in-law probed for a pellet.

My ear was still plugged up and probably would be for some time, but the hurt had started to go away. I'd always had good hearing and I hoped one ear could do the job for two until the other one healed.

"What size shoes do you wear?" I asked Lloyd.

"Eleven and a half," he replied. "Why?"

"Close enough," I said. I held up my shoeless foot. "Mind if I borrow a pair?"

"I let you take my daughter, I guess a pair of shoes isn't that big a deal."

I wandered into his bedroom and peered into the closet. Most of the shoes were formal and slipons, and ugly, but I noticed a relatively new pair of Adidas high-tops in one corner. With a wry smile on my face I shook my head and grabbed the high-tops. No one said anything about my new shoes when I went back into the kitchen. Lucky for them. I let Lloyd keep my one shoe for good luck.

Bob's shirt and Steve's pants and socks were pretty much history, so my father-in-law loaned them some clothes. They fit pretty decently, too, although Steve didn't seem too fond of brown corduroy.

"Are you pussies done getting worked on?" Ron said, walking into the kitchen with a big smile on his face.

"I'd beat the shit out of you if I thought it'd be any kind of challenge," Bob retorted tiredly.

My mother-in-law made another appearance after Lloyd assured her it was okay. I introduced everybody again and she offered to make us something to eat. I declined and she didn't seem too disappointed. Lloyd handed me a huge bottle of antibiotics and directed us all to take copious quantities of them or else risk serious infection. We made the proper sounds of agreement. I promised to have Kelly call them and then we left.

Failure Drill

Bob was favoring his left arm and Steve had a permanent grimace on his face when he walked, but on the whole we were in good shape. Especially considering how we could've looked if we hadn't made it out of the stairwell.

"Where now, home?" Steve asked. The four of us sat in the car in front of my father-in-law's house, gathering our energies for yet another car ride together.

"Yeah. We're still not any closer to finding Jerry, but at the moment I can't think of anyplace else to look, and he can always find us there." They nodded their heads in agreement.

"If this keeps up," Bob said, "maybe we can win by attrition. What are we now, five and oh?"

"Hah hah," Steve said dully. Ron started the car and we left.

By the time we made it back to Ron's house we were all starving. George came out of the barn as we pulled up, saw Jerry wasn't with us, and shook his head to let us know he hadn't had any luck either. A few choice words were muttered by all.

Bob had soaked the bloodstains out of his windbreaker, and I'd sponged off my jacket, but George still noticed the bandages and the new clothes. He also had eyes to see Steve's limping and Bob's arm hanging strangely.

"What happened?" George said warily.

"We ran into a little trouble," Bob said. "Again," he added needlessly. "I'll explain while we eat."

We had grilled ham and cheese sandwiches and potato salad while Bob told the story. We all ate like cops at a free buffet. Adrenaline must do something to the appetite, probably a leftover survival trait.

"If I live long enough, I'll get fat eating over here all the time," I said when Bob had finished his tale.

"What are you going to do now?" George asked.

"I have absolutely no idea," I said profoundly. "Which seems to be a recurring theme in my life. I've reached the sitting on my ass and waiting stage. Anybody else has any ideas, let me know."

"I have some work to do on the Jeep," Ron said, "so I'll be here if Sleepy calls. Take care of what you have to do, maybe one of us will think of something."

"I have to make an appearance at my house sometime this week anyway," Bob said. "I haven't seen my parents in eight months. If I came home for a week and never stopped by the house, my dad would find me and hold me down so my mother could break my legs. I was there to grab my clothes last night but they weren't so it doesn't count." He smiled. "But first, I have to make up a story about how I got this," he continued, tapping the bandage on the side of his head. I looked at Steve.

"I have no interest in hanging around the house with my parents or going to work," he said, "so I might as well play chauffeur some more if you need it."

"I know this thought probably hasn't crossed any of your so-called minds," I said, "but you can still bow out of this. After today I wouldn't blame you. I'm sort of surprised you haven't."

"You shouldn't be," Steve said. "Jerry isn't a fair-weather friend. What happened today scared the shit out of us, but it sure as hell wasn't something that we weren't expecting." He paused a second and replayed that over in his mind, making sure it'd come out right with the double negative.

"You forget, bwana," Bob said to me, "backing out now wouldn't do any good anyway. We killed those guys today, not you. If they saw anyone grabbing Valenti, it was us. That makes us targets now, if not by Bufonte -- who may or may not find out -- then by the feds or whoever will be investigating our handiwork up at State. Christ, I guess that means I've got to dump my .44," he cursed.

"Your nine, too," I told Steve. "Although you left a bunch of cases in that stairwell with your prints on 'em."

Steve shook his head. "I wore gloves when I loaded my magazines," he told me.

I could only stare at him. "Who *are* you guys?" I said.

"Play it out to the end," George said to me. "You got no choice, now. None of you."

"Yippee kiyay," I said, giving them a lackluster toast with a can of Diet Coke. "If we're gonna split up tonight, then, don't forget to watch your backs."

"Paranoid is my middle name," Bob said.

"I thought it was Erwin," Ron said with a grin.

"God I wish I drank," I said to the ceiling. I thought about my plans for the evening. "I should call my office, see if there are any messages on my machine."

There were two. One was from Weatherspoon, which contained a demand that I call him in and phrases like 'pointing a loaded weapon at a federal agent' and 'destruction of government property' in and amongst a lot of really creative profanity. The other one was from Kang Distributing telling me my order had arrived and could I please come down to the warehouse in person and pick it up.

"Anything?" Bob asked when I hung up the phone.

"Maybe," I said. "I'll find out soon enough. C'mon, Kato," I said to Steve. We headed outside, Ron behind us with some rags and a toolbox in his hands. As we walked past the Dodge parked by the barn, Steve stopped and looked at the car.

"Hey Ron!" he said. "These supposed to be here?" I looked and saw three round holes punched in the right rear quarter panel of the Dodge.

"Hunh," I said.

"What?" Ron asked, and came around the end of the car. When he saw the bulletholes he stopped short.

"Are those what I think they are?" Steve said.

"Probably," I replied. "Can't think what else they'd be."

Ron bent down and touched the holes in his car. "Shit!" Ron shouted. "Shit!" He threw down the rags and toolbox and pulled out his car keys from his pocket. He yanked open the trunk and peered inside. I leaned over the edge and did too. Surprisingly, none of the rounds had pierced the inner lining of the trunk.

"Hunh," I said again. "Must've been thirty-eights or something like that without a lot of power. You're lucky."

"Goddammit!" Ron said. He didn't appear to be feeling very lucky. "You work months on a car, treat it like a baby, and *this* fucking happens! Why couldn't they have hit a window? Because those are cheaper and easier to replace, that's why! Now it's gonna take me a couple weeks to fill in those goddamned holes and sand them and paint them and God knows what else."

"Poor baby," I said. "Maybe they should've shot you in the head instead."

"Need less Bondo to fix it, that's for sure," Steve observed

We walked over to my car and climbed in. Steve was driving, if for no other reason than because he figured the bad guys would shoot the driver first, and I was more important to finding Jerry than he was. I would've argued if I'd thought it would do any good, or if I had half the energy necessary to either drive *or* argue.

"Where?" he asked.

"Head for I-75, southbound," I said. "I'll direct you from there."

"Great. Another long drive."

"Just shut up and drive, you whiny bitch," I said, fighting back a smile. I looked out the windshield. After a few seconds of nothing, I looked back at him.

Steve was staring out the windshield, but I don't think he was seeing Ron's yard. He blinked strangely a few times. "I was in a gun fight," he said in seeming disbelief. His face screwed up and it looked for a second as if he was going to cry, and his hands started shaking violently. He grabbed the steering wheel to still them. "Holy shit," he nearly whispered, then looked at me.

"Yeah," was all I said.

Chapter Twenty-Seven

OLD FRIENDS

Charlie Kang, as Kang Distributing, owned a warehouse with a small parking lot, part of the latter overshadowed by the maze of ramps connecting the Southfield Freeway to I-96. The area looked like a set from Escape From New York, but the rent had to be cheap.

I had Steve stay in the car and walked to the warehouse alone. The secretary in the small office up front wore make-up like Tammy Faye Bakker and had a hairstyle that was thirty years out of date. The office smelled like she'd last bathed when her haircut was in style. I told her who I was and that Charlie was expecting me. She buzzed me through a door in the wall behind her. On the other side I found myself in the warehouse proper, just one huge area, larger than it looked from the outside, with too few windows and a high vaulted ceiling. There was a lot of hustle and bustle, more than I'd expected from the still parking lot. Two fork-lifts were busy unloading a couple of semis, stacking pallets loaded with boxes against one far wall. I looked at the boxes and recognized a lot of brand names. Too bad I wasn't in the market for electronic equipment. Charlie was standing in the middle of the activity, watching, and waved me over when he saw me.

Charlie had a bland, forgettable face with lively, darting eyes and, as always, wore an impeccably tailored suit. He stood about five feet eight with a wiry body and a permanently courteous demeanor. Even when he'd been beating the crap out of that guy in the bar he'd been polite, calling him "Sir" as he littered the floor with his teeth. A small scar on his left cheek gave his face a little distinction.

"You're still keeping in shape, I see," he said.

I shrugged. "You have some news?"

Charlie smiled like a politician. "My, my, impatient, aren't we? I guess that's understandable." He waved his hand around at the busy forklifts and a man in a hardhat using a drill in a far corner. "No one can bug us in here, at least," he said. "Not that they'd ever have reason to." I let him see a small smile.

He continued. "I found out some things I think you'll find very interesting."

"The chase, the chase, cut to the chase," I entreated him. He smiled with a corner of his mouth, then laid it on me.

"Pietro Bufonte is *not* trying to have you killed," he said. He waited for my reaction with a smile.

"I'd hate to see what would happen to me if he was," I said. "He must use tactical nukes. What the fuck are you talking about?" His inscrutable act only went so far with me.

"Mr. Bufonte does not want you dead. He was, in fact, unaware of your very existence until this morning." Charlie, the born storyteller, stopped for a dramatic pause. My head was spinning too fast for me to object.

"You are in no danger from Mr. Bufonte," Charlie went on. "However, you aren't so lucky when it comes to Reginald Kellogg."

"I'm not . . . I don't get it," I said. "Who?"

"Let me tell you a story," Charlie said with a grin. "Once upon a time there was a right-hand man to an important figure in organized crime. This figure, however, was growing old. His aforementioned right-hand man began to think that maybe he could do a better job of running the company, so to speak. The problem, though, was that he didn't have the money or the manpower to take over the position. And he is *such* an impatient man. So, he dabbles in a few transactions here and there, making money, a lot of it, and friends, too. Pretty soon, he's made enough dough to think he has a chance to go it on his own. The idea was to establish a power base before he attempted, shall we say, a 'hostile takeover.'

"There was a snag, though, for in his business dealings, which he made behind his boss' back, using his boss' name, his clients came to think, reasonably enough, that they were doing business with the Boss, Grand Guinea Number One himself. You see, not many people would have the stones to do business behind the back of this guy, and this right-hand man knew it, used this to his advantage. I suppose it wasn't too hard to make people think that everything was on the up and up. Even the stone-faced guys in the sunglasses and off-the-rack grey suits were fooled." He smiled again.

"When some of these clients turned witness for the feds, for whatever reason, and the feds began poking their noses around even more than usual, this right-hand man started getting nervous. He wasn't ready to step up to the throne yet, he was still gathering money and support. Then the shit hit the fan. These clients turning witness found out they'd been working for Goombah Two instead of Goombah Number One. They found this out while they were under protection, supposedly safe and secure. It suddenly dawned on them that if Kellogg found out that they knew about his dealings behind his boss' back, he might want quite badly to kill them to keep their mouths shut. And that Bufonte might want to kill them because they'd inadvertently helped Kellogg in his rush for power." Charlie paused a second. "They must've been idiots. Apparently the fact that a lot of Italian-type people in the area might want to kill them as soon as they found out these guys were turning stool pigeon, no matter what the other factors in the equation were, never occurred to them. The unknown in this is what exactly made these guys, these prospective witnesses, think the federales couldn't adequately protect them. Treachery? Incompetence? Your guess is as good as mine. But I assume they considered the threat a very real one. I would. And, as you might expect in such a case, they took off."

"They rabbitted, and now two of the three guys are dead," I said. At least now I had the whole story. It made me feel a little better, even though my situation hadn't improved any.

"Three," Charlie said. "All three of them are dead now, as of last night. It seems someone shot the last remaining hotfoot seven times as he came out of a restaurant. Police are calling it a gang related drive-by shooting." *Of course at a restaurant*, I thought. *Where else?*

"Kellogg would want me dead," I reasoned aloud, "because I was looking for Jerry, who witnessed his guys kill Potential Witness Number One. I'm not a cop, so they figure I'm a nobody, they can whack me without drawing any heat. With me gone, they can find Jerry at their leisure, make sure he doesn't do any talking. At least as to who did the hit, he'd be able to ID people. How did you find out about all this?" I asked Charlie.

"A little bird told me," he answered. "It told me sometime this morning, right after Bufonte somehow found out what Kellogg was planning. Maybe one of Kellogg's recruits was getting cold feet after seeing how miserably his new boss was faring against one lousy part-time P.I. with a juvenile taste in shoes." I looked down at the high-tops I had on and smiled. "Bufonte didn't take kindly to the fact that his protégé was planning to usurp the throne, although that is how he himself got to the top."

"What time this morning did this happen?" I asked him. "When did you find out about it?"

"It all came down about six hours ago," Charlie said. "I found out about it shortly thereafter. Why?"

"That should've been plenty of time for him to call off his dogs," I said to myself. I told Charlie, "Less than four hours ago two of Kellogg's men tried to kill me, and now I can't figure out why. If Kellogg's double-dealing was public knowledge by then, what reason would he still have to kill me? I can't believe revenge, or even frustration. That would be too wasteful of people, a resource he needs right now more than ever." I didn't get it. "Where is Kellogg right now?" I asked him.

"If I knew that, I'd make a lot of money selling Bufonte the address. No, no one knows where he is. He's gone into hiding, I assume so he can regroup and try to figure out if he can still overthrow Bufonte, now that he knows it's coming. Personally, I don't think he can. Not enough resources. But he has to try, there's no going back."

"Then I don't get it," I said. "Why the hit today? Bad communication? The guys that came after me left before the news broke?"

"Maybe," Charlie said with a twinkle in his eye, "because it's rumored that the first ex-witness had something in his possession that belonged to Kellogg. Something worth a great deal of money."

"What?"

He shook his head. "I wish I knew. My guess is that since Kellogg is still after you, he thinks this kid, or even you, has whatever it is that he wants."

"Great," I said. "Listen, can you give me a black box for my phone to keep out unwanted listeners? Office phone. Buy or rent, hopefully I won't need it for too long, but I'm gonna need it quick."

"It will be in your office and hooked up before the sun sets," he said poetically.

"How are you going to get into -- never mind, I don't want to know. How do you find out all this stuff? About Kellogg," I said, amazed at his intelligence network.

"A little bird told me, I said that already," he replied with a smile.

"And why are you telling me all this?" I asked. "I know you could make a lot of money selling this information to some people."

"Out of the kindness of my heart?" he said hopefully.

"No such animal, my friend," I said. "Your main motivation is greed." I paused and the simple answer came to me. "I know why," I said. "Could it be that if I stir up Bufonte and Kellogg enough they'll start a war with each other, and you can be there to step in and take over their business? You ready to move up from the wholesale industry?"

"What can I say? The enemy of my enemy is my friend, as the saying goes. And you have been doing remarkably well, I'll grant you that. Keep it up. But perhaps you overestimate me. After all, I am only a simple Chinaman." I knew his simple Chinaman story word for word, and already had a lot to think about, so I begged off and said goodbye. He wished me luck, the bastard.

"Anything?" Steve asked when I got back to the car.

"Everything," I said, and proceeded to tell him all I'd learned, even though I knew I'd have to tell it at least once more. I had to tell someone.

"So you think whatever Kellogg wants back, Jerry has?" he asked me. "Where would he have gotten it?"

"Beats the shit out of me," I said. "Kellogg would've had someone check the personal effects of the two guys Jerry killed. I'm assuming that what he wanted was supposed to be there and wasn't. Something those guys took off the target at the Burger King after they whacked him. Jerry took a gun off one of the guys, maybe he took the thing, too. Either that, or Jerry's had other run-ins with Kellogg's people that we don't know about and snagged it then."

"What do you think it is?"

"I'd guess it's something incriminating Kellogg in something illegal, otherwise why would he go to all this trouble to get it back?"

"Why hasn't Jer turned it into the cops then? It would take the heat off him."

"Fuck if I know," I said. "Maybe he doesn't know what he has. Maybe he's seen too many mob movies, doesn't think he can trust the cops 'cause there's bound to be one on the take. Also, remember, he saw the hit. He killed the two guys we think did it, but the cops didn't find an abandoned car in the area. That means there was probably a third guy, a driver, that got away along with the murder weapon. Jerry could finger him, so he's technically still a threat to Kellogg and his people even if he doesn't turn in this missing evidence."

"Great."

"Very," I agreed. We stopped at a gas station about a block away from the warehouse and I called the number Weatherspoon had left on my machine amid the four letter words. He answered on the second ring.

"You rang?" I said.

"Who is this?" he demanded gruffly.

"John Phault."

"You, my friend, are in very serious trouble," he said to me. Like that was a big news flash.

"You must've been talking to my wife," I said. "What do you want?"

"I want to talk to you. In person. Where are you now?"

"Unh-unh," I said. "You wouldn't like the area, you might get mugged. I'll meet you somewhere." He gave me directions and I said I'd meet him there in forty-five minutes.

"What does he want?" Steve said.

"Probably wants to yell at me for destroying government property," I replied, remembering a transmission lever that used to be attached to a grey Ford. "Or arrest me, he's sure got probable cause. But he didn't even mention that, so I'm not sure. Guess we'll find out."

"You seem awful cheerful for a guy who might be getting arrested."

I smiled at my companion. "I'm just happy I finally know what the hell is going on."

The meet was at an Arby's on Mound Road in Sterling Heights. I wasn't surprised. It seemed like I'd spent half of my recent life in fast food restaurants. It felt like I was getting close to the end of this thing, Jerry Phillips or no Jerry Phillips. Weatherspoon and Gaines were sitting side by side in a booth in a corner, two cups of coffee untouched on the table in front of them. They both wore sour looks.

"My, don't we look chipper," I said. I left Steve in the car. It was better if he didn't show his face. Too bad I didn't have that option.

"Sit down and shut up," Weatherspoon said. They were obviously in no mood for banter, so I made nice and sat down.

"If you would've told me about your involvement in this at the beginning, it would've made my life a lot easier," Weatherspoon said. He scowled at me.

"At the beginning of this I didn't know I *was* involved," I said. "Since then I've been kinda busy to sit down for a fireside chat."

"Speaking of your being busy, you wouldn't know anything about a double homicide up at Michigan State earlier today, would you? It happened right after you vandalized the vehicle of two of my agents and left them stranded."

"A complete accident on my part," I explained. "A slip of the hand. If you like, I'll pay for all the damages." He waved a hand, dismissing the idea.

"Two guys were shot dead in a stairwell in a dorm up there," he said. "One was shot in the chest and again in the head with what looked like a cannon they tell me, half his brains were on the wall behind him. The other guy was shot six or seven times. When Harding and Campbell heard the sirens they had to run over on foot to see what was happening. They took over from the MSU Department of Public Safety, pissing off about seventy people, when they recognized one of the dead guys as a known associate of Bufonte. They tell me the two dead guys had sawed-off shotguns, and the stairwell was littered with shot and some blood that probably wasn't from either of the two stiffs, as well as a bunch of nine-millimeter empties."

"Hunh," I said.

"Listen, wise ass," he snarled, leaning over the table at me. "I can cuff you right here. Take your gun. You know I've got probable cause. How'd you like that? Do you really want me checking your gun's ballistics against that of the murder weapons up there?"

If he'd wanted to arrest me I'd already be in the back of his car. He didn't want me so much as what I knew, and he wasn't sure what that was. Maybe I wouldn't have been so cocky if bullets from my gun had actually found their way into anyone. As for Weatherspoon, he was probably measuring the length of his future with the DOJ in days.

"Do it," I said. "Or don't do it. But don't waste my time with threats. While you're checking the rifling on my gun the clock'll still be ticking."

Weatherspoon apparently didn't want my ass just yet, because he sat back and brooded for a while.

"Harding and Campbell were the ones who actually identified the bodies," he told me after a minute. "At least one of the stiffs worked for Bufonte."

"Yeah, you said that."

"Actually," Weatherspoon corrected himself, "they *used* to work for Bufonte. Nowadays it seems they were doing a lot of work on the side for Reginald Kellogg."

"Curiouser and curiouser," I said.

"Do you know about Kellogg?" Gaines asked me, speaking for the first time since I'd sat down.

"If you mean about his going into business for himself, yeah, I just found out," I said.

"We were this close to nailing him and Pietro," Weatherspoon said with a sigh. "You heard our third witness got popped?"

I nodded. "So you have no case now."

"Maybe. That's why I wanted to talk to you. You want the kid that's missing. Kellogg wants the kid too. Badly. Badly enough to try and kill you to keep from finding him first. I still don't know why, and I really don't care, but if I can, I'm gonna turn it to my advantage." I wondered absentmindedly if Weatherspoon's informant was the same person giving Charlie his information. "It was the search for the kid, you know, that alerted Bufonte that something was up. Kellogg was using too many of his people and old Pietro got suspicious, nosed around, and found out what was up. It could be that Kellogg just wants to kill the kid out of revenge. He ain't Italian, but he's been around them long enough to know what a vendetta is. But I'm not buying it. He's too smart for that. Do you know why he's still after the kid?" he asked me.

I shook my head. "What do you want from me?"

"I want you to find the kid," Weatherspoon said.

"I've been working on that," I said. "So far I haven't had much luck."

"Find the kid," Weatherspoon said. "Then we can use the kid to draw out Kellogg. Entice him either with the kid or whatever the kid has that he wants. Then maybe we can nail him."

I shook my head, disgusted. "You want me to help you use the Phillips kid as bait because you fucked up. That's great. Like he doesn't have enough problems already."

Weatherspoon shrugged. "Kellogg's going after him already," he said. "What does he have to lose?"

I could've told him, told him that Jerry would be safer with me and his friends than with Weatherspoon's people, if Harding and Campbell were any example of the Justice Department today, but it wouldn't have done any good.

"Fuck," I said. "And I took this case as a favor to someone, too. Okay," I told them. "I don't see as I have any choice." Helping the feds was the only smart move I had left. I knew that, and he knew I knew that. Jerry's friends wouldn't fit into any equation he would put together, so he'd have no reason to believe I wasn't sincere. I needed to keep Weatherspoon off my back for another day or two. Things were moving too fast to last much longer than that. "When I find Phillips I'll let you use him as bait. But I want a couple things first," I told them.

"Of course you do," Weatherspoon said, rolling his eyes at Gaines. They'd been expecting some sort of quid pro quo.

"One," I began, "I want you out of it. Don't tap my phone, don't follow me, or I'll make what I did to Harding to Campbell look like a self-confidence seminar for agents." They didn't say anything, so I continued.

"Also, I've been working with some people," I began.

"People?" Weatherspoon laughed. "From what I hear they're just kids."

"Kids or not, you *know* what happened up at State. A first-year agent could look at that scene and figure it out. Call it another drug-related shooting involving a suspected on-campus drug ring, and then bury it." It was a totally justified shooting, but between our fleeing the scene and the boys' lack of CCWs there was no shortage of things we could go to jail for. "Believe me when I say you'll never be able to get anybody on murder charges for what happened there. That's an old building, with no interior security cameras, especially not in the stairwell, and eyewitnesses are notoriously unreliable. There aren't any guns to match those bullets to. The only people that know what happened in that stairwell aren't going to tell the authorities anything that'll help get them put in jail. In fact, they won't be saying anything without a lawyer present. Trust me on that." Weatherspoon hadn't said anything, I couldn't tell whether he was in shock from my demands or what, but I decided to press my luck.

"They weren't there," I told him. "I want your promise on that."

"Now, I don't—" Weatherspoon began.

"It's the deal, I said flatly. If he managed to keep his job, he'd be able to maneuver the murder investigation in any direction he chose. "I want them left alone as you can leave them. They've saved my ass more than once already, and if they had badges they'd be up for commendations. I don't want their lives ruined by an arrest on their records."

Weatherspoon's face was a deep purple, but he didn't say anything so I kept on. "I have a feeling we're going to be seeing some more shit together before this is all over. If you think they're out of control now you're wrong, but if they think they're facing serious prison terms I can't tell you how they'll react. Leave them alone or when Phillips pops up neither one of us will ever see him or his friends again. You think I'm wrong? Look at these kids' goddamn track record. They're lucky and stubborn and smart. See how far you get trying to dig up Kellogg if they split with Phillips."

We both knew Kellogg would show up eventually, but if Weatherspoon brought him in it would look a hell of a lot better to his superiors than if Bufonte left his bullet-riddled body in the middle of a street somewhere. Weatherspoon stared daggers at me and sat there visibly trying to calm himself. Probably counting to ten.

"Not out of control?" he said slowly, repeating my words. "What do you call Donald Valenti?" I didn't even blink when he said the name. He sighed and sipped some coffee, looking out the window.

"What's the matter with your head?" Gaines asked me, pointing.

"Gunpowder tattooing," I told him.

Weatherspoon jerked his head away from the window and stared at me. He leaned sideways a bit to see what Gaines was looking at. The powderburns didn't look like much, just black speckles, but maybe a thread of cotton had worked free and was sticking out of my ear.

He and Gaines glanced at each other. I couldn't read their expressions, but some signal must've passed between them.

"All right," he said. "But you do this wrong, if it goes down twisted, you'll be in so much trouble along with your playmates, your heads will roll so fast you'll think you stepped onto fucking ground zero. Both of us know that if this thing squirrels any more out of our hands you and your buddies are going to take a major fall no matter what promises I make." He stopped and sipped some coffee, then continued at a slower pace. "I'm going to pretend I've never heard of Donald Valenti," he said. "It'll save us both a lot of hassle, and he should've been killed a long time ago, anyway. I've never heard of him, that is, until you fuck up. Then the investigation starts, search warrants and all." He gave me a pointed look. "But your little buddies? Don't let them bump into some dumb beat cop, 'cause if they get caught carrying it's their asses. I've got enough headaches.

And try to keep them from shooting anybody else, if that's possible."

Another sip of coffee, and he said, "I can't believe I'm doing this. Christ."

Neither could I, but I knew why he was -- he liked his job and wanted to keep it. That, and he was probably still trying to ferret out the leak in his organization. He was backed into a corner just like I was. He made getting up motions. "Anything else?" he said to me.

"Yeah," I said. "Second Chance, if you've got 'em, but either way I need five bulletproof vests. Size Large."

Chapter Twenty-Eight

EVEN A BLIND HOG....

"Well?" Steve said when I got back to the car.

"We're out of the frying pan for the mess up at State," I said, "although whether that's permanently or not I don't know. He recommends we don't do it again. Oh, and just for the record, the two guys up at State were Kellogg's."

"How the hell did you arrange that?" he wondered.

"I agreed to set up Jerry as bait if and when I found him. They want Bufonte and Kellogg so bad they can't see straight."

"You what?"

"Don't worry about it," I reassured him. "About the only thing I can guarantee is that that's not going to happen." I sighed, then pulled the small recorder out of my jacket pocket. I hit the Stop button.

"What's that?"

"Audio recording of a federal agent agreeing to cover up a double homicide." I shrugged. "It's vague and of limited legal value, definitely not enough to put him in jail, but it's great leverage if I need it. He won't remember exactly what he said, so I'm sure he'll imagine it's a lot more incriminating than what it actually is."

"Damn," he said admiringly.

"Find another phone," I told him. "I've got to call Ron."

"Why?"

"Listen and learn," I told him. He scowled at me, but we found a phone and I called the Kelly's. Ron answered after two rings and said hello hesitantly.

"It's John," I said. "Any news from Jerry?"

"No, nothing." I shook my head at Steve and he scowled again.

"I didn't think I'd be that lucky," I said. "Listen. There's going to be a package delivered there in a little while."

"What?"

"I'm getting five Kevlar vests delivered to your house, compliments of the Department of Justice and Special Agent Weatherspoon. I didn't want you airing out the delivery boy so I told them to use a grey Ford like the one we had fun with earlier today." God, that was only earlier today? It seemed like last week. "The feds have more grey Fords than you'd care to know about. Don't answer the door. Officially, they were never there. And keep your eyes peeled. If you remember, Weatherspoon's the one that lost the witness that started this whole shebang. We're both betting he's got a leak in his department. I told him to use someone he trusts, since I don't want Kellogg finding out where I am, but you never know."

"My dad should be around for a while, he can watch my back," Ron said.

"Later," I said, and hung up. I pursed my lips and looked at the car. It was a simple problem, really. I could drive it to where Jerry was and pick him up and take him back to his friends, if only I knew where he was. It was the simple problems that made life a real bitch.

"We go anywhere else and we're going to have to get some gas," Steve said, seeing where I was looking. I chewed my lips for a while, thinking, then nodded.

"All right, I need money too, and time to think," I said. "Let's go."

"Where?" Steve asked.

Where turned out to be the ATM in Royal Oak where Jerry had been four days before. The bank was long since closed, and Steve parked in the lot with extreme disregard for the lines on the blacktop. We got out and I stretched with more energy than I thought I had left. Then I fell back against the front of the car, my energy reserves exhausted. I'd hoped going to the bank would give me a fresh angle on where Jerry might be. As I stared at the empty parking lot, I realized I should've known better.

The ATM was set into the bank's wall, surrounded by a booth. It was about thirty feet from me, which was about thirty feet farther than I wanted to walk. With a grunt I got up anyway and started toward the booth, just two spare walls and a roof to protect the user from the elements. I pulled my bank card from my wallet as I made the seemingly endless trek to the machine. My ear throbbed with pain, and I had a headache that wouldn't quit. I'd taken a handful of Tylenol, but they'd barely even taken the edge off.

Done feeling sorry for myself, I stepped into the enclosure and fed my card into the machine. It digested the piece of plastic and hummed for a while. I punched in my personal identification number and it hummed some more. I looked around the stall as I waited.

The walls of the booth were done less than tastefully in

textured aluminum, built to withstand graffiti instead of look good. It was a neat idea, but man had yet to create a material that could withstand the attack of a pimply-faced fourteen-year-old with a five dollar knife.

The walls were, in fact, completely covered with the scratchings and doodlings of bored bank customers. I punched a few more numbers into the machine and entertained myself by reading the offered prose.

Most of the scratchings in the aluminum were either homophobic or denigrating to females, and it made me wonder what the hell was the age limit for issuance of an ATM card. Led Zeppelin, a perennial favorite, made quite a few appearances, along with a few other strange word combinations I assumed were bands of the heavy metal genre. END IGNORANCE -- KILL A MORON and HITLER HAD IT RIGHT were a few examples of what passed for biting social commentary.

I punched in some more numbers and the machine began to spit out twenties at me. In large, deeply cut block letters near the machine were the words, STUPID PEOPLE SHOUDNT BREED. Next to that was scratched, SLEEPY WAS HERE 8/21 1500.

I picked up my money, grabbed my card and receipt, and was halfway out of the booth before it hit me. I went back and looked at the graffiti again. It still said SLEEPY WAS HERE 8/21 1500. I looked at my watch and saw it was almost six, and said something that would've shocked a Marine. Then I saw the line through 8/21 1500. Below that was scratched 8/22 1500 in slightly fainter lines. They looked very fresh. I stood up slowly, a wide grin spreading across my face. I suddenly didn't feel very tired any more.

"That in-depth, hardcore detective work will do it every time," I said to myself. I did a goofy two-step and stuck my head around the corner of the partition and curled a finger at Steve.

"Oh Steve dear," I called out to him, "would you come here, please?" He grumbled something, but got off the hood and walked over. I stuck a finger at the graffiti and leaned back against the other wall, my arms folded. Steve bent down to read what was cut into the aluminum. I saw his back stiffen, then he checked his watch.

He stood up, grinning, and looked at me. I grinned back. We stood there grinning at each other like a couple of fools for a while. If I had any rhythm I'd have asked him to dance. After a minute I said, "Aren't you glad you have a world-class detective such as myself to help you crack this case?" I thought his face was going to split, his grin was so wide.

"Better to be lucky than good," he said. At that, we both broke into laughter and I walked back to the car laughing so hard I thought I'd pass out.

Chapter Twenty-Nine

SATAN COMES TO CALL

We pulled into Ron's driveway and saw him bent over under the hood of the Jeep, just inside the barn door. He stood up as we shut off the car and walked over.

"Problems?" Steve asked. He was still smiling.

"No, I'm just jerry-rigging a platform for the battery," Ron said. "The other one's rusted through." A shotgun was leaning against the Jeep's fender, a step away from Ron.

Steve still couldn't wipe the grin off of his face. I wasn't having much luck either. Ron grunted and started to bend back down over the car, but stopped halfway and stared at us.

"What's with you two?" he said. "You look like you just got laid or something."

"Nothing much," Steve said nonchalantly. "Just that we know where Jer is going to be at three o'clock tomorrow afternoon." Ron soon had an identical goofy grin on his face.

"Damn," he said. "Jer must've figured we'd find out about him using his money card, or someone would, but he left the message in a sort of code so only we'd know it was from him."

"You're lucky I knew his nickname," I said. "Although he probably wouldn't have rescheduled a rendezvous too many more times. If we didn't -- if *you* didn't show up for the second meeting I bet he'd have finally called here. We'll know tomorrow, hopefully. Did the package come?" I asked Ron.

"Yeah, the vests are inside. How come there's five?"

"One for me, because I need to keep this jacket open in front to get to the gun under my arm, but an open jacket isn't giving me any protection in front. I figured that out in the brief second I was staring down the muzzle of that sawed-off shotgun. Adrenaline's real good for those bursts of intellect. Vests for the three of you, so you don't become statistics, and one for Jerry if and when we find him."

"Don't say if, say when," Ron said. "And when is three o'clock tomorrow in Royal Oak."

"Don't have your wet dream yet," I said. "We still have a lot of other problems."

"Nothing that can't be solved with a suitable application of high explosives," Ron said with a grin.

"This ain't no guardhouse gate, dufus," I told him, and headed inside the house, leaving him wondering how I knew about his high school adventures. When I used the phone I found there was a message from Mrs. Phillips on my machine, asking if there were any new developments. She tried to sound angry that I hadn't turned him up yet, but she just came off sounding scared and worried. Technically her three day retainer had run out, so I didn't feel quite as bad as I might've for not calling her back. I called home on a whim and Kelly answered.

"Hi," I said, surprised.

"Hi," she said back. "Are you coming home?"

"Not yet," I replied. "Soon, hopefully. Another day or so and a lot of my questions should have answers. Don't tell me you're alone in the house?" I said, a hint of worry creeping into my voice.

"Don't worry, I'm fine. Scott has two men guarding me in shifts. In fact, I just talked to him a little while ago. He said to tell you that Justice was breathing down his neck and he had to throw them a little meat to keep them satisfied. Does that make any sense to you?"

"Yeah," I said. I was surprised it hadn't happened sooner, but Scott's neck could take a lot of heat.

"Do you still want me to head to my parents'?" Kelly asked me. "This is shit here. I can't go to work, I can't go out, I'm sitting here watching talk shows and MTV all day, I can't concentrate enough to read. It literally is torture. At least at my parents I'll have someone to talk to besides cops."

"No, I don't think it's a good idea anymore," I told her. "Besides, can you see your mother with two cops in the house? Down here, at least you'll be close. Hold on a little while longer, I'm doing the best I can. I don't think the house or you will be a target anymore, the guy after me can't really show his face, but you never can tell. He might think it's worth it to kidnap you to get some leverage on me. It's best if you just stay put. Who's guarding you?"

"MacPherson and Stevenson. I assume they're cops, at least they act like it, but Scott really didn't say. One of them looks familiar."

"Burglar broke into MacPherson's apartment in the middle of the night. Mac says the guy jumped out the window trying to escape. Burglar says he was thrown. Bad guy's paralyzed from the waist down, since Mac lived on the third floor, and is now suing Mac and the apartment complex for umpteen millions. MacPherson is going to need all the money he can make for his legal bills."

"I saw that on the news."

"All over the news."

Stevenson I didn't know, but if Scott was using him he was okay. There wasn't much more I could say to Kelly, and if I stayed on the phone too much longer I'd start to miss her too much, so we said goodbye and I hung up.

It was after six and I was beginning to get tired again. I looked around wearily and saw the stack of vests on the kitchen counter. There were rated for threat level IIA, which meant they'd stop most pistol bullets up to a .44 Magnum. Of course, no soft body armor made would stop a rifle bullet, but luckily shoulder arms weren't in vogue with the majority of bad guys. Hard to conceal an assault rifle inside a pair of low-rider jeans. I didn't think I was in any danger in the kitchen, so I left them on the counter, laying my jacket down beside them.

Steve called up Bob to tell him the news about Jerry. They talked for a few minutes, then Steve hung up and told me Bob would be over later that night after he'd had dinner with his parents. Apparently they hadn't asked him about the holes in his head. They knew better.

I found some Italian sausage in the freezer and some green peppers, cheese, and French bread in the refrigerator and made myself a sandwich; grilling the sausage, melting the mozzarella, and toasting the bread. It tasted better than it had any right to, given my degree of culinary skill. The diet Coke was cold, which meant it tasted just a little bit horrible.

Ron rolled in and together with Steve heated and ate three large frozen pizzas and split four beers. While they were doing that I revealed all that I'd learned from Charlie Kang about who was really after Jerry, and the tentative why, as well as the details of my conversation with Weatherspoon and Gaines. Most of it was old news to Steve but he got excited again anyway, hoping that the end was in sight.

Around ten o'clock Steve left to pick up Bob. I assumed he was successful because Bob was sleeping on the other couch when I woke up at one-thirty, my contact lenses sticking to my eyes and my back sore where my shoulder holster was digging into it. I stumbled into the bathroom, took out my contacts, used the facilities, and stumbled back out into the family room, passing Steve who had guard duty and the shotgun. It took me forever to fall back asleep, somewhere close to two minutes. I dreamt someone kept chasing me with a gong and hammer. Every once in a while they would catch up and bang it right next to my ear. The dream changed and suddenly I was in a car with faulty brakes hurtling down a road at a hundred and fifty miles an hour. I was just about to collide head-on with a grey Ford when I woke up with a jerk. Bob was gliding through the motions of *T'ai Chi Chuan* in the middle of the room again, the bandages from his head and arm removed to show dark red spots and streaks where the pellets had hit. They didn't seem to bother him.

"Good morning," he said after he'd finished. "You really zonked out last night."

"It's my advanced age and deteriorating physical condition," I said. "How's the head and arm?"

"Sore and stiff, but I'll live." I nodded and struggled to get up off the couch. With a few grunts I was vertical and headed off to take a shower.

Still wet behind the ears, I put on the last of the clean clothes I'd stashed at Ron's. Under my baggy T-shirt I strapped on one of the vests that I'd grabbed as I went through the kitchen. With the Velcro straps adjusted right, unless I bent over it didn't show at all under the shirt. When I headed back out, I was alone except for a single Kevlar vest on the kitchen counter. I slid it over to one side; it wouldn't be needed until three o'clock, if then.

I heard movement upstairs, but didn't see anyone. I grabbed the last bagel from the refrigerator, slapped some cream cheese on it, and began to eat as I wandered through the house. It was quite large and I wondered what George did for a living to be able to afford it, especially with the odd hours he kept. A top of the line computer occupied desk space in the library. Law books filled the shelves next to the computer. I shook my head in confusion. He sure as hell wasn't a lawyer.

When about half the bagel was gone I found myself in the living room. I peered out one of the bay windows into the front yard and observed two squirrels maniacally chasing each other through bushes, trees, and over the lawn. Moving so quickly I could barely follow them with my eyes they circled around a tree, shot up it, shot down, then darted across the lawn toward the driveway. Just as they scurried across the gravel drive into some bushes I noticed a car turning into the driveway.

I stopped chewing. "Hey, Ron," I called out. "Do you know anyone who has a new, brown, Cadillac DTS?" The noises upstairs stopped as I waited for an answer.

"No," he said warily. "Why?"

"Because someone who has a Caddy knows you," I said. The car slid slowly to a stop in front of the house and I moved away from the window, drawing my gun. The Caddy was immaculate -- it looked like it had just been driven out of a dealer's showroom. There were two men inside but I couldn't see them too clearly because the car's windows were tinted.

Three seconds after the car stopped, the driver stepped out, shut his door, and walked toward the house. He was a slim, dark haired man in his late thirties and was wearing a grey pinstripe double-breasted suit that fit him perfectly. It looked much too warm for the season, but he wasn't sweating. The suit, his white shirt with French cuffs, and salmon colored tie had set him back the cost of a decent used car if I knew anything about clothes. I got a distinctly bad feeling from him, maybe due to my growing paranoia of all strangers, maybe not. My gun was in the best place it could be if I was expecting trouble, in any case.

I heard movement behind me and Ron appeared, shotgun in hand. As our visitor rang the doorbell, Ron shouldered the shotgun and placed the muzzle against the glass of the front window with a slight click. I could see that the man on the porch heard the click, but had enough self-control not to look in its direction. If he was what I thought he was, he probably could guess what had made the noise.

As the doorbell chimes faded, I said loudly through the closed door, "Can I help you?" I sensed someone and turned to see Bob watching the stranger through the window.

"I am looking for Mr. John Phault," the thin man said loud enough to be heard inside.

"Never heard of him," I said.

"I was under the impression that he was at this address."

"And what makes you so sure you have the right address?" Ron said, keeping his cheek against the stock of the shotgun.

"Mr. Pietro Bufonte would very much like to talk to you, Mr. Phault," the man said, smooth as silk. "He was kind enough to send his favorite car." He stood patiently on the porch and waited, his hands clasped in front of his body, looking like he had all the time in the world. We both knew that wasn't so. I looked at him for a few more seconds and then went into the kitchen for my jacket.

"How do you know it's not a trick?" Ron hissed. "He could be from Kellogg!" Steve had appeared and was standing in the foyer looking at me.

"I don't think so," I said. "I don't know why, a hunch maybe. This isn't Kellogg's style. He seems more prone to violence than subterfuge."

"If you go, I'm coming with you," Bob said. I nodded and opened the front door. The man on the step smiled at me with less emotion than most mannequins displayed.

"This way please," he said, making a small sweeping motion with his arm toward the car. I opened the screen door and stepped out, Bob behind me. Ron still stood where he'd been and I made sure not to get between him and our surprise guest. The man put the palm of his hand against Bob's chest and clucked apologetically.

"Just Mr. Phault, please," he said.

"You want me, you get him," I said flatly.

The man held his hand on Bob's chest for a second as he considered this new situation, then smiled without warmth again and bowed his head slightly to Bob, removing his hand. He opened the rear doors on both sides of the car and waved us in, shutting the doors behind us. I sat behind the passenger, who was white and muscular as far as I could tell from his neck and head, and Bob sat behind the suit who drove.

Chapter Thirty

IN THE SPIDER'S LAIR

Riding in the Caddy was like floating in a womb: soft, silent, and smooth. Even as we turned onto I-75 and headed toward Detroit, doing seventy miles an hour, I couldn't hear the Caddy's engine. Neither of our hosts spoke a word during the entire trip. I tried not to think about Jimmy Hoffa, who got his last Caddy ride not ten miles from where I'd been picked up. Or was that a Lincoln? Details, details.

We coasted south on the freeway straight into the heart of Detroit, our driver handling the car like it was an extension of his own body. The glass towers of the Renaissance Center gleamed magnificently in the morning sun, almost making me forget that Lewis and Clark would get lost in the maze of its lower levels.

The thin man steered the DTS into the heart of Greektown, one of Detroit's few tourist attractions, past Trapper's Alley and several high-end Greek restaurants. I kept an eye out; I knew the area, and wanted to know exactly where I was in case I had to make a quick exit.

We rolled to a stop in front of an impressively decorated

Greek restaurant, with its name written in artsy blue neon above the door. I was still trying to read the name when our two hosts got out on either side of the car.

The passenger in the front seat, who I hadn't been able to see clearly before, stood up when he climbed out of the car. And up. He was at least six-six, and probably weighed in around two-eighty. I got out of the car and stood next to him, not liking the sensation of someone his size next to me. I heard Bob open and close his door as I checked out the surrounding area. There was a little foot traffic on the sidewalks, and some passing cars, but no one seemed to take an inordinate interest in us.

"Follow me, please," the slim man said, coming around the front of the car and striding toward the brass encrusted doors of the establishment. He opened one of the large doors and waved Bob and me into the dark interior. I stopped at the entranceway to let my eyes adjust to the light and got a wave of hot breath on my neck from the Incredible Hulk behind me. I ignored him and followed the thin man into the rear of the restaurant, moving between booths and tables carved from expensive, stained oak. Bob kept beside me, saying nothing, but I could tell he was on edge. I didn't blame him; it was more my territory than his and I didn't have a clue what I was doing.

Almost at the back wall of the restaurant, sitting alone in a luxuriously padded booth, was Pietro Bufonte. He had a plate of something in front of him that I couldn't recognize in the dim light. I could hear him chewing. After a moment, he stopped and looked up at us.

"Nothing better than Greek food," he said with only a trace of an accent. "Beats Italian any day, far as I'm concerned. Pasta, that's what you eat when you run out of food. Hey Frankie!" he called out to one of the waiters.

"You trying to make me go blind? Turn on some lights." Frankie went into a back room and light flicked on all over the restaurant.

Bufonte was wearing an expensive dark blue suit with small gold cufflinks and an ear to ear smile that tried to convince me he was someone I could trust. I wasn't buying. He looked like a guy that used to kill people wearing an expensive suit.

"Well?" I said, after he'd studied me for a while. "You called me." Only a flicker of displeasure crossed his features, but it was there. The big man wasn't used to uppity guests, but he really must've wanted to talk to me -- no one had even asked if we were armed.

"Watch it," the giant said warningly behind me.

I turned and looked at him. He was my age or younger, with scar tissue around one eye and a nose that had been broken and set badly. I was guessing college offensive lineman that hadn't been good enough for the pros and had fallen in with the wrong company. Bob was sizing him up like he was a piece of fruit on a corner stand. The thin man was standing off to one side, hands clasped in front of him. Except for his eyelids occasionally moving, he was doing the perfect imitation of a coma victim. If anything was going to happen, he'd be the one to watch. I'd be willing to bet he was much more dangerous than the giant, appearances notwithstanding.

"Now August," Bufonte said, "is that any way to speak to our guests?" He slid an ingratiating smile my way. "He's young and foolish yet," he explained to me, "but he's loyal."

Geez, he must really be in trouble, chastising his help in front of strangers. Kellogg must have a real chance. Next he's going to start pumping me for Kellogg's whereabouts. I decided to push him, see just how far I could go.

"Really? I had a dog like that once," I said.

"Does he do any tricks?" Bob asked Bufonte. There it was again, another flicker of displeasure or annoyance. Now we'd done it, the mafia Don wouldn't invite us back.

"I'll show you a trick, you little fuck," August said, moving close to Bob and flexing. He towered over Bob, making him seem almost undersized. Almost. The two of them squared off, with Bob looking up into August's glowering face with a bright, inquisitive smile. It was the steroid version of David and Goliath.

"Butch, Spike," I said. "Heel."

"I have business to discuss with these gentlemen, August," Bufonte said calmly but firmly. "Now is not the time." August glanced from Bufonte to Bob and scowled. Bob smiled back handsomely.

When I saw nothing was going to happen I slid into the booth across from Bufonte without asking. I was probably violating seventeen different Rules For Dealing With High Ranking Members Of Organized Crime, but after the week I'd had I just didn't care.

"What business?" I said.

"I was hoping you might have some information that I need," he said warmly, my best friend in the whole world.

"Let me guess, you want to know where your protege is," I said. "Please, tell me if I'm wrong." He smiled at me again. Somehow I didn't swoon.

"I'm in a unique situation," he said. "I managed to disrupt my colleague's plans early enough for him not to establish more than a base from which to operate. It is this same base, however, that enables him to remain hidden from me. And this is my problem. In order to keep face, as it were, with my other business associates, I must find my associate and demonstrate my disapproval of his actions.

This type of activity musn't be encouraged. I would reward you highly, of course, for such information." He looked like a retired low-rent kneebreaker, but he sounded more like Walter Cronkite. Actually, he sounded like a kneebreaker *trying* to sound like Walter Cronkite. The big words seemed a little too much for him.

"What makes you think I know where he is?" I said.

"I did not say that you did," he replied. He spread his hands expansively. "You have survived, even excelled, in the face of several attempts he's made on your life, or so I've heard," Bufonte went on. "You've disrupted his plans and in fact, it was in part your actions that helped reveal Mr. Kellogg's machinations to me. This leads me to believe that either you're very lucky or very good. And since I don't believe in luck . . . ." He spread his hands again as I choked back a laugh.

"You seemed to find me easily enough," I said. "Why can't he? Why can't you find him yourself?"

"Ah," he said. "A question we both know the answer to. With the ease at which I found you, it's obvious you intended to lure Mr. Kellogg into making another or in fact a series of rash moves that would expose him to yourself. You knew that I would also be watching for Mr. Kellogg to make said rash moves. He undoubtedly knows where you are, as you intended, but cannot move against you as he knows I will be watching. Have been watching, for several days." He peered at me intently to see my reaction.

"You've had people watching the house for over a day," I repeated, trying to conceal my disbelief. Something about it rang false, but I couldn't put my finger on what just yet.

"Of course," he said warmly, beaming. He spread his hands. "They are good, are they not, to have not been spotted. Of course you would assume you were being watched, though."

"Of course," I said, playing his game. A minute later I'd figured out what was bothering me about Bufonte claiming he'd known where I was for several days, but I couldn't figure out why he was lying about it, unless he wanted to sweat me a little for being rude to him in his own restaurant.

"But I still don't understand your involvement of these children," he said. "Are they not trouble?"

Trouble? I thought. *You have no idea.*

"These 'children,'" I said, "are almost as good as I am. In five years they'll be better." He didn't understand what I was saying but he pushed the confusion out of his eyes.

"So you're telling me that you in fact *don't* know where Mr. Kellogg is at the present time?" Bufonte didn't seem too pleased.

"If I did, I would've already acted on the information," I said. He got my meaning.

Bufonte pursed his lips. "That does seem more logical," he said. "But it is distressing. It means that I will have to increase my efforts to locate him. It isn't a job I enjoy, but one rather that I am forced -- compelled -- to perform. He was once as a son to me." There was a brief bit of sadness in his features that could have been genuine and then it was whisked away to parts unknown.

"If you are misleading me, and do in fact know the whereabouts of my associate, I would indeed be highly displeased."

"You can answer a question for me," I said, ignoring his last comment. "The answer might help me locate your associate." He spread his hands at me again.

"If it is possible," he said carefully.

"Why is Kellogg still sending men after me, even when

his betrayal of you is public knowledge? I've heard rumors, but don't have anything solid as yet."

Bufonte smiled pleasantly. "I've known Reginald Kellogg for many years," he said. "He is brilliant, daring, and resourceful, but most of all he is vengeful. He carries a grudge forever. You got in his way of finding this witness, this child, and it was partly your fault that he had to move against me before he was ready. Nothing he has tried has stopped you. There were even rumors that one of the men, a man that was mine before Kellogg poisoned his mind, that this man was tortured. Had all this happened to me, and I assure you I am quite level-headed, I would take it very badly. To Reginald I would imagine that now it has become a matter of pride. He knows he doesn't have the manpower to overthrow my organization, and it's only a matter of time before one of my people discovers where he's been hiding. The only thing left for him is revenge."

"Great," I said.

Bufonte went on. "Three men he last did business with, the men who thought they were dealing with Reginald only as an extension of my organization panicked when they found out that Reginald was working on his own. They were afraid of retribution from me, so, stupidly, they decided to run. There is a rumor that before they ran they secured a tape detailing some illegal activity Reginald was involved in. If such a tape exists, this youth you are looking for must have it. Everyone assumes that if it exists he has it, so it does not matter whether that is the truth or not. Actually, I'm amazed he's lasted this long. I have information that Mr. Kellogg has conducted quite a thorough search for him."

"Him and me both," I said. "I've had about as much luck." Bufonte spread his hands and shrugged.

"Personally," he told me, "I don't think there is a tape,

or similar piece of evidence tying Reginald to anything. Not only because he is meticulously careful, but if these people had such a tape, why didn't they give it to the police or federal agents when they were in custody, under their protection?" He smiled. "If I thought there was a tape, I'd be looking for it too, on the off chance that my name was mentioned. I'd hate to have my good name slandered." *Yeah, that'd be about right*, I thought. More *people with guns looking for Jerry*.

I was getting tired of Bufonte's act although, I had to admit, for someone with a sixth-grade education who started out breaking thumbs, he put on one hell of a front. Maybe he'd missed his calling in Hollywood. I slid out of the booth and stood up.

"If you find Kellogg before he finds me," I said, "give him my regards." Bufonte's smile faded a little and he nodded.

I walked back to the Caddy with Bob and the Thin Man. August stayed in the restaurant, at Bufonte's request, probably to minimize the potential for bloodshed.

We rode back to Ron's in silence, our driver weaving in and out of what traffic there was with little difficulty. He dropped us off at Ron's door and drove away without a word. Bob and I stood there for a minute, soaking up sunlight. He let his eyes wander over the house, barn, yard.

"You buy his story about knowing you were here for a couple days?" he asked me.

"No," I said. "He didn't know I existed until just a little while ago. Besides, too many of Bufonte's people are now Kellogg's people, someone would've told Kellogg where I was if Bufonte knew that long ago. If he was that interested in revenge, a florist's truck filled with guys with shotguns would have visited by now. This place is too isolated for him to pass up."

"Now *that* would've been interesting," Bob said. He looked around, maybe hoping a florist's truck would appear over the horizon.

"He probably found out where I was from the leak in Weatherspoon's department, he's the only one I know of that knew where I was. Hell, I had him deliver those vests right to the door. The timetable is right for that to have happened. I think Bufonte was just blowing smoke."

"Why?"

"Who knows? To see how I'd react, probably. To test me. I'm the guy that's been beating his best man, maybe he wants to see what I'm made of." I kicked at the gravel driveway. "The problem now, though, is that Bufonte knows I'm here, no question."

"So? Kellogg's the problem, not Bufonte. Oh."

"Yeah. Organized crime isn't filled with that many loyal men, no matter what Mario Puzo says. If Bufonte knows where I am, Kellogg does too. If not already, very soon."

"Exactly when do you figure Bufonte found out you were here?"

"He probably sent the car over as soon as he found out about you guys, where Ron lived. He doesn't have that much time to waste, nowadays. He's smooth, though, I'll give him that. Real smooth. But then I guess he should be, to have gotten where he is."

"He sounded like he just found a dictionary and wanted to try out a bunch of new words. Fat fuck looked like a garbageman that hit the Lotto, but I guess to get where he is he had to have some balls. Okay, so working from the theory that Kellogg knows where you are?" Bob asked. I thought that one over for a while.

"My best bet is to stay here. Unless you guys have had enough and want out." He looked at me the way I thought he would. "All right then. I'll stay here at least one more night. It's too late for you guys to get out of this anyway. Unnoticed, that is. The mob's not much for squad assaults or thousand yard snipers, and the layout of the land here pretty much precludes anything else."

"Plus you got us here to watch your back."

"Plus I got you here to watch my back," I agreed. "And, after our little talk with his former boss, he'll know that we now know that he knows we're here, if that makes any sense. I doubt he'll try anything," I sighed and moved toward the front door, "but the next twenty-four hours should be interesting," I said.

Chapter Thirty-One

MEETING TIME

"Is anybody else sweating like a pig under their vest?" Ron asked.

"That's a stupid question," Steve said. He pulled at his T-shirt where it was sticking to his neck as we walked toward the Diplomat. I felt a trickle of sweat run down my back and smiled. The vests would stay on no matter how hot it got.

Ron hawked and spat on the ground, then wiped the palm of his hand across his forehead. "Saddle up," he called out. We climbed into the car and Ron pulled out of the driveway with a spray of gravel.

No one was talking, we were all wrapped up in our own thoughts. I was finally at the end of the string I'd begun tugging at five days earlier. Finding Jerry wouldn't solve all my problems, but the ones I'd have left would look a lot simpler. The puzzle was what I would do with him when I found him. Weatherspoon wanted me to use him as bait. Kellogg had no problems with turning Jerry into bait, but his definition of the term was slightly different from Weatherspoon's. And the boys, especially Bob, were just about ready to hunt down Kellogg themselves. What finally happened would depend on who found who first. In any case, I could assume the location of my hideout was common knowledge, so my immediate future was destined to be interesting. I tried not to think about it.

Ron turned into the bank's congested lot, managed to find a space, and shut off the car. I looked at my watch. 2:45. I'd wanted to be early, just in case. The four of us climbed out of the Dodge and stood. I didn't know about them, but my heart was beating way too fast.

"You look like a bunch of cherry bank robbers," I told them after surveying the situation. "One of the customers is going to see us, scream to a teller, and then we'll have six cops breathing down our necks asking why we're standing out here setting off metal detectors at the courthouse downtown. One of you go stand somewhere or something." Steve ambled over to the money machine and stood inside the booth. Bob moved to the sidewalk along the street and leaned against a light pole.

"Jesus Christ, now doesn't that look inconspicuous," I said. Someday, maybe, they'd learn better how to disappear into the ebb and flow, but for the moment their obviousness was to our advantage. I wanted Jerry to have no problems spotting them. The four of us played rubberneck for a while, checking out every car that pulled into the lot and every customer that went into or came out of the bank. At two minutes to three, Steve had to leave the shelter of the money machine booth when a large middle-aged woman came to use it and kept shooting him suspicious looks. She kept her hand inside her purse, probably ready to Mace him at any second. He strolled over to Ron and I and shook his head.

"Zip," he said. "So far. Jer is usually on time."

"He's had a rough week," I said. "Don't fault him too much if he's a bit late."

Steve shrugged and leaned against the front fender of the car next to ours. Jerry stepped out from behind it and said into Steve's ear, "It would have been tougher sneaking up on a sock." Steve jumped and spun around.

Bob appeared out of nowhere behind Jerry. "Maybe," he said.

A slow smile spread across Jerry's face and he turned slightly to look at Bob. He had several days growth of beard on his face and looked like he hadn't been sleeping well, if at all. There was a small black dufflebag over his shoulder and he was wearing a black windbreaker over a dingy grey T-shirt. His hand kept unconsciously straying towards his left armpit whenever there was a sudden noise from the street. I hadn't noticed it before, but we were all doing that.

"I saw you the whole time," Steve said with a grin on his face.

Bob was grinning too, a small, warm smile that didn't mean a lot unless you knew how rarely he smiled and meant it. He slowly stuck out his hand and Jerry slowly took and held it. No one else moved or said anything. Jerry let go of Bob's hand and looked at the rest of them, his eyes glistening.

"Goddamn," he said, his voice choked with emotion. He said it again, quietly, and shook his head. Seeing him, finally, I understood how he felt.

"You, butthead, have a lot of explaining to do," Ron finally said, a broad smile on his face. "Where the fuck have you been? We're your friends, remember? You're supposed to talk to us if you get into trouble, not take off and disappear. Especially with trouble like this."

"I know, I know. At first I just ran, I wasn't really thinking. Later on I thought about calling you. I decided I'd better wait to drag you all into this, at least until you knew what was going on or met some people who did. I assume that's you," he said to me. "Cop?"

"Private investigator," I said, "hired by your parents."

He smiled and nodded his head. "I was wondering if you guys would get my message. If you didn't show up for this meeting I was going to call one of you up."

"I want to hear the whole story," I said to him, "but I don't feel the middle of a parking lot is the best place for it."

"I'm hungry as fuck," Jerry said. "There's a Wendy's down the street, let's talk there." I groaned inwardly at the thought of more fast food.

"There's something in the car I want you to put on first," I said to him. He half-heard me, paying more attention to Bob.

"What the hell happened to your head?" Jerry said. Bob smiled and wiggled just the one eyebrow and the stitches above it.

Chapter Thirty-Two

CATCHING UP

"So what happened, exactly, from the time you left for lunch on Wednesday til now?" I asked Jerry after he'd eaten his fill of burgers and fries at a speed faster than I thought humanly possible. The boys had formally introduced us, and from Jerry's attitude, probably put in a good word for me as well. "Don't leave anything out," I instructed him. "It could be important."

"Okay," Jerry said, wiping burger slime off his face, "here goes. I was working Wednesday at the nursery, everything's kosher, and I head out to lunch. I've got a coupon for a Whopper, so I decide to go to the Burger King down Rochester. When I pull into a space I almost got clipped by this semi. The guy driving it must've had shit for brains, or was a new driver or something, 'cause he tried to go through the drive-thru and got stuck."

"Someone tried to go through the drive-thru in a semi?" Ron said. "What a bonehead."

Jerry nodded his head. "Yeah. It wasn't a full-size semi, but it had twelve wheels if it had two. Anyway, this guy got kinda stuck, because there wasn't enough room to make the turn, and he kept jockeying back and forth, grinding the gears. He made one hell of a racket. Anyway," he said, drawing in a deep breath, "I get out of my car to go inside and the wind blows the coupon right out of my hand and under the car next to mine. So I get down on my hands and knees and try to reach it, but of course I can't. I end up having to get on my back and slide halfway under the car to reach the damn thing, and then it almost got away again." He slurped some pop through a straw and shrugged his shoulders. "Do your vests make you guys sweat a lot?" he said.

I couldn't help but smile, it felt like I'd won the lottery all over again.

"Like a pig," Ron said. "Tell the damn story."

"So I finally reach the coupon and I'm about to slide out from under the car when I see a pair of feet walk up to the car next to the one I'm under and get in. I decide to wait until he's pulled out until I get up. He sees someone slide out from under a car in a parking lot and for all I know he'll freak out, think I'm a rapist waiting for a woman to walk up so I can abduct her. Stranger things have happened. Well, barely a second later, not even, two other pairs of feet walk up to the car, one on each side of it, and I hear two pops and see two shell casings fall on the ground. I knew right then, somehow I just *knew*, what had happened. There was no doubt in my mind. Well, one of those damn cases rolls under the car where I'm stretched out. You believe my fucking luck? I can still see it, real clearly. It was a three-eighty auto, and I could even see the Winchester headstamp on the brass. If I never remember anything else, I'll remember that, laying on the pavement and watching that damn thing rolling back and forth. I just froze up, just stayed there and looked at it while one of the guys says 'Check his pockets and grab anything you find,' and the other guy grunts. A few seconds later I hear keys jingling, like maybe they took the guys keys out of his pocket or out of the ignition, and then I hear one of them say 'Cases.' I barely heard him over the noise of the semi which sounded like it was finally pulling out of the lot. So the guy on my side of the car bends down to pick up the empty cases and I'm staring him in the face like a moron, under the car with a fucking Whopper coupon in my hand.

"I scrambled out from under the car and got into mine and drove off, as fast as I could and without looking around. I think I heard the guy say 'Hey' or something, but I was sort of panicking so I'm not sure." Jerry gave a quick smile. "Surprised the fuck out of him to see me staring him in the mush when he looked under that car. I got a brief glimpse of the guy I think they shot, he was slumped over in a red car."

"Dead," I said. "Shot in the eye and neck."

"Let me put this as simply as possible," Jerry said. "Who was he, who shot him, why, and should I still be running?"

"Later," I said. "Finish your story first, we've all been waiting to hear it. Trust me," I said to his scowl. He looked to his friends but they nodded that he should continue.

"Okay, you anal retentive dickheads," he said, peeved, "so now I'm driving down Rochester Road. I'm freaked, panicking, I'm not driving too well and in short order I discover that I'm being followed by a car with three guys in it."

Jerry took a breath and continued. "I'm sitting there trying to think of what I should do. I can't go home, they'd just follow me and kill me and probably whoever else was home. They're in a damn Trans Am, no way I'm gonna outrun 'em. I can't go to a police station, the guys behind me would just disappear, and they'd already have my license number. I heard enough laying under that car to figure out those guys had done this kind of thing before, so I had to assume they had my plate. One night they'd show up at my house uninvited and kill me and whoever else saw them, and my parents are light sleepers. I wracked my brain, but I couldn't figure out what to do, meanwhile I've already passed Champion and these guys are glued to my bumper with at least one gun and three people and all I've got is a pocketknife."

"You should've driven to my house, butthead," Ron said.

"What if no one was home?" Jerry said. "Your place would be a nice secluded area for them to kill me, douchebag. Besides, I didn't think of it." He shook his head. "It doesn't matter, now. I kept going, and before I knew it I was in Royal Oak. I figured that would be as good a place as any to play it out, whatever happened."

"You should've gone to a police station," I said. "Better odds." He shrugged again.

"Next time I'm being followed by a bunch of hitmen, I'll keep that in mind," he said sarcastically. "At the time, the more I thought about it, the more Oakridge seemed to be the best solution. It's right on a corner, and a lot of traffic goes by. If I got onto the playground, in the open, they wouldn't shoot me because of potential witnesses. They'd probably just try to threaten me into their car. If I went, *then* they'd shoot me."

"They didn't seem to have too many reservations about shooting someone in the parking lot of a Burger King," Bob pointed out. "You took a risk."

"I had no choice," Jerry said. "They started speeding

up, changing lanes, like they were gonna try to force me off the road. I beat them out at the light on the corner and pulled in front of the school. I got out and walked about forty feet onto the lawn and waited. They screeched up about a second later and the two guys hopped out and ran over. Who were they, mob?" I nodded.

"One of them says to me, 'Get in the car,' and flips open his coat to show me a revolver in a shoulder holster. I was trying to act scared and it wasn't too hard. But these guys, they were real cocky and got too close to me, I guess trying to intimidate me. I said, 'Let me see that again,' and this guy, this moron, he shrugs and pulls open his jacket again and I punched him in the throat with my knife. The other guy must not have seen the knife and thought I was foolin' around, 'cause he reached for me instead of his gun. I slashed him across the throat." Jerry looked down at the table and shivered, for the first time showing some real emotion about what he had done. "God, I didn't know there'd be that much blood. And it just squirted out, straight out," he said, sickened. "He grabbed at his neck and I stabbed him in the chest. Both of them went down at the same time, blood everywhere. It was like a movie. The guy driving the Trans Am smoked his tires getting out of there." Jerry shook his head and shivered again.

"I didn't know what to do," he went on. "I'm standing in the middle of a playground, the playground that I played on when I was in *grade school*, for Christ's sake, with two dead guys on the ground still bleeding and twitching all over the place. I wiped off the blood on my hand and knife as well as I could and searched them both." His voice went very quiet.

"I've never touched a dead body before," he said. "Hell, I've never seen a dead body, much less killed anyone. I don't even get in fights."

"Stop it," Bob snapped at him. "You know better." Jerry raised his head and looked at him for a second. "We've already had to kill four people trying to find you. You know the rules of this fucking game, they haven't changed. Shit happens. Life sucks and then you die. Deal with it. You managed to make it this far, I know you can handle it. You have handled it."

Jerry stared at him for a few seconds, took a deep hesitant breath, let it out slowly, and nodded in slow motion.

"Five," I said. For some reason, getting the number right was important to me. "Not four, five people," I told Bob. He thought for a minute, then nodded. He'd forgotten about Freddie the Knife. Jerry gave me a questioning look.

"Finish your story first," I told him. "Ours'll take a while to tell." A wry smile snuck across his face at my insistence.

"You guys really want to know what happened, don't you?" he said. "Five people, seriously? You're not fucking with me? Jesus. Anyway, I searched them, and found this. I think it's the one they took off the guy at Burger King." He set a keyring on the table. There were six keys on it, two to a GM car, three for unknown locks, and one plastic-and-metal key with a number stamped on it that looked like every other locker key I'd ever seen.

Wow. Just wow.

He takes out two armed, experienced guys with a pocketknife and then has the presence of mind to search the bodies, in full view of God and anyone else in Royal Oak that day who might happen to glance in his direction. I could've used him on some of the hairy raids I went on down in Miami. I picked up the keyring and looked closer at the locker key.

"I think that one key is something they might've been

interested in," Jerry was saying. "It looks like a key to a locker, number five-forty-seven, but where that locker is I don't know. Or what's in it."

"This key was made by the same manufacturer that makes the lockers in Greyhound bus stations," I said.

"Are you sure?" Steve asked.

"I ought to be," I said. "I spent half of each week for nearly six months in a Greyhound station in Florida waiting for one of my CI's -- that's a confidential informant. Big case, and the guy refuses to use a phone, always wants to meet in person, then the fucker's always late. Real late. I was almost glad when he got killed. The big question, though, is whether the Greyhound stations up here use the same brand lockers as in Florida."

"Even if they don't, can't you find out which places around here use those kinds of lockers by having a locksmith look up the serial number on the key?" Ron said.

"Yeah," I said. "That is, if you can find a locksmith in this city that has those reference books at his store. Trust me, they usually end up having to write to the manufacturer, send them a copy of their locksmith license. Big, slow pain in the ass. I'll do it if it comes to that, but if this is the key, we'll want what's in that locker sooner than we'd get it that way."

"What's in the locker?" Jerry said.

"Finish your story," Bob said. "Then we'll fill you in."

"Christ," Jerry muttered, but went on with his tale. "I also took one of the guys' guns," he said. "It was only a snubnose thirty-eight, but that's better than nothing. I figured the guy in the car that took off had my license number but it would take him some time to track down where I lived, so I drove home as fast as I could. I changed my clothes, grabbed my forty-five, its holster, a double mag pouch, some extra mags, and all the ammo I had, which wasn't much. I threw some underwear and stuff into my bag here," he nudged the shoulder bag next to him, "grabbed some food, and was out the door less than five minutes after I'd come in."

"Where'd you put your car?" I asked. "The police have had an eye out for it for a while now. Us, too."

"I went straight from my house to the long-term lot at Metro Airport," Jerry said. "I figured my best bet was to disappear for about three or four days, until my parents or you guys got worried and started looking for me. I expected cops, not a private eye," he said to me.

"Friend of a friend of the family," I said. "I'm close with Lieutenant Scott Copley, your parents asked him for help. Know him?"

He nodded. "Vaguely," he said. "So now I'm disappeared," he went on. "I thought four days would be long enough for someone to figure out what was going on. I only thought of leaving the message at the money machine later."

"And for the last five days -- excuse me, six?" Steve said.

"In the past six days I've had quite an experience," Jerry said. "I spent three nights in three different shelters for the homeless in Detroit, and only had to pull my gun once. I spent the night in a twenty-four-hour-a-day porno theater, getting regularly propositioned, I went to the range in Royal Oak and stocked up on mags and ammo. I cut myself shaving several times in the bathrooms of several different Denny's restaurants until I finally gave up, and I managed to sneak one shower three days ago from a YMCA in Highland Park. I also watched my back every single minute of every single day. All in all I've had a rather splendid week."

"I'll bet," Steve said. He sniffed. "Are you sure you've had one shower?" Jerry flipped him off.

"Just wait 'til you find out how much it's going to cost to get your car out of the long-term lot," I told him.

"Forget that," Jerry said. "I want to know what you guys have been doing that you've had to kill five people. Who's after me? And who's the guy that got killed at BK?"

"Hell, we didn't even know you were missing until this bozo showed up last Saturday and asked us if we'd seen you or knew where you were," Ron said, pointing a thumb at me. "Your mom called looking for you but I just figured you were over at Jodi's getting a piece."

"Oh shit!" Jerry said, a look of terror on his face. "Jodi's going to kill me for not calling her. I never even thought about it. Not that I would've called her anyway, but it's the thought that counts."

"C'mon guys," I interrupted. "Let's get out of here. I don't feel comfortable sitting in one place for very long anymore." Jerry's 'Oh shit' had made me reach toward my gun and I realized that if anything sudden happened in the restaurant, we were all so wired we'd kill half of Royal Oak. The four of them automatically swung their heads around, scanning the room for trouble.

I could see chagrined expressions form on their faces as they realized how wired they indeed were. Hands came out of jackets, reluctantly letting go of their pistols. Maybe all four of them, especially Bob, were hoping for a confrontation, to either end it or at least help blow off a little steam.

"All right," Steve said for the group. The five of us got up together and headed toward the door. Ron led the way, talking to Jerry.

"Waitaminit," Jerry said. "Thursday, Friday, Saturday. I

was missing for three days and you guys didn't even know I was gone?"

"I told you, I figured you were over at Jodi's getting a piece," Ron said, pushing open the door.

"If I ever got it for three solid days without a break I wouldn't be able to walk," I heard Jerry say as he stepped outside behind Ron. "Neither would Jodi."

I heard a squeal of rubber, loud even inside the restaurant, and saw a tan sedan hurtle up beside Ron and Jerry outside. As the driver of the car stood on the brakes, someone in the backseat threw open a door and caught Jerry in the back of the knees. He hit the concrete hard.

A man appeared at the open rear door of the car and fired a pistol at Ron, who clutched at his side and fell. The man then stuck his gun against the back of Jerry's head as he lay on the ground, yanked him to his feet, and threw him into the back seat of the car. I caught a glimpse of Jerry's eyes, wide with fear, as the man pulled him upright.

Bob and I were halfway out the door, running, when the man fired three times in our direction. Glass flew everywhere, and by the time we ducked, recovered, and got outside the man had dived into the car which was now roaring away across the parking lot. Bob let loose with a round from his .44 that spiderwebbed the back window of the car. I knocked his arm up before he could fire again.

"You'll hit Jerry!" I yelled at him.

"He's dead already!" he yelled back. We watched the sedan squeal out onto Woodward and roar away. Bob snapped his head back to look at me, his eyes blazing. I held up the keyring in front of his face.

"They weren't trying to kill him," I said. If they'd just wanted Jerry dead his brains would've been on the sidewalk in front of me.

Behind us a woman with blood on her face and arm was screaming. The window in front of her was half gone, and glass decorated the table she was sitting at. Below the ruined window Steve was bent over Ron, who was clutching at his lower back, a grimace of pain on his face. A few steps and I was at his side.

"How bad is it?" I asked. I pulled his hand away and saw a hole through his jacket and shirt six inches above his belt, about four inches to the left of his spine. I yanked up the jacket and shirt and saw the slug still imbedded in the Kevlar body armor.

"What do you think?" Ron spat out. "It hurts like a bitch! Shit!"

"Do you want to be here when the cops show up?" Bob said rapidfire into my ear. "This is going to take a lot of explaining and we don't have the time." I looked around at the crowd that had gathered around us. A bearded man had wrapped a rag around the screaming woman's arm and was trying to get her to calm down, or at least shut up. A lot more people milled around them, staring at her, the window, and the four of us. The questions would start any second.

"No," I said. "Can you walk?" I asked Ron.

"I'll sure as hell try," he said. With Steve helping him a little we managed to push through the crowd to our car. No one protested our leaving, probably because Bob still had his .44 out.

"Police officers!" I yelled. "Back away from the crime scene! This man's been shot, we have to rush him to a hospital. Patrol cars should be here in a minute, all of you were eyewitnesses, we'll want a full statement from you all!"

"Gimmee the keys," I said quietly to Ron as we made the last few steps to the Dodge. Already some of the bystanders, at the words "eyewitnesses" and "statement", were drifting away. I hoped none of the civicly minded ones who stayed remembered our license plate number. Ron dug out the keys with some difficulty and tossed them to me. I started the Diplomat up and backed out of the space as soon as everyone was inside. At least it looked like a cop car. Too bad Ron didn't have a siren or a blue light, the car had everything else.

The tires chirped when I pulled onto Woodward but that was due to my inexperience with the overpowered engine; I was trying to maintain a low profile to keep from being pulled over. A mile and a half down Woodward doing the speed limit, with Ron swearing up a storm in the back seat, two squads with lights and sirens going rocketed past us.

I wasn't sure where I was going, or for that matter where I should go. After a while I looked where the car was pointing and saw I was headed in the general direction of my office. As I let the Dodge take the reins I tried not to think about how stupid we'd been not to circle and double back in the car to check for a tail. How stupid *I'd* been.

The boys didn't know anything, they couldn't be expected to think of that stuff, but I should've known better. The more I tried not to think about my stupidity the more upset I got. After having Jerry right in my hands, I'd had him ripped away as if I wasn't even there. I punched the steering wheel, succeeding only in bruising my knuckles. The boys were in the same mood FDR had been in after Pearl Harbor.

I parked the car and we headed up to my office. I didn't recognize the security guard, but we looked like we knew where we were going so he didn't challenge us. It could also have been because we looked like the Four Horsemen of the

Apocalypse. None of us said a word as we rode the elevator up to my office.

I unlocked the office door, collected the mail on the floor and threw it on my desk. The boys sank dejectedly into the couch and chairs. Bob reloaded his .44.

"What now?" Ron said. He was still standing, just inside the door, stooped over and holding his side.

"C'mere," I said. I had him take off his jacket and shirt and sit on the edge of the desk. I undid the Velcro straps and pulled the vest off over his head. On the lower left side of his back, near the floating ribs, was a purple-red bruise the size of a silver dollar. I probed it gently with my fingers and Ron sucked in some air with a hiss. I'd had some experience with bullet bruises, and knew it was going to get bigger and turn darker and uglier and hurt more before it got any better, which it would.

I went over to my filing cabinet and dug through its top drawer. Inside was a lot of junk I'd collected the last few years, as well as a couple first aid items. I found half a roll of bandage and some tape to secure it and went to work on Ron.

"Are they broken?" he asked me, trying not to breathe.

"They might be fractured, I'm not sure," I said. I had him lift his arms and I wrapped tape and bandages tight around his ribcage. He grunted with pain once and then I was done.

"That'll make it not hurt so much," I told him. "Hopefully it'll hold you for a while. You'll know soon enough if they're fractured." He took a few tentative breaths and nodded. "You'll probably also piss blood for a week, even if your ribs aren't cracked," I added. Throughout the whole procedure Bob and Steve had been sitting quietly, staring morosely at the floor.

"What's next?" Steve said. He sounded like a cancer patient that'd just been told the chemotherapy wasn't working.

I went behind my desk and sat down. Ron stood and with some difficulty put his vest and shirt back on, then dug the slug out of the vest. He stared at it for a long time, then stuck it in his pocket.

"Kellogg has Jerry," I said. "He wanted Jerry, but he also wanted this." I held up the locker key. "We know now for sure that he wanted this, because if he didn't, Jerry would've been shot, not grabbed. Chances are Kellogg'll try and set up a deal to trade Jerry for the key, once he finds out where it is. Jerry'll tell him, he's smart, he'll figure out they'll want to set up a swap."

Bob had been staring at the floor, but then he raised his head and looked at me with stony eyes.

"He'll kill Jerry, and the rest of us if given half a chance, the minute he gets that key," Bob said. "Or sooner. He's at the ass end of desperate."

"I'll want to see if we can find the locker that fits this key," I said. "It'll give us a better position to deal from, because we'll know what's in the locker and have it and Kellogg won't know."

"You're not listening," Bob said slowly. "Kellogg wants Jerry dead. He wants you dead. We've stuck our noses in it so now he probably wants us dead too. Whether he gets the key or not."

"Yeah, you're right," I said. "We'll just have to see that he doesn't do that."

"And how are we supposed to do that?" Steve said. He rubbed at his forehead with a knuckle.

"If we have to," I said, "by killing him first, as soon as we set eyes on him. I hope it doesn't come to that, because I don't know what our chances are. Who knows how many people he's got. Six? Sixty? If he didn't have Jerry I might think about calling Weatherspoon, but now that would only get Jer killed." I massaged my temples. I could feel a large headache brewing.

"I never figured on living very long," Bob said resignedly.

"I did," I said. "I planned on having kids. A son. And leading a long and fruitful life, dying in my sleep when I was ninety four. I'd still like that, but it doesn't look like the odds are so good, now."

"Life's a bitch," Ron said, hunched over, holding his back like a senior citizen.

"Shut the fuck up, would you?" Steve snapped at him, then scowled at nothing in particular.

Chapter Thirty-Three

WAITING GAME

"So we just wait until Kellogg calls us?" Steve said. "How do you know he'll call at all?"

"I don't," I said. "It all depends on what's in the locker, or what he thinks is in the locker. If it's the incriminating evidence against him, he'll bargain for it. Or at least make the motions, while he tries to figure out how best to kill us, if he's still interested in that."

"How does he know that we won't just turn it over to the police?" Ron asked me.

"The same way we know that he won't kill Jerry," I replied. "We each have something the other wants. I hope," I added. "We need to find out what's in that locker."

"Give me the key," Ron said. "I'll go to the Greyhound terminal downtown and see if I can get lucky while you wait here for Kellogg to call. How do you know he'll call here, anyway?"

"He'll call here, your house, or my house," I said. "He'll know we'll be waiting by a phone somewhere. This is as good a place as any." I looked at the little black box that sat on the desk next to my phone, on loan from Charlie Kang. Any uninvited listeners would get an earful of static.

"I'll go with you," Bob told Ron. "No use getting stupid this far along." He looked to me and I nodded. They went through the door slowly, Bob holding it open for the slower moving Ron.

"C'mon, grandpa. You need a walker?"

"Fuck you and the whore you rode in on," Ron muttered.

"Good luck," I said.

To help pass the time I repacked the cotton in my ear. I still couldn't hear a thing out of it, but the throbs of pain were a lot less frequent. I hoped it was healing but I didn't have the time to worry much about it if it wasn't. I had the rest of my body to look after.

I bustled around my office as long as I could, trying to feel useful, then finally had to sit down. Steve and I stared at each other, at my office furniture, and at nothing in particular for over an hour. I was too wired to do any of the paperwork that I'd let pile up in the past week. After an hour and a half I summed up all my feelings by saying "Shit." Steve glanced up at me briefly then went back to studying his shoelaces.

I heard footsteps outside the door and Steve and I pointed our pistols in that direction. The door opened and Ron came through, Bob close behind. My heart did a quick mariachi when I saw the briefcase in Bob's hand. I put my gun away as he shut the door, then walked over and set the case on my desk. I stared at the case for a second and licked my lips. It was the intangible turned solid and I needed a moment to adjust to its presence.

"Did you open it?" I said finally, looking up at Bob and Ron.

"We figured that was your right more than ours," Ron said. Steve got up and came over to stand in front of my desk next to his friends. All three of them stared at the case intently, as if it would tell them where Jerry was.

I turned the oversized briefcase around slowly so that the locks were facing me. I took a deep breath and with my thumbs tried the two catches. The latches flipped open with a double click.

"Not even locked," Ron said, sounding a bit disappointed.

I lifted the case lid partway and looked inside. I stayed in that position, without moving, for quite a long time. Then I flipped the lid open the rest of the way and spun the case around so they could get a good look inside. They stared at its interior for a while without speaking. Finally Bob reached out and picked up the cassette tape that was inside. It was tiny, the type used in hand-held personal recorders.

"Do you have a player?" he asked. In response I pulled open a drawer of my desk, reached inside, and handed him a small recorder I probably hadn't touched in a year.

"What about the rest of it?" Ron said in a hushed voice. I glanced at the bundles of cash that filled the case. Then I shrugged.

"Count it," I suggested.

Bob stuck the tape in the player and pressed Play. Surprisingly, the batteries still had a charge left, for faint static came out with the sounds of traffic. A second later a man's voice came on.

"Don't tell me the deal's off," the voice said. It was a deep voice, from a man in his forties or older. "I decide when the deal's off. What the hell is your problem now?" He wasn't yelling, his voice was even and strong, but it was obvious he was angry.

"You changed the deal, that's the problem," a second male voice said. It was louder than the first voice, which might or might not mean he was the one with the recorder. "We agreed on one point two, not seven-fifty. That's barely more than half. We delivered the merchandise on time, I can't believe you'd do business like this. Has Bufonte approved this? I can't believe he would. I said I wanted to deal with him in the first place, so this kind of shit wouldn't happen."

"You don't concern yourself with Bufonte. I'm handling the business here, not him, you have to deal with me," the first voice said. "You think he wants to hear about your problems?"

"I won't do it," the second voice said. "My partners will agree with me on this. We shook on one-point-two mil, not a lousy seven-fifty. The deal's off. We want our merch back or the other four-fifty you owe us."

"Your merch?" the first one said derisively. "Your merch? You gotta be fucking kidding me. What, are you that stupid?" He was getting louder and angrier now. "You think you can order me around like a waiter, you dork? I took Silverberg out when he double-crossed me, and he was the president of a bank, you think a keyboard fondler like you has a chance in hell of making me do something I don't want? I'll squash you like a fucking bug. They'll never find your fucking body, you hear what I'm saying? You'll take the seven-fifty and be glad I'm giving you that much. And don't call me again. I'm too busy to be meeting you at two o'clock in the fucking morning in a Kmart parking lot. Kmart, for Chrissakes. Have a little class. Jesus." There was a pause, then the sound of a car door opening, and the voice came back, a bit fainter.

"Your merch," he said, and snorted. "Watch a few more fucking Godfather movies, why don't you. Me, I went to U of M." I heard a car door close, and the sound of a car driving off, the engine fading away. A click on the tape signaled when the original recorder was stopped. I reached over to my recorder on the desk where Bob had set it and stopped the tape.

"Kellogg?" Steve asked. He was sitting on the couch next to Ron, a large pile of green in front of them.

"I'd bet that money on it," I said. "Admitting to complicity in the killing of Arthur Silverberg three months ago."

"Who's Arthur Silverberg?" Bob said.

"The president -- excuse me -- ex-president of Chemical Bank of Midland. They found him in the trunk of his car, hog-tied and shot twice in the head. No one knew who did it or why, until now."

"Somehow Kellogg must've found out about the tape," Bob said. "Who was the guy that made it?"

"One of Weatherspoon's witnesses, I'll bet," I said. "Make that ex-witnesses. Not necessarily the one that had the locker key, but one of 'em. They probably decided to turn on Kellogg after he stiffed them on their cash."

"Why'd they go out on their own?"

"I don't know," I said. "Maybe they just had second thoughts. Maybe they found out that Kellogg found out about the tape. Maybe they discovered that the deal had been made behind Bufonte's back and he was after their heads. I don't think that was ever true, but they might've heard it."

"I thought Witness was clean, safe from people that

would sell out the location of these witnesses to the bad guys," Bob said.

"Probably," I said. "But would you believe it or have faith in a bunch of strangers, working for the *government* no less, when you knew a well-connected mob honcho was after your butt?"

"Probably not."

I took the tape out of the recorder and slipped it into my pocket. The ruffle of bills continued undaunted, pausing only when Ron or Steve would scribble on a pad in front of them. After about ten minutes they finished counting and went into hushed conference.

"Well, shit," I heard Ron say, impressed.

"How much?" I asked.

"Six hundred and thirty-nine thousand, four hundred and twenty dollars," Ron announced.

"Shit," Bob said, shocked.

"Baloney," I said. "That briefcase is sorta big, but there's no way you could fit that much money in twenties and fifties into it. I've seen enough briefcases filled with cash to know. Count it again."

"There were a few used twenties and fifties on top," Steve said, "maybe ten grand worth. The rest was all brand-spanking-new hundred dollar bills. Still in the bank wraps."

"Shit," I said.

"Beats the Lotto," Steve told me. "No taxes." The phone rang then and we all whipped our heads around and stared at it. On the second ring the three of them turned their heads to look at me. I took a deep breath and punched the call up on the speaker phone. I saw the receiver was still cracked from when I slammed it down after hearing about Kelly.

"Hello, John Phault here," I said. My voice didn't sound tense, I reassured myself, I just had a frog in my throat.

"Well, Mr. Phault, I finally get to talk to you," a familiar voice said. Bob made eyes at me and I nodded. It was the same voice from the tape.

"Mr. Reginald Kellogg, I presume. I was just thinking about you," I said with a glance at the cracked phone. "What a pleasure to hear your voice."

"Yeah, right. Listen, I believe we have some business to take care of?" From the crackling on the line it sounded like he was using a cellular phone, just in case I was stupid enough to bring the cops in and attempt a trace.

"How pleasantly you put it," I said. "No one would know that you'd just kidnapped one of my acquaintances. I don't suppose you've called his mother to tell her he's safe?"

"I'm sure I don't know what you're talking about," I heard him say. "But I am looking for a key. I believe you have it, since I haven't found it here, and believe me, I've had a real thorough search done. He says he doesn't even know what I'm talking about, but since the guys down at the morgue didn't have it and he was the last person to talk to them, I can only assume he took it and either hid it or gave it to you. Other than telling me to call you, he won't say a word, and believe me, my guys have been giving him plenty of encouragement to talk. Tough little snot. Reminds me of me when I was young. Why don't you save him some grief and let me have the key. Trade, even up."

"I've got the key," I told him. "It's to some locker somewhere, right? Why's it so important?" *And how did you even learn of its existence?* I wanted to ask him.

"What am I, Alex Trebek?" he said. "Just meet me and give me the damn key and I'll give you what you want and we'll be square. You've caused me a lot of trouble, but at this point I don't care. I just want to get this over with before more shit goes wrong." Bob shook his head and gave the phone the bird.

"Gee, I hate to sound doubtful," I said, "but aren't you the same person that has repeatedly tried to have me killed this past week? Miserably failing every time, I might add. Why should I trust you now?"

"Unless you're stupider than I thought," he said, "you know that I was only interested in keeping my . . . moonlighting a secret from my employer. That, however, is no longer an option. I do still need that key, though. It will lead me to some . . . important business documents, let's say. Besides, you've got no choice. I've got the kid, remember? You still want him, right? You've sure been acting like you do. Now, let's not make this any more difficult than we have to. I can be reasonable. Why don't you meet me tonight at the corner of – "

"Sorry," I broke in. "I don't want to rock your boat, but I'd rather pick the meeting place, if you don't mind. It's this silly sense of self-preservation that I have."

"Not a chance," he said. "I have an acute allergy to pork."

"Who am I going to call?" I said. "One word from you and the kid's dead. I've gone through too much trying to find that little fucker to let that happen. And I know if I call in the blues the word will trickle down to you. Hell, if I was going to call the cops, I'd have done it already. There'd be twenty of 'em in the room with me right now, trying to trace this call."

"As far as I know, there are," he said.

"The name Donald Valenti ring a bell? If there were any cops here, they'd sure be interested in the fact that I

tortured him to death, then dumped his body in a ditch."
God I hope that little black box is working, I thought. I could feel the sweat running down my ribs. "All I want is for the meet to be on ground I'm familiar with." If I let him choose the meeting spot I'd be dead three seconds after he saw I had the tape.

"It's that or no deal," I went on. "I want the kid back but I'm not putting my head in a noose to do it. I'll compose a topnotch sympathy note for my client about the loss of her son and mail the key to the boys over at the McNamara Building." I knew he wouldn't want that; the FBI has a perpetual hard-on for organized crime and he knew that firsthand.

"Okay, okay," he said after a short pause. "But I see one cop and the kid gets a third eye. I got nothing left to lose. Where?"

"Uh . . . ." I began, then stopped. I hadn't thought that far ahead, I had no idea where I could meet him safely. I'd been more concerned with making sure I wasn't meeting him at a place of his choosing. That way at least he most likely wouldn't try to kill me at the meet – he'd wait until I got home. I looked around the room for an inspiration and saw Steve waving at me frantically. He scribbled something quickly on the pad in front of him and tossed it onto my desk. Among the numbers randomly spaced on the paper, generated when he and Ron added up the cash, were the words "NorthStar Mall, Troy, 3AM tonite." When I looked at Steve again he nodded vigorously and jabbed his finger at the piece of paper in my hands.

"Okay," I said. "Here's the deal. Meet me at the North-Star Mall, tonight at three."

After a pause, Kellogg's voice inquired from the speaker, "Where at the mall? The place is huge."

"I don't think the parking lot will be too crowded at three in the morning," I said. "Just be there on time, you'll find me. Since you know it's huge, you should also know that you'll be able to see if there are any cops with me, you can see half a mile in any direction across that damn parking lot." I thought for a second. "And there's seventeen hundred exits, there's no way they'll be able to cover them all without you spotting something."

I wondered what he was thinking. A crowded meeting place would be what a normal person in my shoes would have requested, to keep Kellogg's men from trying to eliminate us right then and there. But there I was, demanding a meet in a deserted parking lot in the middle of the night. He must either think I was crazy or stupid, or have an angle on how to have him hooked by the police. My bet was that he had at least one cop giving him info, so he should be satisfied before gametime that we had no law enforcement snares set for him. What was in our minds, though, he would just have to guess.

"I don't know why you're making this so difficult," Kellogg said, "it isn't. It's just a simple trade. Just remember that if you pull anything stupid --" "I know, I know," I said. "You mail his parts home to Mommy one at a time. Speaking of his parts, I'd like to hear from his mouth. Just to make sure all his parts are still connected. You know the drill."

"You've been watching too many movies," he said angrily.

"Put him on or you'll be doing Lancaster in The Birdman of Alcatraz," I said. "You're probably a better actor. How he got so far with so little skill is beyond me." I heard some grumbling and swearing and after a wait of several minutes I heard Jerry on the other end of the line.

"Hello," I heard him say. It sounded like he was talking through puffy lips.

"We're all here, Jerry," I said. "How are you?"

"Beautiful. In fact, I'd like to quote some poetry by Robert Frost. 'The woods are lovely, dark, and deep, but I have --'" his voice abruptly faded as the phone was yanked away.

"I don't know whether this kid has titanium balls or is just crazy," Kellogg said, once more on the line. "You better be there tonight, or my boys just might lose patience with him and do permanent damage."

"We'll be there," I said. The line clicked and went dead. I punched the speaker off and looked at the three of them.

"What the fuck is this 'woods' shit?" I said. "Did they bat his brain loose?" Bob shook his head and Ron and Steve shrugged their shoulders.

"The woods are lovely, dark, and deep," Ron repeated.

"It sounds familiar," Bob said hopefully. Steve brows were knitted in thought. Suddenly he raised his eyebrows and such a look of understanding showed on his face a light bulb should have popped on over his head.

He said, "The woods are lovely, dark, and deep, but I have promises to keep, and miles to go before I sleep, and miles to go before I sleep."

"I've heard that before," I said. "What is it?"

"Stopping By Woods On a Snowy Evening. Robert Frost," Steve said. "A poem. The last stanza or whatever they call it."

"That's great," Bob said sarcastically. "So what does it mean?"

"You never were that big of a movie nut," Steve said.

"Oh shit," Ron said, sitting back on the couch. "I get it. I remember."

"Ahem," I said. "Mind enlightening me as to why Jerry would quote Robert Frost, and why it has any bearing on *fucking anything!*" They gave me a bunch of startled looks, and I sat back, as surprised as they were with my outburst. I guess I was under more stress, and feeling it, than I was willing to admit to myself.

"*Telefon*," Steve said after a few seconds, ignoring my interruption. "Charles Bronson, Donald Pleasance, came out about nineteen-seventy-seven. Story's about how a Russian spy is ordering people to blow up important things in the US. The people he's using seem like ordinary US citizens until he calls them and says that part of the poem and then you find out they're Russian moles and that they've been preprogrammed and the poem's their trigger."

"I remember now," Bob said. "We watched it at Ron's one day."

"Right," Steve said, pleased with himself.

"So what's your point?" I said.

"We were still in high school, I think. Maybe even junior high. We were all sitting there watching this movie and someone, maybe even Jerry, said that the poem would make a good signal if you were in trouble. You know how you come up with all these neat ideas when you're young. I mean, we picked what book we'd use for a written book code, all sorts of stuff."

"'The Five Fingers', by Gayle Rivers," Bob said. "Paperback version."

"A signal for what?" I said. "Maybe I'm old and slow, but I don't get it." I glanced at Bob curiously. I'd read that book, but I couldn't remember what it was about.

"What Jerry was doing by reciting that poem," Bob said, "was letting us know that he knows what's going on. He knows that Kellogg isn't just going to let him go when he gets the key, that there's going to be some more killing before this is all over. It was him telling us that he'd be ready if we came in shooting."

"Like the Russian moles in the movie." I said.

"Right."

"You guys are killing me," I told them.

Chapter Thirty-Four

A DIRE PLAN

"You never said anything about the money to Kellogg," Ron said. "Why?"

"What's the point?" I said. "He won't know we have it until he opens the locker. But once he gets the key he's going to want us dead anyway. The least we can do is cheat him out of the money in case we don't make it." An idea popped into my head.

"Hell," I said, "he probably doesn't know about the cash being in the locker. That six-thirty-nine has gotta be what's left of the seven-fifty he paid his now-dead business partners. I'd bet he figures the money is long gone by now, lost forever in safe deposit boxes or off-shore bank accounts."

"What should we do with it then?" Ron said. I looked at the three of them, the expressions on their faces.

"The legal thing to do," I said, "would be to turn it over to the proper authorities." I almost smiled at the looks of dismay on their faces. I waited as long as I dared, then said, "However, I haven't had much luck lately in doing the legal thing."

"We can keep it?" Ron said, like a kid with a new puppy in his lap.

"If we happen to live through the next twelve hours, I figure you guys will have earned it. You'll have more fun with it than Uncle Sam would anyway."

"Yesss!" Ron shouted, doing a little boogie with his butt on the couch. He immediately regretted it and held his side, grimacing.

"Let's see," Steve was writing furiously on the notepad, "six-thirty-nine-four-two-oh divided by four--"

"Five," Bob said. "Jerry gets a share. This is his party, remember?"

"Four," I said. "I don't need any more money, I already get more than I can spend from the damn Florida State Lottery Commission."

"Sure?" Bob asked. "This is your party too. "We're just along for the ride."

Just along for the ride my ass, I thought. They were the ride, and I was white-knuckled in my seat waiting for the next corkscrew on this coaster.

"You guys will find more inventive ways of spending that dough than I could ever think of," I told them. "But don't count your chickens yet. Somehow in the extremely near future we have to rescue your friend, put myself, my wife, and you all out of danger, and put Kellogg out of commission. And do it in such a way that it gets the feds off my back and keeps us out of jail."

"One hundred and fifty-seven thousand, eight hundred and five dollars apiece," Steve announced.

"Shit," Ron said.

"What's with the mall?" I finally said, turning to look at Steve. "And at three in the goddamn morning?"

"I work there during the summer," he said, "as a security guard. It's where I *haven't* been working for the past week. I might still have a job, if I beg real nice."

"And?" I prompted.

"And nothing. It's a good place for a meet. The parking lot out back, by the movie theaters, is wide open. No chance of surprises. The cops cruise through the parking lot at one-twenty and again at four, like clockwork. You could set a watch by 'em. Other than those times it's completely empty, out of view of the road, and no close neighbors to call in a loitering report to the cops. The meet's at three – even if they're a little late we should be done by the next roll-through by the cops. If we're still there at four it'll be as corpses. I'll know whoever's working so I can make sure we won't get hassled by mall security. And I can get one of us up on the roof."

A thought that had been nudging at me rose to the surface when Steve mentioned the roof. It was something I didn't want to acknowledge, maybe even to myself, but Steve's comment told me that I wasn't the only one who was thinking it.

"So what? Why do we need someone on the roof?" Ron asked, puzzled.

"Backup," Steve explained. "Whoever goes up there takes your M-1 and makes sure we don't get any surprises. And to make sure that we get the last word in, if it comes to that. Sniper," he said simply, summing it all up in one word, a word that spoke volumes to me. The rest of them let his statement lie, untouched for the moment.

"What time is it?" Bob asked. I looked at my watch.

"Ten after six," I told him. "Why?"

"I have to take care of some stuff before tonight," he said.

"Me too," Ron added. "I have to go home. Why don't

we all meet there? I'd rather not stay here now anyway. Kellogg knows for sure we're here, and even though he's agreed to meet us later, killing us now might be an idea that'll pop into his teeny U of M educated brain."

"Fine," I agreed. "But remember he knows about your house now, too."

"He gets past my dad and he's a better man than any of us," Ron stated.

"Amen to that," Bob agreed reverentially.

Both Steve and I were as ready as we were ever going to be, so after Ron dropped Bob off at his parents' house, an attractive single-story ranch on the east side of Rochester Hills, he took the two of us back to his house.

"What is it that you need to do?" I asked Bob as he stood in the driveway of his parent's house. Above us, white clouds were beginning to roll in from the west as the sky darkened.

"Rock and Roll," he said with a wink and smacked the side of the Diplomat. Steve gave a wave as we pulled away from the curb.

"Do you know?" I asked Steve, thinking that a normal person, in Bob's situation, might be going to put his affairs in order just in case he died. I was sure that Bob had nothing like that in mind.

"Probably," he said. "You won't like it."

"How did I know you were going to say that?"

We made it back to Ron's house without incident. George was still keeping funny hours, because as soon as we walked in the door he grabbed a duffle bag and headed out the door, not even waiting to hear about Jerry. It was rather strange, but he had his own life to live, and raising Ron would've been more stressful that should be allowed by law – who was to say how it had affected his personal habits?

Ron's mother was still absent. Apparently she and his father hadn't ironed out their differences yet. Steve and I made ourselves comfortable at the kitchen table while Ron tossed his keys onto it and went into another room. A few seconds later he came back with a shotgun in his hands. This was a Remington 1100, a semi-automatic instead of the pump he'd been carting around for the past few days. Beautiful engraving decorated both sides of the receiver, graceful hunting scenes highlighted in gold inlay. I'd bought cars for less than what it was worth. The wood gleamed with reflected light and the dark blue steel of the barrel shone with purpose.

"That's a beautiful weapon," I said admiringly.

"Not for long," he replied. "There's a Russian screwdriver in the drawer behind you, can you toss it here?" I found the hammer and handed it to him. He dug around in another drawer close to the floor and pulled out a small hacksaw.

"What are you doing?" I said. "Why don't you cut down your pump? It cost a hell of a lot less than that thing."

"I don't like it any better than you do," he said, "but I want a gun I can fire with one hand. I've already been shot once, it could get a lot worse. And a replacement barrel for this ain't too hard to find." He touched the end of the saw to his forehead in a salute and went down the stairs to the basement. Soon afterward I heard the sawing start.

With a shake of my head I pulled out both my Smith & Wesson and my Colt and laid them on a placemat. I checked that they were both clean, blew out the dust, worked the actions a few times, then reloaded them and put them away. Both Steve and Bob had taken apart and wiped down their weapons early that morning, so now Steve just checked his nine-millimeter over the same as I had done, adding a little oil to the slide rails. He'd just put the pistol away, a second Taurus identical to the first, which he'd ditched, when Ron came back up the stairs.

The barrel of the shotgun was cut back so that it was flush with the forend. It wasn't pretty, but it was a lot shorter. The barrel was now about four inches shorter than the legal limit, and the gun was more or less useless for hunting the waterfowl it was intended for. But with the right loads, namely buckshot and slugs, it would be devastating on humans out to about twenty yards. Beyond that the pattern would widen too much to guarantee good hits.

"I drilled out the gas ports, so hopefully it'll still cycle with the shorter barrel, but there's only one way to know for sure," he said. He dug through yet another drawer and came up with a handful of shotgun shells. He didn't bother closing the sliding door all the way as he touched them off on the deck, and both Steve and I jumped with each blast.

"Perfect," Ron said, coming back inside, a big smile on his face.

"What, no pistol grip on it?" I said facetiously. "Not even a perforated heat shield." I was intending humor, but Ron took me seriously.

"A pistol grip is useless for control if I've only got the use of one hand," he told me. "Even with a full stock I can hide this thing under a raincoat, and it'll be a lot easier to control shooting it off the shoulder than if I used a pistol grip. And those heatshields, man, they're not worth the money. Complete rip-off. If the barrel's hot, stupid, don't touch it."

I sat there speechless for a moment. The outrageousness, almost absurdity, of my situation suddenly became clear. I was probably going to die soon, violently, and there

I was with kids barely out of high school ready to trade lead with organized crime figures. The funny thing, though, was that they were taking all of it as well, if not better, than I was. Like they expected it, or it was *normal*. And I couldn't chalk all of that up to youthful ignorance, no matter how much I wanted to. The most absurd thing of all, though, was that I actually thought they had a chance. The sheer lust for life they exhibited made me harbor a glimmer of hope for their -- and my -- survival. They felt invincible, and God's penchant for fools and drunks is well documented. On the other hand, their lust for life seemed evenly balanced with an apparent death wish.

"You guys are an experience," I told them. A big understatement, but they pretty much had me beyond words. "How do you think Jerry's holding up?"

They looked at me, then at each other. Finally Ron shrugged.

"He's enduring," Ron said. "Nothing much else to do. He's sure as hell not crying or begging to be released. Hell, we all still believe that we're never going to die. Never underestimate the bullheaded ignorance of youth."

"They could put that on a poster underneath your picture," Steve told him, then looked at me. "You never met Jer before today, but I could tell he's changed, just in the past five days. Matured, or something. After he graduates he was planning on joining the army for a couple years, but if he makes it through this week, the army shouldn't be any trouble for him at all. Most of Basic is mental, anyway, and how the hell's a drill sergeant gonna intimidate someone that was on the run for a week from Mafia hitmen? I guess killing someone or having people try to kill you has a tendency to mature a person."

"You've still got some way to go," I said. They both gave me dirty looks.

"Bang, you're dead," Bob said to us, coming into the kitchen, an athletic bag in one hand. I had to stop the quick draw reflex I'd been developing when he spoke suddenly from behind me. My heart rate took a few seconds to even out.

Bob set the bag on the table with a clunk, but, of course, every single bag they had went "clunk." He went back into the kitchen, grabbed a dish towel, and spread it out on the table in front of us. Then he began unloading firearms onto the towel.

First Bob took his Browning Hi-Power out from behind his back, unloaded and field stripped it in about half a second, and laid the parts on one corner of the towel. Next he removed the already broken down components of some weapon that looked slightly familiar but that I couldn't identify in its current state. Lastly he pulled out a rag and some gun cleaning supplies, and set the gym bag on the floor next to his chair.

Bob quickly cleaned and oiled the Browning. In four seconds he had the Browning put back together, loaded, cocked and locked, and concealed behind his back. The three of us watched his smooth, precise movements quietly.

He didn't look at us and he didn't let anything disturb him, he just worked silently with a blank look on his face. I opened my mouth to say something to him once, but reconsidered and stayed quiet. His brow was furrowed and the blank look had turned into a scowl. If he'd been normal I might've thought he was mildly pissed, but since Bob's reaction to high-tension situations was normally a gut-busting smile, I didn't know what to make of his expression.

I heard a familiar noise and looked out the window to

see raindrops beginning to dot the wood of Ron's deck. The rain came hard and steady, and in just a few minutes there were puddles standing on the cedar planks. The sky was overcast with clouds, but they were whiter than the dark grey I expected for such a heavy rain.

Bob glanced out the window briefly at the rain coming down, but there was no change in his expression. He finished cleaning and oiling the mystery weapon and began assembling it. A black, deadly looking firearm began to take shape. As he slapped the collapsible stock closed, I recognized what it was.

"Where the hell did you get that?" I asked him.

He looked up at me, no humor in him anymore, and no evidence that there ever had been.

"Fort Bragg is the Grand Central Station of illegal arms sales in the U.S.," he said. "What else have I got to spend money on?" He worked the bolt of the weapon a few times, then set it down on the towel.

It was a Heckler and Koch MP5 nine-millimeter submachinegun, considered by most armed professionals to be the best SMG in the world. Bob took out three magazines for the MP5, checked their springs with his thumb, then began loading all three from fresh boxes of Federal Hydra-Shoks he pulled from his bag. When the magazines were full and the two boxes were near empty he sat back and massaged his thumbs.

"I hate to rain on your parade," I said, "but Kellogg will take one look at you with that in your hands and make a U-turn back to the Bat-Cave, stopping only to dump Jerry's body in a ditch."

Without answering Bob bent down to his gym bag, which seemed to hold an infinite number of surprises, and pulled out what looked like a five inch strip of black cloth.

He tied one end of the cloth to the protective ring around the subgun's front sight, then took off his jacket, revealing the leather shoulder rig for his .44. Taking one of the MP5's magazines, Bob slapped it into place in the SMG, making sure not to chamber a round. Then he handed the MP5 to Ron and turned around. Ron took the loose strip of cloth hanging from the front of the HK and circled it around the leather of Bob's shoulder holster just behind his neck, pressing the ends of it together. When he pulled his hands away the gun hung there, suspended, and I realized there must be Velcro on the strip of cloth. Bob carefully put on his jacket over the MP5, concealing it from view. The outline of the weapon was still visible through the jacket, but I realized that wasn't important unless he turned his back on someone who cared. Unlikely. From the front no sign of the weapon could be seen.

Facing us, Bob relaxed and placed his hands on his hips. With no change of expression, his right hand darted off his hip and disappeared behind his back. I heard the unmistakable sound of Velcro separating and then I was staring at the business end of the MP5 as Bob aimed it at the wall to one side of me. He quickly averted the muzzle and set the subgun back on the table, nodding once.

"That should work," he said, more to himself than to any of us.

"Kellogg is going to try to kill us," Ron said. "Again," he added needlessly. "Sooner or later. Do you think he'll try tonight?"

"I don't know," I said. I hadn't thought about our predicament from Kellogg's point of view yet. "He could just want the key, have you considered that possibility?"

"Yes," Bob spoke up. "He's had bad luck so far, trying to hit us. Now he's got us all together in a deserted parking lot at three in the morning. I'd try to kill us if I were him. We have to be proactive. We have to plan for what he can do, which is kill us, not for what he might do. If we leave it to chance, and we're wrong, we're dead. If anyone has to die unnecessarily I'd rather it be him."

I knew instinctively what he was saying was true; maybe I'd avoided thinking it myself because I knew what would follow. I looked at Bob and saw him staring at me. I nodded, not because I liked the obvious conclusion but rather in acceptance of the inevitable.

"If this is the best chance for Kellogg to kill us . . ." Steve began.

"It's an even better chance for us to kill Kellogg," Ron finished for him. He looked at me. "Do you think there's any way we could do it other than a straight-out cold-blooded killing?" he asked. *Well, that's the Sixty-Four-Thousand-Dollar Question you've been thinking about all day,* I told myself. *Better answer it truthfully.*

"No," I told him. "Not if you want Jerry to live. You've got to shoot first. Action's faster than reaction."

He chewed that over for a while, and looking at him I almost missed the faint nod Bob directed my way, for telling the truth. Hell, lying wouldn't have done any good. *Not with these guys.*

"Kellogg won't be expecting it," I explained to them, "because in his mind we're supposed to be the good guys, or a reasonable facsimile. He's used to dealing with feds, the FBI, guys who have to fill out forms in triplicate before they can even consider taking their guns out of their holsters. In his world, the good guys don't shoot first." Sighing, I rubbed my eyes and said, "Who gets the roof?"

"It's my rifle," Ron said of his M-1. "So you go," he said to Steve.

"Okay," Steve said. "I'm a better shot than you are anyway."

"What a load of horseshit," Ron said. "It's because you're going to have to go inside the mall anyway to smooth over your security buds."

"The scope isn't zeroed for me," Steve pointed out.

"No, but it is zeroed," Ron said, "and at the distance you'll be shooting the difference between me and you behind the glass won't matter. Go for center mass, none of us have done enough of this stuff to be so cool as to go for head shots." He tilted his head at Bob -- I guess he figured Bob might be a cool enough customer, but my bet was Bob wanted to be on the ground, face to face with Kellogg for the meet. "A thirty-ought-six will blow his heart out his back, you're only gonna need to use one round per customer." Steve nodded and stared at his fingertips in thought. Bob bent down and took the loaded magazine out of the MP5 and laid it beside the weapon on the table. He checked twice to make sure the weapon's chamber was empty, flicked the safety off then on again, then left it alone.

The rain continued to pour down outside, turning the back yard into a mudfield. Our visibility out over the fields, on a sunny day well over half a mile until the trees popped up, was cut to near zero with the rain coming down in sheets. Between the rain and the darkness a cavalry regiment could be standing at parade rest a hundred yards away and I wouldn't be able to see them, but I wasn't worried. The only people with guns within a hundred miles of me crazy enough to go out in weather like that were sitting next to me. I looked at my watch. Eight-thirty.

"You guys might as well get some sleep," I said. "I want to get there early, about one-thirty, but that still leaves us over four hours before we have to leave."

"I doubt if I can sleep," Ron said, "and I don't know if I'll like my dreams if I can. But I'll try." He wandered over to a couch and laid down, staring up at the ceiling. Bob went over to a chair by the window and sat down. He stared intently at the rain falling, the light almost gone. I looked from Bob to Steve, and Steve shook his head.

"He is *not* liking this," he said very quietly, so Bob couldn't overhear. "Not at all. He is really mad. If it wasn't for Jerry being in trouble, he might almost be enjoying himself, but right now he's worried about him, and he hates having to worry." He shook his head again, then got up and foraged in the refrigerator for something to eat. I got up slowly from the table and sat down on the couch not occupied by Ron. There was no way I was going to be able to sleep, and I doubted they would either.

I stood up abruptly and strode past Steve in the kitchen. I was looking for a phone that had a little privacy, and I found one on the desk in the little library. It only rang twice before she picked up.

"Hi," I said.

"John!" Kelly said. "Are you okay?"

"Yeah, I'm fine," I said tiredly. "How you doing?"

"I'm bored out of my mind, you bastard. When are you coming home?" God, she sounded great. Anxious and worried, yeah, and more than a little bit pissed at me, but hearing her buoyed me like nothing else could.

"This should all be over by tomorrow at the latest," I said. "I've got everything pretty much figured out, now it's just a matter of time."

"What's really going on? Can you tell me? The TV news is just going nuts with all sorts of wild stuff."

"Not right now," I said. For all I knew my whole house was bugged.

"I'm worried about you. You sound terrible. Where are you calling from?"

"I'd better not say. Don't worry about me, I'm fine, I'm just tired is all."

"Then what's the matter? Why'd you call?"

I swallowed the lump in my throat and squeezed my eyelids tight. "Just checking in with the boss, that's all," I told her. I coughed in a futile attempt to get rid of the squeezing sensation in my chest. "Your bodyguards still there?"

"Yeah, Scott's here right now. He's in the bathroom, you want to talk to him?"

"No!" I said quickly. Contact right now was the last thing either Scott or I wanted. He was past being able to do me any favors, and things might be so bad for him that he might have to tell someone that he talked to me. "I better go," I told my wife.

"Are you going to call tomorrow?"

"You'll see me tomorrow," I assured her. *One way or another*, I added silently. "I love you."

"I love you too."

I hung up and did my best to stop shaking. It was a few minutes before I was able to stand up. A new headache was just forming behind my eyebrows, and promised to be a doozy. I headed back out to the couch and sat down.

I slouched there on the couch and listened to the rain on the roof. I thought about things, my life in particular. I didn't want it to end, at least not that night. Preferably not ever, but I had to take what I could get. I had a wife I loved, who I planned to have children with. I had friends, like Scott, that I would miss. And, if I died, I'd never get a shot at Jennifer Aniston. Or Jeanna Fine, for that matter. Not that I had much of a chance anyway, but what the hell, hope springs eternal.

Even though I knew it was pointless to worry about my death, I couldn't help it. I was human, after all. I wondered whether society would care much – or even notice – if I was killed, for whatever reason. The specifics of my case didn't really matter. What mattered was whether I was doing what I thought was right. I was. If there actually was a God, the question was whether *He* would approve of my actions. *Well, if I screw up tonight, and He is hanging around upstairs, I'll find out soon enough whether or not I did the right thing.*

At some point during the evening I jealously wondered where Bob had gotten the MP5, and how much he'd paid for it. I considered what kind of people I was hanging around with that would invent telephone distress code words while still in high school. I wondered how long Scott would have to stay in the hospital after I beat him half to death for giving me this case, provided I lived through the meeting with Kellogg.

I sat there, staring at the walls and thinking, while Ron stayed horizontal on the other couch and stared at the ceiling. I didn't hear him move, so I assumed Bob still sat in the chair and stared out the window, silent as a ghost. Steve was off somewhere in the house, dealing on his own with the thought that he might die in a few short hours. Then again, he could be playing with himself in the upstairs bathroom. I seemed more worried about dying than any of them, probably because I'd had a bigger taste of life and knew better what I'd be missing. Or maybe they knew and it just didn't matter to them, because they were doing what they had to do, for Jerry.

I wondered how soldiers, of any era dealt with the realization that they might die. That there were people, "out there", that wanted them dead. I remembered what one of my fellow agents, a Vietnam vet, used to say whenever the shit hit the fan unexpectedly. "Hey man," he'd say, "ain't nothin' but a thing." He always drove me nuts when he said that, and repeating it to myself on the couch didn't make me feel any better. Then again, I didn't expect it to. But it did make me realize what *would* make me feel better.

Killing Kellogg.

Chapter Thirty-Five

PREPARING THE GROUND

"Everybody got what they need?" I asked. I looked at each one of their faces in turn, searching for I don't know what, and got a nod from each of them. We were standing in the foyer by the front door, on our way out.

Steve had the straps of a soft-sided gun case in his left hand, the M-1 inside. Ron had donned an overcoat which came down to his knees. The pockets in the coat went all the way through, and he'd practiced holding the Remington, his hand through the pocket pressing the gun firmly against his side. He'd found that trying to mount the shotgun with his hand still entwined in the coat bunched it up uncomfortably, but it was possible for him to go from a nonthreatening stance, hands in the pockets of an open overcoat, to a low-ready position with the scattergun mounted and snug against his shoulder in less than a second. Now he had it in his left hand, ready to stash it in the Dodge's trunk as soon as we went outside.

Bob had the MP5 in one hand and the magazines for it in the other. He didn't want to have to sit on it in the car so he was going to wait until we arrived at the mall before he hooked it onto his shoulder harness. He was the last one to respond to my question with a nod.

"You?" he said to me.

"This is insane," I told him. "Like, legitimately off-the-rails crazy insane stupid."

"Yeah, so?"

I shook my head and pulled open the front door. We trudged out to the Dodge and piled in, stashing what gear we had. The rain was still coming down, but not as hard as before. With Ron driving the speed limit we rode in silence through the streets of Rochester Hills to the expressway. The streets shone in the glare of the streetlights, giving the illusion they were clean. So many things in life were just illusion. Things like safety, security, things I used to take for granted. I thought how radically my perspective of the world had changed in the past week as we slid up the entrance ramp to the freeway. We had the road to ourselves; not many people come out at one a.m. on a Tuesday night.

The wipers ran across the windshield regularly, the only constant in my life at that point other than my love for Kelly. That and my fervent hope that I was on vacation in Hawaii, lying on the beach asleep, having a nightmare because of a bad margarita.

I was surprised when I heard music come on over the Dodge's speakers. I didn't think any of them were in a suitable mood to appreciate any sort of melody. After a few seconds of listening, I glanced at the car's dash. The indicator arrow on the tape player was glowing.

"Which one of you assholes put this morbid fucking song in the fucking tape player?" I said. One of them had plugged "The End", by The Doors, an eleven-minute dirge about incest, murder, and drug use, into the car's sound system.

"This is the end, my only friend, the end," moaned Jim Morrison into my ear as Bob turned a huge grin in my direction. I shook my head.

"Sick bastards," I said. Steve and Ron were chuckling and snorting as Ron ejected the tape.

In short order I saw the lit face of the mall and the banners hanging listlessly from the lightpoles dotting its huge parking lots. We glided down the exit ramp into consumer heaven. Overall, the mall and its surrounding lots weren't much larger than Rhode Island. The mall had a full size Sears, Marshall Fields, J. C. Penney, and close to a hundred other stores, including a ten-screen theater complex in the rear, which was where we headed as soon as we turned into the lot. Ron followed the drive that circled the periphery of the asphalt expanse, cruising slowly so we could get a good look around. The lot was empty of cars, a major contrast to the housewife shopping hell that persisted from dawn to dusk.

There were half a dozen cars parked near the front entrance, but Steve assured me that they belonged to the security guards and cleaning crew he'd mentioned would be on the job. As we circled around Marshall Fields toward the back of the mall and the future scene of our meet, I looked down at my watch. One-thirty on the dot. I looked up and my heart hit my throat.

"What the fuck is this?" I nearly shouted. There were fifty or so cars parked near the entrance to the theater. Light spilled out of its doors, and I could faintly see the outline of bodies moving around inside. I looked at my watch again, hoping I had read the time wrong. I hadn't.

Failure Drill

"You work here, do you know what all these people are doing here?" I demanded of Steve. He shook his head.

"I'm clueless," he said. "It's been four days since I worked, though. The theater might be having a midnight movie or something. I don't remember."

"On a Tuesday night?" Ron said incredulously. He pulled into a space about fifteen feet from the last car in the row, about a hundred yards from the theater doors.

"Find out what's going on," I told Steve. He climbed out of the car and walked swiftly toward the theater entrance. The rain had slowed to not much more than a fine mist. As we sat in the idling car Ron intermittently ran the wipers across the windshield.

I looked over the dark facade of the mall. The nose of the Dodge was pointing toward the theater. The dark glassed-in rear entrance of Marshall Fields was about seventy-five yards away to our right. The asphalt to the left of the Dodge ran away for perhaps three hundred yards until I saw a chain link fence glinting in the light of the parking lot's lamps. Beyond the fence were some dim buildings, dark shapes with uncertain outlines, a small industrial park if I remembered correctly.

We were parked halfway between two of the light poles that dotted the huge parking lot and bathed it in an eerie blue-white glow. Ron had picked a good spot -- we had enough light to see by, but weren't sitting like targets right under a light pole. We were on a small rise, too, which didn't hurt. I looked down the gentle slope to the theater and saw Steve walking back. The three of us sat in the car and watched him come closer, his hair shining as it collected droplets of water from the light mist. He opened the passenger door and stuck his head in.

"It's a Clint Eastwood film marathon," he told us, "if

you can believe that. Why they picked a Tuesday night for it I'm not sure, I think it's 'cause it's his birthday or something. Let's hope the cops don't decide to make an extra visit tonight. I talked to one of the ushers, he said the last film ends at two-ten. That should give everybody, even the theater employees, enough time to get out of here before three."

"Let's hope so," I said.

"I also talked to the guy in charge of security tonight. I got him to agree to let me up on the roof and shut off the alarms up there. He thinks I'm bringing a girl. He'll have second thoughts big time when he sees the rifle case, but he's smart enough to know I'm not the kind to go nutso and start shooting people without a good reason. Besides, he can always say I forced him at gunpoint. Which I will, if I have to."

I handed Steve a card with a phone number on it. "Call this after it hits the fan," I told him. "Tell whoever answers what happened. Then call nine-one-one, because *someone's* going to need an ambulance."

"Who is it?" he asked, looking at the number printed on the card.

"The feds," I said. "I promised to let them know when I made contact with Kellogg or found Jerry. I figure better late than never."

"Sounds about right," Ron said. He got out of the front seat and unlocked the trunk for Steve.

"I pray that it won't come to it," I said to Steve, "but if I run my left hand through my hair, like this," I demonstrated, "shoot either the closest bad guy to Jerry, or, if that's not feasible, the guy that looks like the biggest threat to us. You think you can do that?" Steve swallowed and nodded. Ron removed the shotgun from the Dodge's trunk and concealed it inside his overcoat, then slammed the trunk. Steve, holding the rifle case down along his leg, started back towards the mall. He angled toward a door away from the theater entrance, barely visible. I watched him reach it and hit it a few times with the palm of his hand. The door swung open, revealing a dark figure and a well-lit corridor, then closed behind Steve.

I climbed out of the car and stretched. The misting rain was barely perceptible, and looking up I thought I could see the glimmerings of a few stars. Probably wishful thinking. Ron climbed into the backseat of the car and helped Bob with the MP5. I heard the click of a magazine being seated, and the sound of a bolt being worked. After that there was the faint sound of Velcro, then nothing until both of them climbed out of the car and stood beside me. I guess none of us wanted to be still sitting inside the car if something unexpected happened.

I could see both of Ron's hands so I assumed the shotgun was still inside the car. The three of us leaned against the driver's side of the car and stared down to our right at the theater doors. I looked at my watch again. One-forty-five. I crossed my arms and stared out over the parking lot.

A slight wind picked up, ruffling my hair. I looked up and saw a lot more stars. I couldn't see the clouds but they seemed to be moving away to the east as the stars were appearing in the west. A few minutes later the moon, half full, came out from behind the clouds and bathed us all in cool white light.

"It's a beautiful night," Bob observed. He moved away from the car, slowly so as not to jostle the submachinegun under his jacket, and began dabbing the toe of his shoe in a puddle. I took a deep breath and cool, sweet night air filled my lungs. Bob was right.

"Steve won't have any trouble seeing, at least," Ron said. "With luck he won't shoot any of us by mistake." I hoped he was joking about Steve's skill with a rifle, but it was too late to raise any objections. I could feel an ulcer forming.

"The Outlaw Josey Wales?" Bob said questioningly.

"Unforgiven," Ron replied confidently.

"What?" I said.

"Best Clint Eastwood movie," Ron explained to me. "What's your vote? The Rookie, Dirty Harry? High Plains Drifter?"

"Bridges of Madison County," I said after much deliberation. They stared at me as if I'd blasphemed before God.

At twelve after two people began to trail out of the theater doors. We only got a few odd glances. Taillights made red trails in the night as the moviegoers made their way home. Quite a few of them were weaving and appeared to be intoxicated, but as long as they didn't drive into the Dodge or us, I didn't care. I had other concerns.

For ten minutes the patrons filed out of the building, then the lot was still and quiet, only a few more cars left, most down close to the theater doors, ones I assumed belonged to the theater employees.

Two figures came stumbling out of the theater doors and made their way up the hill toward us and the remaining assortment of vehicles. The way they weaved across the pavement, I figured they'd either kill someone or get killed driving home, if they ever found their way out of the parking lot.

The two drunken teens stumbled past car after car until it became obvious that theirs was the one closest to us, a blue Escort GT five spaces down the hill from ours that had

Failure Drill

seen better days. As they reached the rear bumper of their car, the smaller of the two half-fell onto the hatchback, gasping like a fish out of water. The other one dug clumsily around in his pockets, presumably for keys, without having much luck.

Finally he found them, got the keys in the door after four tries, and pulled the rusty door open with a loud screech. The driver grabbed his small friend and wrestled him into the car, then started the Escort up with a rattling roar and accompanying cloud of blue smoke.

The driver squealed the tires of the Escort as he powered it in a high speed slide around a light pole, nearly clipping a fender, and was out of sight a few seconds later. The Escort's roaring exhaust echoed off the brick of the mall once and then the parking lot was quiet again. Jesus, had I ever been that young and stupid and carefree?

"Escort *GT*," Ron said, disgusted. "That's like turbocharging a toaster."

Fifteen minutes later the last of the theater employees had left. The last one shut off all the lights but a token few and locked the main doors. He eyed us warily as he walked to his car, then drove off to leave us alone on the sea of blacktop. I looked at my watch. Two-forty. My heart began to beat a little faster and a little spurt of adrenaline shot into my bloodstream. Ron looked at his watch, opened the back door of the Dodge, and picked the shotgun off the floor. He worked the Remington's bolt, chambering a round, refilled the magazine with a shell from an overcoat pocket, then concealed the shotgun beneath his coat. He held it with his right hand through the coat's pocket, the coat hanging slightly open in front. Bob unzipped his jacket the rest of the way and pulled it away from his back. He stuck his hand under his jacket and extended the MP5's stock into the open position, so that four inches of it hung below the hem of his jacket. Then he leaned back against the car.

I reached under my arm and unsnapped my Smith and Wesson from its holster. I clicked off its safety, made sure there was a round in the chamber, then cocked the hammer. I slid it back under my arm but didn't snap the holster shut around it. It hung beneath my armpit, more of a weight on my mind than anywhere else. I looked at my watch again. Two-forty-four.

"Whatever happens, follow my lead," I told both of them.

Ron nodded, but all I got out of Bob was a stare.

Sounds of traffic hung in the distance, the hum of tires on wet pavement, the occasional faint howl of a siren. I could see the distant headlights of cars on the freeway, few and far between. The blinking lights of a jet passed by far overhead, too high up to be heard. I'd always liked to work midnights, be awake when others were asleep, aware of what was going on in the world when others were not. Hopefully no cops would take it upon themselves to explore the dark side of their world tonight, especially that part of the mall parking lot where we'd decided to make our stand.

Relenting, I turned around and studied the edge of the mall's roof. I couldn't see Steve at all. He would either be above the theater, which was closer, or above Marshall Fields, where he could get a better view of the lot. I turned back around and looked at my watch. Two-fifty-one.

Ten excruciatingly long, blindingly quick minutes later, a powder blue Lincoln Town Car coasted silently around the corner of Marshall Fields, flashed its brights to illuminate the parking lot better, then headed toward us. I wasn't glad to see it.

"Something wicked this way comes," Bob said.

Chapter Thirty-Six

FACING THE DEVIL

The Lincoln moved slowly as the driver and whatever occupants there were scanned the area for unwanted visitors. Finally, it glided to a stop parallel to the Dodge, its passenger side toward us and about thirty-five feet away. I looked at how low the Lincoln was riding on its shocks and figured it for armor plating. The windows were deeply tinted and I couldn't tell how many people were inside.

"Follow my lead," I repeated myself, mostly for Bob's benefit. "You hear me?" He glanced at me, looking more at peace with himself than at any time since we'd met, then returned his gaze once more to the Lincoln.

"Some goals are so worthy, it's glorious even to fail," he said softly, maybe to me, maybe to himself, I wasn't sure.

The driver cut the engine but left the lights on. After a few seconds, the passenger door opened and a blond man in a neat suit stepped out. He slowly surveyed the parking lot and the mall, turning his head and scanning each object carefully with total concentration. When he was satisfied he rapped on the back window with a knuckle.

A husky man got out of the back seat on the driver's side of the car, shut his door, and walked around the trunk of the car to face us. He opened the rear door on our side and Kellogg emerged. He wore a grey pinstripe suit that made him look like a million bucks and had a calm, serene expression on his face. With the air of stoic superiority he was broadcasting he could've been the maitre'd in an expensive French restaurant, impervious to anything mere mortals might undertake. A large automatic, looking quite out of place, was stuck in his belt.

The driver of the Lincoln then got out of the car and stood in the angle of his door, looking the three of us over. It was August, and he smiled a dirty, evil little smile when he saw Bob. I snuck a peek at Bob, but his face was devoid of any expression.

Kellogg stood in the open doorway of the Lincoln and contemplated the three of us, me in particular. A small smile tugged at the corner of his mouth. After a while he swung his gaze over the area. The interior of the car was black behind him.

"Mr. Phault, I presume," he said to me finally, giving a mock bow.

"Moriarty," I said. I looked him and his three companions over, trying to read the expressions on their faces.

"You have something for me?" Kellogg said firmly, a man used to getting what he wanted.

"Where's the kid?" I said calmly, determined to keep my emotions in check.

Reginald Kellogg once more scanned the parking lot and the face of the mall, his face thoughtful. Evidently he determined that we weren't going to play games with Jerry's life, because he nodded to himself and pulled a cell phone

Failure Drill

out of the Lincoln. He dialed a number, said two quiet words to whoever answered, then tossed the phone into the car's backseat and waited patiently. The three of us stared at the four of them for several minutes until a Buick sedan pulled up behind the Lincoln. The driver of the Buick came around to our side and pulled Jerry out of the back seat with the help of yet another thug who came out of the door behind Jerry. That made the odds six to four in their favor, not counting Jerry who had his hands cuffed behind his back. His face and shirt were covered in blood, most of it dried. One of his eyes was swollen shut, and his lips and cheeks looked like hamburger. The way he moved told me his face wasn't the only part of his body that had taken some abuse.

"Son of a bitch," I heard Ron say under his breath. I looked over, worried that he'd do something presumptive, but he kept still. Jerry stood quietly, staring at us with one expectant, wary eye.

"Exhibit A," Kellogg said, holding a hand out to Jerry.

"Exhibit B," I replied, pulling the locker key out of my pocket and holding it up with my left hand. Kellogg held out his hand for it and wiggled his fingers.

"Not quite," I said. "I get the kid in my car first." Kellogg looked down at the ground, shook his head, and clucked his tongue.

"The brat stays with me until I have the key in my hand," Kellogg said apologetically. "Sorry."

I knew it probably would happen. Impasse. Neither of us would give up his prize first, because we didn't trust each other and because we were going to try and kill each other, although each of us hoped the other didn't suspect it. I'd thought all night about what I'd do when it happened, trying to think up the least dangerous solution to my problems. A solution that would guarantee that if there was going to be shooting, only the right people got shot. I hadn't come up with anything. I hadn't expected to.

"Kellogg," I heard Bob say in a dead voice. I whipped my head around to stare at him, to glare him back into silence. He had his head lowered when he spoke, eyes on the ground, but now slowly raised his head to stare at Kellogg. I noticed without much surprise that Bob's hands had gravitated to his hips. Kellogg looked at him like he was a pleasant but mentally retarded relative, interrupting an important business meeting.

"Did you see the sun rise this morning?" Bob asked him. Kellogg's forehead creased in confusion. Mine did, too, as my mind raced. What sunrise? It was still night. Did he mean yesterday morning? It didn't –

Then, suddenly, I knew. Bob was going to do it. Something about what he'd said clicked in my head, it was a quote from I don't know what, but I knew it was going to happen.

I jerked my head around and everything started happening at once. Kellogg's look of irritation vanishing as something in Bob's tone hit a chord. Jerry's one good eye opening wide as he recognized the quote. Ron, starting to hunch, his overcoat bunching around his arms. Out of the corner of my eye I saw Bob, in what seemed like slow motion, raise the MP5 that had appeared magically in his hands. I grabbed for my gun and dived to the ground as Kellogg's men began to react and reach for their weapons. Jerry, hands still cuffed behind his back, threw himself to the ground at almost the same time I did.

My chest slammed into the pavement at the exact moment Bob opened up with the MP5. I heard the stuttering blasts and watched the rounds saw across the blond man's chest as I pointed my pistol at the husky guy and started pulling the trigger, elbows locked and planted on the blacktop. He'd already fished out a large revolver and was firing. I felt several sharp jabs of pain in my face as the asphalt exploded in front of me. He finally went down after five or six good hits to the torso and I sought out a new target. In my peripheral vision I saw the man to Jerry's right start to point the pistol he'd drawn at Jerry's prostrate form. Before I could react a fountain of red erupted from the back of his head and he was falling sideways as I heard the report of the M-1 echoing across the parking lot. The driver of the car that had brought Jerry slammed back into the side of the Buick as I heard the roar of Ron's shotgun. I fired once more at him for good measure then swung my pistol around to point at Kellogg. I caught a glimpse of Kellogg through the gunsmoke as he went down, a pistol firing in one hand and blood covering his face and arms.

August had a pistol out and was shooting over the roof of the car at Bob. I fired at him once but was too low and the slug buried itself in the passenger window. And stayed there. Bulletproof glass.

Bob fired the MP5 from a crouch, its stock planted against his shoulder, and I saw the glass of the Lincoln's passenger side windows spiderwebbing just below August's exposed head. I heard sharp, warbling noises as the subgun's rounds skidded across the roof of the Lincoln. August traded fire unflinchingly with Bob over the car. I saw Bob's jacket puff out behind him and two holes appeared in it, but he didn't seem to notice.

August suddenly spun to his left, and I saw through the window a hole appear in his jacket over his massive left shoulder. A fraction of a second later I heard the crack of a high-powered rifle bullet screaming past at Mach three. August stumbled back and dropped his pistol onto the roof of the Lincoln. Bob held his fire and watched, only to see August grit his teeth and slide through the open driver's door.

"*No!*" Bob cried out in animal rage. The Lincoln roared to life, then slipped into gear and started forward with a lurch. Bob leveled the MP5 at it and opened up. Rounds chewed up the right rear window and the rear windshield, then the MP5's hammer clicked on an empty chamber as the magazine ran dry. Bob threw it to the ground and yanked his Browning out from under his jacket. He let off two rounds that smashed into and further spiderwebbed the already damaged rear window. I fired once too, emptying my pistol. None of our rounds penetrated the car's interior.

I heard two cracks as a rifle fired and the thwocking sound of metal being punctured. August, his shape outlined inside the car by the parking lot's lamps, slumped over sideways. The Lincoln continued to roll down the slight hill, now solely obeying the pull of gravity. I pushed myself off the asphalt and climbed to my feet.

Bob and I watched the car for a second or two as it slowly rolled toward the theater entrance. I couldn't believe the car's customizer had forgotten, or neglected, to armor the roof. Then I saw movement to my left and swung my pistol around to bear on it, forgetting for a second that my pistol was empty with the slide locked back. The movement was Kellogg, covered in blood and trying to stand. Bob brought his Browning around and pointed it at him. I executed a speed reload and lined up my sights with Kellogg's head.

Blood ran down Kellogg's face and both his arms as he levered himself up slowly. He held a .45 automatic in his hand, alongside his leg. Blood ran down his hand, across the gun, and dripped onto the ground.

He tried to raise the gun and point it. The effort must've caused him unbelievable pain, for a grimace etched itself into his features and his whole arm shook as he tried to lift the gun. Bob watched him stone-faced, the Browning rock steady in his hands.

Kellogg managed to raise his arm to a 45 degree angle, then stopped, the pain too much for him. His other arm hung useless at his side, and I lowered my gun and waited to see what he would do. He looked at us, in agony, and grinned horribly. He was done, and he knew it.

"No quarter asked and none given, you **FUCK!**" Bob yelled at him over the Browning.

Kellogg focused on him with some difficulty, swaying slightly with the pain, then he fired twice into Jerry as he lay on the pavement before him. Bob and I stood there in shock, motionless, seeing Jerry arch up off the blacktop and writhe in pain. Then Bob fired at the same instant I heard the crack from Steve's rifle. Kellogg's head exploded like a watermelon dropped from a tenth floor window. His body and what little was left of his head fell to his right and hit the pavement with a thud. I hurried over to Jerry, stuffing my automatic into my belt.

He was on his stomach, head to one side, eyes squeezed shut in pain. There were two holes in his shirt just above his belt. I pulled up the shirt carefully and saw the two large slugs gleaming in the Kevlar of his vest. I gave a great big sigh and shook my head. Jerry coughed, spit out some gravel, and opened his eyes. A quick glance was all he needed to see that none of the bad guys were still standing.

"How are you?" I said.

"Well, other than being on the run for five days,

kidnapped, handcuffed, beat up, and shot with my own gun," he groaned through puffy lips, "I'm fine. How 'bout you?"

I laughed with relief and slapped him on the thigh, then lifted him onto his feet. He could barely stand, and probably would need a wheelchair for a week.

There was a crash and tinkle of glass, and I looked to see where the Lincoln had rammed into the theater doors. I could barely discern August still slumped over in the front seat.

"Loyal, huh?" I said, remembering Bufonte's words. Then I looked around.

It seemed like hours since it had all started, but the time between Bob pulling out his MP5 and August climbing back into the car had been at most five seconds. I swiveled my head around and ran my eyes over the bodies. So much death in so little time. I almost began congratulating myself, then I heard a groan. There Ron was, sprawled on the ground with his back against the rear bumper of the Dodge, and I ran to his side and squatted down. There were numerous ragged holes in his shirt and blood covering his right thigh. The shotgun lay by his legs, forgotten.

"Jesus," he said, and coughed. The cough made him double over in pain, agony etched in his features. Bob was at my side and handed me a knife which I used to cut open Ron's shirtfront. His vest had stopped four bullets, undoubtedly saving his life. I felt along his abdomen and he yelped in pain.

"More broken ribs," I said. I moved to his thigh, which was covered in sticky blood. There was a large hole in the meaty part of his leg, halfway between his groin and knee, but no corresponding exit wound in the back of his thigh. The blood flow was steady, but not spurting, so the bullet

Failure Drill

hadn't hit any major artery, but I'd have been willing to bet his femur was broken. Using the ripped portion of his shirt and Bob's knife I fashioned a pressure bandage. It would do until help arrived, which, if Steve had made the call, would be any moment.

Ron hissed as I pulled the bandage tight and tied it. He looked from me to Bob and Jerry standing behind me.

"Don't tell me I got shot to shit and you guys didn't even get a scratch," Ron complained weakly.

"Wait'll you see how many rounds your car caught," Jerry said with a smile, still hunched over in pain with his hands cuffed.

"Fuck," Ron panted, then passed out. I checked his respiration and pulse, both of which were stronger than they had any right to be. With the pressure bandage in place the bleeding seemed to have slowed to a trickle.

"Is he gonna be okay?" Jerry said worriedly.

"He passed out from shock or pain," I said. "Steve should've called the cops and an ambulance by now, it won't take them too long to get here. Then he'll be fine." *I hope*, I added silently.

I stood up and turned to face Bob. He'd put his Browning away and was standing there silently, looking at Ron.

"Did he ever see the sun rise?" I asked him.

"Classic Magnum P.I. episode," he told me. "Two hour movie. After he says it Magnum executes a guy who killed one of his friends. Told ya you should watch more TV."

I hit him in the face as hard as I'd ever hit anyone in my life and knocked him on his ass.

"Don't you *EVER fucking do that again!*" I yelled at him, jabbing at finger at his face. I held a fist ready and waited for him to get up so I could hit him again. He sat on the pavement motionless, a huge smile on his face and blood running freely from his nose. I kept scowling at him and he kept smiling at me until I finally shook my head, forced the smile from my own face, and offered him a hand. He took it and I pulled him to his feet. He grinned at me some more and wandered over to where the dead bodies lay, methodically treating each of them with a kick to weed out anyone playing possum.

"I think I broke my hand," I said aloud to myself, and massaged it with my non-aching left.

Bob began digging around in the pockets of Kellogg's jacket, getting gore on his hands, until he finally fished out the key to Jerry's cuffs. He freed Jerry, tossed the cuffs to the ground, and went to pick up the MP5. After he inspected it for any nicks or scrapes and pulled out the empty magazine he walked back toward me, holding the submachinegun down along his leg. Jerry knelt on the pavement beside Ron and put pressure on his wound just to be on the safe side.

"Your face looks like a pizza," Bob said to me. I suddenly realized my face hurt and reached up to touch it. Mistake. The side mirror of the Dodge had a bullet hole through it but was still whole enough for me to see the small black chunks of asphalt embedded in my cheeks and forehead. I carefully picked out what pieces I could, letting blood ooze out, then gave up and waited for the paramedics which I could only hope had been called.

As I stood there surveying the destruction all around me, I realized for the first time how much damage had been done to the Dodge. All its windows had bullet holes, both tires on the driver's side were flat, and the car's entire left side was punctuated by neat holes of varying caliber. I was surprised -- I hadn't noticed Kellogg and his men firing at us all that much, but I guess I was too busy at the time to pay attention to anything other than my front sight.

I heard a distant sound and turned to see Steve emerge from the same door in the mall's facade that he'd entered a lifetime ago. He approached the Lincoln and stopped nearby, rifle in hand. One close look at August was all he needed and then he started again toward us.

I looked at the bodies in the awkward positions of death, the strikingly large pools of blood, the spent shell casings littering the ground and shining in the dim light like brass fireflies. Next to me Bob clapped Jerry on the shoulder, then made appropriate noises of comfort as Jerry cried out in pain from the shock to his bulletbruised back. The wide grin was on Bob's face once more as he set the MP5 on the Diplomat's roof, and I got another look at the large caliber holes sieving his jacket. I shook my head in disbelief at him, at the carnage, at the fact we were all alive.

"Shine on you crazy diamond," I said to Bob.

I found that it hurt my face to talk, so I shut up. Bob pulled the Browning from its holster and dropped the mag on the car roof, then racked the live round out of the chamber. When he saw my questioning look he nodded his head past my shoulder and laced his fingers together on top of his head.

When I turned the sirens that had gradually been growing louder and louder finally registered on my brain. Then I saw a grey Ford Crown Victoria come skidding around the corner of Marshall Fields, a police car with its flashers on right behind it. As I placed my two pistols on the roof of the Dodge next to Bob's Browning I could hear their engines straining as they raced toward us.

"Here comes the circus," Steve said as he stepped up beside us. "You okay?" he asked Jerry, and got a nod in return. Steve set the M-1 on the Dodge's hood, surveyed the scene, and rubbed his eyes slowly. "Anybody got any aspirin?" he said.

"Not one word to anybody," I said, staring at the approaching vehicles. I looked around at my companions. "Not one single syllable. I mean it. You're done. This is my show now."

Epilogue

I turned onto Thornridge Drive and put the setting sun behind me. The shadow of my car leading the way, I headed up the slight hill toward the Kelly's. It was difficult for me to see the potholes because of the angle the sun was hitting the road, so the nose of my car bounced up and down continuously.

"Congratulations," my wife said beside me.

"Thanks," I said. "For what?"

"So far you've managed to hit every single hole in the road. Amazing."

"Shut up, you ungrateful wench," I told her. "And me taking you to a party and everything."

"Are they even old enough to legally drink the beer we brought?" she said, a quirky smile on her face.

"You gonna stop 'em?" I asked. Across the road from Ron's house a field had been cleared of brush, a large sign declaring the impending arrival of the Thornridge Subdivision. Several large earth movers were parked in the field for the night.

I pulled into the circular driveway and parked behind a brand new ghost grey Mustang GT. Kelly and I climbed out of my Cavalier and I took a little time to peer into the 'Stang. It was loaded. I straightened up and was turning toward the house when I noticed a factory fresh Kawasaki just inside the barn doors. A little smile curled the corners of my mouth. The Diplomat was also just inside the barn doors, shining and gleaming and whole once more. Someone had told me that it had caught thirteen rounds, but sitting there it looked fresh from the dealer's showroom.

"Is that the barn you said they had?" Kelly asked, pointing at it.

I stared at the barn a while before I nodded.

"Doesn't look anything like I pictured," she commented, tilting her head and examining it in the fading light. I took her hand in mine and led her to the front door.

With one of my hands in Kelly's and my other holding a cold case of Labatt Blue we walked across the lawn and Kelly rang the doorbell. The door was opened promptly by Ron, who pushed wide the screen door with a grin and waved us inside.

"Mrs. Phault, I presume," he said graciously to my wife.

"Kelly," she told him with a smile. He nodded and looked at me.

"Hell boy!" I said, "ain't you healed yet? It's been four weeks!" I set the case of beer in his lap and he rolled the wheelchair out of the way so we could get past him in the hallway. His right leg stuck straight out, held tight in a sort of half-splint, half-cast.

"Two more weeks," he said. "I'm counting the minutes til they take this damn thing off." He smacked his leg and I smiled. "The ribs are just about normal, though."

"I see they've started on the subdivision," I remarked.

"Yeah. But the funny thing is, in about two weeks their vehicles are going to start breaking down and getting flat tires."

"Imagine that," I said. "Some people just don't have any luck." His effort would be futile, pointless, and juvenile, and he knew it, but that wouldn't matter. I jerked my head toward the barn.

"I thought you were going to wait until you healed so you could do the work on the Diplomat yourself," I said.

"Yeah, I was, but I couldn't stand to see her like that, all shot up. I know a couple good guys in Davison, run a body shop, they did her up right for me for an honest price."

"Repairing thirteen bullet holes? I doubt the thought of screwing you ever popped into their heads. Hell, video of your shot-up car was all over TV for a week. The mechanics probably took pictures of each other standing next to it. That your bike I saw in the barn?" He nodded. "How fast does it go?"

"About zero to a billion in half a second," he said. "I haven't been able to ride it yet, obviously, but Steve's had it up to one-forty on Lapeer Road a couple times. He helped me buy it, I've had my eye on it for a while but just didn't have the cash. I couldn't stand the thought of someone else getting it before I healed up."

"You know," I told him, "they make more than just one bike when they come out with a new model."

He gave me a dirty look. "Did you see Steve's new toy?" He grinned. "Like he wasn't dangerous enough with that piece of shit RX-7. C'mon, let's head into the family room. That's where everybody is."

I swept my arm for him to lead and Kelly and I followed

Ron as he rolled on four wheels to the back of the house. The cast on his leg reached from his crotch to his ankle and made it difficult to turn corners, and the chair barely fit through the doorways, but he made do. As it was, he was lucky the cast was only going to be on for two weeks more. The slug his thigh'd caught had cracked his femur and done more damage than I'd thought, but none of it would be permanent except the scar. A few of the doctors at the hospital where he'd stayed for nearly a week felt he'd have complete recovery in his leg, so he ignored the ones that kept insisting he'd have a limp for the rest of his life.

"You met Bob before he left, didn't you?" Ron asked my wife.

"Yes," she replied with a smile. In fact, she'd given him a big kiss on the lips, a thank you for what he'd done. To my complete and utter surprise, he'd blushed a deep crimson and stayed tongue-tied for fifteen minutes afterward.

I was greeted by a chorus of yells and catcalls as I stepped into the kitchen. Steve was there, as well as Jerry, and a girl I recognized as his girlfriend, Jodi. I never had gotten around to talking to her. Seeing her, I felt I might've made a mistake.

"You're late!" Steve yelled loudly, three feet from me. Apparently I wasn't the only one to have brought alcohol. I pointed a finger at Kelly.

"Blame her," I said with a smile. She punched me in the shoulder. Steve laughed and shook my hand. I took the case of Labatt out of Ron's lap and handed it to him.

"Happy birthday," I said sincerely. "What are you now, seventeen?"

"Ha," he said. "Is this yours?" he asked, giving me the finger behind my wife's back. He set the case on the kitchen counter, extracted a bottle, twisted off its cap, and quickly extinguished half the contents. He smiled contentedly and then belched loudly.

"See?" I nudged my wife. "Class all the way."

"So are you two parents-to-be yet or what?" Ron asked in his usual subtle manner. He opened the fridge and moved beer out of the way to make room for the beer I'd brought, then backed his wheelchair up against the kitchen cabinets and crossed his arms.

"Not yet," I said, "but we'd get an A for effort."

Kelly turned beet red and flashed me a scowl. Steve drank some more beer with a smile. Jerry and Jodi were whispering to each other in the family room sprawled on the couch. I couldn't see his hands but it looked like she knew where they were. Apparently his safe return home had been warmly received. Somewhere in the background Led Zeppelin was playing.

"I saw your barn," Kelly said to Ron. "Do you have any horses?" My wife missed the quick glance he threw my way.

"Why yes indeedy," Ron answered. "Would you like to see them?"

Kelly nodded, finally breaking down and grabbing a handful of Doritos from a bowl on the counter. Apparently her attempt to stare them down had failed.

"Okay, but part of the deal is that you have to wheel me around outside. It's a bitch moving this thing in gravel by yourself."

"I don't know, after that crack you made," Kelly replied. "But if you're willing to trust me . . . ."

Ron rolled out of the kitchen with her in tow, headed for the front door.

"I'll only roll you through a little horse shit," I heard my wife say as they disappeared from sight. With a smile on my face I took a bottle out of the fridge and popped it open, then leaned on the counter next to Steve and relaxed. The more I thought about it, the drunker I wanted to get. With everything that had happened after the mall, it was the first chance I'd had to see the guys outside of the hospital or an antagonistic police presence.

"Nice car," I said. "You pay cash?"

"Now, now, I'm not that stupid," Steve said. "I did what you said. Regular monthly payments that don't attract any attention. Parents co-signed on the loan and everything."

"Good boy," I said. We drank some more beer while Jerry and Jodi talked and snuggled on the couch.

"I'd tell them to get a room," Steve confided to me, jerking his head at the couch, "but that'd be the last we saw of them for hours." He took a big swig from the bottle. "So, what's the final word? Nobody with a badge has knocked on my door in four days. I think they finally ran out of people, I must've been yelled at by every local, state, and federal law enforcement officer between here and Memphis. Can we dare hope that this thing is finished?

"As finished as it's ever going to get," I told him. "Nobody's as happy as they want to be but I think they're gonna settle with the way things are now. For a long time there Weatherspoon and the State Police guys wanted to put us all on trial for multiple homicides, but that was mostly 'cause Weatherspoon was pissed I hadn't called him when I found Jerry. And we killed all the guys the Staties have been trying to put away for years. They had thousands of man-hours invested. And cops get all territorial when citizens kill citizens, even if it might be justified. Lot of 'em think they're the only ones who should be carrying guns anyway. They had you guys all set up to take the fall for murder, possession of illegal and/or automatic weapons, illegal carrying of concealed weapons, littering, unlicensed dogwalking, you name it. I didn't rank much higher in their estimation, either. Hell, you know how pissed they were, you got to experience the wonderful world of police interrogations."

"That and the Oakland County fucking Jail," Jerry called from the couch. Both Steve and I nodded at that unpleasant memory.

"So what changed their minds?" Steve asked.

"It took a couple of days for their tempers to cool down and their brains to start working. Then I told them, once again, what happened. How Kellogg called me at the last minute, said he had Jerry hostage, and wanted to meet, I didn't and still don't know why. I explained that as soon as we pulled up, armed with legally owned pistols and one rifle, Kellogg and his guys opened fire. We returned fire, in defense of our lives, in mortal fear, and killed all of them in an impressive display of gunhandling. Afterward we placed our guns on the car, as well as the shotgun and submachinegun the bad guys brought that Ron and Bob managed to wrestle away and use amazingly well to our advantage."

"Do you think they bought it?" Steve asked.

"Oh, hell no," I said, laughing, and opened up another beer. "You could drive a truck through the holes in that ridiculous story. For one thing, there were bulletholes in the Lincoln's roof, and the Medical Examiner noted in the autopsies that several of the bullet tracks in several of the bad guys were at a downward angle, like someone had shot them from and elevated position, like the roof. But you guys did what I told you, you didn't say a single goddamn word for a week, so my story was the only version of what happened that they got from us. Thank God Ron ground off the serial numbers on that Remington, or the ATF would own him for a decade."

"DeWayne, my buddy working security that night, denied that anyone had been on the roof. He said the alarms would've gone off, and they didn't. Course, that's 'cause he shut them off. I'd like to think he's lying to the cops because he knows I'm a great guy, but it's really that he'd lose his job if he admitted he let anyone up on the roof, even a fellow guard, and he needs the money."

"Good thing you grabbed the spent cases off the roof," I said.

"Those guys were so pissed off when I wouldn't talk to them," Jerry said. "Two days straight locked up in that fucking jail, them coming up every few hours and dragging me down to an interview room. I guess they figured they could intimidate me into talking, or that I was dumb enough to blab, since I never called a lawyer. Ron missed all the fun, being in the hospital."

"No need for a lawyer," Steve said, weaving a little. "Didn't say nothing, and that's most of what a lawyer would do anyway, tell you what and what not to say. And charge two hundred bucks an hour." He shrugged. "Jail wasn't as bad as I thought it might be. No rape attempts, nobody trying to beat me up…."

Jerry snorted. "Dude, we came in covered in blood and smelling like gunfire, after having just murdered half a dozen mob guys. Video of Kellogg's Lincoln and the swiss-cheesed Diplomat was all over the local news, and every cell's got a TV. We're getting interrogated by the just about every law enforcement agency there is from the FBI on down. Half the guys in jail were there for drunk driving or petty theft or beating on their girlfriend. We were rock stars. Nobody was going to touch us."

"Really?"

Jerry nodded. "So if they didn't believe a word of the story, why weren't we charged?" he asked me.

"Lot of things," I told him. "First, it basically comes down to our word against Kellogg's as to who fired first and all the other specifics. And he ain't talking. The cops have a pretty good idea of who shot who from all the physical evidence we left strewn around, but they can't prove why, or disprove our story of self-defense. You guys stayed clammed up and I repeated that stupid story to anybody that asked until I was sick of hearing myself talk. Nobody liked it, but they all knew that the chance of a conviction without opponent testimony was slim to none."

"Ladies and Gentlemen of the jury," Jerry began, "we're here today to try a capital case. We have vague circumstantial physical evidence that these defendants murdered -- in cold blood -- six members of Detroit's organized crime community. Who had guns, and, by the way, had just kidnapped one of their friends and might have started shooting first, we're not sure." He snorted. "I guarantee you, at least one of those jurors would refuse to believe that a crime had been committed."

"That's exactly what the Oakland County Prosecutor was thinking," I told them. "I assured him numerous times that if this went to trial I'd go up on the stand and make sure every juror knew that the dead guys were *bad* guys, mafia, who'd kidnapped a college kid because he saw a murder."

"And the feds found me such a disappointing witness," Jerry said with a smile.

Jerry had recognized the driver of the Buick that had taken him to the meet at the mall as the same guy that had driven the Trans Am that'd followed him from Burger King.

Now that that guy was dead, Jerry couldn't be a witness against anyone, and stayed silent when he was peppered with questions about why Kellogg's men had grabbed him instead of shot him. Any kind of a response on his part would have just opened the door to more questions.

"If Weatherspoon hadn't been so worked up," I told them, "it wouldn't have taken me so long to get through to him. He'd wanted to nail Kellogg, or Bufonte, get the credit, grab the headlines, and ended up with nothing but dead bodies. We were the only target he had left. That's when he started all that talk about federal weapons violations. He wanted my ass so bad he could taste it." That didn't sound quite right but I pressed on. "Even the fact that he found out who the leak in his department was by examining Kellogg's private phone book didn't snap him out of it completely."

"So what changed his mind, finally?" Steve said.

"He finally started listening to what I had to say. He realized that there was no way he could take any of us to court if he wanted to stay employed and keep the reputation of the WPP intact. Every newspaper and TV station in the state, and eventually the national network news, would learn how three people had to leave the protection of the Witness Protection Program because there was a federal agent on the take, selling their addresses. And they still ended up getting killed for their trouble. The trial transcript would have been public record, and I assured him that I'd air *all* of his dirty laundry. Including a recording I may or may not have made of him agreeing to cover up a double homicide at State. And how all the Kevlar vests you guys were wearing had serial numbers which could be traced back to him. If everything came out he would get the blame and Witness would be out of business. Why should a bad guy turn snitch if the damn government can't even insure his safety?"

"Kellogg had Jerry, beating and abusing him, and he killed those three witnesses, and still they wouldn't believe us when we said we pulled our guns only in self-defense. Unbelievable," Jerry said.

I couldn't tell if he was being serious or not. "Well, Bob sure as hell didn't help our cause any when he asked Weatherspoon if he could keep the MP5 that he'd 'found,'" I told them with a frown. "Weatherspoon about turned purple when he heard *that*. Look up 'apoplectic' in a dictionary and you would've seen his picture."

"Bob probably has another one by now anyway," Steve remarked, handing me another beer.

"I'm sure of it," I said. What better way to pay Charlie back than to steer a cash-rich customer his way? "You know," I continued, "Weatherspoon wasn't the only one surprised when he found out all your pistols were legally registered. Of course, they were being carried illegally, but they were properly registered."

"Yeah, and when the hell are we going to get them back?" Jerry asked me.

"Try never," I told him.

"What?"

"You heard me."

"But they're not going to charge us! That forty-five is legally mine, goddammit. I want it back. Besides, who says I was carrying it concealed? Open carry is legal in this state. They can't prove anything!" He leaned toward me and in what he probably thought was a whisper said, "We even replaced the floor in the barn. Burned all the old wood."

I smiled. "Welcome to the real world," I told him. "You guys want your guns back, you better be prepared to sue.

But I'd bet you money that they've already been destroyed. Weatherspoon had to have some fun."

"That is such bullshit," Jerry grumbled.

"What are you crying about?" Steve asked him. "It's not like you're broke." Jerry immediately brightened when he thought of his newfound cash.

"How's Bob?" I asked. "Have you heard from him since he went back down to Bragg?"

"Yeah. He's doing fine, as usual. He says pushups are a bitch with shotgun pellets in your shoulder, though."

"I bet," I said.

Already I was feeling the alcohol. The nurse at the hospital had spent an hour digging out chunks of asphalt from my face and telling me how lucky I was none had hit my eyes. I knew how right she was so I took the pain without complaint. The scabs on my face had healed quickly, but Kelly had taunted me unmercifully for a week, saying I looked like a teenager with acne. I'd told her that I was like a teenager in a lot of other ways too, with the end result usually being a pile of clothes on the floor and both of us gasping for breath. I never realized how important some things were to me until I thought I was going to lose them forever. Nothing's trivial when you understand how close to death we all are. I guess we're fools for thinking otherwise.

Surprisingly, I found out that my ear was healing fine on its own and wouldn't require any surgery. That I found out by paying a specialist $150 and having him look in my ear with a penlight for five minutes. My hearing had begun to return, but I still had to wash it out daily with a solution to keep it from getting infected.

"Did you see the news last night?" Steve said before

chugging down the rest of his beer. "They found two more bodies."

I nodded soberly, which was an effort. Bufonte had been busy the past few weeks hunting down and killing the remnants of Kellogg's men in especially messy ways, those who'd been his people but switched sides. The police would find a new body, or part of one, usually in an alley or in the trunk of a car, about every three days. The local networks were trying to outdo each other with video of the unlucky victims, calling it the "Crimson Tide".

Citizen groups were pressuring the mayor of Detroit to crack down on organized crime, not understanding that the bloodbath could've been a lot worse if Kellogg had lived. I wondered how Charlie Kang was faring in his now stormy business world, if he was riding on top of new waves of business or getting dragged under.

The turncoats that hadn't yet been caught by Bufonte were keeping the phone lines at Justice tied up, asking for protection in exchange for testimony or depositions or phone numbers or whatever they could give that might convince the government that they were worth protecting. Weatherspoon, I noticed, didn't thank me for the extra business.

Ron and Kelly came back into the house and made their way into the kitchen, chatting amiably.

"Have you seen their horses?" Kelly asked me. "They're beautiful."

I thought about the last time I'd been inside the barn. The image of blood dripping from an eye socket popped into my head.

"No," I said, and emptied my bottle.

Kelly started into the family room and began talking to Jerry and Jodi. I handed Ron a fresh beer and said, "You know, I did some checking, and I found that there were no unsolved homicides in this area the whole time you were in high school. That story you gave me about shooting the burglar, that was just a goddamned story, wasn't it?" Ron took a long swig and looked at me over the bottle.

"Got you to let me tag along though, didn't it?" He smiled at me.

"Oh, man," I said, disgusted with myself. "I can't believe . . . I can't believe I fell for that. One of these days I'll figure out how your mind works," I told him.

"What are you going to do in the meantime?" he said.

"Well, I'm getting sued," I said. He lowered the beer he'd started to raise.

"Sued? By who?"

"By the family of Leroy Hawkins, the famous RedMan," I told him. "Wrongful death suit. And not just me, they're suing Scott Copley too."

"But they ruled it was a justified shooting!" cried Jerry, sitting up.

"In criminal court," I explained. "This is a civil lawsuit. They're claiming we violated his civil rights, wrongfully killed him, ruined his perfectly good army jacket, made him drop his shotgun, you name it. They're asking for twelve million in punitive damages. And since the department's shooting board ruled the shooting justified the department is paying all of Scott's legal fees. Any legal fees I have, however, come straight out of my pocket."

"Wait a second," Steve said. "If I remember correctly, Scott didn't even shoot Hawkins, did he? Wasn't he the guy up by the register?"

"Scott never even pointed his gun at the guy," I said. "The plaintiffs are saying that he should've somehow prevented me from shooting the bastard, and therefore contributed negligence or some such bullshit."

"Jesus, I can't fucking believe that," Ron said to me. "What's this country coming to, can't even shoot someone anymore without getting sued. He *was* the guy up on the counter, right? With the sawed-off? What're they claiming, that he was going after rats that lived in the ceiling? Fuckin' assholes. You need any money? I know where I can lay my hands on some cash," he said with a smile.

"Nah, I'll make do," I said. "We'll beat it, it's just a pain in the ass. Their lawyer is one of those assholes that advertises for slip and fall cases on TV, can you fucking believe it?"

"What do you call a hundred lawyers at the bottom of the ocean?" Steve said. "A good start!" He laughed drunkenly at his joke.

"You know they're using lawyers in laboratory experiments now?" Ron told us. "Yeah. I guess there's some things rats just won't do." Lawyer jokes bounced back and forth across the room for a while. I reached for another beer, realizing I'd lost count of how many I'd had. Well, Kelly could drive home.

"Come on in here," Jerry called from the family room. Those of us in the kitchen migrated over to him and Jodi. "We've got ribs and pizza and birthday cake, for dessert," Jerry said, "but first we're going to watch one of two kick-ass movies. The other one we'll watch after." He picked up two DVDs and read their labels to us. "*Red Dawn* and *Conan the Barbarian*."

"Yecch," Jodi and Kelly said at the same time.

"You just don't know a classic when you see one," Ron said.

"Where's your dad?" I asked him.

"He and my mom had a reconciliation," he explained. "So they took a little vacation and are in a hotel somewhere up north for a couple days."

"What the hell does your dad do for a living, anyway," I said, "that he works such weird hours and can take time off without any warning?"

"Don't ask," Ron and Jerry told me at the same time.

"I don't want to have to sit through two hours of blood and guts before I eat," Jodi complained.

"Sounds like a basic flaw in your character," Jerry said. He fed the tape into the player while fending off blows from his sweetheart.

"Afterwards," he said to me, "we can teach you a drinking game we invented. It's called Bill Murray. Don't ask me why it's called that, I don't remember, I was drunk at the time. But it's great, you'll get blasted."

"I'm not really having a lot of trouble intoxicating myself," I told him, hoisting a bottle to his blurry image. I sat Kelly down on the couch and fit in beside her. I noticed the Colt on my hip a little more than I would've the Sig, which still hadn't been returned by the cops, but after the past month I was willing to trade a little comfort for more caliber. The Smith and Wesson .357 LadySmith now resided in Kelly's purse, a CCW she'd thought she'd never want lying beside it, courtesy of Scott.

"I want to thank you guys for what you did for me and John," Kelly said. "I don't know if we would've made it without you. Not many people would've done what you did."

"Well, we did it more for butthead here than for you," Steve said, jabbing his thumb at Jerry, "but thanks anyway."

"If you guys ever need anything, anything at all," I said as seriously as I could in my condition, "call me." The

Failure Drill

movie started on the TV and Ron turned down the volume with a remote control. All three of them, Ron, Jerry, and Steve, were looking at me.

"Hell," Ron said, "you call us. You might be surprised at what we'd do for a friend."

I looked at them for a few seconds, all of us smiling, then nodded.

"Now, shut up and watch the movie," Ron said.

Next in the James Tarr Conspiracy Thriller series

vinci-books.com/splashback

A missing father with ties to U.S. intelligence. A private eye caught in a web of espionage and murder.

In post-9/11 Detroit, ex-DEA agent turned P.I., John Phault, is drawn into a sinister mystery when a friend's father vanishes, leaving behind a house full of secrets.

Turn the page for a free preview…

Splashback: Chapter One

FRIDAY

7:41 a.m.

She kissed me passionately, breath hot on my cheeks, her lips pressed firmly against mine. She was insistent, demanding, her tongue fighting to get into my mouth. When that didn't work she nuzzled my ear, licked the earlobe once to get my attention, then came back to my mouth once more. Her tongue was relentless, and she pressed against my chest, holding me down. I felt myself begin to respond finally, and her tongue found its way into my mouth.

I opened my eyes to see two beautiful brown eyes staring lovingly at me. She licked my lips playfully.

"Aaack!" I spat, and brought up a hand to block the tongue as it snaked out again. "Get off me! Leave me alone, dog." She wagged her tail enthusiastically and bounded off the bed, looking for a chew toy to bring back to me so I could throw it for her.

"What the hell is going on over there?" I heard sleepily from the other side of the bed. I rolled my head over and saw my wife. She lay on her side, turned away from me.

"Guess," I said, wiping dog spit from my face with the sheet. My wife turned her head and looked at me over her shoulder.

"Just think how many other guys would like to be sleeping with two women at once," she told me. I heard sounds of approaching dog and looked up to see her appear in the doorway, red rubber barbell in mouth. She looked at me expectantly, tail wagging fiercely.

"She probably licked her butt before she kissed me, too," I said. "Jesus, what time is it? The sun's not even all the way up yet."

"Stop your bitching. You're the one that wanted a dog," she told me. "Get up and let her outside, that's probably why she's hyper, she has to go to the bathroom." I groaned theatrically and struggled to right myself.

"Jeez, am I sure I want kids?" I said after I made it unsteadily to my feet. Kelly rolled onto her back and I saw the bedcovers pushed upward by her distended pregnant belly. It looked like two Cub Scouts had pitched a tent on her stomach.

"You back out now and I'll disembowel you," she told me sweetly.

1:13 p.m.

Jerry Phillips walked into my office without a word and dropped into the chair I leave in front of my desk for clients. I checked my desk calendar and shook my head slowly.

"No wonder this country's going to hell in a handbasket," I said to him. "December ninth, and you're off for Christmas vacation already. You don't have to be back until what, the third or fourth?" Jerry shot me a wide smile, with no hint of guilt whatsoever. In another six months he'd be graduating with a Criminal Justice degree from MSU, with Honors no less, but he still hadn't started sending out job applications. I think he just didn't know exactly where he wanted to go – uniformed or plainclothes, local, state, or federal.

"Tough life, ain't it?" he said. "And Ron got done with his finals before me, he's been home for a day and a half already. So," he said, changing the subject, "we still on for tomorrow?"

"Is it tomorrow already?" I said, and checked my calendar again.

"Oh no, don't start that shit with me," he said, leaning forward in the chair to stick a finger at me. "You knew it was tomorrow, and you're going. Don't *even* try to pull some lame excuse out of your butt." He crossed his arms and sat back. I grinned at him.

I was a private investigator, a former Special Agent with the Drug Enforcement Administration, and before that I was in the Army. Married, with a baby on the way. Jerry and his friends, who had become my friends—Ron Kelly, Bob Grinnand, and Steve Reath—were fifteen years my junior. All of them but Bob still in college. Even I had to admit the five of us made an odd group.

Everyone knows the phrase "politics makes for strange bedfellows". The original quote, as so many do, comes from Shakespeare, *The Tempest*: "Misery acquaints a man with strange bedfellows." I had definitely shared misery with these young men, and we'd bonded in a way that most people will never experience. That transcended our ages or position in the world. Even if we could tell the story, I doubt anyone would believe it. In truth, I was still amazed we hadn't found ourselves the semi-permanent guests of the Michigan Department of Corrections.

"You lose weight or something?" I asked him. "You look different." He was a little over six foot and slender, with brown hair in a slightly long brushcut.

"I've been working out a lot lately," he told me. "Seems like I always get into this workout thing from around the start of school until Christmas vacation. I've replaced about eight pounds of fat with five pounds of muscle. Me and Jodi've been working out a lot together, giving each other moral support." Jodi was his girlfriend, also attending Michigan State. She was barely old enough to drink, gorgeous, and had a naturally abundant physique my old college roommate would have described as 'topheavy'. Imagining her jogging, or maybe doing aerobics...oof. Anyway, moving on, nothing to see here, happily married man.

"Sounds like me," I told him. "Except for me it started when I hit thirty. I get into these six-month cycles. Work out hard for six months, get in good shape, then slack off for about six months until guilt drives me back to the gym."

"Where are you now?" he asked.

"About four months into the working out part. Kelly can't work out 'cause she's pregnant, so I feel obligated to be working out for the both of us. Because I can, don't have any excuses. Are you going to be working over the break?" I asked him.

"Yeah. Selling Christmas trees over at Champion again. This'll make it five years in a row I'm dumb enough to stand outside in December freezing my ass off and getting frostbite on my fingers. So, what kind of holster are you going to be using?" Jerry asked me, getting back to the subject at hand.

I'd agreed to go to a shooting match with him and put my money where my mouth was. He'd been doing a lot of competitive shooting lately and kept browbeating me to come along and use the pistol he and the guys had given me for my thirty-fifth birthday a few months back. That 'misery' we'd shared had involved a kidnapping attempt and several gunfights with members of Detroit organized crime, so a gift of a gun wasn't as weird as you might think. Besides, the guns we'd used were still in the evidence lockup at the Oakland County Sheriff's Department, and likely to remain there forever.

The match was a monthly event put on by a local sportsmen's club. It was an I.P.S.C. event, a "combat" pistol match that wasn't quite realistic and yet was better than anything else around for practicing defensive pistol skills. I'd never competed in one but had read up on them and felt confident I could kick Jerry's butt. After all, I'd been through the DEA Academy at Quantico, which is where the FBI has their Academy. The FBI Academy is several weeks longer than ours, because those courses teaching them how to be egotistical officious pricks add a lot of classroom hours.

"I was gonna work from a Safariland paddle holster," I told him. "It's what they gave us in the DEA, I never had any problems with 'em."

"Good, that's good," he said. "Secure, no snaps or flaps to slow you down, rides a little high but it's a real-world holster, not one of those erector sets some of these gamers strap onto their hips. You talk to Bob recently?" he asked me.

"Yeah, I just talked to him yesterday," I said. "He's looking forward to coming home, but I don't know how they talked him into taking a vacation."

Failure Drill

I'd met Bob about the same time I ran across Jerry. They'd graduated high school together, then Bob'd joined the 82nd Airborne. Since then he'd moved on and had spent most of the last year romping through the world with a green beret atop his head. It was barely more than a year since Nine-Eleven, and everyone in the U.S. military seemed to be overseas or en route. Bob had been out of contact for months at a time. Blond and built like Mike Tyson in fighting trim, but more skilled with his hands, Bob'd told me over the phone that he was back at Fort Bragg on leave, which seemed odd, as the smart money was on us jumping into Iraq inside of a month or two. Then again, maybe this was the calm before the storm for him. "He sounded a bit weird on the phone," I commented to Jerry.

"Yeah, I noticed that too, last time I talked to him. I don't know what's up but I'm sure we'll find out when he gets here. He was in gunfights before he ever deployed for the Army, but God only knows where he's been or what kind of *Heart of Darkness* shit he's seen. Does he need anybody to pick him up at the airport? I haven't been able to get ahold of him lately, they're not real big on leaving messages down there."

"Naw, he's driving, he's not flying. I guess he's leaving early Sunday and will be pulling in late that night. Helluva drive from Bragg."

"Driving? Why the hell is he driving? Between the five of us we can spare a car for him to use on leave."

"He said he bought a new truck he wanted to show everyone," I explained.

"So bring a goddamn picture and save yourself a sore butt and a hundred bucks each way in gas money," Jerry said.

"Set off fewer airport metal detectors this way," I speculated.

Jerry slapped a hand to his forehead.

"Christ, what was I thinking?" he said.

4:45 p.m.

My office mail was in a pile on the corner of my desk and I decided to go through it just to kill time until five o'clock. Nothing much, just a few bills and a lot of junk mail aimed more at corporate-type enterprises than me and my little one-man company. I looked blearily around the office to see if anything else needed to be done, found nothing, and started to pack it in. I'd just grabbed my coat off the chair and was heading toward the door when the phone rang. With a short but choice word I strode across my office and snagged the receiver just before the machine picked up.

"John Phault, Security and Investigations," I said.

"Hey."

"Yeah, what do you want?" I said tiredly.

"My, we're in a good mood, aren't we? Your dog bite you or something?"

"Just a long day." Lieutenant Scott Copley, Oakland County Sheriff's Department, a long-time friend and general pain-in-the-ass, a workaholic with no home life to speak of and not many friends at or outside of work besides me. "So what's all the big buzz I've been hearing coming from the County about the new Prosecutor? He seems to be on TV an awful lot."

"Same shit, different day, that's all. Hendricks, the old Oakland County Prosecutor, decided to retire in mid-term, and now we have Mr. Steve Shields to deal with. Smart as a whip, sly as a fox, compassion of the Terminator. Will not deviate from the letter of the law for anyone. That is, unless they're someone that can do him a favor. He's the new kid on the block and looking to make a name for himself, and boy did he hit the ground running. Too bad Kevorkian's in jail, he could go after him next, that seems to go with the position."

"Hendricks retired, huh? Too bad. At least he knew his ass from a hole in the ground."

"Shields knows from asses. He spends half the day kissing them and half the day kicking them. Hey, how's Kelly? She like being fat?"

"Tell you what. You ask my wife that, face to face, without changing the wording, and see how she replies. I promise I'll send flowers."

"When is she due anyway?"

"February third. But I think she'll be early, 'cause that's still almost two months away and she's huge. She decided to take off work early. She's got a lot of leave saved up, and it's getting hard for her to get in and out of chairs. Friday was her last day."

"Are you sure it's not twins? I saw her two weeks ago and she couldn't fit through doorways." I knew Scott well enough to hear the barely contained laughter just beneath his words.

"It's not twins. We've had ultrasounds done and amniocentesis and they all say one kid. I even have an ultrasound picture of it, though the damn thing could be a moonscape for all I can make of it."

"I can't relate to that," Scott said, "being a father-to-be. I can't even imagine what that's like."

"Me neither. I'm making it up as I go along. This is the easy part, though. All I have to do is make Kelly feel wanted and loved and attractive, to help minimize those hairy hormonal fits. Once the kid arrives, though, all bets are off. A puppy was a pain in the ass but I have a feeling it was nothing compared to what this kid's gonna be like."

"I bet."

"Now all that's left is getting you hitched," I said to him. "Settle you down. Soothe the savage beast of bachelorhood."

"No way. I'm planning to be in the delivery room when Kelly's in labor. Seeing her screaming and spitting, speaking in tongues and levitating shit will stifle any paternal feelings I might be developing."

"God, what an image you just put into my head."

"It's not too late," he told me. "We could still run away and become porn stars. How 'bout it?"

"It's waaaay too late," I told him. Realizing I was still holding my coat in my arm I asked him, "Did you call me for any particular reason?"

"No, not really," he said. "Just working late, stuck in the office and bored."

"What I figured," I said. "I'm late leaving for home, and you know how I've been dancing around Kelly lately to keep her on an even keel, so I gotta go. Bye."

5:19 p.m.

Kelly had her back turned toward me as she stirred something in a pot on top of the stove. The dog sat at attention behind Kelly, every atom of her being focused on the pot Kelly was fiddling with. The dog took the time to make sure I wasn't a burglar lunging for her mother and then glued her attention back onto the stove lest she miss a chance to eat some tasty People Food. I nuzzled Kelly's ear and hugged her. It took some effort to get my arms all the way around her.

"Hi baby," I said. "What are you making?"

"It's my mother's recipe for spaghetti sauce," she told me.

"I take it that we're having spaghetti for dinner, then," I said.

"I feel vindicated. I kept telling everyone that you weren't as stupid as you looked," she commented, still stirring the contents of the pot.

"Thanks," I said. She kept stirring awhile, with my arms around her and my chin on her shoulder.

"Is there something else that you wanted?" she asked finally.

"Would you like to go upstairs with me and make a baby?" I asked her. She looked at me out of the corner of her eye.

"We already did that," she replied.

"Well, maybe we could just practice for the next one, then." I looked at her and wiggled my eyebrows up and down. It's a patented technique, known to make women around the world swoon. She turned her body slightly towards me.

"Are you doing this just to make me feel like I'm still attractive and not just one big house-sized blob?" she asked suspiciously.

"You forget who you're talking to," I said. "Since when have I done anything just to make someone other than myself feel better?" She looked at me for a few seconds. I was trying hard not to stare at her chest, which had grown remarkably over the past few weeks, but I can't exactly say I was successful. Kelly looked at me, looked down at her chest, then back up at me, rolling her eyes.

"Do you even know what subtle means?" she asked, then leaned backward and kissed me. I could taste the spaghetti sauce on her lips. She reached over and shut the burner off, then took me by the hand.

"Just be gentle," I said as she led me toward the stairs. "Remember, I have a weak constitution." The dog stayed rooted to her spot, looking at the stove, then us, then back at the stove in case the pot of sauce tried to make a break for it.

"Shut up or I'll sit on you," my wife told me sweetly.

"Actually…" I began.

Splashback: Chapter Two

SATURDAY

8:32 a.m.

"I can't believe I'm up this early on a Saturday," I said to no one in particular.

"This is gonna be fun, so shut up," Jerry told me.

We were standing with a small group of people at the rear of a large indoor range, gearing up for the match. Jerry was beside me buckling on a holster and magazine pouches, but we weren't in a designated "Safe" area so no one was touching any pistols. The match safety rules were very strict; the gun I normally carried everywhere I'd left in the car. As strange as it sounds bringing a loaded gun to a shooting match was Number 1 on the no-no list and would've gotten me ejected.

"Too bad it's so cold out, this is a lot more fun when it's outside," Jerry was telling me. "If you like this, you should come to some more matches with me. It'll keep your shooting skills sharp."

"If I remember, my shooting skills were sharp enough two years ago to save your pimpled butt," I told him, feeling a bit intimidated by the unfamiliar surroundings. I hadn't been around this many heavily armed and presumably skilled shooters since Quantico. One of the guys near us gave me a curious glance but said nothing.

Jerry and I moved to a side table and began loading magazines for the match. A lot of magazines. Jerry'd said most of the matches had a lot higher shot count than the real world gunfight average of 4 rounds, although the shooting was divided up into several different stages. Besides, he'd said to me on the way over, who'd want to drive twenty or thirty minutes each way to only shoot half a dozen rounds?

"Remind me again of how this is supposed to work," I told Jerry, looking at the array of targets downrange.

"It's simple," he told me. He pointed to the cardboard silhouettes with square heads that were the standard targets of the International Practical Shooting Confederation. "The tan targets with no visible aiming point, no bullseye, just like real people, get two rounds each unless stated otherwise. The closer to the center the better, because there *are* scoring rings on 'em, you just can't see 'em from here. The white silhouettes are hostages, or innocent bystanders, what-have-you. Don't shoot them, they're just there to make your job harder. Where the tan silhouettes are painted black it's considered hard cover, like the person is standing behind a brick wall or something. A hole in the black won't get you any points, and you get points deducted for the miss. Some days we have falling steel plates to shoot at, Pepper Poppers, but it doesn't look like we'll have any today." He peered at the shooting course laid out on the range. "Stage three looks like fun, shoot and move, shoot and move, duck under the table and shoot again. All at close targets. You practice at all to get ready for today, Mr. Hot Shot?" he asked me.

Failure Drill

"A little," I said. What a lie. I'd gone to the range by my house three times in the past two weeks in preparation for the match. I wasn't about to let myself get beat by a snot-nosed kid not even out of college.

"You like this, I'll have to take you to one of the 3-gun matches a club out in Livingston puts on," he told me.

"A 3-gun match?" I said.

"Yeah. Pistol, shotgun, and rifle. I don't know if I like 'em any better, but they're a change of pace and real good to keep your skills sharp on the long guns. Not many other places around where you can shoot shotgun or rifle in combat scenarios. I took Ron a couple of times to those matches, he likes playing around with his new shotgun."

"I haven't shot a rifle in years," I said. "Maybe not since the DEA Academy. Shotgun, yeah, but not rifle."

We moved to the Safe area and uncased our weapons. The pistol Jerry and his friends had presented to me on my birthday was a customized Colt 1911 .45 ACP Government Model, first choice of the FBI's Hostage Rescue Team, LAPD SWAT, 'Delta' Force; pretty much everybody who took their job seriously. Not to mention most of the people milling around me, although a lot of the people I'd be competing against had accessories on their guns like electronic red-dot scopes and recoil compensators, things not suitable for actual day to day use but rather designed specifically for high-speed competition. Jerry'd said the real world guns were scored in a different class from what he called the 'race' guns, so I shouldn't worry. Something like handicapping in golf, I supposed.

The 1911 had become the weapon of choice due more to its ease of customization and mode of operation than anything else—it had the best trigger pull by far, and could be made amazingly accurate. It was also meant to be carried with the hammer cocked and the safety on, which meant someone familiar with its use could get a quicker, more controlled first shot off with a Colt, or its copies, than with any other type of pistol.

I practiced a few draws from my holster and then left the Colt in it, empty, hammer down, reassured once more with my reasonable competence in gunhandling. Over the past two weeks I'd fired close to six hundred rounds through the Colt. I'd draw it, fire one, two, or three rounds at a silhouette, sometimes close, sometimes far, and then do my best to reholster while still looking downrange like they'd taught me all those years ago at Quantico. I watched Jerry practice a few draws of his own and he almost looked like he might be quicker than me from the holster, but the real test would be whether or not he could hit the target.

"Line's going hot!" The range officer yelled out, and everybody made sure their ear and eye protection was in place. The first competitor of the day stepped into the designated shooting box, a four foot square on the floor made of two-by-twos. She'd have to stand inside the box while shooting the first part of the stage. She blew on her hands and wiped her palms on her thighs, then nodded to the R.O. when he asked if she understood the course of fire.

"Load and make ready," he told her. After staring at her for a few seconds I realized that she reminded me of one of my aunts. However, I couldn't picture my aunt Josie ever picking up a gun unless someone trampled her prize rose garden. The female shootist confidently drew and loaded her pistol, then set it in her barely there competition holster, cocked and locked, eyes focused downrange.

"Shooter ready?" the R.O. asked her. As she nodded he held up an electronic timer close behind her head that

Jerry'd told me "heard" the gunshots and recorded the shooter's time down to the hundredth of a second. "Stand by!" he called out, and a second later pressed a button on the timer, which emitted an electronic beep.

The woman's hands were a blur as she scooped up her gun and brought it to bear on the leftmost target. The very second she was on target she began firing, loud staccato blasts that were so close together I'd have thought she was using a submachinegun if I hadn't seen her pistol with my own eyes. She dropped her empty mag and sprinted through her still-airborne empty cases to the next shooting box, reloading on the run, the R.O. glued to her heels with the timer held high. No sooner had her feet crossed into the second box than she opened up on the remaining targets, her empty brass pelting the crowd to her right rear. Done firing, she stood there, panting just a bit, and scanned the targets. No misses.

"If the shooter is finished, unload and show clear," the R.O. told her. "Hammer down, and holster." When she had done so and holstered her now empty gun, the two of them walked downrange with a scorer to check the targets.

As the scorer began recording the mostly A-zone hits that the R.O. was calling out Jerry nodded his head in admiration.

"Damn," he said. "I'm gonna have to watch myself. She gets any better and she'll get bumped up into my class and that'll be one more person I'll have to beat. So," he said, turning to me, "what do you think so far?"

"Jesus Christ," was all I could think to say.

"Goddamnit," I heard someone beside me curse. A middle-aged man was rubbing his cheek just below his impact-resistant shooting glasses. A divot the diameter of a pencil lead was welling blood. "Fucking splashback." He pulled his hand away from his smarting cheek and looked at his fingertips. "Hey, I'm bleeding!"

Angled steel louvers at the end of the range directed the flying bullets down into a sand bank. Occasionally a bullet would hit the front edge of a louver and shrapnel would fly backwards, sometimes all the way to the shooter. It was an uncommon occurrence, but not so rare I hadn't seen it happen before. That's why everyone always wore eye protection.

"Oh, quit your whining, Frank," one of the other shooters said. "You want to participate in something that's inherently dangerous, don't complain if you get bit."

Grab your copy…
vinci-books.com/splashback

About the Author

James Tarr is a regular contributor to numerous firearms/outdoor publications and has appeared on or hosted numerous shows on The Sportsman Channel cable network including *Handguns and Defensive Weapons* and *Guns & Ammo TV*. He is also the author of fourteen books (and counting), including the critically-acclaimed *Dogsoldiers*, *Whorl*, *Bestiarii*, and *Carnivore* (with Dillard Johnson), which was featured on The O'Reilly Factor. He lives in Michigan with his fiancée, two sons and three dogs.